Hostile Territory

D.N. SIMMONS

HOSTILE TERRITORY
THE KNIGHTS OF THE DARKNESS CHRONICLES

2008

Hostile Territory

Knights of the Darkness Chronicles

Desires Unleashed
The Guilty Innocent
The Royal Flush
Hostile Territory
The Lion's Den (2008)

Dedication And Acknowledgements

*I Would Like To Dedicate This Novel To My Absolutely
Wonderful, Loyal, Understanding And Truly Patient
Readership. Writing These Books For You Has Been One
Of My Greatest Pleasures And I Am Thrilled To Have
You All As Readers.*

*As Always, I Would Also Like The Thank My Editor,
Vicky Hughes, For Helping Me Keep My Sanity While
Editing This Novel. I'd Like To Thank My Mother
For Being The Wonderful Person You Are, Honestly, I
Wouldn't Be Here Without You. Last, But Not Least, I'd
Like To Send A Special "Thank You" To All Of You Who
Have Supported Me.*

Love Always
D.n.

CHAPTER ONE

Sergio drove his Python XL30 sports car down the long, winding driveway of the luxurious three-story mansion he shared with the other sixteen members of his Pride. Killing the engine, he quickly climbed out of the sleek automobile. He stretched his limbs, flexing his lean muscles, relieving his body of all tension, before heading to the front door. Before he could slide his key into the lock, the door was yanked open and he was immediately accosted by his seventeen-year-old son, Sebastian, which confirmed one thing for Sergio...Sebastian wanted something...and he wanted it badly.

"Hey Dad! How was your day?" Sebastian greeted his father enthusiastically.

"Oh yeah, you're up to something, what did you do? Or what do you want?" Sergio asked suspiciously as he slid his way past his son into the mansion.

"Can't a loving and obedient son be concerned about how great his dad's day went?" Sebastian shrugged one shoulder, playing up to his father.

Sergio gave him another sideways glance. "Alright, I'll play along, if only to see where you're going with this."

He chuckled. Opening the closet, he removed his leather jacket, slipping it on a hanger on the rod. Turning, he wrapped a muscular arm around his son's shoulders. "Let's see, how did my day go? Well, I woke up, stretched a bit. I had a great breakfast, steak, eggs, pancakes, it was delicious. Once I was done with that, I headed upstairs to get dressed, and as you know, I love to wear flat front pants to work. It took me all of ten minutes to find the right shirt, because-what? why are you looking at me like that?"

Sebastian was frowning, knowing his father was only doing that to torture him. "Dad, you know you're wrong for this...boring me to death with silly details."

"Hey, you said you wanted to know how my day went. You're the one beating around the bush, you know damn well you weren't thinking about my day at work. Now spill it, or I'll keep talking."

Sebastian held both hands up in surrender. "No, no, don't do that. I'll come on out with it. Can I have twenty dollars...please?"

Another chuckle bubbled up from Sergio's throat. "Why?"

"I want to take a girl out tonight, show her a good time."

"Show her a *good* time?"

"Yeah."

"With only *twenty* dollars?"

"Should I have more?" Sebastian crossed his fingers behind his back, hoping to hear the answer he wanted.

Sergio arched an eyebrow. "That depends. How old is this girl? Where are you taking her and how long have you known her?" he questioned.

"Dang Dad, what is this, an interrogation?"

"Yes, that's exactly what it is." Sergio pushed his son into the plush chair in their living room. Tilting the lampshade a little, he shined the brightness into Sebastian's face. "Now answer my questions, boy!"

Sebastian shaded his eyes. "Geez Dad! Come on, enough with the light!"

Sergio chuckled, but did what he asked, releasing his grip on the shade. "I'm waiting." He sat down on the sofa.

"She's seventeen, same age as me. I'm hoping to take her to the movies and out to dinner providing I can get the funds and I've known her for two months, just recently working up the courage to ask her out." Sebastian looked at his dad, hoping he had satisfied his curiosity.

"Well, unless you plan of taking her to some fast food place, like *Mendy's* for the dollar meal menu specials, you're going to need more than twenty dollars. If you're trying to impress this girl, being a cheap ass is the last thing you want to be remembered for." Sergio reached into his back pocket pulling out his black leather wallet. He opened the wallet and began to remove a fifty dollar bill from the money pocket, then hesitated. He looked at his son's perked up expression and laughed. "Better yet, get a job." He shoved the fifty-dollar bill back into his wallet and pushed his son lightly, playfully.

"Dad, come on, stop playing!" Sebastian began to laugh as he hooked onto Sergio, playfully wrestling his father, attempting to pry the leather wallet from his vise grip.

"Oh, you're trying to rob me now? This girl must be pretty hot for you to commit a crime for her!" Sergio speculated with a chuckle.

Sebastian stopped play wrestling with his dad, he looked at him. "Yeah, she's pretty hot-totally hot, to be exact. She's new, transferred in from another school in California. From the moment she arrived at Brentwood Academy, all of the other guys have been trying to hook up with her, but she hasn't paid them any attention. Lucky me that I was paired up with her in science class for the entire school year. The past few weeks gave me an opportunity to get to know her better, if you know what I mean." He winked at his dad, who chuckled.

"I know one thing, your ass better had been paying attention in class. I'm not paying a shit-load of money for you to make goo-goo eyes at this girl," Sergio said, one eyebrow raised.

"See, this is why I can't talk to you." Sebastian smirked.

Sergio laughed. "Why is that?"

"I'm trying to come to you on a man to man issue."

"Don't you mean, 'boy to man' issue? I mean, you did ask *me* for money to take *your* date out. I don't think you've reached the 'man to man' stage yet." Sergio continued to chuckle.

"Case. In. Point.," Sebastian said, making sure to give his father a scolding look.

"Is this you trying to chastise me?" Sergio's smile grew wider as he watched his son. He marveled at Sebastian. A memory flashed

3

through his mind of his son being born and how small and precious he was as he held him in his arms, to the young man he'd become sitting before him. He was proud, as proud as any father could be of their child.

"Dad, I'm serious. I really like this girl."

"Okay, okay, I'll take it easy on you. I'm all ears." Sergio made himself more comfortable on the sofa, resting his right ankle on his left knee.

"We like the same things, such as, the same music, movies and food. She is so beautiful and smart, she has the most gorgeous blue eyes. I was pretty excited when she said she'd go out with me." Sebastian smiled. "Not only that, but some of my friends are so jealous!" he said with a wicked glee.

Again, Sergio raised one eyebrow, then he sighed. "Here." He removed seventy-five dollars from his wallet and handed it to his son, who took the money quickly as if fearing his father would play another trick on him by snatching it away. "Now, you have a curfew, don't take any liberties that you know will piss me off, I expect you to be responsible. Don't do anything you know I don't want you doing and you know what I mean, so get that goofy look off your face."

Sebastian changed his facial expression to one his father would be satisfied with.

"That's better. Okay, have fun and remember, home by curfew."

"Thanks Dad!" Sebastian said happily before sprinting up the stairs to his bedroom to get ready. Sergio watched his son disappear up the stairs then he rose from the sofa, making his way toward the kitchen in the direction of the succulent aroma he was smelling.

"Why did you make that boy suffer like that?" Madeleine asked with a giggle as she rose from the table with a bowl of green beans she was preparing for dinner, snapping each green bean stem into two pieces.

Sergio snorted as he made an offhand gesture. "That's my son, he can handle it. Besides, I had fun teasing him. Man, can you believe it, going on his first real date. It seems like only seventeen years ago he was a newborn baby I held in my hands."

Madeleine chuckled. "Only seventeen years, you say? That would be exact. I remember, he was such a sweet baby, so adorable."

Sergio chuckled. "You think all babies are sweet and adorable."

Madeleine placed one hand on her hip, her other hand holding firmly to the bowl of green beans. "Are you trying to say our son wasn't adorable?"

It was Sergio's turn to hold up his hands in surrender, now. "No, no, that's not what I'm saying. Our boy was adorable, he's perfect."

Madeline smiled sweetly. "He is, isn't he. Back to what you were saying, I do believe all babies are adorable. Their innocence is beautiful."

Sergio shook his head. "I beg to differ. You forget, I'm a pediatrician. I've seen some ugly-ass babies. Sometimes I have to stop myself from jumping back!" he laughed outright.

"Are you sure you're not in the wrong line of work?" Madeleine teased. She knew that he loved his job and was a wonderful doctor.

"Yeah, the kids love me, I enjoy them, too." He looked around casually, then back to Madeleine. "Still, time has gone by so fast. Soon, he'll be going through his first change," Sergio stated, thinking about his son's maturity.

"Oh goodness, I know! It seems like only yesterday, he was learning how to walk and talk," Madeleine said with another soft giggle.

Sergio nodded. "Yeah, I remember." He looked at the bowl of green beans in her hand. "What's for dinner?"

"Your hungry self!" Madeleine ribbed.

"Damn right, I'm starving!" Sergio growled playfully, baring the whiteness of his teeth. "You've been hanging around Natasha too much, you're starting to sound like her."

"She's good people to hang around with, a blast. But you should have picked up something to eat on your way home. Dinner's not even halfway done."

Sergio pouted. "What's for dinner?" he repeated.

"Meatloaf, string beans and baked potatoes along with potato soup and Caesar salad. Sound appetizing enough for you?" she asked with a coy smile.

"I can hardly stop the drool from sliding between my lips," Sergio responded with a hint of anticipation.

"I knew you'd say that."

"No you didn't," Sergio replied, smiling devilishly.

"Yes, I did."

Sergio continued to smile as he left the kitchen, heading up the staircase for the bedroom he shared with Elise. He opened the door, his gaze immediately settling on Elise who was sitting on the bed painting her toenails with light pink nail polish.

"Hello darling," Elise greeted Sergio as she eyed him from head to toe.

"Hey baby. Damn, did I miss you today!" He tossed himself down on the bed next to her, causing her to cease her activity.

"That would have been disastrous had I not paused," she said with a coy smile.

"Oh no, we can't have that. Let me." Sergio took the nail polish bottle from Elise and sitting up on the bed, he lifted her foot gently, resting it in his lap. He began to paint her remaining toenails delicately, making sure no mistakes were made.

Elise watched him intently with a mixture of lust and love. "Our children drove me completely insane today. Neither one wanted to take a nap, I finally got them to go to sleep about thirty minutes ago!"

Sergio chuckled deeply. "You just had to deal with two, I had to deal with seventeen screaming kids today...all were late on their immunization shots, so I'm sure I looked like the bogeyman to them."

Elise giggled. "I'm sure," she continued to watch him until he finished. He screwed the top on to the nail polish bottle and handed it to Elise, who placed the bottle on her nightstand. She turned to face her lover, who was watching her with a lust-filled gaze.

"You know you were wrong last night. That certainly wasn't the proper way to treat your man, letting me hang like that," Sergio stated.

Elise gasped. "I was exhausted! The kids-they wore me out!"

"Sure, blame it on the kids."

"Well," she slid her legs off of the bed and moved closer to him, placing her hands on his thighs and slowly slid up, toward his crotch. "Is there any way I can make it up to you?" she asked seductively.

"Oh, I don't know...what do you have in mind?" Sergio flirted.

"Well, I can do a number of things to make up for disappointing you. Something like this..." Elise's fingers began to slowly unbutton Sergio's shirt, sliding it seductively off his shoulders and tossing it onto the floor. Her eyes roamed appraisingly over his muscular torso.

"I think I like where this is going," Sergio commented with a wolfish grin.

"Oh yes, I have a few ideas on how to make it up to you." She leaned forward, planting tender kisses along the base of his neck. Soft moans escaped his throat as he relished the gentle touch of Elise's supple lips. Her hands found his pecs and began to caress the firm flesh, her fingers kneading the muscles underneath. She lowered her head, planting delicate, wet kisses along his chest, her soft tongue and lips suckled his tender, erect nipples causing Sergio to jerk slightly. She giggled at his reaction before moving downward across his stomach, pausing to tickle his navel with the tip of her tongue.

Sergio released a shuddering moan, his chest heaving with anticipation. Elise unbuttoned his pants and he shifted his body allowing her to slide them off. She tossed the pants into a nearby chair then returned her attentions to his body, brushing her fingertips over his erection, causing him to jerk once again. Elise smiled as she leaned forward, kissing her lover fervently, their tongues caressing each other as their bodies radiated an intense heat which stroked their inner fire. She pulled away from his hungry mouth, her hand pressing gently on his heaving chest. She leaned forward, her tongue snaking between her lips to lap at the thin line of sweat that had beaded his torso. She moved lower and lower, past his stomach toward his groin. Her tongue trail wetness over Sergio's sensitive head, licking away the sticky moisture that had gathered causing him to moan and quiver with pleasure.

A spasm ran through him and he inhaled sharply, before allowing his body to relax. Elise smiled sweetly at him, then lowered her head, her lips parting to take him into her mouth. He moaned loudly as he raised his hips to meet her skillful lips and tongue. She continued to tantalize him as he sank back on the bed, unable to contain his erratic moans of ecstasy. Both lost track of time as Elise's lips stroked Sergio until he could no longer hold back. His back arched high off the bed, fingers gripping handfuls of her long, dark brown locks. His breath came in labored gasps as he rode the raging waves of his orgasm.

Moments passed before he collapsed onto the fluffy white comforter, struggling to regain his composure. Elise raised her head, her aqua-green eyes studying him. His eyes were half closed, his chest continued to heave, only a bit more slowly. He began to smile. With a cat-like gracefulness, Elise crawled upward the length of his body, until she was face-to-face with him. Sergio, lifting his head, pressed his lips firmly to hers as his hand held her head to his. He slid his fingers down the length of her spine, sending tingles over her flesh. His other hand began to remove her pink satin robe with the sequined trim, sliding the robe off one shoulder. He leaned forward, kissing her newly bared flesh, slowly at first, then more passionately. She climbed onto his lap, moaning in response to his lust as the hardness between his legs met the sultry heat between hers. His hand slid the robe down to her waist, baring Elise's breasts. His mouth teased her nipple running his tongue over the tender flesh, sending ecstatic tingles down her spine. Sergio relished the heat that pulsated from between her legs. He fought the urge to plow himself deeply into her, he wanted to be gentle.

He rolled Elise onto her back, his hand untied the belt to her robe, exposing her completely. Giving Elise all of his attention, Sergio traveled further downward, past her stomach. She gasped loudly as his tongue teased her opening. His hands underneath her buttock pressed her closer to him as his lips and tongue brought forth screams of ecstasy from Elise as she writhed on the comforter.

She cried out as her climax exploded from her. Her thin fingers gripped the short cropped, curly locks of Sergio's thick, black hair, pressing his face all the more harder to her flesh. He rode her until she fell back onto the bed, panting, exhilarated. He released her, and with his own cat-like agility, covered her body with his own, sliding himself deeply inside her. She quaked as he entered her, wrapping her arms around his shoulders as he thrust deeper inside her in a smooth, sensuous rhythm, sending them both to the heights of their pleasure. They continued, their bodies slick with sweat, their animalistic auras mingled together as they made love. Sergio's mouth pressed roughly, passionately to Elise's. They began to feel another orgasm building, stronger than the first. Sergio increased his speed as he felt his climax spreading throughout his limbs. She gripped him tightly, nails scratching his back, drawing only the thinnest line of blood. The moment was almost unbearable as they shared their climaxes, rocking hard against each other until the spasms of pleasure began to fade away, leaving them both spent...sated. Sergio collapsed on top of Elise, breathless, exhausted.

"I love you so fucking much!" Sergio declared when he was able to catch his breath.

She sighed. "I love you, too, darling."

The two of them laid in each other's arms for a while before Sergio broke the silence. "I know this is a crazy way to end this perfect moment, but...I'm hungry...the food smells like it's done."

Elise giggled again. "Alright, let's go."

They unwrapped their limbs and climbed out of the bed.

"Perhaps we should shower first," she suggested.

Sergio looked at her, his wolfish grin growing more toothy. "I like that scent on you." He stepped closer to her leaning forward, inhaling deeply. "Ahhh, the scent of my loins."

Elise struck him playfully, punching his left pectoral. "You're so uncouth!" she stated with a chuckle.

Sergio laughed, then pulled her closer for another passionate kiss. He released her and headed to the bathroom. "Taking a shower is more respectful than showing up for dinner as we are...so I'll play along on this night." He turned and disappeared into the bathroom. Elise heard the shower running. She smiled to herself, then followed Sergio inside the shower. They finished quickly, then headed downstairs toward the dining room. Miranda and Daniel walked into the room after Elise and Sergio. Rachel and Carmen had completed setting the table. The remaining eleven Pride members sat down and began feasting.

"So, Sebastian had a hot date tonight, eh?" Devin asked as he stuffed a healthy helping of string beans into his mouth.

"Yeah, I told him to have fun," Sergio replied as he chomped down on a huge piece of meatloaf.

"Bet you were glad it was a girl he's seeing, aren't you?" Daniel asked in a playful manner. Everyone knew about Sergio's "touch" of homophobia.

"Shut the hell up and eat," Sergio responded before tossing a glance at Devin and Angela, whom were both gay.

Devin giggled. "He's got another son...you never know."

Angela laughed. "You're going to give Sergio a heart attack, stop it."

"You two can shut up at any time. Besides, I'm going to love my kids all the same, no matter what their sexual orientation is. But I am happy that he's straight. I feel like I can help him out on his relationships better this way. Shit, I don't know what kind of advice to give him about fucking some dude!" Sergio stated.

"Basically the same...only not the same. Hmmm, I get what

you mean, I see where you're coming from." Devin commented with a sweet smile.

"How wonderful for you and me," Sergio responded sarcastically. "Shall we sing, Kum Bah Yah, now?"

"Devin, shut the hell up and eat," Miranda said, chuckling at both him and Sergio.

Devin snorted, then did just that. Everyone finished their meals quickly, clearing the table afterwards, putting the dishes into the dishwasher for the evening. Several members entered the den to watch a few movies. Sergio and Elise went back to their bedroom, Miranda and Daniel returned to the bedroom they now shared. Devin left to go to Desires Unleashed. He wanted to see his lover, John Fallon, before his shift started.

CHAPTER TWO

Darian sat by the window watching the setting sun disappear into the beautiful multicolored red, purple and bright orange horizon. He smiled as he thought back to the day when his master, Kysen, had given him the gift to watch this amazing evening spectacle. He glanced over at Xavier as he rested, still unable to witness such a sight. He watched the sun set until it completely disappeared, leaving the sky an indigo blue speckled with sparkling stars. He returned his gaze to his young male lover who was now stirring on the bed as he came to.

"It's about time," Darian teased.

"It's only five o'clock…that's about normal for me this time of year," Xavier responded as he sat up on the bed, brushing the white satin sheets to the side. "Is Tasha home?"

"No. She called to inform us that she would be running a little late." Darian watched him climbed out of the bed. His eyes scanned over Xavier's muscular physique, smiling as the younger vampire ran his fingers through his long, brown locks.

Xavier glanced at Darian. "What?" he asked, curiously. A second later, he chuckled softly. "Don't bother answering."

"I wasn't going to."

Xavier shook his head. "I'm going to take a quick shower. What time did Tasha say she'd be home?"

"She didn't say…but I suspect she'll be home before seven. Besides, she knows that you'll want to feed and we promised to let her watch, I'm sure she won't be much longer."

Xavier chuckled at the thought of Natasha wanting to watch them in one of their most intimate moments. He flashed Darian a wicked smile before entering the bathroom.

Darian listened as Xavier turned on the water, he rose from his seat, following his lover inside the shower.

Xavier smiled, but didn't turn to face him. "I knew you'd follow me, can't I have a moment's peace without you barging in on me?" he joked.

"I'm afraid not. I simply cannot give you a single moment of peace. Sorry."

Xavier laughed outright, then he tossed Darian a seductive glance over his shoulder. "You know…Natasha isn't going to be happy if she comes home and finds out we're still not ready."

"Life is full of little disappointments."

"I'm going to tell her you said that."

"Tell her," Darian replied, then he leaned forward, pressing his body against Xavier's back. "I want you, now!" he whispered passionately into the inner shell of Xavier's ear.

Xavier turned around, facing Darian. "Why don't you let me have my way with you tonight?" he asked, his voice was as smooth as silk.

Darian's eyes shifted to Xavier's. "Mmmm, what a tempting notion," he stated with a most beguiling smile.

"That's not an answer," Xavier positioned himself behind Darian, pressing him against the shower wall. He placed his hands on Darian's shoulders, keeping him pinned.

"No, it wasn't," Darian agreed, smiling at his lover's lusty aggression.

"Well?"

Darian smiled as Xavier pressed him harder against the shower wall. His breathing quicken as his lover's fingers traced wavy patterns down his back, traveling down past his firm buttocks. Xavier begin to caress his cheeks, parting them slowly. Darian moaned as Xavier's fingers began massaging his sensitive opening.

Xavier leaned closer towards Darian's ear. "I love that sound you make." His fingers entered Darian slowly, stroking him as his other hand began to caress Darian's strong pecs, causing him to shudder with pleasure. Xavier licked the outer shell of his lover's ear as his hand found his erection. Slowly, almost torturously, he began to stroke Darian's hardness, circling his fingers over the tip. Darian's back arched, his body twitching slightly as if begging his lover to continue. Xavier chuckled as he pulled his fingers free. He kneeled down behind Darian, his tongue replacing his fingers as he gently licked the soft, warm opening, tracing numerous patterns over his lover's sensitive flesh as his fingers continued stroking Darian's erection, causing him to gasp and wither against the tiles.

Darian moaned louder as his hands pressed firmly against the shower wall. His eyes closed in ecstasy as he relished the sensations. Xavier continued his dual assault, sending waves of pleasure coursing throughout Darian's limbs. Water ran over the two men, plastering Darian's long, wavy, jet-black locks to his face and torso. Xavier's skillful strokes worked Darian over, bringing him closer to his climax. Darian began to moan louder as his body heated up, preparing to erupt.

All of a sudden, the pleasure ceased.

"Tasha's home," Xavier announced as he rose to his feet, looking toward the bedroom.

"How rude!" Darian complained, regarding Xavier's abrupt cessation of their lovemaking.

"She's going to be mad that we're not dressed." Xavier smiled wickedly, knowing full well what he'd just done would no doubt warrant payback.

"This is what I get for allowing you to seduce me," Darian scolded playfully as he forced himself to calm down.

"Hey, I don't recall inviting you to shower with me. Nonetheless, I love you and I'll make it up to you," Xavier whispered passionately with a hint of mischievousness.

Darian looked at him. "I know. You're most precious to me for many reasons. Rest assured, your love is returned, my beautiful inamorato." He kissed Xavier deeply then pulled himself away. "I'm still going to get you back for this one," he warned.

Xavier laughed. "Oh, don't hold a grudge, we really do need to get ready," he said.

Darian looked at him with a sigh. "I've been around for sixteen hundred and fifty years. I'm far too old and wise to be holding petty little grudges." He climbed out of the shower, and turning, shook his head. "On second thought, I think I'll do so just this once. Vengeance will be mine...that was just cruel." His smile held wicked promise.

Xavier laughed as he walked to his closet. "I'll make it up to you," he repeated before opening the doors, searching for the perfect outfit. Darian stretched out his long form on the bed, allowing the air in the room to dry his body.

"She's almost here," Xavier said as he neatly laid his clothes on the edge of the bed. Both men looked toward the door just as Natasha walked through.

"I'm so tired! You guys would not believe the day I've had!" she declared as she tossed her coat in a nearby chair.

"Why don't you tell us about it?" Darian suggested.

Natasha looked at Darian's naked form. "Aren't you supposed to be dressed by now?"

"Yes."

"Well?"

"I was just relaxing, but I'll get dressed now."

"Relaxing?" Natasha looked at both men. "Geez, I can't leave you two alone for a second!" She playfully pushed Darian as he rose from the bed. "Go on, get dressed! I expect you both to be dapper by the time I get out of the shower. I just need twenty minutes to get ready, so no more funny business!" She walked into the bathroom, tying her hair up along the way. She figured the reason neither man was dressed was due to their "physical excursions", as Darian had once called it. She would have been jealous otherwise, had she not accepted their relationship prior to getting involved and falling in love.

"Well, if I had my way, I'd be even more relaxed by now. But Xavier is such a romantic, he didn't want to keep you waiting," Darian said.

"Well, I'm glad someone was looking out for little ol' me," Natasha commented, turning on the water. *Okay, so they weren't getting busy.* she thought to herself. *But not for lack of trying.*

"I'm always thinking of you, my darling," Xavier said.

"I look out for you...it's just...let's say that Xavier left me in a rather compromising predicament," Darian said in his defense.

"It's your own fault for following me into the shower," Xavier commented, chuckling.

Darian tossed him a seductive glance, then walked to his own closet. Both men dressed quickly. Darian chose a smoke-gray suit with a black button-up shirt. Xavier wore a black suit with a smoke-gray button-up shirt. They each wore their matching ties with the black, silver and white pattern which Natasha had picked out for them. Both men tied their long hair into single ponytails. Natasha exited the bathroom, a white towel wrapped tightly around her torso.

"Xavier, can you get my strappy black dress from my closet, the one with the pearls on the straps? Oh! I need my black strappy heels, too."

"You have several pairs of black "strappy" heels, which pair do you want?" Xavier asked.

"The ones with the criss-cross straps that go up my ankle."

"You have several pairs of those-"

"Oh, never mind! I'll get them myself! I'll be all day trying to get you to get the right pair of shoes," Natasha stated with a chuckle.

"The trick is to act clueless," Xavier whispered to Darian with a sly smile.

Natasha chuckled. "Let me guess, you're hoping that I'll be too reluctant to send you on more errands. Ha! Don't bet on it...you forget, I'm lazy."

Both men laughed as she removed the dress and heels from her closet.

"Give me twenty minutes, and I'll be ready."

"That's what you said thirty minutes ago before you took your shower," Darian reminded her, one eyebrow raised.

Natasha giggled. "So, I may have taken longer than expected. I'm going to be with you two gorgeous fiends tonight, I want to look halfway decent!"

"I prefer you naked," Darian stated with a lecherous grin.

"I'm sure you do, with your freaky ass!" Natasha replied.

"I just have superior taste, is all," Darian joked.

"Sure you do, but try as I may, I just can't see my birthday ensemble being appropriate for a night out in the city," she said, mimicking Darian's tone.

Darian laughed freely, his dimpled schoolboy grin making her blush.

Natasha slipped on her gown, then strapped on her heels. When she was completely dressed, she made sure to spray on her very own perfume scent from *Anisi* that Darian had especially designed for her, respectfully labeled: *Natasha*. It was a gift that had completely surprised her, not to say that all of their gifts to her didn't blow her away. Both men bombarded her with lavish gifts, twice as many on special occasions. Needless to say, Natasha felt that she was becoming pleasantly spoiled.

"Are you ready yet?" Xavier asked as he sprawled lazily over the cushioned chair by the bed, one leg draped over the armrest.

"Yeah," Natasha looked at both men. "See, I told you I wouldn't take long." She reached for her cashmere coat hanging in the closet.

"Oh no, not long at all...only one hour and seventeen minutes," Darian teased, although he was correct on the time it had taken her to get ready. He pulled on his own long black cashmere trench coat.

"I see you've got jokes! You're regular comedian! Taking your act on the road, are ya? Hush your trap, let's go," Natasha bantered playfully. Both men chuckled as they headed out of the bedroom. Xavier pulled his gray trench coat from the closet by the front door.

"You two look so gorgeous. I love those suits on you." Natasha gazed lustfully at both men.

"As do you my dear." Darian leaned forward, kissing Natasha softly on her lips.

"Are you going to feed?" she asked, her eyes shifted from one man to the other.

"But of course. I have the perfect place in mind. But first, we want to make sure that you have eaten," Darian said.

"Are you sure, I don't want you two to feel any discomfort, I know you must be hungry." Natasha looked at Xavier.

"Don't worry, Tasha. I'm a lot more resistant to the hunger than I was before. I'll be alright," Xavier assured her with a tender smile.

"Okay." She didn't say anything else on the matter, figuring they knew their situation best.

The three walked toward Darian's brand new Anaconda Pavilion. He had traded the older model in for the newer one as he did with most of the cars in his two-story garage. He navigated the car smoothly passing other automobiles on the expressway. Forty minutes passed before they arrived at their destination.

Two valet attendants trotted toward Darian's car, opening the doors at once. One offered Natasha his hand and he assisted her out of the car. The two vampires stepped closer to her, Darian tipped the valet a twenty dollar bill which was the smallest currency he had in his wallet.

"I love this restaurant! Elise brought me here two weeks ago for lunch. They have some really good food." Natasha beamed as they entered.

"Only the best for you. I've heard that *Angelino's* made the top five restaurants list in the *Chicago Word* recently. Trust Elise to have chosen to bring you here," Xavier said with a chuckle.

"I know, the three of you have excellent taste," Natasha said.

"As I stated earlier," Darian said.

"O-kay, Darian...you have the most wonderful taste in the world, happy now," she asked, rolling her eyes playfully.

"Not really, there's something about the way you just praised my exceptional attributes which sort of cheapens everything." He smirked.

"You're ridiculous."

"See what I mean?"

"Okay you two, enough already, let's go inside," Xavier interrupted, laughing at the two of them.

They entered the parlor foyer and were greeted by a female employee, who asked, "May I take your coats?"

"Yes, please," Natasha said. Xavier assisted her in removing her long trench coat. "Thank you."

"My pleasure." He smiled.

The female hostess took their coats. Once she checked in their coats, she handed Darian the reclaim ticket. "Enjoy your meal." she said with a courteous smile.

"I'm sure we will, thank you." Darian flashed her his million-dollar smile before turning to greet the Maitre d'.

"Good evening and welcome to *Angelino's*. What is the name of your party?" the Maitre d' asked.

"Alexander." Darian replied as he stood beside the podium.

The Maitre d' looked down at his reservation book. "Ah, yes. Mr. Alexander, party of three. Right this way. Please follow me." The Maitre d' led the way to a table by the window reserved for very special guests. As they made their way to their table, Natasha looked around the beautifully decorated restaurant's interior. Huge crystal chandeliers hung from the ceiling, illuminating the dining area. Cream colored table clothes covered each table with matching chiffon drapes adorning every window. Beautiful and exotic cream, yellow and white flowers were sitting in vases planted on every table. The floor was layered with a thick cream and white contemporary designed marble-pattern carpet. After directing them to one of the best tables in the restaurant, the Maitre d' spoke. "Someone will be with you shortly, please enjoy your meal." With that, he returned to his post.

Xavier took his seat beside Natasha.

Natasha looked at her two men. "This place is so beautiful."

Both men looked around at the interior.

"It's lovely," Xavier said with a smile.

"Not quite as extravagant as some restaurants I've been to, but the decor is rather elegant...contemporary by many standards," Darian commented in a blasé manner.

"Okay, Darian. What is the most beautiful place you've ever visited?" Natasha asked, genuinely curious.

"Oh, this should be interesting," Xavier said, watching Darian from across the table.

Before Darian could speak, a waitress approached their table carrying three menus. "Hello, how are you this evening?" she asked with a bright smile.

"Oh, we're doing just fine," Natasha replied with a bright smile of her own.

"Wonderful! Here are your menus, and can I get you anything to drink?" the waitress asked as her eyes scanned their faces.

"I'm fine right now," Natasha said.

"I'm fine, thank you," Darian said.

"Nothing for now, thanks." Xavier smiled.

"Well, if you change your mind, just let me know. I'll give you a few minutes to decide on what you want, I'll return to take your orders," the waitress said with another pleasant smile and nod, then she attended to her other customers.

Natasha looked over her menu while Darian and Xavier left theirs untouched.

"Ooh, I think I want the same thing I had before but I like to try new things every once in a while. I'm trying not to order the lobster, even though that's where my heart's at," Natasha said as she flipped through the menu.

"Why not order the lobster, and whatever else you want to try," Darian suggested as he relaxed more comfortably into the cushioned chair.

"You don't mind?" Natasha asked in a soft voice.

Xavier chuckled. "I don't think you're going to dissolve our funds anytime soon."

Darian nodded in agreement. "Order whatever you want, darling."

Feeling a bit like a pampered princess, Natasha smiled. "There's only one problem. Elise knew about my love affair with lobster, so she ordered for me because the menu is in Italian." She looked up at her lovers, hoping one of them would translate the menu.

Darian chuckled as he picked up his own menu, opening it to the entrée page. "What are you in the mood for?"

"What sounds good to you?" Natasha replied. Still wanting to be daring in her food choices, but more than willing to be advised.

Darian mention an item in Italian.

"Speak English." Natasha reached across the table, poking him lightly in his chest.

Darian shifted the menu to the side, peeking at her from around the edge. "It's sautéed duck over a bed of lightly seasoned angel hair pasta, drizzled with a rosemary and red pepper cream sauce."

"Sounds like something you'd enjoy," Xavier added.

Natasha shrugged. "Well, I like duck, and I like pasta. Why not." She smiled. Both she and Darian placed their menus down on the table to let her waitress know that she was, in fact, ready to place her order. The waitress looked in their direction noting the closed menus. She walked over to them, smiling.

"I take it you are all ready to order?" she asked.

"Yes." Natasha picked up the menu opening it to the first page. Remembering how to pronounce the first entrée she wanted, she ordered her beloved lobster dish. She also informed the waitress that she wanted to place another order to go.

The waitress's hand jotted down Natasha's requests. She nodded her head. "Sure, that won't be a problem, ma'am."

"Great. Thank you."

"Excellent choices by the way, ma'am." The waitress smiled, then looked at the two men. "May I take your orders?"

"No, thank you," Xavier and Darian said in unison. The waitress looked at them a bit confused.

"We've already eaten, now we're just spoiling her," Xavier said with a flash of his charming smile.

"Oh, very well." The waitress looked at Natasha. "I'll have your appetizer here in a few minutes." She gathered the menus and walked away.

"My eyes might be bigger than my stomach, but I'm going to eat like a pig tonight," Natasha said with anticipation.

"You won't get past the appetizer!" Xavier teased.

"Oh yes she will. Restaurants such as this one only offer you a taste of what you really want. They hope that you're starved enough, because when you are, you'll get full fast when you finally do eat something. You'll believe that you actually had a generous cuisine, when in fact, you only nibbled your way through dinner," Darian stated.

"That's why I ate that candy bar on the way over here," Natasha said. "I'm prepared to chow down."

"Good," Xavier responded, then he looked at Darian. "You never answered the question."

"Ah, yes. The most beautiful place I have ever visited. Let me think...the list is so long." He mentioned the name of the world's most famous and luxurious ocean liner. "It was most beautiful, quite before it's time...so tragic – its fate." He paused for a second, remembering that fateful night. He decided to continue. "I must say that my master, Kysen, had the most wondrous palace I have ever been in. Why, even the mansion in which he resides now rivals my own home."

Natasha asked Darian about the ship he mentioned, amazed that she was actually speaking with a survivor from that presumed "unsinkable" luxury liner which had sunk on its maiden voyage.

"Are you surprised?" Xavier inquired. "It was supposed to be the most beautiful luxury liner on the ocean. Of course Darian wouldn't miss its maiden voyage."

"When you put it that way, no, I shouldn't be surprised," Natasha agreed. She looked at Darian. "So tell me about it?"

Darian chuckled. "The liner was a work of art, but guided by arrogant men who caused its demise." He spoke of his experience on the doomed liner, the banquets he attended, the encounters he'd had. "I lost over a half of million dollars in property when the ship sank into the Atlantic. After it went under, I flew away with the one person I had granted eternal life to."

"Where is he now?" Xavier asked curiously.

"He's alive, but I haven't searched for him, so I don't know where he is," Darian said as he gazed unseeingly at his empty saucer.

"That's both sad and amazing at the same time," Natasha commented softly as she reflected on what Darian had told them.

"That's life." Darian looked toward the waitress as she approached their table carrying Natasha's appetizers.

"Here you are." The waitress set the plate on the table. "Is there anything else that I can get for you?"

"No, nothing right now. Thank you," Natasha said as she eyed her plate.

The waitress nodded, then walked away, but not before giving her the obligatory "hope you enjoy your meal" line. Natasha began to eat the appetizer, releasing a barely audible moan as she enjoyed the flavorful dish.

"I take it that the food is delicious?" Xavier stated more than questioned as he watched Natasha eat. She nodded as she speared the last stuffed shrimp with her fork, scooping it from the plate, sliding it into her mouth with delight.

Darian chuckled. "There's no doubt about it, you crave seafood. I should take you to Florence, Italy. They have wonderful seafood restaurants that I think you would enjoy. And that would only be the beginning."

Natasha swallowed. "That's something I'm looking forward to." She enjoyed her dinner and the conversation. They discussed her busy work day among other things and both men were disappointed to know that she had received disciplinary action for her tardiness.

"You don't have to accept that kind of treatment. You do know that, don't you?" Xavier asked, obviously agitated by the news.

"Yeah, I know. Don't worry, I still enjoy my job, but I'm in the wrong here, I have been tardy far too often as of late," Natasha admitted.

"Still," Xavier continued. "You don't have to be bothered at all. We can take care of you."

"I know, but I kind of like having something constructive to do during the day."

"What about free-lance? Going into business for yourself, perhaps opening a photography studio?" Xavier suggested.

"I'd like to do that sometime in the future. I'm still learning so much about the business, I want to soak it all up before I take on that kind of venture," Natasha said.

"Very well. As long as you're satisfied," Darian added. Natasha nodded. The three of them continued their discussion until they were ready to leave. They exited the restaurant after Darian left a huge tip for the server. The cold, biting wind hit them instantly upon leaving the restaurant, which affected Natasha more than it did the two vampires. They didn't seem at all bothered by the brisk breeze. Darian sent a valet to retrieve his automobile and they stood waiting for his return.

"Natasha?!" a male voice called out causing her to turn in its direction. She saw her ex-boyfriend, accompanied by another woman approaching. He came closer, stopping in front of the trio.

"Wow, fancy meeting you here," he said as he eyed her new physique appraisingly.

"Tell me about it. How have you been, Montell?" Natasha asked politely, not really caring to hear his answer. Darian and Xavier assessed Montell and his female companion, objectively. The vampires telepathically scanned the minds of the male and female to find their own preconceptions were confirmed. They now knew that this man standing in front of them, only two feet away, was the man who had broken Natasha's heart almost three years ago.

"Oh, nothing much. I see you're looking pretty good," Montell said as his eyes traveled down the length of her body.

"Well, Annette helped me get back into shape."

"Oh, how's Annette anyway?"

"Annette died. She was murdered actually, almost two years ago. It was all over the news."

Montell gave her his most convincing shocked expression. "Oh shit! I'm sorry to hear that."

Natasha nodded, exhaling slowly. "I'm sure," she said dryly.

"Hey now, sure, it's no secret that we didn't get along."

"She thought you were dog shit, and that I could do better," Natasha said.

Montell scoffed. "It's no secret that I didn't like her and she didn't like me, but it's still bad news that she was killed. That's all I'm saying." His gaze darted over to Darian and Xavier.

Natasha followed his gaze, she smiled. "Oh, how rude of me. Let me introduce you to my boyfriends. Darian...Xavier, this is Montell, my–"

"Ex," Darian said, interjecting.

Montell's eyes bulged. "Your boyfriends?"

Natasha nodded.

The female who stood beside Montell snorted. "What kind of a woman has two boyfriends."

"A very fortunate one," Xavier replied. He looked at Montell. "We really must thank you."

Montell glared at Xavier, a slight sneer on his lips. "Why?" he asked harshly.

"Because, thanks to your foolish decision to leave this lovely woman, we were given the opportunity to swoop her into our arms and treat her the way she deserves to be treated." Xavier flashed Montell and his female companion his most charming smile. Darian chuckled.

Montell's jaw tightened. "Yeah, whatever," he snapped.

The valet pulled Darian's expensive luxury car in front of them and climbed out, leaving the car running for convenience. Darian reached into his wallet as the valet attendant approached him. He handed the young man a hundred dollar bill, which pleased the attendant greatly.

"Thank you, sir!" the attendant said with great enthusiasm. Darian nodded. The attendant walked back to the car and stood by the passenger door, waiting to assist Natasha inside.

Montell's companion looked at Darian's car, her eyes rolling upward. "I still say if you were any kind of woman, you would have been able to keep a good man like him. You wouldn't need two," she snapped.

Natasha turned to face her. "You're right. I'm not 'any kind of woman', you are, and you can keep his sorry ass!" She looked at Montell. "Well, I would like to say that it was nice to see you again, but...it wasn't. Take care." She smiled as she made her way to the car. Darian took over for the valet attendant and assisted her into her seat. Xavier climbed into the back, behind Natasha while Darian slid comfortably behind the steering wheel. He drove off, leaving both Montell and his female companion staring angrily at their taillights as he traveled down the street.

"Oh my God! That was sweet! Did you see the look on his stupid face?!" Natasha asked, bubbling with glee.

"He's handsome, but not very bright," Darian stated as he drove the car at an increasingly high speed with ease.

"I can't believe you said that!" Natasha exclaimed to Xavier.

"Well, it was the truth." Xavier shrugged one shoulder.

"I know! I loved the look on his face after you said it. That was priceless! Oh! I wish I'd had a camera!" Natasha beamed as her mind replayed the scene over again in her head. She laughed delightedly.

Xavier looked over at Darian. "I don't think I've ever seen you tip a valet so much money before."

"That's because I don't. I was...how would you say it... showboating." Darian laughed softly.

"I wish Annette were here, I could tell her how dumb he looked when he found out that I have two gorgeous, rich men who actually love me for me, by my side, the bastard!"

"I think that made Tasha's night," Xavier said with a chuckle.

"I believe you're right. I don't think anything we could do for the rest of the evening is going to top that," Darian replied as he threw a glance at Natasha.

"What? I can't be petty? I can't enjoy a little retribution?" Natasha giggled once more.

"We didn't say anything," Xavier said, smiling.

"Yes you did, plus you gave me a 'look', but it's cool, I'm over it." She grinned.

Both men looked at her, each raised an eyebrow.

"What? I swear, the rest of this evening is about us. Where to now?" she asked.

"My club. We still haven't fed."

"Oh yeah," Natasha said.

"I want to dance," Xavier said from the back seat.

"Well, *Desires Unleashed* is the hottest spot in town," Natasha stated as Darian drove toward his night club.

The three of them arrived, the valet jogged over to the driver's side of the car as Darian opened the door.

"Hello Mr. Alexander," the valet greeted him.

"Good evening, Michael," Darian replied. Xavier climbed out of the back seat, stepping over to open the door for Natasha. She exited the automobile as the valet attendant sat behind the steering wheel. The three of them walked past the bouncer into the club which was filled with the gyrating bodies of about eight hundred club goers as the music blasted from dozens of speakers throughout the dance area.

"I love this song!" Natasha declared as they made their way past the vibrant, dancing club goers.

"I know, you've only played this song ninety times in the past week," Xavier teased.

"No I didn't, I just bought the CD yesterday."

"Then it's worse than I thought," Xavier chuckled.

"Oh hush!" Natasha slapped Xavier playfully on the arm as he continued to laugh. "Well anyway, I'm ready to dance."

"I need to feed," Xavier said as he kissed Natasha softly on the temple.

"Oh, that's right. Okay, you guys go and take care of your business," Natasha said.

"You're not coming? You don't want to watch?" Xavier asked.

"I do and I don't. Does that make any sense to you?"

"Yes and no." Xavier took her hand into his. "Why not?"

Darian stepped closer to her. "It's one thing to watch us feed from another being, be them vampire, shifter or human, for pleasure. It's another to bear witness to us feeding from humans for nourishment. Would that assumption be correct?"

Natasha nodded. "I have nothing against you doing what you have to do. I understand, and it helps that I know you don't kill your human victims just to feed. But the more I thought about watching the two of you tonight, the less appealing it became, the less excited I was to see it happen. I realize that I only like watching you feed in *that* way. Especially when you do it to each other." She looked off to the side, eyebrows creased. "That didn't exactly come out the way I wanted it to."

Xavier chuckled. "I think I understand."

"Very well, I'll make sure to, umm, 'do it' to Xavier tonight when we get home, just for you." Darian winked as he smiled boyishly, his dimples making him appear even more mischievous.

"Now, that, I can look forward to. Alright, I'll still be here when you two are done. Don't keep me waiting long," she said, then turned, grabbing hold of the nearest man next to her, prompting him to dance.

Xavier smiled, pleased to see that Natasha's level of confidence had risen. He remembered when she wasn't so bold and couldn't help but think that living with them, sharing their life had something to do with it. He turned, following Darian as he led the way through the sea of people toward the employees-only entrance. Once inside Darian's office, Xavier sat on the edge of the three-sectioned, marbled desk. Darian sat in his leather chair behind his desk, he picked up his telephone pressing one button on his speed dial.

"Send them up," Darian ordered, ending the call.

"Send who up?" Xavier asked.

"Two very willing mortals that will provide us with warm,

fresh blood," Darian said as he ran a finger down the length of Xavier's thigh.

"Oh, I thought since Natasha wasn't going to be watching us, you'd want to hunt?"

"Not tonight, we still have her with us. I figured we'd just feed here." Darian smiled wickedly.

"Well, there's always tomorrow night."

"Indeed," Darian replied. There was a knock at the door. "Come in," he called out.

John walked into the office with two mortals following behind him. Both male and handsome, one was blond with green eyes standing six-feet tall with golden tanned skin. The other was six-feet-three with brown eyes, dark brown hair with a chocolate skin tone. Both men wondered just how much pleasure vampire bites produced. Especially a bite from a powerful master vampire such as Darian, they each hoped that the rumors would prove themselves to be more than just rumors.

"Excellent John, you may leave us," Darian said. John bowed to Darian and left the office, closing the door behind him. Xavier watched the door close. It never ceased to amaze him how different the vampires in Darian's coven behaved when they were in Darian's presence as opposed to anyone else's. Tony, John, Gary, Annabelle, April, and Miko were always humble in Darian's presence. There was no doubt in Xavier's mind that they had only the utmost respect for Darian. In his experience, most masters ruled their covens with cruelty and oppression. Darian was quite the opposite. He was a fair master, very relaxed and approachable. He had three simple rules that were never to be broken. If his rules were violated, the price that was to be paid for such a violation was high. In reality, the vampires in his coven loved, respected and even feared him because he was who he was. They understood him and each gave him their loyalty free of will. It was easy to give Darian their loyalty, because he was a man of his word and he took great care of them, protected them, provided for them, gave them a place to belong.

Darian approached the two men, letting his gaze scan over

their bodies approvingly. "So, you wish to feel the rapture of the vampire's bite?" he asked the men.

Both blushed, one answered. "Y-yes," the blond stammered.

Darian chuckled seductively. "Of course you do." His exotic forest-green eyes held both of the men's gazes.

Xavier watched their faces blush even more. "I want the blond," he requested.

Darian turned to face Xavier. "As you wish."

Xavier rose and made his way over to the tall blond man, who was becoming a bit more nervous. He leaned closer to him, brushing his lips along the soft, fragrant skin of the man's neck, causing him to tense even more. Xavier could hear the man's heart beating furiously inside his heaving chest as his desire rose.

"Why are you tensing, this is what you wanted. Don't worry, there's nothing to be afraid of," Xavier whispered softly into the man's ear. "Do you want to sit down?" He motioned to the sofa. The man nodded and sat down. Xavier stood over him, smiling, knowing the man was growing increasingly more nervous.

Darian stepped behind the other man, sliding his arms around the man's torso, pressing his body against his own. The man seemed to become rigid, but made no struggle against him.

"Watch," Darian instructed his victim as he inclined his head in the direction of sofa.

Xavier sat on the sofa next to the blond, his left hand gently took hold of the man's chin. The blond panicked, grabbing hold of Xavier's hand.

"I don't think I want to do this," he said in a rush of words, unable to hide his fear any longer.

"Don't you? I'm sure this is a decision you thought long and hard about. You came here tonight hoping to be chosen. You wanted to feel an extraordinary pleasure unlike no other. I can give you that if you're brave and daring enough to accept my gift," Xavier whispered softly as his sparkling gray eyes peered into the pale green of the other man's eyes.

"Yes," The blond man said softly, almost absently as he gave into Xavier. The man closed his eyes as Xavier leaned closer to him, pressing his face into the man's neck. The blond gasped, wincing as Xavier's fangs pierced his flesh. His hands gripped Xavier's arms as he held him closer. His expression became euphoric, more relaxed as his body responded to the pleasure that the union was creating. He began to moan softly as the feeding continued, his breathing came in ragged breaths until his body let loose one violent quake, falling still seconds later. Xavier pulled away, his tongue running smoothly along his lips, licking away any blood that might have escaped his thirst.

"Is…is…is he dead?!" The other mortal man asked in a shaky voice.

Darian chuckled, he leaned closer to the man's ear. "No, but he is in heaven. Your turn." Without further delay, he plunged his long, razor sharp fangs into the man's pulsating vein causing him to arch as he cried out from the initial pain. Darian's eyes closed as he began to feast. Xavier watched from the sofa, sated…calm. The man in Darian's arms began to pant heavily, soft whimpering moans seeped from his throat. The bulge in the front of his black pants became very apparent as Darian continued to drink from him. A few more seconds passed before the man released a long shuddering moan as his body begin to spasm with ecstasy. When his body grew still and limp, Darian retracted his fangs, lifting the man. Xavier rose from the sofa as Darian laid the mortal down gently next to the other.

Darian straightened himself, looking at Xavier. "Well that was very enjoyable," he said. "You know, I find it humorous that Natasha enjoys watching us feed from each other."

"I know what you mean. I would have never thought that she would enjoy it, but I understand why. The entire experience is very erotic, which is why we have so many mortals who are more than willing to watch as well as donate. I'm actually happy that this doesn't bother her, it makes me feel even more close to her."

"Don't you have a clever way of putting things into perspective," Darian stated with a chuckle.

Xavier looked at the two sleeping men. "Are we going to leave them there?" he asked.

"For now," Darian said as he gazed at them. "Why don't you go enjoy yourself, there are some matters that I must attend to."

Xavier flashed Darian a knowing look. *"Friday Night's Bloodiest Fights?"* He knew what "matters" Darian was attending to. It was Friday night and the *Tournament of Champions* was just beginning in the underground arena Darian rightfully labeled the "Coliseum".

"Catchy title."

"It was completely unintentional, but I'd have to agree." Xavier smiled.

"I missed last week's tournament completely, because of our vacation." Darian gave him a boyish grin.

"Yeah, yeah. Have fun." Xavier chuckled then left the office, heading for the dance club section. There he saw Natasha sitting by the bar speaking with Devin and Tony. He made his way over to them. She smiled as he approached, and moved one seat over, making room for him so that he could join them.

"Having fun, darling?" Xavier asked as he slid into to the empty bar stool.

Xavier looked at Devin and Tony. "Hello fellas."

"Hey cutie!" Devin greeted with a toothy grin.

"Eyes off my man!" Natasha warned playfully.

"Aww, you have plenty to spare. Most of us in the world only have one lover," Devin teased.

"Don't hate...it's ugly," Natasha joked, giggling.

"Who's hating? I'm envious, there's a difference." Devin winked flirtatiously at Xavier followed by boisterous laughter.

"Whatever, boytoy. Keep on, I'll tell your man," Natasha said as all four laughed.

"You don't have to go there! So, where's your *other* significant other?" Devin asked Natasha.

"I'm sure he's extremely busy," Tony commented as he tossed Xavier a knowing look.

"What was that all about?" Natasha asked.

Xavier looked at Tony, his eyes widening slightly as they bored into the other man's. Tony knew full well the meaning behind that stare. Darian didn't really want Natasha knowing about his guilty pleasure for fear she'd want him to end the tournaments, which he didn't want to do because he enjoyed them a great deal. He assumed Natasha would go on endlessly about the moral atrocities the Coliseum encouraged until he gave in. In the end, he decided to keep the Coliseum and all that goes on inside, a secret.

"Nothing, don't worry about it," Xavier replied.

"Hmmm, must be a vampire thing," Devin speculated. "Well anyway, how was the vacation?"

Natasha decided to let it go, thinking it wasn't a big deal. She turned to face Devin. "Oh, it was a lot of fun. Paris is beautiful! I want to go back so badly!"

Xavier chuckled softly. "Don't worry darling, we will." He looked at Tony, "So when are you and Gary going on your little vacation?"

Tony smirked. "Whenever my boss gives me the big O-K."

Devin laughed. "Something really needs to be done about your boss not letting any of you go on vacations," he said, throwing an accusing glance toward Xavier.

"It's your own fault for making yourself such a hot commodity. You won't share your secrets and no one can put on a spectacle quite like you," Xavier said. "With that special drink of yours, you've made yourself indispensable."

"Is that it? I just thought you guys were serious when you said I wouldn't get any benefit time with this job," Tony said, one eyebrow raised.

Xavier laughed. "Yeah, well there's that, too." He took a sip of the drink Tony had made for him.

"Well, If I do get the opportunity, I plan on taking him to Greece. I think he'd have a great time," Tony responded. "Besides,

I've never been and I'd like to see the place where Darian was born."

"It's beautiful. Good choice," Xavier commented.

"Yeah, sounds like a great vacation spot. I'd like to go there myself," Natasha stated. She looked at Devin. "What about you and John?"

Devin finished off his drink, placing the glass back down on the bar. "Well, it'd be nice to get away with my baby, but he has this warlord boss that never gives him a moment of peace, works him like a dog—he does! It's terrible," he stared accusingly, but teasingly at Xavier.

"He has hours to make up for all of the times I let you two have the night together," Xavier reminded with a wink.

"Hogwash!" Devin threw his hands in the air.

"So how's your little girl doing?" Natasha asked Devin.

"She's doing fine. I bought her the cutest little outfits. Just perfect for a little bit like herself. I got her these cute little pink gym shoes." Devin held his hands together a few inches apart to emphasize how small the sneakers were. "You know she's walking now and getting into all sorts of shit. Of course, Madeleine talked about me for buying the shoes. She said that they don't support her feet and she called them expensive baby accessories."

"She's kinda right," Natasha stated.

"Well, I say nothing is too good for my little princess!"

"I'm sure. But you're right, she is just a little pink princess. I hope you guys buy her more clothes in other colors. The world is big enough for only one Elise and all of her pink," Natasha said as she sipped her virgin daiquiri.

"You ain't never lied!" Devin stated, chuckling as he reflected on Elise's massive pink wardrobe. He turned when he sensed John approaching.

"What in the hell does that mean?" Tony asked.

Devin looked back at him. "What?"

"What you said, 'you ain't never lied', what does that mean?"

"Oh," Devin chuckled. "I just means that I think what she said makes a lot of sense and just something I hold to be true. That's all."

Tony nodded, acknowledging that he understood the urban slang term.

John walked over to Devin. "Hey." He leaned forward kissing him passionately.

"Hmm, I miss that. When can we hang out?" Devin asked, once the kiss was broken.

John shrugged. "As soon as I get the time." He looked at the others. "Hello everybody. The whole gang is almost here, I see."

"Yeah, except for Adrian and Nicole," Natasha said.

"This is normally their night to get out of the pound," John said.

"I resent that comment." Devin rolled his eyes with a snort.

"Don't be that way, I didn't mean anything by it. I'll make it up to you," John winked.

"That's better. In any case, wherever they are, I'm sure they're having fun," Devin said as he tossed a seductive glance at John who smiled wolfishly.

"Exactly what we should be doing." Natasha slid off of the bar stool taking hold of Xavier's hand leading him onto the dance floor. He pressed himself against her as she rocked her hips against his body.

"I love the way you move, so seductive, you're very graceful," he said as he observed the hypnotic sway of her hips.

"Thanks babe. I, of course, love the way you do everything that you do." She turned around, wrapping her arms around Xavier's neck, pulling him down to her. She locked her lips to his as he held her closer.

The two continued to dance and mingle with the others for a few more hours, until Natasha began to feel exhausted. Natasha yawned. "Okay, I'm done for the night. I know when to throw in the towel, unlike the rest of you." She pointed at the others as they chuckled.

"Awww, you just can't hang with the big dogs!" Devin teased.

"Don't you mean prissy cat?" Natasha retorted.

"Touché. I have a comeback, but I'll save it for later and then unleash it when you least expect it." Devin smiled.

Natasha gave him a sly look as Xavier wrapped his arm around her waist.

"Come on, darling. Say goodnight to the nice people," Xavier joked, assisting her off the stool.

"Bye."

Devin cleared his throat. "I'm fairly certain he said to say 'goodnight', not 'bye'."

"You know what?" Natasha paused.

Smiling devilishly, Devin leaned forward. "What?"

"If you weren't so cute, I'd have you beaten, skinned and made into a handbag." Natasha blew him a kiss.

Devin curled his fingers and clawed the air, making sure to make aggressive "cat" sounds. "Lucky for me, you love me. Night Tasha."

"Yeah, lucky you." Natasha laughed and waved to everyone before leaving the club. "Where's Darian?" she asked once they were outside.

Xavier beckoned for the valet to bring their car around. He looked down at Natasha. "Darian had to tend to some other issues."

Natasha nodded her head, satisfied with the answer. She didn't really question Darian's business issues. She felt that Darian and Xavier did what they had to do. Being with them for nearly two years and witnessing all of the dangerous events that complicated their lives, she fully understood why they had to do the things that they did, even if it meant breaking all of the laws.

"Okay. Man! I'm so sleepy!" She yawned loudly, causing Xavier to laugh.

"Don't worry, I'll get you home as soon as possible," he said. She smiled as she linked one arm with his, pulling him closer.

The valet pulled Darian's Anaconda Pavilion in front of them. He climbed out of the car, handing Xavier the keys.

Xavier helped Natasha into the passenger side then climbed in behind the wheel. He drove the car home, arriving at the mansion in less than forty minutes. He looked over at Natasha, who was fast asleep.

He chuckled. "Just like a baby," he whispered, then climbed out of the driver's seat. Rounding the car to her side, he opened the door and gently pulled her out. He entered the mansion with Natasha cradled lovingly in his arms. Reaching the bedroom without disturbing her, he laid her gently on the bed. Removing her clothes, he replaced them with her favorite blue silk nightgown-a gift from Elise. Once he was finished with Natasha, he undressed himself, discarding his clothes in the dirty clothes hamper located in the bathroom. He climbed in the bed next to Natasha, sliding very close to her so that their bodies touched. A few minutes later, he heard the door open, before Darian entered.

Darian looked at Natasha sleeping and chuckled. "I thought she wanted to see me 'do it' to you, as promised."

"The night became too long," Xavier gave Darian an accusing look. "Or could it be, you took too long to come home."

"That could be the reason, we'll never know."

Xavier smirked. "She missed you tonight," he whispered.

"Ah, but she had you to keep her company, my love," Darian responded as he began to undress.

"Yes, but she still missed you."

Darian chuckled softly as he hung his clothes in his huge walk in closet. "I see. Well, I'll try not to let my other "issues" interfere with our time again, sound good to you?"

"Sounds fair enough." Xavier watched Darian climb in beside Natasha. He leaned forward, kissing Xavier softly, then lowered his head, kissing Natasha tenderly on the forehead.

"She's so warm," Darian said softly.

"I know, and soft," Xavier agreed as he let his fingers slide lightly down the length of her arm. He looked at Darian. "Would you ever turn her?"

Darian's eyes focused on him. "I honestly don't know. I don't think that she wants our life...yet, I have no idea how I feel about letting her die a human's death. I can't answer that." He looked down at Natasha's sleeping form, then back up at Xavier. "Can you?"

"I could, but like you, I don't think she would appreciate that," Xavier laid his head down next to hers.

"I suppose we should present the possibility to her," Darian suggested as he laid his head down on the pillow.

"I suppose," Xavier agreed, then he grew quiet. Both men relaxed their minds and bodies as they waited for the sun to rise.

CHAPTER THREE

Warren panted heavily in Matthew's ear as he fought to regain his strength. Gently, he pushed himself away from Matthew, rolling over onto his side. His chest heaved slightly as his breathing returned to normal.

Matthew lay next to him, one leg tangled in the blue linen sheets. He ran both hands over his face to clear away the numerous beads of sweat that threatened to blur his vision. He turned, smiling, looking at Warren.

"That was amazing…as usual." He leaned forward, kissing Warren softly on his nipple, sucking it lightly.

Warren chuckled. "Don't start something you don't have the energy to finish."

"Who says I don't have the energy?" Matthew asked teasingly. "You're the one out of breath, not me."

Warren laughed. "You're right, you definitely have energy. You were amazing, I mean, damn! That was fucking great!"

"I love you," Matthew said as he gazed lovingly at Warren, who turned to face him.

"I love you, too."

The two men laid in each others arms for several minutes before the telephone started ringing. Warren picked up the cordless handset, glancing at the little digital LCD screen to check the caller ID.

"Shit…it's the job," he muttered.

"It's our day off!" Matthew complained.

"I'm not going to answer this shit!" Warren began to place the handset back on the nightstand when Matthew stopped him.

"Wait," he placed his hand on Warren's arm. "What if it's really important?"

"Someone else who's on shift can deal with it. Right now, I just want to eat you up…in that good, sexual way."

Warren dropped the telephone on the nightstand and immediately wrapped his arms around Matthew, burying his face close to his neck with a sexy growl, causing his lover to belt out a throaty laugh.

"Stop!" he playfully protested through chortles.

"Ain't no stopping once I get started!" Warren declared, as he climbed on top of Matthew, pulling the sheets over them. He started to seductively kiss a trail downward to Matthew's groin when both of their pagers began beeping in its distinctive emergency-alert tone.

"Fuck!" Warren cursed as he threw the covers off, climbing out of bed. He reached into both of their pants pockets, retrieving the pagers, tossing Matthew his as he viewed his own.

"I've got a 911 emergency, you too?" Matthew asked.

Warren nodded. "What's so fucking important?"

Matthew shrugged as he reached over to the nightstand grabbing the telephone, dialing the S.U.I.T. precinct.

"Supernatural Unit Investigation Team," a male voice greeted.

"Is this Williams?" Matthew asked.

"Yeah," Officer Williams responded.

"Hey, this is Detective Eric, we were just paged, what's up?"

"Oh, Matt, Captain wants you and Warren in here, pronto. Something about a suspicious DB. City cops don't know what to make of it either, they suspect it's our neck of the woods."

"Did they say why?" Matthew asked.

"From what I'm hearing, silver may have been involved."

"What?" Matthew was shocked by the possibility of a shifter death.

"I know…first case like this if it is…at least in the state of Illinois. Don't know about you, but I'm excited. You two better get down here right away."

"Gotcha, we're on our way." Matthew hung up the telephone, looking up at Warren, who nodded his head. "What do you think it means?" he asked.

"What do you mean?" Warren questioned.

"Well, it's suspected that the corpse of a shape-shifter has just been discovered...what could that mean?"

"Right now, I'm not sure. Could be we just have a human based crime or another shape-shifter one. I can't determine anything without seeing the body first. I'll tell you what, though, I sure didn't need this shit! Come on, let's get ready." Warren walked into the bathroom, wasting no time taking a quick shower. Matthew showered while Warren dressed in a black t-shirt and dark blue colored jeans. When Matthew finished showering, he dressed in a green button up shirt and black slacks. Both men pulled on their black leather jackets before heading out of the door.

When they arrived at the precinct, both detectives went to their captain's office. Warren knocked.

"Come in," the captain instructed. Both men entered. She looked up at them from behind her cluttered desk.

She was dressed in a gray skirt and a white blouse, exposing just the barest hint of cleavage. Her blonde hair draped over her shoulders, flowing past her breasts. She reached into a folder, retrieving a sheet of paper as she began to speak. "Great, I'm glad that you two are finally here. Listen up, we've got ourselves a possible 2-14. It's the first this precinct has ever had and if this turns out to be what we think it is, I want my best on the case."

"Oh quit with the much deserved praise. You still owe us for the Rogers Park case," Warren reminded as he loomed over her desk, arms folded across his chest.

"Oh, I almost forgot about that one!" Matthew agreed.

"Think I owe you two a 'good job'? I do believe I gave you one of those once the case was wrapped up. But this is serious and as two S.U.I.T. officers, this is your jobs. Now whether or not I give you a cookie afterward is inconsequential. Getting the job done need be your only reward."

"Wow, okay, nothing like getting a tongue lashing to put things into perspective. Now, about the case...," Warren said, tossing a look to Matthew.

"Glad you're on board," the captain stated sarcastically.

"Always. Where was the body found?" Matthew asked.

"Here's the address. Go there, see what you can find out and get back to me with any new information." She handed Warren a slip of paper with the location of the body. Both men look over the paper.

"This is in Peoria," Warren commented, somewhat agitated, knowing he had a long drive ahead.

"Yeah, so? You know that we cover the entire state of Illinois," the captain said, crossing one long leg over the other.

"That's not what I meant, I'm just noting the location of the body," Warren stated, attempting to cover his blunder.

"Oh? For a moment there, I thought you were going to complain about the three hour-plus drive it's going to take during rush hour traffic to get there."

"Now that you mention it...."

"No time. The person who discovered the body is still there, so why are you two still here? Go on, get going."

Their captain shooed them out of her office. They left, wasting no time as they made their way to the front desk.

"Let's take a DC, I'm not putting those miles on my ride. I also don't like the feeling I'm getting about this one," Warren said, eyebrows creased, lips curled downward in a frown.

"Sure," Matthew agreed. "What kind of feeling are you getting?" he asked.

"Not sure, can't really place my finger on it. Let's just get down there."

Matthew nodded as he signed out one of the detective cars. Both men climbed inside and drove to Peoria at breakneck speed, with the siren blaring to make their way through traffic as fast and safely as possible. Once they arrived at the location, they walked toward the crime scene. Red S.U.I.T. tape with white lettering blocked off access to the body. Warren stopped walking immediately when he scented the victim was a coyote shape-shifter. Matthew had stopped a step after Warren, looking back at him curiously.

Shaking his head slightly, Warren said in a low voice, "I'll tell you later." Matthew nodded as they continued to approach the scene, bending down low, dipping under the tape to find a uniformed police officer advancing their way. After identifying themselves, the office escorted the two men to a local police officer who greeted them.

"Hey, my name is Officer Johnson, I was the first to arrive at the scene." The six foot Officer Johnson looked to be about twenty-five years old; dark brown close cropped haircut, brown eyes and milk chocolate-toned complexion.

Both detectives shook his hand. "Is the scene as you found it?" Matthew asked. "Nothing's been touched or moved?"

Officer Johnson nodded. "Yeah, er, yes sir, as far as I know, nothing's been touched. I asked the lady who found the...it, if she moved it or touched it in any way, she said she didn't do anything, just called 9-1-1."

"'It'," Warren repeated with a hint of agitation.

"I'm just saying that, well, it's a corpse, not alive anymore and it for damn sure wasn't human."

"Do you know that for certain, or are you just talking out of your ass?" Warren asked.

The officer was caught off guard by Warren's comment. "I'll tell you what, I've never seen a human body sizzle from a silver bullet like this one. Come on, you guys of all people should know that these monsters are just freaks of nature with human faces. Some good Samaritan probably just shot it dead because he was scared and with good cause."

Matthew looked at Warren, a worried expression on his face. He knew how much Warren hated the amount of intolerance and ignorance that was directed toward the supernaturals.

Warren's jaw muscles tightened, he bit hard on his tongue, struggling to control his mounting temper. When he thought he had enough control, he spoke. "Last I checked, the most recent psychopathic murdering son-of-a-bitch that was finally caught after gruesomely killing seven women, was a human being. Who are you to call another being a 'monster' just because you're shit-pissed scared of what you don't understand?!"

"Hey, calm down, I'm just saying. Who are you, their spokesperson?" The officer took two steps backward.

Warren started to respond when Matthew interjected, "Let's not get into this. We're on the same side, we're just fighting different battles. We see different sides of everyone. Besides, we don't have time," he said, looking from one man to the other.

Warren glanced at Matthew and nodded.

"Good. Listen, we can take it from here. Oh and a word of advice, Officer. You should try to keep your personal feelings apart from your job," Matthew advised.

The young officer looked at him, then gave Warren one last glare, then nodded and walked away.

Matthew turned toward to Warren. "Are you trying to raise suspicion?"

"No. But I hate ignorant assholes like that!"

"I understand, you know I do, but this isn't the time or place for anyone to stand on their soapbox."

Warren chuckled wryly. "You're right." He exhaled. "Let's go do some investigating."

Both men slid on pairs of latex gloves as they approached the naked body for examination. Warren could smell the enticing scent of the blood as it dried in a pool around the corpse's head. Upon a closer inspection, the two detectives concluded that the shifter was shot in the back of the head by the size of the exit wound. The bullet had managed to blast out the victim's left eye. Bits of brain matter and tiny shards of white bone spilled out of the damaged eye socket onto the pavement. The other eye stared forward blankly. A thin white film covered the pupil, letting the two detectives know that the victim must have been dead for a few hours.

Both detectives noted pieces of silver still burning away the shifter's flesh. Warren looked at the victim's face again, noting that he was a young Caucasian with black hair. Warren guessed that the victim was close to six feet, approximately twenty years of age, and not a natural born.

Matthew looked over the body for any tattoos or scars, prior to his transformation, that could possibly help them identify the victim, but didn't find any.

"They must have taken his clothes to remove any lingering evidence, you think?" Matthew asked, mentally trying to come up with several scenarios on how the crime happened.

"Could be. Or maybe it was some prank. You know, get him out here, naked. He thinks it's all fun and games and then, bam! Shot down dead," Warren speculated. "Or maybe it's something else entirely. Regardless, it's murder anyway you slice it."

"So what do you think this means?" Matthew asked Warren.

"Not sure yet. The killer knew what he was, they had access to silver, " Warren replied, leaning closer to peer into the gruesome, bloody gaping wound.

"Yeah, I see." Matthew leaned closer to get a better look. "We're going to need that bullet analyzed. We also need to see if we can lift any epithelial off the body. I want to know if there's anything on this DB that can lead us to his killer."

Warren nodded. "CSI should be here soon. I'm going to look around the area, see what I can find." He scoped out the vicinity, sniffing, hoping to catch a scent.

Matthew finished writing down a few notes about the body and decided to join Warren. "Did you smell anything that raises hairs?"

"I caught the scent of several coyotes on the body, which lets me know he either belonged to a Pack or was possibly killed by one. There was also four distinct human scents on his body, three I smelled on a trail that led from the body toward that alley," Warren said, pointing to the opening of an alleyway. He walked a few paces forward, following the trail. "They must have checked the victim out to make sure he was dead then ran back to their vehicle." Warren stood still, both hands on his waist as he pondered the situation.

"I'm still wondering why he was here?" Matthew questioned. "Why the parking lot of this restaurant, was he waiting for someone?"

Warren bit his bottom lip, contemplating the question. He shook his head. "I'm wondering who those three human scents belong to. Were they responsible for killing him? Or were they the first to discover the body but then freaked out and ran away. I don't know." He turned toward the corpse. "The angle from the alley doesn't add up with the gunshot wound or the way he fell."

"I'd have to agree. Think it was close range, one shot to the head, execution style?" Matthew looked at the body again.

"Possibly, for that kind of damage to be done to the victim's skull."

"It's one of many possibilities." Matthew looked back toward the trail Warren had pointed out, trying to find answers to their questions. They continued to bounce ideas off of each other, trying to figure out what happened.

"I was thinking that also. A high-powered rifle would also do the trick. And there's plenty of locations where he could have fired from," Warren said, turning to face Matthew.

Matthew locked eyes with him, then glanced down at the blood splatter and brain matter surrounding the victims head. "I'm not a blood expert, but I'm willing to bet once forensics gets here, we'll have more answers to our questions. About the victim, we can probably rule out a close range attack. I mean, It can't be easy to sneak up behind a shape-shifter and blow their brains out."

"Impossible, is more like it," Warren stated, displeased with the situation.

Matthew stepped next to him. "Do you think we have a human rebel group on our hands? Think this murder is a message?"

Warren nodded. "Quite possibly, but we can't be too sure. Listen, I'm going to call Xander and let him know about this."

"Good idea. He might need a head's up if it is," Matthew agreed.

Both men turned to see the forensic team arriving. Marshall Galen, the official S.U.I.T. Medical Examiner for Illinois, wasted no time investigating the scene and the corpse. He knelt beside the body, the shutter of his camera clicking repeatedly as he took multiple photographs.

Both men walked over to him. "Got anything you can tell us?" Matthew asked.

Marshall looked up at Matthew. "Although, without me, you guys would be chasing your tails and I know that I am the greatest, but I've just arrived at the scene. Give me a minute to gather my thoughts here."

"Okay, you've got one minute." Warren gave Marshall a slight smile.

"I can tell you something right now, though. There's no doubt this is a shifter. Silver shrapnel's still smoking," Marshall said, peering into the bloody crevice of the skull and noting the still searing flesh.

"Yeah, we figured that part out all on our own. Anything else?" Warren asked, a hint of sarcasm.

"Later." Marshall busied himself with his inspection, working the scene. After a few minutes, Marshall cleared his throat, which was never a good sign. "Well fellas, I've got some good news and bad news, which do you want to hear first?"

"The bad," Warren said as he came closer.

"Well, the bad news is; you two have your work cut out for you. The people who took out this guy were some real pros. He's definitely a shape-shifter and he was shot from at least three-hundred feet away."

"I suspected as much, although the wound looks like a close range impact," Warren pointed out.

"That's because a shredder silver bullet was used. Although, I can see why you would think that. A 'shredder' bullet can give a wound like this that kind of appearance. But if you look here," Marshall pointed to the wound, "I can tell by the entry wound of the bullet that it was shot from afar. The shooter was positioned high enough to create this trajectory. The scorching around the edges is just the effect of the silver's damage to shape-shifter flesh." Marshall adjusted his glasses, pushing them further onto the bridge of his nose.

"Well damn," Matthew said, puzzled and impressed.

"See, that's why they pay me less than what I'm worth at the S.U.I.T., gentlemen." Marshall smiled.

"Hell, we're all in that boat!" Matthew stated. "So basically, this guy was caught off guard. I wonder who he is?"

"Then that would mean someone was waiting for him. It's starting to make some sense now. I wonder...?" Warren trailed off, pondering a new notion.

Matthew remembered all that Warren had told him about the various scents, the trail and what Marshall had just confirmed. "So could it be the people shot him them drove up to make sure he was dead?"

"It's possible. We need to pinpoint a possible location where the sniper fired from." Warren said, mentally working out the scenario.

"What vehicle and who are *they?*" Marshall Galen interrupted, curious as to how the two detectives came up with multiple killers in an automobile.

"What about the 'good' news?" Matthew asked Marshall, ignoring the question, hoping to distract the rather intuitive and efficient pathologist.

Marshall sighed, allowing the two detectives to bypass his question. "Nothing you two haven't figured out on your own."

"Meaning?" Warren asked.

"Meaning, this poor bastard was probably lured here. Someone suspected what he was and they wanted him dead. And they are working with some pretty heavy artillery. You might want to check any gun shops who may have sold a very expensive high-powered rifle." Marshall gave them the names of a few rifles he suspected capable of causing that kind of damage. "Check the registries, and the rebel human rights groups we have on file, at least that's a start," he said, removing a handkerchief from his pocket and wiping his glasses clean.

"Do you have anything else for us?" Matthew asked.

"Give me a few hours, I have to examine all of the evidence closer. I want to try and discover what kind of shifter we have here, might be able to track his family or pack or whatever the hell. I'll be able to tell you a lot more after having gone over everything...get back to me later." With that, Marshall rose to his feet, nodded at the two detectives, then walked away to continue going over the scene.

Warren looked at Matthew. "Let's go speak to the person who found the body."

Matthew nodded. "Good idea."

Both men removed their gloves as they walked over to a pretty brunette with a creamy skin tone who had discovered the body. Her fearful hazel eyes locked onto the two detectives as they made their way closer.

"Hello Ma'am, I'm Detective Eric, this is Detective Davis." Matthew gestured to Warren. "We know that you're shaken up over this whole experience, but we need you to answer a few questions. Do you think you can do that?" he asked her in a soft, compassionate tone.

She nodded slowly then cleared her throat. "Y-yes sir," she answered softly.

Matthew smiled and nodded. "Thank you, Ma'am. First off, what is your name?"

"Samantha Waters," she replied.

"Mind if I call you Samantha? You can call me Matthew." He hoped to relax her so that she'd be more willing to cooperate.

She nodded.

"Good. Okay, what were you doing at the time you discovered the body?"

"I was pulling into the parking lot. I'm supposed to open up for today, so I was the only one here at the time."

"Okay. Now, was the body as it is now, exactly the same way as when you found it?"

"Yes, I refused to touch it…I just called the police." She held herself tighter as she glanced in the direction of the corpse. "It was so gross."

Warren placed his arm gently around her shoulders and slowly turned her away from the corpse and forensic team. "You've seen enough of that, haven't you?"

She smiled shakily as she nodded.

Matthew continued. "You did the right thing calling the police."

Warren looked at her. "How long have you been working here?"

The young woman looked up at Warren. "Three months."

Warren stood over her, with both arms crossed over his chest. "According to the police report, you stated that you found the body at 9:33 this morning, correct?" he asked with a stern stare.

"Yes. I called the police immediately. I've already told you that."

"That's funny, because the report says that you contacted the Illinois S.U.I.T. division, then the police. It was a dead body, why didn't you just call the police and let them determine whether or not to contact us?"

Samantha stared at Warren for several seconds before answering. "I was just trying to do the right thing. You never know who to call these days, I just thought I'd call both, I didn't know that was a crime."

Warren ignored her sarcasm and decided to ask one more question. "And you stated in the report that you didn't touch the body at any time, is this also correct?"

"Yes, we went through all of this! I can't stand dead things, I mean, he's laying there all bloody, naked and nasty! He wasn't moving and he looked dead. I didn't even get close enough to see if he was really dead, I just called the police, okay!" The young woman stated more forcefully. She appeared to grow agitated. "Look Officers, I've answered your questions, I don't know anything. I just saw the dead body and called all the police I knew! I don't have anything else to tell you. May I please go? I'm really upset about all of this and I just want to get away from this place right now."

Matthew looked at Warren's cold stare, then back at the female. "Yes, but we may have to contact you later if we need to ask more questions."

Samantha nodded. "Sure." She rose from her seat and walked away. Both detectives watched her leave, then Matthew turned to Warren.

"What was that all about?" he asked.

"Her scent is on the body."

"Shit!" Matthew looked back at the girl as she drove away. "How the hell are we going to bust her on that?"

"We can't, not yet at least. And we won't be able to if Galen doesn't find anything on the body to connect her to the crime. My word won't count for shit. Remember, I'm not supposed to have been able to smell her scent. We're just going to have to bring her in and break her, find out what's really going on, especially if she keeps to her story."

"That's why you asked her if she touched the body."

Warren nodded. "Her scent being on the body also made me question why she knew to call the S.U.I.T., most people just call the local PD."

"You have to call Xander right now," Matthew stated.

Warren nodded, then they walked off toward their car. Both men climbed in, Matthew behind the wheel. Warren pulled out his small silver cellular phone, dialing his Pack Alpha. The phone rang several times before someone answered.

"Hello?" A female voice spoke.

"Hey Nicole, this is Warren. I need to speak with Xander, ASAP."

"Sure, one minute." Nicole placed the him on hold, then went to inform Xander, who was reading old English literature in his study.

"Xander, Warren's on the phone. Needs to speak with you, sounds important," Nicole announced upon barging in.

Xander looked up, closing his book. "I'll take it in here. Which line?"

"Line two."

"Thank you."

Nicole left, closing the door behind herself.

"Yes, Warren," Xander acknowledged, once he picked up the line.

"Xander, we have a problem. This morning, we found a dead body of a coyote-male, really young...bitten. He was killed with a XG15."

"Come again?"

"It's a new bullet specifically designed to shred into tiny shards upon contact with its target."

"Shredding silver ammunition...," Xander mumbled, both frightened and appalled by the continued advancement in human weaponry.

Warren snorted. "Yeah, new and improved from the K-15's. I smelled four human scent traces on him and a host of other coyote shifter scents. And get this, one of the human scents belongs to a young female who supposedly discovered the body. Even though she swears she never touched him, never went near the corpse. I couldn't discredit her because, well, you know why not. What do you think is going on?"

"This could be the work of a human rebel group. At least, that is what it looks like for now. I'll call a few other shifter communities, see if I can find out any information. Keep me up to date, Warren," Xander said.

"Will do." Warren ended the phone call.

After spending a little more time investigating and finding little else to help their case, they decided to head back to Chicago.

"So what is Xander going to do?" asked Matthew as he navigated the car.

"He's going to make some phone calls to a few other Packs or Prides, see what he can come up with."

"We need to grab something to eat before heading back to the precinct, and in a few hours, check in with Marshall. That should give him enough time to see if he's discovered anything new."

Warren agreed.

CHAPTER FOUR

Xander sat in the leather chair behind his redwood desk flipping through his phone book, finally settling on a few pages he'd marked with paperclips. He dialed one of the numbers and waited for a response.

"Hello?" a male voice answered.

"Hello, Bernard, this is Xander."

"Ahhh, nice to hear from you. Wow, the last time we've spoken was five years ago, was it not?"

"I do believe so," Xander chuckled.

"We really shouldn't let so much time pass between us."

"I agree. Listen, I called on an important matter. Tell me, do you know, or have you heard of any emerging human rebel groups?"

"No. Not that I know of. Why?"

"Well, a male shifter was found dead in Peoria, which isn't too far from your neck of the woods."

"A shifter was found dead!? How was he killed? What kind?"

"From what I've been told, he was shot with an XG-15 bullet. He was a coyote. I apologize for not mentioning his breed earlier."

"My goodness, why do they make these weapons so easily available to the criminal element? I swear, we were safer when we were unknown!"

Xander chuckled; he agreed.

"I don't know anything about it, but I'm going to do some investigating on my end to see what comes up," Bernard said.

"Very well. Keep me informed if you find out anything. I'll continue to do the same on my end." The two men ended their conversation and Xander continued to call several other Packs and

Prides, including Elise's, to inquire about any human rebel groups. He finally called the last contact located in Maine.

Their Pack Alpha was given the telephone. "What can I do for you?" he asked in a deep, masculine voice.

"Hello Victor, this is Xander Peter–"

"I know who you are, why are you calling?" His tone was slightly harsh. Xander smiled to himself. Eighty years ago, he and Victor had battled over the Chicago-Illinois territory. Xander had won, forcing the other Pack to leave, thus forever creating an enemy.

"Very well, I'll cut right to the chase. Are you aware of any human rebel group activity?"

"What's the matter, can't keep your shit together over there?"

"Victor please, let's put our past behind us. We have more pressing matters to deal with. Please, just answer the question," Xander implored in his gentlemanly manner.

Victor huffed, but decided to cooperate. "I am aware of a human rebel group who call themselves the 'Soldiers of Humanity'. Word has it that they are stirring up trouble, but nobody knows what. I have a Pack member employed with the S.U.I.T. division here in Maine who's keeping an eye on them. A few years ago, some members were arrested for vandalizing several supernatural-owned businesses, but that was the extent of their threat as far as I know. I haven't heard anything more."

"Thank you for the information."

"What happened?" Victor asked with a slightly haughty tone.

Xander paused for a second, then decided that it would be in all of their best interests if each shifter community knew of the possible danger. He decided to inform Victor of the incident in Peoria so that he too could be prepared.

"Well, I've told you what I know. Keep in touch," Victor said without any haughtiness at all. He was far too concerned with the current situation to maintain the attitude.

Xander agreed to keep Victor up to date before ending his call. Next, he called Warren who was at his desk when his cell phone rang. He answered it immediately.

"Hey Xander, did you find out anything?"

"Yes. But there is still no telling how much of this pertains to your case." Xander relayed to Warren what Victor had told him.

"Well, that's more than what we had. I'll look into some of our files to see what comes up. I'll call you back."

"Warren…,"

"Yes, Xander?"

"Come home soon, it's a *Lunar* tonight and you can't afford to be on the clock right now."

"I know, I will."

With that, both men hung up.

***

Warren told his partner everything that his Pack Alpha had told him. Matthew turned to his computer to begin looking up files on that particular rebel group.

"It says here that this group, better known as S.O.H. pronounced 'so'." Matthew snorted, eyes rolling upwards, "have had several members indicted on charges of weapons smuggling, and bashing victims who happened to be into the whole 'goth' vibe. They've burned down several vampire and shape-shifter establishments. One member is in jail on two counts of murder." He looked at Warren. "The last known location of their base is in New York City. Before that, it was Maine, but that's all they know. The information isn't current and their group relocates constantly."

"Fuck me!" Warren hissed under his breath. "Matt, print that up for me and let's go see if Marshall has anything for us."

Matthew nodded and did just that, handing Warren the freshly printed paper. Warren folded the paper, sliding it into his back pocket. Both men headed for the morgue.

Marshall was bent over the body of the decomposing shifter with scalpel and tweezers. He was looking at the corpse through a magnifying glass attached to a band he wore on his head. He looked up when both detectives entered.

"I was waiting on you two. I'm sad to say, but I don't really have anything right now," Marshall said, by way of a greeting.

"Nothing?" Warren asked, obviously disappointed.

"Not one thing. Who ever removed his clothes were probably wearing gloves. There was no scuffle, so I can't find any blood or skin under his fingernails. Only thing you have is the type of bullet used." He told them the caliber of the bullet that was used. "Oh, there is one thing, I did discover what kind of shifter he was, a coyote. I suppose you can check to see if any coyote Packs are missing a member. Although, he may be what you might call a stray."

Warren stood with one hand on his waist, the other brushed his bangs from his eyes. "I don't think so," he said.

He loathed the human terminology to describe a lone shifter. He felt the term "Stray" was demeaning. The shifter community preferred to label a Pack-less, Pride-less shifter as a Rogue, if the shifter chose to leave of their own free will. The other term was, Pariah; if they were forced to leave. Warren had to agree, the two names gave a more definitive title to such a being.

"Why do you think that?" Marshall asked, a curious expression on his face.

"Think what?" Warren asked, cursing himself for letting his thoughts wander. Now he was struggling to remember exactly what he'd said that had Galen questioning him.

"You said, you think he may not be a stray? I was wondering what makes you think that's a possibility?"

Eyes studied the young detective closely.

Warren looked at Matthew, then back at Marshall. "Oh... well...," he struggled for a feasible answer to the inquisitive scientist's question.

"He may belong to a Pack, we don't want to rule that out," Matthew interjected, coming to Warren's rescue.

"That's true, or even a Pride. As a matter of fact, the only wolf Pack that we know of, that's listed, is in DeKalb. Do you think that some Packs and Prides choose to stay anonymous?" Marshall asked as he looked at both men.

"That's a possibility," Warren agreed. He turned to Matthew, nodding his head in the direction of the door. "We should get going."

The two detectives headed toward the door. Warren turned to Marshall, who was still watching them. "Galen, let us know if you find anything else."

"But of course, Warren." Marshall smiled at the two officers then went back to examining the body.

Outside the morgue, Matthew scolded Warren. "I realize that this is hitting too close to home for you, but you have to seriously watch what you say and how you say it!"

"Don't you think I know that?"

"Do you? You know, this is not the first time you've slipped up."

"Spare me the lecture, please."

Matthew held up both hands in surrender. "Fine." He lowered his hands. "I'm just saying you're slipping around the wrong people. I'm done. What now?"

"Now, I should be heading to Xander's mansion. I'm starting to feel the effects of the *Lunar*."

"What do they feel like?" Matthew asked, genuinely curious.

"I feel weak, my senses are heightening, which is somewhat annoying...and I'm very hungry."

"Interesting. All right, you go on to Xander's, I'll cover for you. I really want to look into this rebel group a little more before I leave here."

"Fine, but get home before the full moon." Warren fought the urge to kiss Matthew. Their relationship was hidden to those with whom they worked with and that was the way they wanted to keep it. If their captain was to discover that they had become lovers, she would most certainly separate them. Deep personal or intimate relationships in the S.U.I.T. division was greatly frowned upon.

"I love you," Warren whispered seductively to Matthew.

"I love you, too, and I'll try to keep myself busy tonight while you're away." Matthew winked and flashed Warren a mischievous smile. The two men went their separate ways. Matthew weeded through numerous files on various human rebel groups in the United States as Warren traveled to Xander's mansion.

CHAPTER FIVE

Warren entered the mansion, immediately greeted by several members of his Pack.

"Hey Warren, how's everything going?" Justin asked. "Haven't seen you here since last month. Ball and chain keeping you busy?"

"Matthew would probably shoot you if he heard you call him that. But yeah, between my personal life and the job, I'm kept pretty busy, little punk." Warren playfully whacked Justin on the back of the head.

Justin laughed. "That's good."

"Hey, where's Xander?"

"Can't you scent him?" Justin asked.

"Yeah, but it's easier if you just tell me."

"His study, lazy ass, where else would he be?" Justin dodged Warren's second blow and dashed up the stairs to his room.

Warren shook his head, chuckling on his way to Xander's soundproofed study, ringing the doorbell once he reached the room.

Xander pressed a button which released the lock on his door, opening it. "Come in."

Warren walked in. He sat in one of Xander's high backed leather chairs, handing his Alpha the file he'd had printed up about the Soldiers of Humanity rebel group.

"Right now, Matt's looking into some other groups to see if they've broken any laws," Warren said, settling more comfortably into the chair.

"That's good. Listen, this young woman whose scent you caught on the body...did you smell blood from the body on her, or just the scent of his flesh?"

"Not a lot of blood, but the scent was on her hands and torso. She lied to us, and I can't prove it without exposing myself."

"Where does she live?"

After Warren gave him her address, Xander dialed an extension on his telephone.

"Who are you calling?" Warren inquired.

"Nagesa. I want him to check out this young lady, interrogate her before the *Lunar* tonight."

Warren remained silent, nodding in agreement. When Nagesa answered his telephone, Xander told him what he wanted him to do; and he agreed. The Pack leader hung up the receiver, he looked at Warren.

"How is Matthew doing, by the way?"

"He's doing just fine, we're both doing just fine."

"This is good." When Xander rose from his chair, Warren did the same. "Why don't you make yourself something to eat. Tatiana has prepared a huge lunch for everyone."

"Great, I'm starving!" Warren exclaimed.

Xander chuckled. "I know, come." They headed toward the dining area where the food was being laid out. All of the other shifters crowded around the table, everyone taking a seat.

Adrian looked at Warren. "I think you should bring a packed lunch since you no longer live here," he teased from across the table.

"Oh shut up, Adrian! I knew the peanut gallery was going to say something!" Warren retorted.

Adrian laughed. "Damn right, damn straggler, how's the love life? Did you break him yet?" he winked. Nicole stepped behind him, whacking him hard on the back of the head.

"Oww!" Adrian exclaimed as he rubbed the sore spot.

"You don't need to be worried about that," Nicole playfully scolded him as she sat down in the chair next to his. "Hi Warren."

The others chuckled.

"Hey Nicky, that's right, keep him in his place!" Warren teased.

"Oh, I will." She smiled.

Tatiana brought the last platter into the dining area and everyone commenced filling their plates from a buffet of veal, string beans, pork cutlets, wild rice and tossed salad.

"You know, this is more like dinner than lunch," Justin stated.

"Well, you can always make yourself a sandwich," Jesse said, rolling her eyes.

"Why don't you make it for me?" Justin retorted.

"Why don't you kiss my ass?" Jesse shot back. The spunky woman was a bitten wolf, turned five years before as she was leaving a rave party. Her long hair cascaded in waves down her back as her light brown eyes remained plastered to the food on her plate.

"Enough," Xander interrupted, ending the conversation before it got out of hand. "There will be no bickering at this table." Both Justin and Jesse lowered their heads submissively as he gave them each his stone-cold stare, letting them know that he meant business. He then looked over the other members. No one was daring enough to challenge his authority. Satisfied, he returned his attention back to his food.

After a few minutes of silence, Adrian spoke. "So what's this I hear about a dead shifter?"

"We're still looking into that," Warren answered.

"Yeah, I'm sure it's on the top of the S.U.I.T.'s list of things to do," Adrian scoffed.

"As a matter of fact, it is." Warren set his fork down, glaring at Adrian. "You know, contrary to what you want to think, Adrian, there are a lot of great officers in the S.U.I.T. division. Great men and women of the law who truly want to see justice served, regardless of species!"

"Spare me the propaganda speech. You sound like a fucking

recruitment commercial. And are we talking about your justice, or theirs?" Adrian shot back.

"Justice. There's only one kind!" Warren was growing annoyed.

"How naive. I'd be hard-pressed to see anyone in the S.U.I.T. besides you, actually track down the one responsible for killing that shifter; they probably think someone's doing them a fucking favor."

"God, I swear, I've heard enough prejudicial bullshit from enough people for one day!" Warren exclaimed.

Xander's fork clinked loudly on his expensive china plate, silencing the two men. He looked at his son Adrian, and Warren. "We will not discuss any of this at the dinner table. Do I make myself clear?"

Both men nodded. Once again, they continued to eat until all the food was devoured. The shifters cleared the table, placing the dishes into the dishwasher. Xander had instructed everyone to meet in the living room. So once the chores were taken care of, the entire Pack filled the living room, sitting in their favorite spots. Xander sat in his favorite burgundy chair, one leg crossed over the other. His wife took her place beside him in her own matching chair.

Making sure he had everyone's attention, Xander started speaking. "Adrian, you brought up the shifter that was found murdered this morning. The fact that Warren detected other shifters' scents on his person, lets us know he might have a Pack or was killed by one. Most likely, it's the first one," he said.

"So he's of the canine species?" Alex asked, picking up on the 'Pack' statement. He had joined Xander's Pack almost two years before, when he'd been turned. He'd been frightened by his new powers and a hunger he didn't understand and had been feeding on the cattle he'd found on certain farms in the rural areas of Illinois. Warren had notified Xander of his whereabouts. He'd been found by Adrian and brought back to the mansion where he now lived and felt he belonged.

"Yes," Xander answered, then continued. "He was killed by a sniper shot with a silver bullet that shredded upon impact, known as XG-15 ammunition. I've made some phone calls, a human rebel group known as the Soldiers of Humanity are suspected to be involved due to their well documented attacks on supernaturals. I've also sent Nagesa to interrogate this young woman, who may have something to do with this shifter's murder."

He looked over his Pack. "Any questions?"

"Do we go after this human group?" Adrian asked.

"We want to make sure that we find the right one responsible. It would not be wise for us to attack various rebel groups," Xander answered.

"Well, I know that you're going to do your best to get to the bottom of this," Tatiana stated, the others nodded.

She leaned over, kissing Xander tenderly.

Xander ended the meeting with a wave of his hand and everyone went on their way, engaging in different activities until nightfall when the shifters began to gather in the privately owned, wooded area adjacent to the mansion.

Nagesa jogged up to Xander, having made it home in time for the *Lunar*. "I believe the address is no longer in use," he reported. "The apartment was empty. I did catch the scent of a female, which could have been hers. It was very faint, days old."

Xander nodded. Warren cursed under his breath.

"Don't worry, we'll figure this out. Now is not the time to discuss this," Xander stated as he looked up to the sky. The shifters stood naked as they awaited the *Lunar* to take over their bodies and force their change. Gray wisps of clouds passed by the full moon as it glowed brightly against the dark blue velvet night sky. When the moment had come and the Pack lowered themselves to all fours, they began to change. Many of them moaning or whimpering in agony as their bodies contorted to accommodate their animal counterparts. Several minutes passed before their group transformation was complete. Xander was the first to regain the strength in his legs. He shook himself all over as the others slowly got to their feet and did the same. Tatiana rubbed against him, licking his muzzle. He returned her affection, nuzzling his muzzle against hers. Each member rubbed the length of their bodies along their Alpha and Matron, sharing their scents and solidifying their loyalty, their bond. Once that was done, Adrian trotted over to a tree marked by his father a month ago. He lifted his leg, releasing a spray of urine, soaking the bark. Xander growled at his son, giving him a warning. Adrian lowered his leg and sprinted off to wrestle with Warren. The two rolled around, playfully snapping at each other.

Xander sniffed the area his son had recently marked. Covering Adrian's mark with his own, he reclaimed his territory. Once he finished, he led the hunt. Some couldn't keep up, but managed to hold the other's scents. Xander spotted a buck a few yards away. With a speed far too fast for the buck to respond to, he and the others attacked the wild deer, dragging him down as a group. Xander's long, jagged teeth plunged deeply into the buck's neck, painfully paralyzing the animal. The others continued to tear into the buck, ripping away chunks of flesh and muscle, feasting greedily. Xander ate his fill as did Tatiana, before settling comfortably together near a tree while the others continued to eat.

Once everyone had eaten their fill of the animal, they began to frolic with one another. Once again, Adrian teasingly challenged his father, tugging his tail repeatedly until Xander rose, catching his son by his scruff, and bringing him down to the ground. The two snarled at each other playfully before the Alpha let him go. The entire Pack played with each other, running, chasing and wrestling one another, enjoying their freedom.

They were reveling in the cool night's breeze when all were frozen by the sound of bullets whizzing through the air. Xander rose to his feet as the others dashed behind trees, not really knowing the direction the bullets were coming from. Xander and Nagesa, remaining concealed amidst the bushes peered in the direction of where they thought the shots were fired. They saw the lights of a truck speeding away. Both raced at amazing speed, struggling to catch up to the vehicle, but to no avail. The huge black SUV was far away from the mansion, merging onto the highway.

Xander and Nagesa sniffed the area, searching for clues and locking in the scents they discovered. Xander released a low, menacing growl as he turned to make his way back to the others with Nagesa following close behind. When they reached the others, they found one of their members lying on his side in a bed of fallen multicolored red, orange and yellow leaves. A thick stream of blood oozed out of a single gunshot wound in his chest. His gray eyes stared straight ahead, all signs of life were gone. Xander knew right away that Alex had been slain by a silver bullet. Everyone crowded around his dead body which was still in wolf form. They all knew he would remain that way since he'd died on a *Lunar* night. The Pack sniffed and nuzzled Alex's corpse, some whimpered and whined. Xander threw his head back, belting out a long mournful howl. The others joined in the sad song echoing throughout the area. Their unified howl was heard several miles away, alarming all of the mortals who heard their grief. Xander ended the howl, quieting the others as they lay around their fallen member, mourning.

***

Elise and the others finished off the last remaining bits and pieces of their prey. Devin decided to climb into a nearby tree, lying lazily on one of the strong branches while the other shifters played gaily with one another. Sergio lay against Elise, fully content. Earlier that day, he had given Sebastian permission to spend the night over at his best friend's house. He didn't feel it necessary to have Sebastian watch the babies on every *Lunar* night. The babies were safe and sound at the babysitter's and Sebastian was free to enjoy himself. Sergio and Elise watched the others purr and rub against one another in their own way of bonding. The friskiest member of their Pride, David—an orphaned tiger, still a child, but fortunate enough to have survived the Change, tugged on Madeleine's tail, urging her to play with him. Madeleine playfully pawed David, rolling him over on to his back, nuzzling his stomach lovingly. David squirmed until he flipped over onto all fours and leaped toward Madeleine just as a bullet pierced the grass where he had been standing. Instantly,

Sergio was on his feet as was Elise, both alert. He, Daniel and Miranda raced toward the gunshots as more bullets were fired. Elise ran further into the woods, leading the others to safety.

The three quickly located a black SUV before it could speed off down the street. Sergio leaped onto the SUV, plunging his muzzle into the roof, denting the thick metal. The driver screamed and swerved the unstable SUV wildly, attempting to throw Sergio off. He had embedded his powerful claws into the roof and was beginning to rip and shred the metal. The other men inside the vehicle began to fire shots erratically, trying desperately to keep the other shifters at bay. One of the wayward bullets struck a tree, exploding on contact, the shrapnel becoming embedded in Miranda's left hind leg causing her to cry out. She faltered, then kept running through the searing pain. When she saw an opening, she leapt forward, aiming for the rear window. A bullet shattered the glass, striking her shoulder, slicing an artery and ending her attack. Daniel ran to her aid, immediately inspecting her for any fatal injuries. He saw all of the blood and began licking. Elise came to her aid and with her claws and teeth, began digging for the silver bullet, finding the one in her shoulder instantly. She bit into Miranda's flesh, locking the bullet between her teeth as she ripped the damaged flesh away along with the bullet causing Miranda to yowl in pain. Elise then went on to work on her wounded leg. Meanwhile, the driver, in a panic, swerved the big SUV one more time, causing Sergio to lose his grip on the slippery metal of the truck's roof.

He scraped at the metal, desperately trying to regain his grip, but to no avail. He was tossed aside, his body slamming into a thick tree with a heavy thud. As the truck tires struggled to gain control on the unpaved road, it fishtailed, the back end slamming hard against Sergio's injured body, pinning him against the tree for a second before the tires regained traction and sped away. Sergio collapsed onto the ground, whimpering softly as he endured the immense pain of eight shattered ribs and multiple internal injuries trying to reconstruct themselves. Daniel walked beside a limping Miranda toward him, both sniffed his body and licked his muzzle. Elise ran to him, placing her fur covered leg next to his mouth, tempting him to bite her, to drink of her healing blood. Sergio refused to bite Elise. He lay on the ground, surrounded by the others for a few minutes as his injuries healed completely. Once he was healed, he rose to all fours, enraged. He turned to Elise, nuzzling her with his muzzle, making sure that she was unharmed. Together, they sniffed the tire tracks and footprints of their attackers, attempting to gather all information that they could before returning to the woods. This time, the Pride traveled deeper into the forest for safety measures. At this point, sunrise was too far away.

CHAPTER SIX

The sun rose slowly over the horizon, shining its soft, heated rays over the city. The Pride lay resting in the cool high, grass. Sergio, Miranda and Elise were awake, watching over the others. Suddenly, the resting shifters were jarred awake by their Transformation. Their bodies slowly began to return to their human state. The fur receded, their bones reformed into human skeletons. Once the transformation was complete, the shifters rose to their feet, angry.

"What the fuck was that?!" Sergio belted out as he paced back and forth.

"That was what Xander warned us about. We have to contact him," Elise stated. She looked at Miranda. "Are you okay?"

"Yes," Miranda answered, still too angry to contemplate their situation. She wanted only one thing…revenge.

Sergio turned, facing the others. "What I don't fucking understand is how in the hell did they find out where we live?!"

"I don't know, but we're going to find out," Elise said through gritted teeth.

"What kind of bullets were those?" Devin asked, returning to the others after examining the remains of the silver bullet embedded in the grass.

Sergio and the others walked back to where the shards were embedded in the trunk of a tree. "Looks like they were using XG-15, a redesigned version of the K-13 ammunition only using silver instead of metal." He rose to his feet, huffing slightly.

"How do you know?" Devin asked.

"I had asked Warren. I like to keep track of what the S.U.I.T. comes up with to kill our kind," Sergio replied.

"Fucking humans! What will they think of next?" Daniel cursed.

"For crying-out-loud, don't speak about it!" Madeleine said as she cradled David in her arms.

Sergio stood, stark naked with both hands on his hips, he looked at the others. "I caught a pretty good glimpse of the sons-of-a-bitches before I was tossed from the truck. We need to contact Warren, he might let me look at some of their files. I also memorized the license plate. We catch the driver, we may be able to get to the bottom of this shit," he suggested.

"Well, hell. Why are we still standing here?" Devin asked as he started walking toward the mansion.

Sergio took one step, just as Madeleine grabbed his arm. "Get our son."

"I'm already on it, I want all of the children here," Sergio replied as he patted Madeleine on the hand. Satisfied, she nodded.

All of the shifters walked into the mansion. Elise immediately snatched up the first cell phone she saw and dialed Xander.

"Hello?" Xander answered the phone in a calm tone.

"I'm glad I've reached you, we were attacked last night. Miranda and Sergio were wounded, but they're all right. Sergio was able to see our attackers and we have a license plate number. Do you think Warren can get Sergio into the precinct to look over a few files?" Elise asked.

"Getting the license plate number is good news. Unfortunately, we were attacked last night also and didn't fare as well. We lost one of our members."

Elise gasped. "Oh my God! I'm so sorry! Who?" she asked softly, saddened by their loss.

"Alex. I am angered by this. He had survived a great deal. The S.U.I.T. had had him on their extinction list when I rescued him, took him in. There was still so much more for him to learn, to see. It is always difficult to deal with a death of a Pack member, as I'm sure you understand."

"I do. I want you to know that you have our condolences. David was almost killed as well, and I'm so grateful that he wasn't. Although, I hate to rush, and I don't want to seem insensitive but we don't have time to spare-"

"Speak no more, I understand. We'll have time to mourn later. Send Sergio over to the precinct, Warren will meet him there. Oh, Elise?"

"Yes."

"The female whom Warren interviewed yesterday has vanished, her apartment...empty. Based on last night's attack, one can only assume the body of the shape-shifter that was found was obviously a message to us."

"I don't succumb too well to threats. This human group will soon discover that. Sergio will meet Warren at the precinct in an hours' time," Elise said with certainty.

"Good. We'll talk later."

"Goodbye." Elise ended the telephone call. She called out to Sergio who came jogging down the elegant staircase. He reached the bottom, heading toward her.

"What did he say?" he asked as he pulled a blue shirt over his head.

"They were attacked as well and lost one of their own. Alex was killed," Elise informed him.

"What?!" Devin exclaimed, incredulous.

"Alex was killed last night in an attack just like our own," Elise repeated.

"I heard you the first time, I just can't fucking believe it!" Devin sat down on the sofa, still in shock.

Sergio looked at Elise for several moments, remaining silent, though the tenseness in his body showed he was far from calm. He turned to Devin. "Were you able to reach Sebastian?"

"Our telephone wires were cut. I was just about to tell you that when I heard the news about Alex."

Sergio became even more incensed. He huffed as he pulled his coat from the hall closet, reaching into his right pocket for his cell phone. He flipped it open, turned it on and dialed his son's cell number. He waited patiently for an answer. The phone rang several times before the voicemail answered. He left a message for his son to get in contact with him. Next, he called the home of his son's best friend, and still no answer.

"No luck? Try the school, don't they serve breakfast? He may be there even though it's a bit early. If not, you could still leave a message for him when he gets there," Devin suggested.

Sergio did just that.

"Brentwood Academy, how may I help you?" The operator said in greeting.

"Hello, this is Sergio Giovanni. If my son, Sebastian Giovanni, is there, I really need to speak with him, this is a family emergency," he said in a tone that bordered on demanding.

"One moment, sir." The operator placed Sergio on hold as she paged for Sebastian. Sergio waited impatiently for her to return with his son. The others' eyes remained locked on Sergio. Elise called the babysitter and was relieved to learn that her children and the sitter herself were unharmed. Elise sent Miranda to retrieve the children with Tiffany, (another member of her Pride) and Carmen as back up.

The operator returned. "I'm sorry sir, but I've paged your son, he didn't respond. He might not have arrived yet. Please call back at seven-thirty when the children are expected to report to their homerooms," she said. Sergio agreed, then ended the call.

"I left Sebastian a message. I'll call the school back in an hour. Until then, keep trying to get in contact with him." Without waiting for a response, he stormed out of the mansion, en route to the precinct. When he arrived, Warren greeted him at the door.

"Hey Sergio, come on." Warren led him to his desk.

"Where's Matthew?" Sergio asked.

"At home. I spoke to him this morning, he's still reading up on this rebel group. He was shocked to find out what happened to us."

"Yeah, I'm sorry to hear about your Pack member." Sergio gave Warren his condolences. Warren nodded, thanking him.

"Okay, let's get right to business. What is the plate number?"

Sergio told him the number and Warren typed it in. A file immediately came up on the monitor. Both men leaned forward, mentally etching every detail into their memory.

"Joseph Harris, thirty-two years old, Caucasian male and he lives in Park Ridge," Sergio read his file aloud.

Warren printed up his information. "He doesn't have a criminal record."

"Until now, not that I plan on pressing charges. I have other plans for him," Sergio commented threateningly.

Warren nodded. When the printer completed the task, Warren snatched the paper out of the tray. "Let's go."

Both he and Sergio headed toward the parking lot. Each man climbed into their own car and drove toward Joseph's apartment.

On the way, Sergio called his son's school once more to check in. The switchboard operator answered. Again, Sergio asked her to page his son.

"Mr. Giovanni, I've paged him globally as well as contacted his homeroom teacher and she tells me that Sebastian did not report to school today."

"What? What do you mean? He's there, check again!" Sergio demanded.

"Sir, if he didn't respond, he's not here."

"Let me speak to the headmaster."

"Very well, sir," the female operator said in a slightly snappish tone, although Sergio could care less if he'd offended her. He waited on the line until the headmaster came to the telephone.

"Good morning, Mr. Giovanni, this is Headmaster Williams. I was briefed on the situation. I've checked again with Sebastian's first period teacher, she said that Sebastian didn't show up for class."

"He's not there?" Sergio repeated in disbelief, suddenly caught off guard and growing more fearful.

"No sir. We will continue to keep an eye out for him, just in case he's late. He normally has excellent attendance," Headmaster Williams said then waited for Sergio's response.

"What about Allen Whales? Did he come into school today?" Sergio asked as he struggled to control his temper.

"Normally, we don't divulge that kind of information, sir… but I'll make an exception for you. One moment." The headmaster checked the first period classroom attendance for Allen. "Mr. Giovanni, Mr Whales is attending school today."

"May I speak with him?" Sergio asked.

The headmaster paused for a few seconds, not sure if he wanted to involve the adolescent in the situation.

"Listen, my son is missing. Allen was the last known person he was with. I just want to ask him some questions, please," Sergio pleaded.

"Very well. One moment, Mr. Giovanni."

Sergio waited several minutes before Allen's voice came over the receiver.

"Hello?" Allen spoke softly through the receiver, hoping he wouldn't be in trouble with Sebastian's father.

"Allen, did Sebastian come over to your house last night for a sleepover?" Sergio asked, getting right to the point.

"Yeah," Allen lied.

"Don't lie, this is important."

Allen paused, then spoke. "No. He went out with this girl he just hooked up with at school. You're not going to tell my parents are you, Mr. Giovanni?" he asked in a shaky, fearful tone.

"That's the least of my worries, tell me more about this girl," Sergio entreated.

"She's hot," Allen began.

Sergio rolled his eyes but remained silent while Allen spoke.

"She came here about two months ago. I don't know too much about her because she pretty much keeps to herself. But she and Sebastian hit it off quickly. He was pretty excited about spending the night with her, said he might 'get some'. He might still be with her."

"Do you know her name?" Sergio asked, mentally kicking himself for not prodding his son for more information before hand.

"Only her first name, it's Crystal. I can't remember her last name. That's all I know about her."

"Thanks." Sergio ended the conversation. He knew the headmaster would never give him the girl's personal information. He was shocked and disappointed to discover that his son had lied to them all. He dialed Madeleine's cell phone. When she picked up, before she could say 'hello', she heard Sergio say, "I'm going to kill Sebastian when I get my hands on him."

"What's going on?" she asked, worried about her son's whereabouts.

"He lied to us. He didn't go to Allen's apartment for a sleepover, he went to some chick's house to get laid. Listen, keep trying to get that boy on his cell. We're on our way to the apartment of one of the men who attacked us. If Sebastian calls home, you know what to do."

"I do, be careful," Madeleine said before they ended the call.

When they were several minutes away from their attacker's location, Warren called Xander to bring him up to speed on the situation.

"Hello?"

"Xander, we have a suspect in the attack. Sergio and I are almost at his apartment right now." Warren proceeded to tell Xander everything that he now knew.

"Excellent. You know what to do."

"Yeah, I know."

"What is expected goes beyond the laws of this government, don't let the S.U.I.T. interfere."

"Xander, you don't have to tell me that. I know I got kind of defensive last night, but the Pack will always come first."

"Good. Stay in touch."

"Will do." Warren hung up his cell.

They parked a block away from Joseph's apartment building. When they reached the outside main door, Warren broke the lock and they made their way up the stairs to apartment 3B. When they reached his apartment, they could smell him inside as well as hear him. Warren looked at Sergio, who nodded. He kicked the door open, gun aimed directly at Joseph's head, stopping him before he could reach for his shotgun.

"Don't fucking move!" Warren stepped into the apartment, Sergio closed the door behind them the best he could considering it was almost unhinged. He slid a chair under the door knob to keep it closed, then turned to face Joseph.

"Step away from the gun!" Warren commanded with a cold-blooded stare.

Joseph followed orders. He slowly stepped away from the shotgun that lay on the sofa.

"Good, now have a seat."

Joseph sat down in a chair.

Sergio reached for the gun, checking the ammunition. "XG-15's." He inspected the rest of the apartment, noting that everything looked to be neatly placed. The apartment was clean and best of all, Joseph was alone.

He came back into the living room, nodding at Warren.

"Where did you get that kind of ammunition?" Warren asked Joseph, his gun still aimed at him.

"I'm not telling you shit, fuck you!" Joseph yelled defiantly, spitting a glob of saliva at Warren who moved swiftly, avoiding contact.

Warren looked at Joseph, then without warning, kicked him hard in the face, knocking out two of his teeth.

Joseph screamed in agonizing wails as he cupped his bleeding mouth. Tears welled up in his eyes as he looked at Warren's and Sergio's no-nonsense expressions.

"I'm going to ask you again. Where did you get that kind of ammunition?" Warren asked.

"I don't know," Joseph muttered through his injured mouth. "I wouldn't know that type of shit. Who are you anyway?"

Sergio slammed the butt of the shotgun into Joseph's shoulder, dislocating it. Joseph screamed again in excruciating pain as he fell to the floor, his good hand clutched over his now injured arm.

"We're asking the fucking questions, got that?" Sergio's voice was forceful, frightening.

Tears poured from Joseph's eyes as he nodded in agreement.

"Why did you attack us?" Sergio asked as both he and Warren awaited an answer.

Joseph panted in feeble gasps as he spoke. "Our organization hates you freaks! We'll purify our country by killing you, ridding the world of the atrocity against nature which is you and all of your kind."

Sergio's jaw tightened as he listened to Joseph's twisted point of view. Warren fought the urge to just kill him, he needed questions answered first.

"How did you know to attack us?" Sergio asked.

"You were just targeted, they don't tell me these sort of things." Joseph struggled to answer their questions. He spit a glob of blood and saliva on the floor to free his mouth. "Look, I just followed orders, I didn't order the fucking hit! What are you going to do to me?"

Sergio looked at Warren, then back down at Joseph. "There's something you're not telling us."

"I'm telling you all I know, I swear!" Joseph pleaded.

"Bullshit. You know more. How did you know how to find us?" Warren asked.

Joseph remained silent. Sergio pushed him down onto the floor, placing his foot on Joseph's injured arm. Applying pressure slowly caused the man to cry out in pain.

"Okay! Okay! Jesus! We had your addresses, okay!" Joseph spat out between raspy gasps.

"Who gave them to you? Is this going to be a tit-for-tat interrogation?" Sergio asked. He leaned forward, which added more pressure on Joseph's arm.

"Ahhhh! No! No! I swear I'm telling you all that I know!" Joseph thrashed on the floor, pleading with Sergio to remove his foot.

"Who gave you our addresses?" Warren asked, growing

ever more impatient and annoyed by the games that Joseph was playing.

"I don't know that kind of stuff!"

Sergio looked at Warren. "Pick him up, put him in the chair."

Warren did just that, slamming Joseph down hard into the wooden chair. Joseph winced, but was pleased that he was finally off of the floor away from the other man's foot. Sergio removed his shirt, then his pants and last his shoes. Warren placed a foot on Joseph's chest, pinning him into the chair. Sergio began to change forms. His body elongated, becoming more muscular, furrier. His hands grew longer, wider, nails turning into claws. His face was the more horrific, half-human, half-leopard. Joseph was frozen with fear, unable to struggle against Warren's foot, or even to scream as he witnessed the half-transformation.

Warren looked back at Joseph. "We're tired of playing your games. Now, I'm really pissed, but he's even more pissed. If you don't start answering our questions, he's going to eat your ass one piece at a time. Are you ready to cooperate?" he asked.

Joseph nodded his head vigorously. "Yes! Yes! Jesus, yes! Keep him the hell away from me!" His eyes grew wide as he watched Sergio approach him. A thin stream of urine flowed from him onto the floor as the sound of Sergio's powerful footsteps echoed throughout the apartment.

"Oh, he doesn't look happy," Warren taunted.

"Please, keep him away!" Joseph begged.

"Who sent you?" Warren demanded.

"I really don't know! I swear! Our boss, Steve Sanders knows. He's in charge of all of our contacts. He's the one that got us the guns, bullets and your addresses!"

"How long have you been planning this?"

"Steve was contacted about the job maybe four or five months ago!"

"What about the shifter left dead in the parking lot?"

"A part of the setup. He was just some freak Steve wanted us to kill and plant there as a message. We knew we were going to attack you on the full moon, where you wouldn't be able to fight back as good. We knew attacking you on the full moon would catch you off guard. I think Steve wanted to throw you off your game, I don't know. I just did what I was told."

That sparked Warren's interest. "By whom? Who gave Steve the shifter to use as bait?"

"I. Don't. Know!" Joseph yelled angrily through gritted teeth. "I told you, I only know what I know and it's not a lot!"

"Where can I find this Steve Sanders?" Warren asked.

Joseph remained silent. Warren looked over his shoulder, prompting Sergio to react. Without a second wasted, Sergio's clawed hand slashed Joseph's thigh, tearing open flesh and shredding muscles. Warren muffled Joseph's screams with the palm of his hand.

"I'm starting to see bloodlust in his eyes, you know how we shape-shifters are when we smell blood. It also doesn't help that he's pretty pissed, remember? Are you going to talk?" Warren asked. Yellow snot ran from Joseph's nose as freely as tears ran from his eyes. A long string of drool connected Warren's palm to Joseph's mouth when he removed his hand. Warren wiped his hand on Joseph's jeans, cleaning away the saliva.

"He's...h-he's," Joseph stammered. Sergio inched closer. "He's at the third location!" he blurted out as he pressed his uninjured hand over his thigh which was now bleeding profusely.

"What's the third location?" Warren asked.

"The mansion of some vampire...something...Alexander!"

"Darian?"

"Yeah! That was his name!"

"Shit!" Warren shot a glance at Sergio who remained still. "What else can you tell me?"

"They're gonna kill him and everyone in his house. That's all I know. I've told you everything, please let me go!" Joseph pleaded.

Warren looked at Sergio, who nodded. He began to change back into his human form. His fur receded, his body returning to its normal size. He dressed quickly.

"We have to tell the others!" Sergio stated as he pulled on his t-shirt.

"I know." Warren looked at Joseph. He knew now, for certain Xander's words were ringing true. What they were doing and what they were going to have to do went beyond the law. Believing he got all of the information he could and not wanting to take Joseph with him, he broke his neck, snapping the bones instantly with an audible crack. Not wanting to waste another second, both men left the apartment after wiping their finger prints clean. They took the back exit, leaving Joseph's broken, crumpled body slouching in the wooden chair.

"We should hurry, we don't want anyone seeing us leave," Warren said as they sprinted to their cars.

"We have to tell the others about their plans now," Sergio said as he opened his car door. Both men climbed into their automobiles, pulled out their cell phones, calling home as they drove toward Darian's mansion.

Sergio waited for Elise to answer, as soon as she did, he started speaking.

"Elise, get over to Darian's right now, he's under attack!" he blurted out before Elise could speak.

"We're on it," she said, hanging up the telephone. She called to the others. Everyone came running to her. As soon as they were all present she told them what they had to do.

"Holy shit! Let's go!" Devin exclaimed as he raced toward the front door with the others following behind him.

All ran to the garage, climbing into two separate SUVs and sped out, heading toward Darian's mansion.

Warren called Sergio on his phone as he sped through busy traffic.

"Yeah?" Sergio asked.

"Did you get in touch with them?" Warren inquired.

"Yeah, their on their way there now. What about you?"

"Xander and the others are also heading to Darian's home. I didn't get a chance to tell them anything else."

"Same here. This shit is all fucked up and I want to get to the bottom of it. Who hired these assholes?!" Sergio wondered.

"I've got a good feeling that we're going to find out soon enough. We need to keep one of these assholes alive for one of the vampires to question later. Something tells me that one of them will probably be able to gather more information."

"Steve Sanders," Sergio suggested.

"Perfect."

CHAPTER SEVEN

Darian lay still in his bed snuggled next to Xavier. Natasha had already left for work two hours earlier. The house was quiet, servants tended to their daily duties; cleaning the house, washing the cars and guarding the resting vampires. The sun shone brightly in the sky, casting soft rays of light over the huge three-story, tan-brick mansion with it's beautiful, lush, sculptured landscape. Seventeen men and women dressed in green army fatigues stealthily scurried across the grass, far enough away as to not be detected, but close enough to fully surround the mansion.

"This is their weakest moment, we have to attack now. Has anybody seen Joseph?" Steve asked as he peered through his binoculars into the mansion windows.

"No, not since last night when those fucking freaks almost got us!" answered Kel, one of the men who had attacked Elise's mansion the night before.

"That's because you didn't follow the plan. Forget about him, we can't wait for him to get here. Now is the time." Steve lifted the walkie-talkie to his mouth pressing the talk button. "Are you ready?"

A garbled, static-laced voice came over the receiver. "Yeah, we're ready, just tell us when."

"Outstanding." Steve signaled for the other people on his team to get into their positions. As they did, some aimed their weapons from a kneeling position, while others chose to lay prone. He gave his team last minute instructions. "Remember, aim for the windows, hitting the building itself won't do us much good. We know that the guards are armed, so expect return fire. They may be human, but they're also traitors to the race, so shoot them anyway if it comes to that, but don't waste time focusing on them. The second and third floor bedrooms are our target, everybody got that?"

They all acknowledged that they understood.

"Good." He clicked the button on his walkie-talkie once again. "Fire at will."

A second later all seventeen attackers began blasting rocket launchers, firing sniper rifles and AK-47's into the windows of Darian's beautiful mansion, shattering glass and instantly destroying furniture inside. Three out of ten of Darian's human servants were killed with the first onslaught of bullets. One rocket crashed into the roof on the west wing, exploding shingles and debris everywhere, completely caving the left section of the roof into the mansion's attic. Inside the mansion, two of the seven remaining servants rushed toward Darian's bedroom, while the other five ran through the mansion, taking positions beside windows for a counterattack. They couldn't see their attackers, but they shot in the direction where the bullets and rockets were being fired from, blasting their own weapons into the trees and bushes that surrounded the property.

Darian was wide awake at the first whiff of smoke and the sound of gunfire. The moment he felt the vibrations of the exploding rockets, he knew that his home was under attack. He struggled against the weakness he suffered in the daylight hours as he quickly wrapped a blanket around Xavier's defenseless form, making sure not one part of his body would be exposed to the sun. As he lifted Xavier from the bed, a highly flammable and deadly rocket crashed through his bedroom window. Thinking quickly, Darian ran into the closet with Xavier in his arms, closing the door behind them at the very moment of impact. He felt the intense heat against the closet door, the flames licking against the wood, burning away the barrier between sunlight and darkness. Darian struggled to keep conscious as he pushed past the clothes toward the back of the closet. He laid Xavier down and began punching away at plaster, wood and cement until he made an opening into the next room, which happened to be John's.

Darian picked Xavier up in his arms, carrying him into the next room, only to collapse onto the floor as two servants ran in, coming to his aid.

"Master!" they screamed in unison.

"Get John!" Darian commanded as he struggled to rise. He was enraged as he saw his luxurious mansion burning down around him. He wondered if any of his coven survived the attack, and what of his servants?

"Master, the house is being completely destroyed! We can't reach the other's bedrooms, there is a wall of fire blocking the hallway!" Tyson informed Darian as they continued to wrap John's body in a heavy quilt.

"Get us to safety, now!" Darian commanded. He could feel himself losing consciousness; it was inevitable. He could no longer keep himself awake. He collapsed onto the floor next to Xavier in a deathlike sleep. His servants rushed to the closet to retrieve another thick blanket to wrap him in for safety. Billy burst into the room, followed by the last two servants remaining. Each quickly surveyed the room, trying to decide on what needed to be done. They ran to Darian's resting form, standing over him as they looked around the room at the flaming carnage.

"Where can we take them? We're completely blocked off from the coffins! The hallway's practically in flames! There's nowhere we can go, we're trapped!!!" One of the frightened men declared.

"He's right!" another added. "If we try to escape out of the window, the blankets won't be enough to protect them! What are we going to do?!"

"We leave them!" Greg exclaimed.

"Are you insane?! We can't leave them!" Billy responded, incensed at the suggestion.

"The hell we can't! Wayne, Don and everyone else are dead and I'm not going to die here with them!" Greg ran to the window. Tyson rushed over to him, latching onto his arm.

"Help us, we need you!"

"You mean, die with us! Fuck that! If you're smart, you'll come with me, leave these vampires to their own!"

"Turncoat!" Ronald yelled. "Bastard!"

Greg snatched his arm away from Tyson. "At least I'll be alive!" He climbed out of the window, carefully maneuvering himself onto the drain pipe, sliding down until his feet touched ground. He didn't wait to see if any of the other four decided to join him. He ran as fast as he could to safety.

Elise and her Pride as well as Xander and his Pack arrived at Darian's mansion, all were in shock to see the three-story estate was a blazing inferno. The attackers were long gone, and they wasted no time running into the fiery hell to save their defenseless friends.

"Shit!" Devin ran toward the building at lightening quick speed as did the others. "We need the coffins!"

"Adrian, Madeleine, Miranda, Carmen, Rachel, come with me!" Sergio ordered as he ran into the scorching hot inferno. The five of them followed Sergio as he leaped over gaping holes, dodged falling timbers and burning drywall. The six shifters raced toward the basement, quickly locating the stash of exquisitely carved coffins.

"Everybody grab one, now!" Sergio ordered. They did. Once they each had a coffin in their possession, they ran toward the bedrooms of the resting vampires.

"Over here, hurry!" Elise called over the roaring flames. "And bring two coffins!"

Sergio and Devin ran toward Elise while the others searched out the rest of the bedrooms. Elise opened the door to the bedroom where the four remaining servants stood over the three resting vampires. Sergio ran to Darian, quickly placing him into the coffin before lifting Xavier, laying him gently on top of Darian. He closed the coffin. Devin had hastily stuffed John inside a coffin slamming the lid closed once he was done.

"Take them to safety," Elise ordered as she pointed to the four servants. Sergio nodded. He walked over to Tyson, wrapping his arm around his waist as he held the coffin in the other arm. He then climbed onto the window's ledge, jumping off, landing lightly on his feet with Tyson screaming the entire fall.

"Stay with the coffin," Sergio ordered as he leaped high, back through the very window he jumped from only seconds before. It took no time at all to return with Ronald and the other coffin containing John. Devin jumped with both Derek and Billy, placing them down next to the other two servants. Then both he and Sergio leaped back into the window and followed Elise to help the others rescue the other vampires.

"There's going to be a backdraft when we open this door," Xander warned Nagesa as the two stood outside of Annabelle's room. Nagesa nodded, then braced himself. Xander opened the door, releasing an engulfing cloud mass of fire. The thick, smoldering black smoke clogged their lungs and blinded their eyes. Their highly sensitive noses burned as they struggled to breathe. Their lungs felt seared as they choked on the thick smoke. Still, both managed to find their way toward Annabelle's bed where half of her body was in flames.

"My god!" Xander exclaimed. "Hurry!" He and Nagesa dashed over to her, instantly smothering the flames with the purple blanket from her bed. Once the flames were extinguished, Xander placed Annabelle inside a coffin. As he lifted the coffin onto his shoulders, the floor crumbled under his feet, tumbling him and the coffin down to the level beneath.

"Are you alright, Xander?!" Nagesa called.

Xander groaned as he removed a large piece of splintered wood from his thigh. "Yes, don't worry about me, get to the others!"

Nagesa followed orders as he ran from the room to find the other vampires. Xander carried the coffin on his shoulders. He ran as fast as he could, causing the fire surrounding him to grow more fierce as wind from his movements created deadly flame funnels. He managed to crash through the window, landing in the soft bed of flowers in Darian's garden. He joined the others, placing the coffin on the ground as he gasped for fresh air. A few seconds later, Adrian and Warren dashed through another window, carrying a coffin each.

"Where are the others?" Xander asked.

"On their way," Adrian answered.

They could hear the sirens of police and fire trucks approaching.

"We need to leave before they get here!" Warren said, still panting.

Xander nodded. "Here they come," he said the moment Elise and the rest of the shifters sprang from the third story window with the last two coffins.

"Good, you're all here. We have to leave, now!" Xander stated. They quickly gathered up all the coffins, the four servants and loaded up their SUVs. They pulled away from the fiery mansion using the rear exit just as the emergency vehicles pulled up through the front.

"Oh boy, that was close as hell!" exclaimed Justin as he wiped soot from his brow.

"You ain't never lied! God, I can't believe this is happening! What's going on?!" Devin asked Xander.

"I'm not sure," Xander said. "The fact that all three of our homes were attacked is alarming. I don't have my home registered as the property of a shape-shifting community."

"It's some strange shit going on, Xander," Warren began.

"Go on," Xander urged.

"Now, I kinda wish I hadn't killed Joseph earlier. But he told me some very disturbing information," Warren proceeded to tell the others what Joseph told him and Sergio.

"My goodness! Who is behind these attacks?" Xander wondered.

"Darian is going to be sooo pissed when he wakes up," Justin stated.

"I know. I almost don't want to be around when he does," Adrian commented.

"I know one thing…we are all in this together at this point. These are not isolated attacks," Warren said.

Nagesa remained silent as he drove the huge SUV.

"Where do we go?" Justin asked from the back seat. "We shouldn't go home because they might burn down our shit, too, trying to kill us again."

Xander turned in his seat, looking at him, then his gaze shifted toward the others. All seemed to be reflecting on what Justin said.

"Good point," Xander responded as he turned back around. "Nagesa, drive to our hangar."

Nagesa tossed Xander a look, then nodded.

Xander pulled out his cell phone to discover that it had been damaged by the fire. "Excellent," he muttered sarcastically, slipping the phone back into his pocket. "Adrian, hand me your cell phone."

"Here." Adrian removed his cell from his inside jacket pocket, handing it to his father. Xander called Elise.

"Yes Adrian," she greeted, recognizing the number on her caller ID.

"It's Xander. Elise, listen it would be best if we did not go to our homes. They may already be compromised. Just follow us."

"I was just thinking the same thing, we'll follow you. Did Warren tell you what he and Sergio found out?" Elise asked.

"Yes, and I find it to be extremely disturbing. I can't quite put my finger on it. I'm wondering who is behind this human rebel group and what do they want with us?"

"We know they want us dead. Burning down Darian's mansion made a clear statement."

"We have to find these humans. When the police clear out, we're going to have to go back to Darian's mansion and search for clues," Xander suggested.

"Good idea. We'll talk more once we're all together," Elise said. Xander agreed and both hung up.

"I hate to bring this up, but I'm starving," Justin said softly as if afraid he was going to be reprimanded.

"I know. Once we get to the hangar, we'll get food. Don't worry." Xander reassured the others who were feeling what Justin was feeling. They drove toward Xander's private airplane hangar. Justin and Adrian climbed out of the truck to open the large metal double doors so that the others could drive the trucks inside. The pitch black hangar was housing the Pack's luxury jetliner. Once inside, Adrian and Justin closed the door, locking the bolt behind them. The shape-shifters climbed out of the trucks, but did not remove the coffins.

Sergio strode gracefully from around the huge Sidewinder SUV, removing his burnt and frayed shirt revealing a strong, muscular chest, with a thin layer of soft black hair. "We have about six hours before sunset. What are we going to do until then?" he asked as he leaned against the truck.

"Well, we were talking about going back to Darian's mansion and looking around for clues," Adrian stated as he sat down on an empty dust-covered crate. "Will somebody turn on the lights?"

"I'm already on it," Andrea said. A moment later the huge hangar became illuminated. "There, that's better." She returned to the others, sitting on a crate next to her Pack member, Adrian.

"I can't believe Greg ran out on us?!" Tyson fumed.

"Who's Greg?" Sergio asked.

"One of Darian's servants," Devin said.

"He was scared," Derek stated.

"And we weren't?" Tyson spat out, growing even more angry. "His punk ass split with his tail between his legs!"

"Well, he wanted to live, can't really fault him for that," Madeleine said as she finger-combed the tangles from her long, luxurious red hair.

"He didn't have any loyalty! Together, we might have been able to do something. Darian's going to be pissed about that, too," Ronald said as he gazed through the window of the SUV, looking at the coffin that contained Darian and Xavier.

"I mean, would any of you run off and leave the other?" Tyson asked the shifters.

"No. Never, but our situation is different from yours. You're just his servants, we have a bond," Sergio stated.

"Not true. Darian is our master, not just our employer. We have a blood oath pledging our allegiance to protect him and the others. For that, he protects us and our families. You just don't betray that!" Tyson said the last sentence through clenched teeth.

"Take it easy Ty, we have to handle the "now" and not dwell on what's happened in the past. We have to figure out what to do next," Billy said, attempting to calm down rising tempers.

"Indeed," Xander added, then he looked at the others. "I'm sure that some of you are extremely hungry-"

"I know that I am, I'll be more than willing to get the food," Justin declared, inadvertently interrupting Xander.

"Me too, my stomach is growling something fierce. For a minute, I thought it was going to attack me!" Devin joked as he also tried to lighten the tense mood. It worked. There was a chuckle from some the others.

"Very well. Rachel, Justin, Carmen and Madeleine, why don't you get us all something to eat, " Elise appointed the four to the task.

"Sure, I don't mind going," Carmen remarked, slightly disappointed that she was designated to fetch the food for everyone.

"Just go," Elise ordered. The others didn't say another word, only walked to one of the SUVs, unloaded the coffins, then climbed inside and left.

Elise turned to Sergio. "Try Sebastian's cell phone again. And I have to call Natasha to let her know what happened. I think it'd be wise if she took the rest of the day off."

Sergio agreed. He called his son and waited impatiently while the cell phone continued to ring. "What the fuck! He's still not answering!" He slammed the little silver phone shut. "Why the hell isn't he answering?!"

"He may not have his cell on. Did you leave a message?" Devin asked.

"Four and he hasn't called me back." Stressed, Sergio ran his fingers through his thick, black, wavy hair, frowning all the while.

Elise came up behind him. Running her long, delicate fingers over his shoulders, she kneaded the tense muscles.

"We'll try him again." She tried her best to calm Sergio down. She hated seeing him this upset but she didn't like the situation, either.

"I don't like this shit, Elise. He's never done this, it's too careless!" Sergio's voice was low, but all of the other shifters heard him loud and clear, and understood his concerns.

"I know," Elise whispered softly as she lay her head against his back.

Sergio took a deep breath. "You'd better call Natasha," he reminded her.

"Oh! yes! Thanks for reminding me." She stepped away from Sergio, pulling out her little cell, calling Natasha, who didn't answer. She decided to leave a message, warning her to not return to the mansion, to call them immediately after receiving the voicemail message.

"She didn't pick up either, eh?" Sergio asked. Elise frowned, shaking her head. Sergio ran his fingers through his hair once more. "Something doesn't feel right…it just doesn't feel right!" he groaned.

"What do you mean?" Nicole asked.

Sergio looked at her. "My son, who has never disobeyed me, and who always checked in with us, is not answering his phone, nor did he go to school this morning. And I'm not getting a good feeling about Natasha either." He looked at Elise.

Elise nodded. "I'm going to call her job." When the automated operator answered, she selected Natasha's extension and was transferred. The telephone rang several times, then Natasha's voicemail picked up the call.

Elise ended the call, choosing not to leave another message. She then called Natasha's job again, only this time selecting a live operator.

A male answered, "Chicago Word, how may I direct your call?"

"Hello, I have a problem. I am a family member of Natasha Hemingway. If she is there, I need to speak with her, it's an emergency."

"Ma'am, I can transfer you to her extension-"

"No. I've tried that. I need to know if she came in to work today." Elise reiterated.

"One moment ma'am, let me check that for you." The operator placed her on hold for two minutes, then returned. "Ma'am, Miss Hemingway has not made it into work today, but you can still leave a message on her voicemail for when she does come in. Would you like to do that?" he asked politely.

"No, I don't think I would, but thank you for your help," Elise said her goodbyes before disconnecting. She looked at Sergio. "I think you're right."

CHAPTER EIGHT

Xander gestured for his son to hand him his cell phone. He dialed home.

"Adrian?" Tatiana answered the telephone, recognizing her son's cell phone number displayed on the caller ID.

"No darling, it's me," Xander replied.

"Oh thank god! Is everything okay?"

"No. We are going to do some more investigating and I want you and the others to meet us at our hangar. Come right away. I'll feel better when I know you're safe."

"Was anyone killed?"

"A few of Darian's human servants were killed."

"Say no more, we're on our way...," Tatiana paused. "Xander?"

"Yes?"

"I love you," she said softly.

"And I love you." With that being said, both of them ended the call. Xander returned the cell phone to his son.

Adrian looked toward the trucks. "Who's going to give Darian the bad news?"

"Shit! Not me, I know that much!" Devin stated adamantly.

"Don't be a scaredy-cat," teased Tiffany, another member of Elise's Pride. "I doubt Darian will hurt you."

"Whatever! You weren't there when Xavier almost died. You didn't see the anger in his face. You didn't feel what we felt when he released his aura. Hell, even Miranda doesn't think he released all of it, but what we did feel was more than enough to let me know that I don't want to be the bearer of bad news!" Devin responded. Tiffany remained quiet. She decided to not make any further jokes on the matter.

"I think both Xander and I are capable of giving Darian the information that he'll need to know," Elise said as she called home to check on the others. Amber let Elise know that the infants were doing fine. Satisfied, Elise ordered the others to join them at the hangar as well.

"Dang, where the hell did they go to get the food?" Nicole asked out loud to no one in particular. Her stomach growled softly as she waited for the others to return.

One hour and twenty minutes later, after shifters from both houses joined the others, the four shape-shifters returned to the huge hangar carrying dozens of bags filled with foods loaded with calories, high proteins and fats.

"It's about time!" Nicole exclaimed as she walked over to where the bags were placed.

"Well, it took us so long to come back because we argued about where to go. I didn't want chicken and Madeleine didn't want hamburgers, but then we weren't sure if any of you guys would, so we just settled on various fast foods," Carmen stated as she searched through the bags for her meal.

"So what did you all get?" Warren asked as he approached, followed by the others.

"Ribs, chicken, burgers, fries, hoagies, fish and...where the hell are my gyros?" Justin searched through the bags until he found his food. "I'm the only one with three gyros, and I'm not sharing, so breathe back!" He walked away with his greasy bag of food, sitting down on an empty crate.

Xander cleared his throat, Elise stood beside him chuckling.

"The rules still apply," Xander stated, meaning that he would be allowed to chose his meal first, as was his right as Pack Alpha. A few of the other wolves pouted, but stepped aside for him to pass through.

"You don't want my gyros, do you?" Justin asked, his voice apprehensive as if he really didn't want to know the answer to his question.

Xander chuckled softly. "No."

Justin exhaled. "Cool."

"You wolves, what a male dominated community," Elise said softly. Xander tossed her a charming smile, then continued to search through the bags until he found something he wanted to eat.

Elise and Tatiana fished through the bags.

"Hmmm, I suppose I'll take this," Elise said referring to two roast beef hoagie sandwiches. After Elise, Tatiana picked out something, then joined Xander and began eating. Everyone else chose their meals and all settled down to eat.

Once they were done, Warren spoke. "Should we go to Darian's mansion now?"

"Yes, but be careful. I want you to go with Nagesa, Adrian and Nicole," Xander instructed.

Elise looked at Sergio. "You should go back to Joseph's apartment, look around more thoroughly, see what you can find."

Sergio nodded and without wasting another second, rose from his seat. He looked over at Miranda. "Why don't you come with me."

Miranda nodded, rising from the dusty crate that she had been sitting on. The six shape-shifters left the hangar to go to their designated locations.

The four wolves drove for forty minutes until they pulled in front of Darian's once beautiful mansion. The home was still undergoing investigation. Officers and firefighters were still on the premises. Red S.U.I.T. tape surrounded the mansion, labeling it a crime scene. Large holes riddled the mansion's smoke-stained walls, windows were broken throughout the estate, part of the roof had collapsed, exposing the inside of the mansion to the sun's dangerous rays. The once manicured lawn was now littered with debris from the attack, destroying its beauty.

"This is fucked up! I hate to say this, but I'm glad they didn't do this shit to our house," Adrian said, surveying the damage.

"I have to agree with you," Warren spoke softly so as to not bring attention to themselves. "I want you three to be as stealthy as possible. I'm going to ask them some questions, but I don't want you guys getting caught snooping around the crime scene."

"Don't worry about us, we've got it covered. Just meet us back here once you're done," Adrian said.

Warren nodded as he stepped over a large piece of what used to be a part of the roof, making his way toward a S.U.I.T. officer to ask some questions, while the others looked around. After their investigation, Warren met up with Adrian and Nicole.

"Find anything useful?" Warren asked.

"Not really. Some scents that go as far as thirty yards that way," Adrian said, pointing in a direction down the road, leading away from Darian's mansion. "And some bullet shells, possibly from an AK-47, but no other clues. What about you?"

"Pretty much the same information, corroborating yours. There's some bullet shells, rocket shells, no silver ammunition, guess they didn't think they'd need any. There are no witnesses, of course, and I'm going to have to agree with Devin. I wouldn't want to be the one to tell Darian that his house is pretty fucked up." He stopped, looking at the others. "I also wouldn't want to be the one to tell them that we can't contact Natasha."

Adrian looked at Warren's worried expression. "How are you feeling about that?"

Warren's eyes locked on Adrian's. "I don't like it, as a matter of fact. Let me call Matthew, tell him to put out an APB." He pulled out his cell phone, calling his partner and lover. The telephone rang several times, but Matthew didn't answer. He hung up, then called the precinct and still there was no answer. He checked to see if Matthew had gone in to work; he hadn't. He tried to call Matthew's cellular. Once again, no answer. He slammed his cell phone shut. "What the hell?! Matthew isn't answering either. This is not a coincidence!" He looked at Nagesa who came closer.

"Wait a fucking minute! Are you telling me that Matthew, Natasha and Sebastian are missing? No one's been in contact with any of them?" Adrian tossed a glance at Nicole who looked to be as worried as they were.

"I'm calling Xander." Warren said, wanting to inform him

about Matthew's disappearance as well as the update on Darian's mansion.

"All three?" Xander paused, Warren waited. "They took the weakest of our households," he said, immediately establishing a pattern.

"How would they even know? Not even our job knows that Matt and I are a couple." Warren asked, obviously outraged.

"They may not know you're a couple, you're close enough as partners." Another pause. "This attack is too precise, surgical. Also, I don't think this human group organized this themselves. However, I don't want to get ahead of the game at this point. Any scenario is possible at it stands now. "

"Whomever is behind this had to have been watching us for a while. But why?"

"Listen, finish your investigation, we'll talk more when you get back." Xander left Warren to his task.

"Tire tracks were left in that direction," Nagesa reported, pointing toward the winding driveway leading to an open gate.

"What did they look like?" Warren asked.

"I know they were driving three trucks. Three separate tracks, two were definitely made by Sidewinder SUVs."

"How much help is that?" Nicole asked as she looked from one man to the other.

"I'm going to go and take a look." Warren walked off in the direction Nagesa had come from. He examined the tire tracks, mentally measuring the width of the tread marks. By looking at how much rubber stained the streets, he knew they were speeding. He also caught a few scents from the attackers and knew they were all human.

"The tires look new, the treads are deep. I memorized the pattern. I think they're GBS tires," Warren said as he approached the others. He made a calculated guess, knowing that GBS was the main supplier providing tires for the automotive company that manufactured Sidewinder SUVs.

"Still, how does that help us?" Nicole asked.

"Right now, who knows?" Adrian stated with a scowl. "It would take us forever to track down their trucks, and who the trucks are registered to-this is ridiculous!" he cursed under his breath, turning from Warren.

"I think the S.U.I.T. will help in tracking down the trucks. We have the tracks, I just need to take pictures for references. I can look up the make and model of the tires to be certain that they're GBS, then see how many people have SUV's with those model tires in the city. That should narrow it down somewhat," Warren said.

"That's only going to get you so far. If they didn't purchase their trucks in Chicago, or even in Illinois, you're looking for a needle in a haystack. It's still the same shitty situation," Adrian said, sighing in frustration. Warren remained silent, realizing he had a point.

"Let's head back," Nagesa suggested, then led the way back toward their vehicle.

***

"Have you tried to call Sebastian again?" Miranda asked. She watched Sergio's stony expression as he drove the car.

"I've called his cell at least twenty-five times already. They've got him. I know it!"

As they drove toward Joseph's apartment, Sergio's phone rang and he answered.

"Yeah?"

"Sergio, I just found out that Matthew's missing as well. So that makes three, one from each of our families," Elise informed him. Sergio was silent, too angry to speak.

"I just thought I'd let you know. Be careful." Elise ended the call. Sergio slipped his phone back into his pocket.

"I heard," Miranda said, looking out of the passenger window. They drove in silence until they reached Joseph's apartment. They entered the unit, inspecting the area. No one had contacted the police. Everything was as he and Warren had left it. Miranda balanced the door, so that it looked almost closed. They stepped further into the living room, Miranda looked at the crumpled, dead body slumped in the wooden chair against the sofa.

"Nice job," she stated.

Joseph's arms dangled over the armrest, one arm clearly dislocated as it was oddly misshaped, bent in a way a human arm shouldn't be able to achieve. Jagged and splintered bones in his neck jutted out from the skin. Blood had dried into a dark red crust over Joseph's lips, chin, shirt front and pants. A puddle of dried blood had formed on the floor where it had dripped from his numerous wounds. His eyes were open, but lifeless.

"He deserved more than that. Warren was being merciful. Listen, I'll check his bedroom, you check these two rooms." Sergio pointed to the living room and dining room.

He walked into the bedroom and immediately began opening dresser drawers. When he didn't find anything useful there, he tried the closet, looking through shoeboxes filled with old bills and letters. He searched pockets of pants, shirts and suit jackets, finding nothing useful. Miranda searched through Joseph's wallet, stashed in his back pocket, fishing through his various credit and membership cards. She then slid it into her pocket and moved on to the sofa, lifting the cushions, looking for any type of clue. She did the same to the chair cushions, buffet drawers, and cabinets. After about half an hour of searching, she heard voices coming up the stairway, down the hall from Joseph's apartment. Two men were talking and appeared to be very angry by their tones. They were wondering why Joseph hadn't joined them that morning.

Miranda softly called out to Sergio.

"Yeah?" he answered, sticking his head out of the bedroom door.

"Two men are coming."

Sergio nodded, exiting the bedroom. Miranda smiled as she walked over to a wall. Her nails grew long and sharp, curving over to form claws. With catlike agility, she climbed the wall, embedding her claws deeply into the drywall until she was poised directly over the doorway. Sergio hid behind the door and they waited for the two men to enter. There was a knock at the door.

"Joseph, you better open this damn door! We know you're home, your truck's outside!" one of the male voices called out. Then he knocked again.

"He's probably passed out drunk in a puddle of his own puke," the second man speculated.

"That's the least of his worries, Steve's pissed!" said the other man as he continued to knock. Sergio chuckled to himself as he had to agree with the man. Being unconscious in a puddle of his own puke and a no-show for an attack was the least of Joseph's worries.

"Fuck this!" The man grew agitated. He began to pick the lock until the door opened, swinging back, dangling from one hinge.

Sergio was relieved that the door hadn't fallen completely off, it still provided his cover for the time being. Both men looked at the broken door, then at each other. They drew their guns as they stepped very cautiously into the living room.

"What the fuck?!" The taller man's mouth dropped open as he looked on in horror at what remained of Joseph.

"Shit, Adam, we need to get the hell out of here!" said the shorter man, growing more nervous with each passing second.

Figuring the moment was perfect for an attack, Miranda leaped from the wall, grabbing the shorter man before he could react. Sergio grabbed the other before he could turn his gun on Miranda. Both men struggled vainly in the shifters' grips, but neither shifter loosened their hold.

"Now listen, I am in no mood for games. You're going to tell us what we want to know." Sergio's voice was deep and measured as he spoke in order to contain his emotions.

"I ain't tellin' you freaks shit!" Adam yelled as he struggled in Sergio's grip. Sergio could smell the fear emanating from them as they struggled to get loose. He was sure Miranda could smell their fear as well. It certainly would explain the smile that was now plastered on her face as she watched the two men.

"What about you, are you going to make this hard?" Sergio asked the other man who had given up trying to break free from Miranda, and simply stood still.

"Go to hell!" the man retorted with less conviction. Sergio felt that the other man would be more willing to cooperate.

"I'm going to ask you this once. Where are the others?" Sergio asked the question out loud, allowing either man to answer. Neither spoke.

Sergio shook his head. "Very well, we'll do this the hard way. You won't talk, perhaps I should give you an incentive." He took hold of his victim's chin, squeezing it slowly until he crushed his jaw. His hand quickly covered the man's mouth, muffling his agonizing screams as he struggled wildly in his arms. Sergio didn't stop there. His eyes stayed locked on the man Miranda held. He watched the man's eyes grow wide with fear, he scented the terror-soaked sweat as it leaked from his pores.

The man was petrified…he would talk.

Sergio waited to see if the man would volunteer information, he didn't.

"You have the answers to my questions, don't you?" Sergio asked the other man, who remained silent, although his eyes gave him away…he was scared enough to answer their questions. "Where are the others?"

"If I tell you, what's in it for me?" The man asked, obviously mentally working out a plan to save himself. He didn't want a shattered jawbone, not like his companion.

"I'm fairly certain I said I wasn't in the fucking mood for games!" Sergio applied more pressure to his grip. The mind-numbing pain in Adam's jaw brought him to tears which flowed freely down his cheeks. He whimpered softly as he struggled to free himself. Sergio held on tightly as he slowly began separating his victim's head from his body. A thin line of blood appeared across Adam's throat as the skin was being ripped apart. Blood began to gush out of the newly gaping wound, spattering over both Miranda and the other man as it poured down Adam's shirt. The other man screamed, Miranda covered his mouth so that he wouldn't draw any attention. Tears flowed from the man's eyes as he fought to get away. It was no use, Miranda held onto him firmly, making sure that he was exposed to the horror before him. Sergio continued to rip Adam's head away until it became completely detached. He dropped the body onto the floor. Still holding onto the decapitated head by the long strands of blond hair. Sergio dangled the head in front of the horrified man, making sure he had his undivided attention.

"Do you want to end up like him?" Sergio asked in a voice as cold as ice. He wanted the other man to understand how serious he was about their situation.

The man shook his head wildly as his bulging eyes focused on the head of his friend as the severed veins hanging like tentacles dripped thick globs of blood on the floor.

"Are you ready to answer our questions truthfully?" Sergio asked.

The man nodded his head frantically. Sergio nodded to Miranda, who removed her hand from the man's mouth. The man gagged and Sergio stepped away quickly, avoiding the foul stream of sour vomit that shot forth from the man's mouth. Miranda released the man as he continued to heave the contents of his stomach onto the blood stained wooden floor. When his stomach could give forth no more, the man scurried away from the hot mess. Shaking and weak, he stared up at the two shape-shifters. Sergio stepped over the vomit, approaching the man in a menacing manner. Terrified, the man began to scoot backward.

"Stay right there!" Sergio demanded.

The man ceased his movement. His eyes were locked onto Sergio as he squatted down in front of him.

"First off, what's your name?" Sergio asked.

"E...Ed...Edward," the man answered.

"Good, now that we're past the pleasantries, what the fuck is going on? Where are our family members and the others, mainly your leader, the one I believe is named, Steve?"

"Are you going to let me live? I mean, I don't want to die." Edward's voice trembled with fear.

Sergio looked at the blood on his fingers. He slipped one finger between his lips. When he pulled his finger away, it was clean.

"Jesus!" Edward exclaimed. Stuttering as he spoke, he gave Sergio the location of his leader and the others of his group.

"Where are the people you kidnapped? And who's behind this attack?"

"I don't know!"

"Don't bullshit me! Answer the fucking questions!"

"I swear I don't know! We were paid twenty-five-thousand dollars each to take you out! A while back, somebody contacted Steve, told him he had this job for us. Steve took the job, it was a lot of money."

Sergio looked back at Miranda. She had propped the door back up while Sergio was talking and now, she stood still as if she were a statue. He turned around to face the man once again. "Where's my son and the others?"

"I don't know what you're talking about?!"

Sergio slapped Edward hard across the face, hard enough to cause pain, but not to cause damage.

Edward groaned. "I swear I don't know anything about that! We didn't take anybody!"

"Then who did?" Sergio demanded.

The man began to cry. "I don't know," he said, his voice breaking between sobs.

"He doesn't know," Miranda stated.

Sergio looked at her, then back to the man once again. "I know. I can tell he's not lying."

"I'm not lying, I really don't know anything about any kidnappings."

"Okay Edward, how many of you are there?"

"Twenty-three...Um, now it's twenty-one," Edward said making sure to give Sergio the accurate number minus Adam and Joseph.

He prayed that Sergio would let him go since he was answering their questions.

"And you say they are all at that location?" Miranda asked.

"Yes! Yes! They're waiting for us to report back!" Edward exclaimed hoping that he could buy himself more time.

"So report back. We don't want them growing suspicious, do we? But when you do, make sure you tell them that everything is okay. Joseph was drunk, I don't know…possibly lying in a puddle of his own puke. Tell them nothing of what's happened. If I sense that you are trying to betray us, I'll rip your throat out. Do we have an understanding?" Sergio asked.

Edward nodded. "Yes. Are you going to let me live?"

"So far, you've been very cooperative, so I'll let you live. But if you double-cross me…," Sergio paused. He looked at Miranda. "Miranda, can you tell him how much I hate double-crosses?"

She stood over Edward, intimidating him. "He really hates double-crosses. You even think about doing it, he'll make you wish you'd died like that guy over there." She pointed to Adam's decapitated corpse.

"I swear, I won't double-cross you. I'm going to do exactly what you told me to do," Edward promised.

"Well, then, we have a deal." Sergio smiled.

"Oh, thank god!" Edward said breathlessly, relieved that he would survive this.

"Okay, make that call," Sergio ordered.

Edward nodded. "What do I tell them about Adam when I don't show up with him?"

"I'm sure you'll be able to think of something to tell them."

"Yeah, I should be able to." Edward could feel a wave of relief wash over him. He began to calm down.

"Get yourself together first, I don't want Steve to think that something's wrong," Sergio said.

Edward nodded, taking several deep breaths, releasing them slowly. He pulled out his cell phone and called his leader.

Steve answered. "About time you called, what's going on with Joseph?"

"Steve, Joseph's drunk as hell. There was a whore in the bed with him, we escorted her out. Want me to leave him here or bring him back with us?" Edward's voice was calm, without a hint of fear.

"Damnit to hell! Yeah, bring his drunk ass back here. And you two don't waste anytime getting back, we've got another hit. This one should be the final one."

Edward looked at Sergio who was urging him to inquire about the next hit.

"What's the other hit? I thought we hit the three homes already?" Edward asked, satisfying Sergio.

"Yeah, we did, but we didn't kill all of those fucking freaky ass shifters. Although, I do believe those bloodsucking bitches are piles of ash." Steve seemed very pleased with himself.

"Are we going to attack the two shifter mansions again, it's not a full moon-"

"Hell no!" Steve interjected. "Much better, we've got all our ducks in a row this time. Mike spotted four of them at the vamp mansion snooping around. He followed them back to this private airplane hangar. We need the entire team on this one, so bring your asses!" he demanded before hanging up the telephone.

Edward slipped his cell phone into his pocket. He looked at Sergio. "Did I do well?" he asked.

Sergio nodded, but he was extremely worried by what he'd heard, as was Miranda. Neither spoke of their concerns out loud.

"Come on, let's go." Sergio rose to his feet and Edward did the same. After wiping the apartment clean of their fingerprints, the three of them left using the back entrance. Sergio climbed into the driver's seat while Miranda shoved Edward in the back seat before slipping in beside him. Sergio called Elise. He waited for her to answer.

"Do you speak Italian?" Sergio asked Edward.

"No. Why?"

"No reason."

When she answered, he started to tell her about what he heard, speaking in Italian so that Edward wouldn't understand him.

"This is good. At least we now know what their next move is. We have to take care of them immediately," Elise said. "Where are you headed to now?"

Sergio told her the address Edward had given him.

"We'll meet you there, wait for us before you attack," Elise ordered.

"Okay, see you in a few." Sergio hung up his cell. He looked at Miranda. Still speaking in Italian, he said, "Elise and the others are going to meet us."

Miranda nodded and the three drove until Edward told them to pull up in front of an insurance company.

"This it?" Sergio asked.

"Yeah, they'll be in the back. I don't have to go in there with you, do I?" Edward asked, obviously worried.

Sergio turned around, facing him. "Don't you think you should? I mean, they are your crew."

"I'm not going to die with them, I'd rather stay here...or better yet, you two can just let me go, I swear I won't spoil your plan!"

Sergio's face contorted, he threw a glance at Miranda, then back to Edward. "Where's your loyalty?"

"My loyalty is to myself...I want to live."

Sergio laughed for a few moments then he grew silent. "This better be the right place. If this is a trap, I'll renege on my promise, you got that?"

Edward nodded. "I told you the truth. I can tell that you're a no-nonsense man. I wouldn't lie to you, not when my life is hanging in the balance. This is the place. They're expecting Adam, Joseph and me to come walking through the door any minute now."

Sergio smiled. "Don't worry, *you* won't disappoint."

"But I don't want to go in," Edward protested, until a stern look from Sergio quieted him.

"The others are here," Miranda announced as she saw Elise and the others pull up in an SUV. Sergio turned around as Elise, Xander, Adrian, Devin and Madeleine climbed out of the vehicle.

"Let's go," Sergio said. He and Miranda exited their car. Miranda motioned for Edward to slide out the back door after her. The three walked over to Xander and Elise who were leading the way.

"I can smell them," Miranda said. "I can tell by their scents they've eaten from here recently." She stepped around to the front of the fast food chicken restaurant a few doors from the insurance building where the human rebels were.

"Oh yeah, I recognize at least two of those scents," Adrian agreed. He tossed a glance at Edward, then stepped closer to him, grabbing him by the collar. "Tell me who shot down one of our members? I'm sure you know which one I'm talking about?"

Edward trembled in Adrian's vise-like grip. "Jacob!" he stammered. "I wasn't even there last night!"

"You piece of shit!" Adrian cursed, shoving the man against the outer-brick wall of the restaurant.

"Keep your head together, Adrian. We have business to take care of," Xander said, urging his son to remain calm and focused. He looked at Edward. "We want to enter through the rear entrance. Lead the way. "

"But, but...I'm not going in there, no fucking way!"

Elise grabbed Edward's chin, applying enough pressure to cause him to squirm.

"This is not up for negotiation. Move it!" Elise released Edward with such force, he stumbled but was able to grab onto a parking meter, allowing him to regain his balance. He turned, shivering at the menacing glares that were all directed at him. He nodded slowly.

"Follow me," he said as he led the way.

"Walk faster!" Sergio demanded as he stepped closer to Edward who had been keeping a slow pace in front of the others.

"There is one thing that I failed to mention," Edward began, standing a few feet away from the back door.

"What's that?" Sergio asked as he looked around, beginning to sense that something was wrong.

"They have cameras all over, so they already know you're coming!" Edward blurted out as he ran toward the back entrance. Several men and woman came spilling into the alleyway, weapons firing. The shifters dodged the flying bullets as they ducked for cover behind huge metal dumpsters. Edward ran toward the others for protection. One of the rebels tossed him a gun and he aimed the barrel at the dumpster where he knew Sergio was taking cover.

Sergio peeked around, then immediately ducked again, barely dodging a silver bullet. "Fuck! That little double-crossing son-of-a-bitch!"

He called out to Devin who turned toward him. He gestured for him to go around the front and to take others with him. Devin nodded, letting Sergio know that he understood. Devin tapped Miranda and Elise on the shoulders, motioning for them to follow him, they nodded. The three of them ran out of the alley, successfully avoiding the barrage of bullets that held the others at bay. Xander ran toward his son. He whispered for Adrian to help him toss one of the dumpsters into the group of rebels.

"That will distract them enough for us to capitalize," Xander stated. Adrian nodded. Both took hold of each end of the dumpster. Springing up, they tossed it toward three humans who were hiding behind a red Viper. The dumpster struck the car, shattering windows and propelling the humans against the ground causing them to drop their weapons in the impact. The shifters used that split second of confusion to launch a counterattack. Sergio ran toward the group, grabbing hold of two members by their hair, smashing their heads together, cracking their skulls. Both of the lifeless bodies fell limp in his grip. He wasted no time as he tossed the bodies into the frightened rebels as they tried to scurry back into the building.

"Catch them, I want Steve alive," Xander called out. "Sergio, don't kill any others until we find him!"

"All we need is one!" Sergio grabbed a hold of a female member who tried to shoot him, snatching the gun from her hand then backhanding her, knocking her unconscious.

"One who can give us the information we need, so don't get overly zealous," Xander stated as he kicked down the back door. All of the shifters converged on the humans inside as bullets whizzed past them. They dodged the gunfire long enough to capture twelve humans, rendering them unconscious while the other rebels had closed themselves off in the back room, each reloading their weapons.

"They're in that room," Devin said, pointing to a steel door.

"Then lets finish this!" Miranda said, stalking toward the door, kicking several times, knocking it down. The heavy, dented steel door fell before her, revealing seven desperate mortals scurrying for cover. With a speed that left the rebels astonished and terrified, the shape-shifters raced around the room, disarming each human and rendering some of them unconscious. Sergio slowly approached Edward who shrank into a corner of the room, trembling as he came closer.

Sergio looked down at him. "You double-crossed us, Edward. And here I was, trusting you to be the disloyal scum I knew you to be, even though you were pretending you wasn't. That's twice you've let me down!" He leaned over, grabbing Edward by the throat, lifting him two feet off of the floor. "Now, I'm going to give you a chance to make it up to me. Which one of these bastards is Steve?"

"Fuck you, you were going to kill me anyway! I ain't telling you shit!" Edward spat in Sergio's face.

"Oh shit! Big mistake! I definitely wouldn't have done that!" Devin stated as he shook his head.

"Indeed," Elise agreed as she stood over several humans. Some were beginning to awaken, while those who were already conscious watched Sergio and Edward curiously, wondering what would happen. Would Edward give Steve up?

Sergio ripped a piece of Edward's shirt off, using the torn fabric to wipe the glob of spittle from his cheek.

"I'm gonna fuck you up for that." Sergio continued to hold Edward with one hand and with his other, he took hold of the man's genitals and squeezed.

Edward screamed and struggled in Sergio's unfailing grip. "Ahhh! God! Stop! Lemme go! Lemme go!" he begged.

"No, not until you tell me what the fuck I want to know!" Sergio twisted Edward's genitals, causing tears to well up in his eyes as he screamed for Sergio to release him.

"He's going to kill you anyway, don't tell him!" A female called out, encouraging Edward's stubbornness.

Miranda walked over to the female, striking her hard across the face, splitting her lip.

Adrian chuckled. "I couldn't have said 'shut the fuck up' better myself."

Sergio never took his eyes from Edward who had not answered his question.

"Tell us what we want to know, you asshole!" Devin exclaimed.

"Sounds like a smart thing to do," Sergio agreed as he began to slowly pull harder on Edward's genitals.

"Ahhh! Okay, okay, he's there, right there, please, lemme go!" Edward pointed to a man lying unconscious next to the female who had told him to remain silent.

Sergio turned to the others. Devin walked over to the man, kicking him in the abdomen. The man woke up, coughing and gasping for air. He looked up at Devin, who smiled.

"Hello, Steve," Devin greeted him.

Steve looked at Edward who was still pointing at him as he whined and moaned in Sergio's grip, his genitals still clamped in the shifter's hand.

"You asshole!" Steve cursed.

"We've got him." Devin grabbed Steve by the back of the neck, making him rise to his feet.

Sergio turned back to Edward. "Are you sure this is Steve?" he asked. "Because, you know, you've lied to me before. I'm having some real trust issues dealing with you." He applied more pressure.

Edward screamed. "Yes! Jesus Christ! Yes!"

Sergio nodded. "Good," he said.

"Please let me go," Edward pleaded.

"Too late for that." Sergio tightened his grip, ripping the man's genitals from his body along with the patch of jeans that used to cover Edward's crotch. Blood gushed from the wound, spattering Sergio's pants and the floor beneath them. Edward screamed, hands automatically going to his crotch, as if hoping to heal it in some way. The pain was intense, far too much for him to bear. Tears and snot ran freely from his eyes and nose. Sergio dug his nails into Edward's throat, tearing away a chunk of flesh along with Edward's vocal cords before letting the body fall to the floor.

"Oh my god!" one of the female humans gasped as she witnessed Edward's death.

"Are we done here?" Devin asked the others who were patiently watching Sergio's "interrogation".

"I know I am. I'm fucking tired of these games. I want my son!" Sergio growled as he wiped his bloody fingers on his blood-splattered shirt.

"Yes, we're done here," Elise said. "Kill them all. We have who we came here for." She walked over to Steve, taking him by the arm, leading him toward the exit as the others killed the rebels.

Miranda and Devin shot fifteen of the rebels who tried to fight back, then they left. Adrian and Sergio broke the necks of the remaining four rebels. Xander looked around the hideout for anything that could give him information on who had hired the humans. He was joined by Sergio who helped search through the cabinets and drawers.

"Nothing!" Sergio growled, growing even more frustrated and angered. "This is pissing me the fuck off!"

"Calm down. It is true, they are very elusive, and have covered their tracks pretty well, but we have the one person who may be able to give us some answers," Xander said.

"I know that you're right. But this shit is driving me crazy." Sergio ran his fingers through his thick, wavy hair.

"I understand." Xander placed his hand on Sergio's shoulder, offering him comfort.

"Let's burn this place." Adrian suggested. "We don't want to leave any evidence."

"Good idea," Sergio agreed and began searching for flammable fluids, the others joining in. Together, they were able to locate several containers of cleansers. They poured the liquid directly on the bodies, on the floor, cabinets, desks, tables, chairs and anything else that would burn.

"Okay, let's go," Sergio stated as he pulled a book of matches from his pocket.

"What are you doing with matches? It's not like you smoke," Adrian asked.

"I always keep a lighter or book of matches on me. You never know when you're going to need them, like now," Sergio answered. "Now, let's get the hell out of here." Everyone else left through the back exit as Sergio lit a match, tossing it on the floor as he walked out.

"What happened to the other truck?" Adrian asked, seeing only one left.

"We'll explain later, we need to go," Elise said from inside the truck. The others climbed into the remaining SUVs and drove back to the hangar. Once inside, they brought everyone up to speed on what had happened.

"Too bad we couldn't have eaten them," Devin said.

"I'm more concern as to where my son is. This jerk over here better tell me what I want to hear." Madeleine said, gesturing to Steve who was being guarded by Elise. Sergio took a seat beside Elise, remaining silent for the time being.

When Steve tried to rise, Elise shoved him back down on the dusty crate. "Sit," she ordered. He did, crossing his arms over his chest as he watched the shifters.

"Should we tie him up?" Justin asked, looking to Xander for an answer.

"Why don't you do the honors," Xander suggested.

"I'd rather rip his arms off his body," Sergio grumbled. "Tell me again why we aren't torturing him?"

"Because he's not going to talk," Elise responded.

Steve watched all of the shifters around him. His eyes stayed locked on Xander and Elise, his confidence shaken by their calm demeanor. He wondered what they were waiting for. He hoped that his partners would come for him before they could do anything permanent to hurt him. Besides, they had a deal.

Tatiana walked over to Xander, taking a seat beside his. "What do you have planned for him?" she asked.

Xander sat, relaxed in a chair. "We'll wait until sundown." He smiled slightly.

"But we need answers now, Xander," Sergio protested.

"We do, but those are answers that he is not going to give us willingly."

"Are you sure about that? I've found that breaking bones and ripping off body parts is a wonderful and very successful interrogation strategy," Sergio said, staring menacingly at Steve, who remained silent, his expression unreadable.

"Something tells me that strategy won't work on this one," Elise said, agreeing with Xander.

"He'd rather die then tell us?" Sergio asked once again.

Xander turned toward Sergio. "I understand that you are desperate to find your son, I do. And this situation is not pleasant for any of us, but do not let that hinder your better judgment and most importantly, your senses."

"How can you be so laidback when these sons-of-bitches killed one of your Pack members!" Sergio argued through gritted teeth.

"Because acting irrationally now will not save those still in need of our help. Rest assured that I am not pleased, nor 'laidback'. I am calm, because I must be calm as you should be until the time comes when we should act," Xander said. He watched as Sergio pondered the message behind his words.

Sergio took several deep breaths, attempting to regain control of his temper. "Tell me," he asked, knowing that Xander and Elise knew something that he didn't know. And whatever they knew about Steve, he wanted to know.

Xander looked at Steve, then back to Sergio. "He does not fear us. Not enough to use his fear against him."

"We can make him fear us," Sergio urged.

Xander shook his head. "No, he is relaxed which is odd. He sits here surrounded by shifters who could kill him within an instant. Supernatural beings that he has attacked on more than one occasion, yet I sense no fear or apprehension in him. He does not fear our retribution."

"You're right," Tatiana said, looking at Steve.

"How can you tell?" Nicole asked.

"My dear, use your senses. Can you taste his fear in the air? Can you smell it?" Xander looked at the others.

Collectively, they shook their heads.

"God, I hate this!" Sergio growled as he walked away from the others. No one bothered to follow him, knowing he needed a moment alone.

"We could torture him, but he wouldn't speak. There is someone else that he fears more than us," Xander said.

"Ahh, so that's why we're waiting for sundown!" Devin nodded. "Shit, that works for me."

Xander smiled.

"Very good decision," Tatiana agreed. She leaned forward kissing her husband on his left cheek.

"Too bad we're not going to torture this one, I bet my interrogation techniques would surpass Sergio's," Adrian said.

"I'm more interested in seeing what Darian will do to this motherfucker once he wakes up," Sergio said as he rejoined the group. "I hope he crushes his bones into dust!" He walked over to Elise. "Have you tried again to contact Natasha?"

Elise nodded. "We've tried to contact Natasha, Sebastian and Matthew, they can't be reached. The only one who will be able to contact Natasha is Darian, for they have a connection."

"This is driving me crazy, Elise," Sergio whispered as he sat down beside her.

She wrapped her arms around his shoulders. "We will save them, darling. Don't worry," she whispered into his ear.

"Where's Miranda, Warren and Nagesa?" Sergio asked, finally realizing the three were missing.

"Xander and I thought it would be a good idea to send them out to search for Sebastian, Natasha and Matthew," Elise said.

"When did that happened?" Sergio asked. "Shit, I should be out there!"

"It happened before we returned to the hangar. Elise sent them off in the other SUV to search the city," Xander replied.

"We need you here. Besides, they are more than capable of handling the task, Sergio." Elise placed her hands on both sides of his face, turning his head toward her so that their eyes met. "Listen to me, Sergio. They are searching locations where they could have taken them to see if any scents were left. Warren went to the school to get the address of the girl Sebastian was last seen with. Once we have that information, we will go from there. I do not want you acting out on emotions that will blind you, do you understand?"

Sergio looked at Elise, studying her expression, he nodded. "Yes. But I want you to know that I don't like being here when my son is out there somewhere. Probably scared, not knowing if he's going to live or die. He needs me."

"I know, but more importantly, he needs you to stay focused." Elise leaned forward kissing Sergio lightly.

They all waited for the others to return and for sundown. Devin and Justin were playing cards with a deck that he had found in the glove compartment of one of the trucks.

"Man, what time is it? I'm starving!" He looked at his watch, seeing that it was still early in the evening. "Damn, that's it!"

"Should have eaten at the chicken shack that was down the street from that insurance building," Adrian teased.

"In retrospect, yes. But since I didn't, can we go and get something to eat?" Devin looked at Sergio and Elise.

"Very well, Devin, take someone with you," Elise said.

"Good! Okay, Justin, and Daniel, let's go," Devin leaped from his chair, followed by Justin.

Daniel groaned. "I suppose I should go with you, we know what happened the last time you two went on a food run."

"Hey, that was like two months ago and we apologized for that," Justin said in his defense.

"Yeah whatever." Daniel turned to the others. "Is pizza good enough for everyone?"

"That will be just fine," Xander said.

Daniel nodded. "Good, okay, pizza it is."

The three shifters left to go to one of Chicago's most famous restaurants for deep dish pizza.

CHAPTER NINE

"Matthew!" Warren vainly called out Matthew's name knowing that his lover was no longer inside the house that they shared. He could smell blood immediately. He ran upstairs to their bedroom, the door flying open as he shot into the room. He saw drops of blood on the sheets, carpet and the dresser.

Nagesa came up behind him, entering the bedroom, surveying the damage.

"There was a struggle, they hurt him!" Warren said, grinding his teeth in anger. He looked at the rumpled sheets that were half off of the mattress. The table lamps had been knocked over and there were empty bullet casings on the floor. Miranda joined the other two. She looked around the room as well and noticed the silver-nitrate gel that had dried on the wallpaper in rivulets from several holes in the wall.

She walked over to the wall. "Silver-nitrate bullets. He knew they were shape-shifters," she stated.

"If shifters are somehow involved, then where do the humans fit in?" Warren asked.

"Elise and Xander need to know this," Nagesa said. "Once we check out Natasha's job and the school to get the girl's information, we'll give them a full report. Let's go." He walked out of the bedroom, followed by Miranda. Warren lingered a few seconds more looking at the blood stained room once again, balling his hands into fist to keep from screaming out in rage. He took several deep breaths then left the room to join the others.

When they arrived at the school, Warren climbed out of the car before leaning into the driver's side window.

"You guys better let me handle this. Working for the S.U.I.T. has its advantages. I'll be back." He walked inside the expensive private prep academy. Upon entering, he was accosted by security.

"Good afternoon sir, how can I help you?" the security officer asked with a pleasant smile.

Warren looked around the extravagant school, beginning to remember his high school years. He and Adrian had shared a lot of the same classes and got into trouble often.

Warren reached into his pocket, removing his leather badge and I.D. holder. He opened the flap of the holder, revealing his silver and gold S.U.I.T. badge and photo I.D.

"Detective Davis, S.U.I.T., I need to speak with the headmaster," Warren said as he slipped his holder back into his pocket.

"Oh, yes sir, er, Officer...one minute please." The Security officer clicked the little button on his walkie-talkie requesting that another officer come to escort Warren to the headmaster's office. A few minutes passed before a second officer clad in a security uniform that consisted of a black shirt and pants combination identical to the entrance security personnel. Both wore a utility belt containing a flashlight, pepper spray and low-shock tazers ideal for stunning individuals only. Warren assumed that Sergio was paying a shit-load of money for his son to attend such a school.

"Detective Davis, please follow me." The other security officer led Warren toward the headmaster's office. Arriving at the office, the two men stood waiting in the doorway. The headmaster, a tall man with graying hair at the top and black sideburns, beckoned them inside. Warren gazed at his chiseled features, thinking he had once been a handsome man, but one could tell that time had taken its toll on him.

Once inside the office, Headmaster Williams looked at the accompanying security officer. "Officer Stone, if you could excuse us."

The security officer nodded and left, leaving Warren and Mr. Williams alone.

The headmaster extended his hand to Warren, who shook it. "Detective Davis, I'm Mr. Williams, the Headmaster here at Brentwood Academy. How may I help you?"

"I'm in the middle of an investigation and I need to ask you some questions about one of your students," Warren began.

The headmaster nodded. "I'd like to be of service, but I have to inform you this academy is of high standards. We don't allow shape-shifter adolescents to become students within these walls for the safety and peace of mind of all of our attendees. Our students' parents, including the board council have forbidden it."

"What does that have to do with anything?" Warren asked, thoroughly insulted and slightly perplexed as to why the headmaster felt the need to inform him of their discriminative practices.

"Well, you're a S.U.I.T. Detective, if I'm not mistaken. Therefore, you deal only with supernaturals, am I correct?"

"You are, but that is irrelevant. I need to know the address and full name of one of your students."

"Do you have a warrant?"

"No. I could get one, but that would take entirely too much time. This is a matter of life and death. Now how much of my time are you going to waste? She could be in danger. Do you really want one of your student's death to be on your conscience?"

The headmaster looked Warren up and down, debating whether he should ignore protocol and offer the information. The detective did say it was a matter of "life and death", and he wouldn't want to be the one responsible for anyone's death. Certainly if the S.U.I.T. was involved, the student was in trouble. He wouldn't be able to forgive himself if he let someone die because of a technicality.

"Listen, I'm going to help you, but this is completely off the record. I don't want anything to come back on me concerning your case. Giving you this student's private information is strictly prohibited and I could get fired, for starters. So I mean it, my name doesn't come up in any reports and you didn't get the information from me, got that?"

Warren held his hands up as if in surrender. "Hey, I got it. I appreciate what you're doing. I know the risks, trust me. I wouldn't ask this of you if I didn't think it was serious."

"That's good to know. Okay, who is the student you're looking for?" Headmaster Williams asked.

Relieved that things were going to go smoothly, Warren gave the only information he knew. Her first name and description. The headmaster seemed to be concentrating, scanning his memory for a student that fit her description.

When he thought he had the answer he snapped two fingers together. "Ah, you must be talking about Crystal Dawners. She's new, transferred in from California. We've been keeping an eye out for her since a lot of the lads have taken quite a liking to her. She's not here today, but I suppose that's why you are." The headmaster looked her information up on his computer. "Here's her address." He wrote her information down on a yellow sticky note and handed it to Warren.

"Thank you for your help, Headmaster Williams," Warren said gratefully.

Headmaster Williams nodded. "Please let me know if everything is okay."

"I will." Warren shook his hand once more before leaving the school.

He climbed back inside the car.

"Were you able to get the information?" Nagesa asked.

Warren nodded, giving Nagesa the address. The three of them headed toward her home. They arrived at a four-condo complex. Warren walked up to the condo where the girl was staying. Nagesa and Miranda leaned against the wall, out of eyesight of anyone who opened the door. Warren rang the bell. No one answered. He rang the bell two more times. When no one came to the door, Miranda stepped in front of Warren. She pulled two hairpins from her hair, letting a few strands fall down her back. Straightening, twisting and bending the hairpins into lock pick tools, she inconspicuously begin to pick the lock. Within seconds, the door was opened. The three of them walked in, closing the door behind them. None of them turned on the light; it wasn't necessary. They didn't want to alarm the neighbors and they hoped that they hadn't already.

The three of them looked around the medium size condo which was nicely decorated in contemporary furnishings. There was a light blue leather sofa and loveseat set along with an ottoman. The set was complete with the oak end tables and coffee table. They surveyed the dining room which was also very nicely furnished with an eight piece redwood dining set.

Nagesa walked over to the buffet cabinet, looking at the china and souvenirs that decorated the glass and wood casing. "This is a one bedroom condo and she lives alone," he said as he further examined the rooms.

"Not only that, but she's had visitors...shifters," Warren added.

Miranda interjected. "Coyotes. That's their scent." She walked into the bedroom, frowning. "Sebastian was here."

Warren came in behind her. "He's no longer a virgin, and she hasn't been for a while." He inhaled deeply. "The coyote's scent is fresh in here. They took them both." He walked into the center of the room, sniffing the air. "There's something else, I recognize her scent."

"You know her? Who is it?" Miranda asked.

Warren pursed his lips as he scanned his memory. He remembered. "Oh Yeah! The girl from my crime scene yesterday! She was supposedly the person who 'found' the body." He made quotation marks in the air as he spoke.

"You think she planted the body?" Miranda asked.

Warren nodded. "I suspected she had something to do with it yesterday. The scent of the body was on her and vice versa, even though she claimed to have never touched it. Now, I know she had something to do with it. She'd told me her name was Samantha Waters; there's really no telling what her real name is."

"Let's stick with Crystal for now," Miranda said.

Nagesa walked into the bedroom, stepping past them, he began to search Crystal's dresser. The others decided to follow his lead. Nagesa found a box of photographs, covered in what they all believed to be Crystal's scent. He tucked the box of photos under his arm, then looked at Warren.

"Did you find anything?" he asked.

Warren shook his head. "The only thing that's here is a few items of comfort and clothes. There are no family photos on the walls, there's no sense of 'home' here."

"Why does she live here alone?" Miranda asked out loud to no one in particular.

"We need to get to Natasha's job," Nagesa said, then he walked out of the condo, followed by the others. They climbed into the car and drove toward the *Chicago Word*, one of the top rated and best-selling newspaper companies in the city.

Upon entering the building, the three shifters immediately picked up on numerous shape-shifters scents. There were so many, they were unable to distinguish one from the other.

"You've got to be fucking kidding me!" Warren said, looking at his other companions. "Are you smelling what I am?"

They nodded.

"We need to check out her work area, that may narrow it down," Miranda said.

"I agree." Warren approached the front desk.

The woman sitting behind the desk looked up, smiling. "Hello, welcome to the *Chicago Word*, how may I help you today?"

"Hi, I was wondering if I can speak with Natasha Hemingway, we're friends of hers," Warren said, offering the woman his most charming smile.

"Sure, let me just call her to let her know you're here."

She picked up the telephone, but Warren reached over, placing his hand over hers.

She looked up at him. "Is there a problem?"

"I'd like to surprise her."

"I'm sorry, but I have to issue you all visitor passes and I still have to let her know you're here."

"I'd really like to-"

"Oh for crying out loud!" Miranda interrupted. She approached the front desk. "Warren just show her your badge. You're S.U.I.T. and we need to get upstairs to her desk. This back and forth is doing nothing but wasting time."

Warren looked at Miranda, shocked. He'd never seen her respond in that way before, he found it refreshing.

He turned to face the customer service representative. "She's right. I need to get to her work station." He showed the woman his badge, wondering why he hadn't thought of doing that first, himself. "It's very important that I do."

The woman tossed Miranda an off-putting expression, then returned her gaze to Warren. She pointed at his two companions. "Are they S.U.I.T. also?"

Warren shook his head. "No."

"Then they stay down here, you may go up." She gave Warren a visitor's pass.

He looked at Nagesa and Miranda. "I'll go check it out."

They nodded and remained standing. Warren walked to the elevators, getting on the first one that opened its doors. He pressed the button for the fifth floor. When the elevator doors opened, he walked to Natasha's work space. He could smell over a dozen shape-shifter scents and not one remotely matched the scents he had detected at the crime scene or at Crystal's house. He looked over Natasha's belongings and paperwork, trying to find anything that might give them a clue. There was nothing.

Disappointed, he returned to the others. "Nothing, not even scents. When they took her, they didn't come here to do it. That tells me Tasha was kidnapped before she came to work today, probably before they attacked Darian's mansion."

"I think you're right. We were so preoccupied with the immediate threat, we didn't even see the real attack taking place. I think everyone would agree that the attacks on our homes, although serious offenses, were just smoke screens to conceal a bigger plan," Nagesa speculated.

"I agree, one that involves shape-shifters," Miranda added. "Let's head back."

The three returned to the hangar. When they opened the door, the strong scent of pizza wafted up to their nostrils causing their stomachs to growl.

Adrian chuckled softly. "Hungry?"

"I wish I could say food was the last thing on my mind, but truth is, it's on my mind. I'm starving, but I'm more worried about Matthew, Tasha and Sebastian," Warren said as he walked over to the many boxes of half eaten pizza. He reached in, grabbing a large slice of pepperoni, sausage and cheese pizza loaded with onions, black olives, green peppers and mushrooms. He shoved the slice of pizza into mouth, greedily chewing and swallowing before chomping down on another bite.

Nagesa looked at Warren, shaking his head. He walked over to Xander, handing him the box of photos he had confiscated from Crystal's condo. "I found this at the condo of the girl who was last with Sebastian."

Sergio rose at the mention of Sebastian's name. "What did you find out?" he asked anxiously.

"We found out a lot and kind of nothing at all, if that makes any sense," Warren began once he'd swallowed. "Matthew was attacked at our house. He managed to get off several shots before they took him. It wasn't easy either, he put up a fight. The room had blood splatters, not a lot, but enough for me to know they hurt him."

Xander nodded. "If there was still any question in our minds whether the three have been kidnapped, it's been answered."

"Yeah. They also got to Natasha before she had a chance to get to work. None of the scents I smelled at my house and Crystal's condo were there." Warren finished his third slice of pizza and reached into the box for another.

"Hold on, they took the girl, too? What's her full name? Does her family know?" Sergio asked, approaching Warren.

Miranda looked at Sergio. "Trust me Sergio, she wasn't innocent. There wasn't a sign of a struggle at her apartment. Everything was neatly in its place. Not only that, but we believe she lived alone after inspecting her apartment." Miranda turned to Elise. "There were no family photos, nothing that proved this girl had a mother or father. It was a single bedroom condo."

"Not to mention, I recognized her scent from my crime scene yesterday. Samantha Waters and Crystal Dawners are one and the same," Warren said.

"That is odd. How did she get into that kind of academy without parental permission?" Madeleine asked. "Sergio and I practically had to give blood and DNA samples to get Sebastian into that damn school!"

"Perhaps she had a little outside help. That isn't all, she and Sebastian had sex, and it wasn't her first time. I don't know if that bit of information is significant now or not," Miranda said, then she reached into a box removing a slice of pizza.

"Well, at least we know how she lured him there," Carmen said. The others nodded.

"There's one more thing. We caught the scent of a coyote throughout the house. It was fresh, possibly only a few hours old." Nagesa settled onto one of the dusty crates. Devin offered him a slice of pizza which he graciously accepted.

"Excellent work," Xander complimented the three. Both he and Elise appeared to reflect on the newfound information. He rubbed his finger along the line of his bottom lip, eyes staring forward.

"I'll say this, I'm not at all happy about the involvement of supernaturals in the least. These crazy ass humans were bad enough, now we have coyotes to worry about?!" Nicole complained.

Nagesa nodded. "I think the attacks on our homes were some sort of diversionary tactic to take our attention away from the kidnappings." He looked at Warren who had finished off four slices of pizza and was now bearing an expression of both worry and anger.

"I think you make a good point, except the attack on our homes wasn't meant to be some sort of distraction, but to coincide with their ultimate plan. We know that a human rebel group was working with a coyote Pack, now we need to know why." Elise said as she placed a reassuring hand on Madeleine's shoulder.

Madeleine looked at Elise. "Thank you." She smiled.

Elise gave her a smile in return. "We'll get to the bottom of this, don't worry. We'll save Sebastian."

"I know."

"So the humans are working with these fucking shifters?!" Justin asked as his eyes darted from Elise and Sergio to Xander and Tatiana.

"We established that about ten minutes ago. Where in the hell have you been?" Adrian said.

"Oh, well I was outside taking a piss, I didn't hear the whole breakdown. I just came in on the end," Justin said, pointing toward the back exit door.

"Why were you taking a piss outside?" Devin asked.

"Because someone is in the bathroom here, and the other toilet is broken," Justin answered.

"Who gives a shit!" Adrian blurted out, silencing the two younger shifters.

"What we need to know now is why are they working together, as Elise said," Xander replied, getting back on the important subjects.

"There could be a number of things that they want, territory, our blood, or they could just be doing this shit for fun!" Sergio openly speculated, offering a number of reasons. Elise nodded.

They all finished eating the pizza and sat down to discuss certain strategies as they waited for the sun to set. A few hours later, the sun was finally setting and the shifters waited impatiently for the vampires to rise.

"Our Master will be rising soon!" Tyson exclaimed with great glee.

"Good, about time," Adrian responded.

A few more minutes passed before all heard a coffin lid open. Elise rose from her seat, approaching the SUV that contained Darian's and Xavier's coffin. Peering inside, she saw Darian unwind the thick burgundy blanket that had been wrapped around him to protect against the sun's deadly rays. Dirty patches of soot covered his body from head to toe. Before he climbed out of the truck, he peered back into the coffin. Still inside was Xavier. Darian unwound the thick, black blanket and gazed down at Xavier's perfect form, untouched by the fire. He smiled, then closed the lid. He emerged from the SUV, taking a quick account of all who were present. He looked around the hangar, realizing where he was. His gaze shifted to Elise who stood before him and the others. Some were standing, while the rest continued to stay seated. It didn't matter to him that he stood before them all, naked.

What mattered was finding out just what was going on.

He let his gaze roam over the room as he spoke. "I want to thank you all for saving us, I owe you a great debt. Now please, tell me what is going on."

One of Darian's servants stepped up to him and bowed. "Master, Greg ran away, he didn't try to help us save you."

Darian looked down at his servant. Very gently, he lifted his face to his. "My concerns do not pertain to Gregory, and you needn't be worried about him. Only know that you did well."

"Yes, Master," Tyson returned to his seat.

Darian looked back at Elise. "What do you know?"

Elise took a deep breath, then proceeded to tell Darian all that they had discovered.

"Natasha's been taken!" Darian fought to contain his rage. He turned away from Elise, exposing his perfect backside. It didn't matter to him at this point that his house was in ruins. What mattered was that several of his human servants had been killed, his woman and friends kidnapped, and people he had grown to care for were murdered or injured. Mentally, he tried to contact Natasha. He couldn't. It occurred to him that she might be asleep, or worse. He didn't want to think of the worst case scenario, that was too close to giving up on her for his comfort. He tried to contact her another way, the same method he used when he entered her visions. He was relieved to discover that she was asleep. Her visions were running rampant, mixing in with her dreams. She was unable to control them or distinguish what was a dream and what wasn't. Darian frowned, not liking Natasha's mental state, but he was happy to know that she was alive.

"Is she alright?" Elise asked, almost in a whisper.

Darian turned toward her. "Yes," he said, wiping away a stain of soot from his brow with the back of his hand.

Xander rose, making his way over to Darian. "We have one of their members, the leader of the human rebel organization actually."

"What has he told you?" Darian asked, his voice was steady, calm.

"We have not asked him anything. He would not tell us if we did, not even under the threat of torture. We left him for you." Xander pointed to Steve, who for the first time since he was taken, showed actual fear.

"Ahh, there's the scent!" Sergio whispered under his breath. His lips curled upward in a sneer, pleased to finally smell and see that their captive was finally terrified.

Darian eyed the man as he approached him, closing the distance quickly. Steve's breathing began to quicken the closer the vampire came to him. His eyes scanned over the master vampire's nakedness which did not seem to bother the vampire in the least. Darian stood before him, incensed. He wrapped his fingers around the man's neck, lifting him and the chair he was bound to several feet off of the floor.

Steve's eyes grew huge as he witnessed the vampire's strength and total lack of regard he had for his human life. Steve's features twisted in a scowl as he forced himself to grow more belligerent, attempting to counter the fear he was feeling with anger. "You think I give a fuck about you, vampire?! You're already dead, you just don't know it yet! You can kill me but that won't help you. You're all gonna-"

Darian drove his long, razor-sharp fangs deeply into his victim's neck as fast as a viper attack. Steve froze, startled by the sudden intense pain the bite caused. He grimaced in agony as Darian's fangs ripped his throat open, spilling blood down the length of his torso.

"Shit!" Devin hissed under his breath.

"He's really pissed!" Justin added. "I've never seen a vampire rip out someone's throat before." He watched, transfixed as Darian continued to drain the last drop of blood from Steve's veins.

Darian pulled away, dropping the body and the chair to the floor. The chair gave away under the heavy weight of the lifeless remains, breaking two of its legs. Both the chair and Steve's corpse toppled onto their sides.

"What have you discovered?" Xander asked. He was still calm when he spoke, unaffected by what he'd witnessed.

Darian turned, looking at him. "He and he alone worked for the shape-shifters. He made a deal with them to spare his life."

"Why would he do a dumb ass thing like that?" Devin asked, genuinely curious.

"Would you let the man talk, Devin, please," Daniel said.

"I'm sorry," Devin apologized, he looked at Darian, "go on."

"He was diagnosed with terminal brain cancer. Doctors gave him a year to live, at the most. His human rebel group, Soldiers of Humanity, had made enough waves where he came from in Houston, Texas, that they caught the attention of a particular group of shifters. One night, a man came to his home, made him an offer he couldn't refuse. He was promised to be turned into a shape-shifter if he could use his rebel group to attack us. Thinning our herd, so to speak, if not flat-out elimination. The shape-shifter contact he had, provided him with our addresses, descriptions and ammunition, but precious little else. He didn't know our names or even our association with each other."

"Where you able to gather the contact's name?" Xander asked.

"Unfortunately, no. The contact didn't use a name. Very clever, if I may say so myself," Darian said.

"Did he know where they've taken Sebastian and the others?" Sergio asked, his voice was strained as he fought his mounting anxiety.

Darian shook his head. "No. He knew nothing about the kidnappings."

Xander walked back to his seat. "I don't believe these shifters are working alone."

"I believe we can narrow it down to them wanting our territory, this is obvious. They've targeted the only supernatural forces in the city and surrounding suburbs that actually poses a threat," Elise stated.

"It could still be other reasons," Adrian stated, not wanting to limit their options for strategic planning.

"Like what?" Devin and Justin asked in unison.

Adrian continued. "For instance, let's not forget about our recent colorful history. They could try to sell us on the black market. And this wouldn't be the first time we've seen shape-shifters turn on each other for money. Ever since we were exposed, humans have come up with a number of ways to make money off of us, some legal, some downright treacherous."

"That doesn't make sense. Hell, vampire blood is the biggest and most expensive thing you can sell and buy on the black market. They were the biggest attack this time around. If we hadn't gotten there in time, chances are Darian and his entire coven would have been decimated," Warren pointed out.

Adrian thought about what Warren said. "Yeah, now that I think about it, that actually makes more sense. I guess Elise is right, it's our territory."

"Still, they're a bold bunch and I believe that they knew these pathetic mortals would not be able to complete the job. I think this group has had a back up plan from the beginning," Tatiana said.

"These dumb ass humans were cannon fodder!" Sergio growled

in rage, turning around, he took a few steps away from the others to cool down.

Elise watched Sergio pace the room, wishing she could help ease his mind. She turned back around to face Darian. "Is there anyone else involved in this?"

"At this point, this is all we know because it was all he knew. He wasn't included in the larger scheme of things, nor did he care past his own part in the plan. I believe our best option at this point is to track down his contact," Darian said.

Xander nodded. "At least we now know that the humans were pawns. Somehow, that knowledge narrows down our list of enemies."

"Pawns or not, those sons-of-bitches did some real fucking damage!" Adrian added. He stood with both hands on his hips as he watched Darian and his father. "What are we going to do now?"

"We're really going to have to watch our every move now. Chances are they already know about this place if the humans did. We should leave here as soon as possible. We also have to keep in mind that they can track our scents as easily as we can track theirs, which I think is the reason why they are keeping their distance," Tatiana said.

"I agree, they must be a small group of shifters to take such drastic and underhanded measures. Their strength isn't in numbers. At least, I don't think so," Elise speculated.

"They may be a small group of shifters, but they're greedy as hell to want the entire Illinois Territory!" Daniel said.

"One thing is certain, we have to keep in mind that they have the most vulnerable of our households. Right now, the ball is in their court," Elise stated.

"Yeah, but if Darian can make contact with Natasha, she might know something, a landmark or their exact location. She would be able to communicate that to him. That's our best hope at the moment," Warren said as he ran his fingers through his black, thick, wavy short-cropped locks. His gray eyes scanned over the faces of the others as they contemplated their situation.

There came the sound of a door opening. Everyone looked in the direction of the SUV and saw Xavier climbing out with the blanket wrapped around his body. He appeared to be confused as his gaze settled on Darian.

"What's going on?" he asked, completely bewildered.

Darian walked over to Xavier. "We were attacked earlier today. They were attacked last night during the *Lunar*." He gestured toward the shape-shifters.

Xavier's eyes widen. "Who, why?!"

"A human rebel group did the deed, but they were acting out on orders given to them by a coyote Pack," Darian said. He sighed softly, a finger running along his eyebrow. He turned away from Xavier, not wanting to have to give his lover the next bit of information.

Xavier's eyebrows creased. Suspicious, he stepped in front of him, keeping eye contact. "Darian?"

Darian gazed focused on Xavier's beautiful soft gray eyes.

"What else?" Xavier asked. He knew there was more and he wanted Darian to tell him everything.

Darian took a deep breath, releasing it slowly. "They have Natasha…Sebastian…and Matthew."

Xavier's face went slack with shock. He was speechless as he let what Darian told him sink in. Natasha, *his Natasha*, was in danger and this had happened when he could not protect her!

"This is not your fault, nor could you have prevented it. Don't dwell on the past, focus on the future and what must be done." Darian cupped Xavier's face, lifting it to his own. *We are facing an enemy that knows more about us than we know about them…now is not the time to let any weakness show.* Darian's mental voice penetrated Xavier's mind and he nodded. Darian was right. He had to be strong. Besides, he was not the only one who had a loved one in danger. They were all in danger and he fought to control his rage as it mingled with the fear that was growing deep within him.

Xavier turned around, facing Elise and the others. "What else happened?"

Xander told him everything that had happened, everything that he wanted to know.

"That is it. Now we have to wait until they make the next move, or until Darian connects with Natasha."

Xavier looked at Darian. "Why can't you connect with her?"

"Because she's unconscious, and her dreams are rampant. She's not controlling them. I think she's been drugged."

"Shit!" Xavier gasped as he ran his fingers through his long chestnut brown hair. He turned to Xander. "Do you have any suspects?"

"As in who?" Xander asked.

"Any other community that you think might have done this, perhaps we can narrow it down."

Xander shook his head. "As you are well aware, Illinois, especially Chicago, is prime territory for any supernatural. My list of enemies is as anonymous and as limitless as yours."

Xavier had to agree with him. There was really no way of tracking down any supernatural who didn't want to be found and who knew how to remain hidden.

"Listen, Darian, your coven is going to have to feed. I don't think it would be safe for them to hunt or even try to find a willing victim at your club. Besides, we need to get you some clothes and get out of here," Elise suggested.

"I have another location were we can rest up and prepare," Darian told them the address to his hotel.

"That's yours!?!" Daniel exclaimed. "It's a palace! I had no idea that you owned it."

Darian smiled slightly. "It was nothing compared to my home."

Those who'd been to that particular hotel had to agree with him. His home had been simply a marvel, beautiful.

The remaining coffins that were laying side by side on the floor begin to open and the rest of Darian's coven climbed out.

Annabelle sat on the lid of her coffin, too weak to stand, her body still badly damaged from the fire. Particles of burnt skin flaked away as she brushed her arms and face delicately with her fingers. The entire coven watched Darian as he mentally conveyed the information to them, letting them know everything.

"You gotta be fucking kidding me!" John's legs buckled and he fell back against the side of the truck. The very thought of him being so close inside the arms of death disturbed and frightened him. Devin went to his side, wrapping an arm around his waist to help steady him.

Miko sat down beside Annabelle, taking her into her arms. She was relieved that Annabelle had survived the fire that burned her so badly. She was hers, only sixty years old. Annabelle had been twenty years old when Miko first saw her sneaking a secret lover from her bedroom window, seconds before her abusive husband walked through the bedroom door. Miko watched from a tree as Annabelle's husband hit her for not having dinner hot and on the table. It didn't matter that he never came home on time, nor did it matter to him that dinner was cooked, his plate already made and set aside for him in the oven. That night, Miko watched Annabelle's husband knock her down, splitting her lip in the act. He pressed her face against the hardwood floor, ripped her gown from her body as she screamed and begged him to stop. Over and over again, he slapped her, raped her, accused her of making a fool out of him. He knew of her infidelities, he swore he'd kill her if she saw "that man" ever again. Tears streamed down her face as he slammed hard and deeply into her. His thrusts were brutal and from the images Miko had gathered from Annabelle's darkest memories, she now knew that his thrusts were always brutal, his kisses always cold, harsh. His heart, untouched. His love, unknown. Miko could take no more. That night, she pulled Annabelle's husband away, knocking him dizzy. She took the frightened woman into her arms, and offered her a better life, one that was everlasting and without fear.

When Annabelle had accepted her gift, that night her husband's rages were quieted forever. Now Miko held Annabelle's burned body in her arms. Someone dared to try to destroy them, a coward who attacked from afar with a human shield. She was furious, and as she looked around the room, the expression on the other's faces mirrored her own. Retribution would be had.

"We have to feed," Miko said softly as she cradled Annabelle, her hand lightly brushing the younger vampire's hair.

"We know. Don't worry, we've got your back," Devin said, "who should I offer myself to first?"

"Miko, so she can heal Annabelle," Darian directed.

Devin nodded, he looked at John. "Are you okay, can you steady yourself?"

"Yeah, I'm fine now, it was just, you know…I guess I freaked out when I found out how close I came to dying. I'll be okay." John gave him a reassuring smile.

Devin approached Miko. She gently released Annabelle, then rose to take him into her arms.

"Thank you, Devin," she said, then she buried her face into his neck, sinking her teeth deeply. He gasped, his body stiffening from the pain. A moment later, his muscles began to loosen, he started to pant and moan from the immeasurable pleasure that coursed through his veins. Miko cradled his head in her hands as she drank from him. Before long, his knees buckled as ferocious waves of ecstasy cascaded through his body causing him to spasm until she pulled away, holding him until he could regain his footing.

"I love the way that feels!" Devin whispered dreamily.

"Devin," John began.

Devin turned to face his lover. "Oh geez, you're terrible!" He was giddy, still drunk off the pleasure of Miko's bite as he approached his lover, slipping his arms around his neck.

John pulled Devin closer. "I'm so glad that you guys were able to save us…thank you so much, baby."

"I'm glad that we were able to save you, thanks to Sergio and Warren." Devin stood on the tips of his toes, leaning forward he pressed his lips to John's in a passionate kiss. A second later, he pulled away. "Drink," he bared his neck for John who leaned in, driving his long fangs deeply into his flesh.

"Ah!" Devin gasped, arms tightening around John's shoulders, then relaxing as the indescribable pleasure coursed through his body once again. Both men began to moan in ecstasy. With each passing second, their moans became louder until they shook with pleasure as dual orgasms rippled through their bodies. John released Devin, but held on to him firmly, not wanting to let him go.

Miko allowed Annabelle to feed from her. With every swallow of Miko's blood, she began to heal faster until all signs of the burnt flesh had disappeared. Daniel watched the two female vampires, he knew that Miko would need to feed to replenish the blood she'd just given. When Miko was done, he offered her his wrist, which she gratefully accepted. Miranda, Nicole, Justin, Madeline, Rachel, and Roland offered their blood to the other vampires.

Roland, a wolf from Xander's Pack, bravely walked up to Darian. "You can feed from me." He offered his wrist to him.

"Thank you," Darian said softly as he reached for Roland's wrist, sinking his fangs into the blue artery, his lips closing round the wound as he began to drink from the shifter. Erotic sounds of the other's moans and pants echoed throughout the hangar as the vampires fed. The blood of a shape-shifter was rich and often left a vampire with the feeling of delirium. The stronger the shifter, the stronger the effect that all vampires relished.

Once everyone was finished, they all took a few moments to regain their senses and strength.

"What do we do now?" Devin asked as he leaned against John.

Darian touched Xavier's arm, bringing him out of his trance. He was still thinking about Natasha. Xavier tried very hard to concentrate on the matters at hand, but he could not put aside his worry over her. Darian knew what his lover was thinking about, he knew that Xavier would worry about Natasha until she was safe. He turned toward the others. "Right now, none of our homes are safe havens. So, we should make our way to my hotel. You're welcome to stay there for as long as needed. May I borrow someone's cell phone so that I can make the arrangements?"

Adrian pulled his cell phone out of his coat pocket. "Here," he stated as he handed it to him.

"Thank you," Darian flipped the cell phone open and dialed his hotel reservation line.

"*Xavier Hotel*, my name is Ashton, how may I help you?" the clerk rattled off in greeting.

"Ashton, this is Darian Alexander."

"Oh, good evening, Mr. Alexander, what may I do for you?"

"I need my suite to be prepared for my arrival. Give my key to Elise DuPre. We will be arriving within the hour."

"Yes sir. Your suite will be ready when you arrive."

"Excellent." Darian ended the call, handing the cell phone back to Adrian.

"All that feeding left me starving!" Devin mumbled.

"Once we've settled into the hotel, feel free to order whatever you like."

"Let's get the hell out of this hangar," Justin said, rising from the dusty crate that he had been using for the past four hours. He was more than happy to give up the uncomfortable seating for the prospect of comfort and room service. "I've been sitting on this dusty box for hours. I suspect that my ass now possesses that ugly crisscross pattern and let me tell ya, that doesn't look good on anyone." He patted the back of his jeans, brushing away all signs of dust and dirt.

"Are you going to walk into the hotel like that?" Warren asked Darian as he pointed out the vampire's nakedness.

Darian looked down at his body and chuckled softly. "Although we Greeks bear not one image conscious thought about our physiques, we do know when to put on clothes."

A few of them chuckled.

"We will be climbing back into the coffins, which is why I arranged for Elise to get the key card to my hotel room."

"Hell, if I wasn't claustrophobic, I'd climb into one of those coffins myself. I look like shit from head to toe," Nicole said, looking over her torn, soot-covered clothes.

"Truth be told, only a few of us look presentable, but I don't care. I just want to get out of here," Daniel said as he made his way toward the doors to open them.

They all climbed into their huge towering SUVs. The vampires settled back into their coffins as the shape-shifters drove toward the very hotel Darian had constructed over thirty years ago which he named after his lover. On the way over, Elise tried her best to tidy her clothes and overall appearance. She ran her fingers through her hair, attempting to untangle her luxurious brown locks. When they reached the hotel, they pulled the trucks to a stop at the front door. Elise climbed out and walked inside. The male receptionist behind the counter smiled as he watched her graceful approach. To him, she looked as though she'd been in an accident of some kind, but it wasn't for him to judge, only to serve.

"Good evening, Ma'am, how may I help you?" He asked as he struggled to keep eye contact, though he wanted to catch a quick glimpse her exposed cleavage. Her attire, though ruined by the patches of soot and ash, did not deter his lecherous thoughts. He had never seen a woman as beautiful as Elise and could hardly keep his eyes off of her.

Elise smiled at the young man. "My name is Elise DuPre, I believe you're expecting me. I'm here to pick up Darian Alexander's key card to his suite."

"Oh, yes. One moment Ma'am." The male reached into a drawer and removed Darian's key card. He handed it to Elise who took it with a charming smile before turning to walk away. He watched her backside as she headed toward the exit, feeling a smidgen of jealousy that a man would have a beautiful woman such as her by his side. He was so deep in thought that he remembered he'd never asked her to show identification. He hoped that the manager did not notice.

Elise walked toward the truck, Sergio leaned toward her. "We have to take the coffins inside, let's go," she said, stepping back from the vehicle.

Sergio and the others climbed out. He walked to the back of the truck, opened the door and pulled out one of the coffins, carrying it on his right shoulder. The other shape-shifters followed in his footsteps. The hotel employees and patrons watched in shocked silence as they witnessed the strength and power of the supernaturals. Elise told the valet attendants to park the SUVs. They obeyed, driving the trucks into the underground garage. Elise and Xander led the way as the other shape-shifters carried the coffins onto the elevators. Once they reached the floor of Darian's suite, they exited the elevators and waited patiently for Elise to open the door. Once inside, they placed the coffins on the floor and looked around. Darian's suite was a two story palace. White marble floors and columns. Cream suede sofas, chairs and a loveseat with glass and marble end tables and a coffee table. There was a large redwood eight piece, buffet and dining set with six chairs upholstered in a cream colored padded fabric.

"Damn! Would you look at this place!" Ronald exclaimed as he strolled through the rooms. "It even has a fireplace! This is a nice hotel room."

The others looked around as well.

Justin was just as impressed as Ronald. "Darian has wonderful taste, I'll tell you that."

Darian opened his coffin as did the other vampires. Each climbed out and stretched their muscles.

He walked over to Elise. "Thank you."

"Don't mention it." She smiled, her eyes trailed over Darian's body, "umm, Darian...?"

Darian smiled. "I'll get dressed."

"Please do," Sergio added as he plopped down on one of the cream suede chairs.

"Didn't think nakedness would make you so uncomfortable, Sergio," Darian looked at him.

"Not nakedness, just *your* nakedness." Sergio winked at Darian, who smiled.

"Please make yourselves at home, order whatever you want to eat from room service," Darian said.

He walked into his bedroom, with Xavier following closely. Xavier closed the door behind them.

"Darian, what are we going to do?" he asked as he stepped closer.

"Xavier, you must calm down. Natasha is still alive."

"I know that you're right, but-"

"No, don't do that. There is no time to panic in this situation. Natasha, Matthew and Sebastian-the youngest, are all in danger. These shape-shifters who kidnapped them are keeping them alive for a reason, one we will find out soon enough."

Darian turned away from Xavier, opening his closet door. He slid clothes back and forth on the rod, looking for something comfortable to wear. Settling on a pair of black slacks and button-up shirt, he dressed quickly.

Xavier reflected on what Darian said. He knew that he was right. Xavier was never one to lose his control, but the thought of Natasha being surrounded by danger was almost too much for him to bear. He cleared his mind of the vicious images that plagued him and decided to clothed himself as well. He dressed quickly in a pair of dark blue jeans and a white t-shirt. Both he and Darian emerged from their bedroom. The other vampires were now fully clothed, and a few of the shifters were also wearing borrowed clothing. Darian walked over to the sofa and sat down, crossing one leg over the other.

Xander was sitting opposite Darian in a recliner. Elise sat next to Sergio on the loveseat. She watched both Darian and Xavier, feeling sad about their entire situation, but not willing to despair. She held one of her infants in her arm, Sergio held the other. Both were feeding the toddlers. Madeleine had settled on the other sofa, with David beside her, his head in her lap as he napped.

"This all started with that fucking dead body!" Warren blurted out.

Adrian looked at him, but said nothing. He knew that Warren was worried sick about Matthew. A little over a year ago, a situation like this might have pleased Adrian, but not now. He had grown to like Matthew and was happy that he and Warren were in love and had each other. Matthew was a part of their family, even though he was human, and Adrian wanted to see him safe.

"This started before the body, Warren," Miranda stated.

"You think?" John asked, sarcastically. "So are we going to do anything about it?'

"What is it exactly that we should be doing at this point, that we haven't already done, John?" Sergio asked, slightly agitated.

"I don't know, something, shit!" John replied, feeling a little bit helpless and anxious at the same time. "I want to get these motherfuckers back!"

"There is nothing that we can do right now. We have searched the entire city and surrounding suburbs with no success and Illinois is too vast a state to search in its entirety. We have no idea how many we're up against or where they are. We have no information in regard to what their ultimate goal is, what their plan entails. We are now at a stalemate. Our only option at this moment is to wait for them to make the next move," Xander said as he held his infant daughter, Mariah in his arms. "Just be patient."

"I want my son safe more than you know, but Xander's right. There's nothing we can do at this point. To go out searching for them would spread ourselves too thin and it might be what they're hoping we do," said Madeline as she held her daughter, Mia, she'd had with Devin. She tentatively stroked David's hair, hoping to keep him napping.

"Do you think they're even in Illinois?" Sergio presented the question to whomever might know the answer.

"They're no longer in Illinois. The mental bond I have with Natasha tells me that much. It feels strained when I try to contact her. I have to try harder to concentrate when those with whom I'm connected with are great distances away from me," Darian said, then he looked at Sergio. "You are quite right, to pinpoint where to look is time consuming and dangerous. If they sense that we are coming close, they could..." Darian trailed off for a number of reasons. The thought of the shifters killing their loved ones disturbed him, but he knew the thought would be far too painful for the others. There was a knock on the door.

"I'll get it," Sergio said as he rose from the sofa. He knew what Darian was going to say and was relieved that he didn't say it. It was an outcome he wasn't willing to accept. He opened the door, he could smell the delicious aroma of the food and he was starving. Three room service staff walked into the room rolling three large carts in front of them. They parked the carts in the middle of the dining area and walked away without even waiting for a tip.

"Damn, I was going to tip them," Sergio commented.

"They will be serving us for the duration of our stay, so there is no need for a tip. They are going to be more than compensated," Darian stated.

Sergio shrugged one shoulder and began uncovering the platters. The shifters crowded around the carts as they prepared their plates. The vampires were settled comfortably throughout the hotel suite.

John looked at Darian. "Do we go to the club tonight?"

Darian turned toward him. "No. I called Angela, left her in charge. I don't want any of you inside the club until we get to the bottom of this. Since they were so bold as to burn down my home, I don't think they would hesitate burning down the club if we were inside."

"Damn, I didn't think of that. So without us there, there's no reason to stake out the club?"

"Wait!" Gary turned to face Darian who seemed to know what he was going to say. "They might be at the club, expecting us to arrive!"

"I don't think so. I'm sure they think we're dead. That one thought is our best defense. Whatever the case, going to the club is a chance I'm not willing to take," Darian replied.

"Not to mention, they said they searched the entire city, that includes the club," John said pointing.

"Yeah, and if you're supposed to be dead, and we're on high alert, the last thing they think we're going to be doing is dancing the night away at *Desires Unleashed*," Adrian stated.

"Another thing is, they don't want us to catch onto their scent. Being covert is what's working best for them," Carmen said.

Darian nodded as he tried to contact Natasha once more, still he was unable to mentally reach her. He said nothing to the others, although he was relieved that she was alive still. The shifters continued to eat and wait for their enemy to make the next move.

CHAPTER TEN

Hmmm?" Julian hung up the telephone.

Scott looked up from his newspaper. "What's wrong?" he asked.

"I've been trying to reach Steve, but he's not answering," Julian replied.

"When was the last time you spoke with him?" Scott asked.

"Earlier today, like around one or two o'clock. He was saying they knew where the shifters had scurried off to and they were going to attack. He wouldn't tell me where though, said he had everything under control, fucking prick." Julian plopped down lazily in a blue chair.

"Were you really expecting him to answer?" Elizabeth asked sarcastically as she sauntered into the room. Her feline gracefulness gave her a sexy sway to her hips with each step she took.

Julian chuckled. "Not if these supernaturals are as skilled as I think they are. I'm pretty sure they've killed him and his miserable lot of fake ass slayers."

"What if they captured him and are torturing him right now for information? Do you think he'd tell them anything?" Scott asked, folding his newspaper.

Elizabeth laughed. "I doubt it! That idiot actually thought we were going to bring him within the fold! Why would we want a turncoat like him? That asshole sold his own people down the river."

"Well, even if he's dead, he served his purpose, that was all he was expected to do," Julian said, lounging even more comfortably in the chair.

"But they weren't able to kill the shifters." Scott was slightly disappointed that their opposition was ever present.

Julian laughed heartily for several seconds. As his laughter tapered off, he looked at Scott. "Did you really think they could? Really, all we wanted them for was to take out the vampires and as a bonus, kill as many shape-shifters as they could."

"Which they failed miserably," Elizabeth scoffed.

"Not exactly. Granted, we had hoped that they would be able to take out more than just one shifter, but the biggest threat is now out of the way and that's the most important," Julian said.

"I don't think he served his purpose. If he's dead, and they were able to get answers out of him, all he did was leave our enemies with more questions. They'll be looking for answers," Scott protested.

"You worry too much, dumbass," Elizabeth said, sneering at Scott. "All we really, really wanted from the very beginning was Darian and his coven eliminated. The shifters were just a bonus. We can take care of them, piece of cake."

"Exactly. With Darian and his coven destroyed, those pups and kittens won't pose that much of a threat," said Jaric, as he entered the room. He was a seven-hundred and sixty year old vampire and second in command in the coven he shared with his lover and maker, Cassandra.

"Why were you guys so scared of Darian anyway?" Scott asked.

Jaric glared at Scott with piercing blue eyes. "Watch yourself, coyote!"

Frightened by Jaric's power, Scott quickly adjusted his tone. "I didn't mean anything by that. I was just curious as to why we had to use those humans to kill them. Aren't you stronger than he is?"

"We can not go solely on Eliana's accounts of Darian or his coven. She's dead now, after she and that idiot lover of hers decided to go on their little killing spree. I believe that Darian killed her even though it was classified as a S.U.I.T. killing."

"Maybe it was," Scott said.

Jaric chuckled. "Yeah, and maybe I'll grow a pussy and tits and change my name to Sally. Your age is speaking louder than your brains, Scott. The S.U.I.T., although very well equipped, couldn't defeat the likes of Eliana. She was powerful even before I gave her my blood. Let's not throw aside the fact that Darian's managed to stay on top in Chicago for some time. This was taken into consideration and was not taken lightly. Cassandra feels that she could easily take Darian, but why bother…let those foolish humans do our dirty work. Can you imagine what their asses must be thinking now?"

Elizabeth chuckled. "You knew that those humans wouldn't be able to kill Alexander's and Elise's crews, didn't you?"

Jaric nodded. "Of course. That goes without saying. That's why we have the back up plan. Right now, those shifters are holed up somewhere, scared and bewildered. They don't know what their next step is going to be and that's exactly how we want them to feel."

"Okay, explain something to me…why did you send Cory out to pick up a human?" Elizabeth asked.

"I have my reasons and you'll soon see," Jaric responded before turning to leave.

Elizabeth watched Jaric walk away. "Arrogant asshole."

"Shhhh, he can still hear you," Scott teased.

"Good. I think Milan's crazy for teaming up with these vampires. The city should be ours," Elizabeth griped.

"I know why our Alpha teamed up with the two of you guys."

Elizabeth cocked her head sideways. "Why? Enlighten me?" she asked sarcastically.

"Well, basically, we couldn't have gotten this far alone or in individual groups. United we stand, divided we-"

"Save the peace crap for someone who gives a shit. Maybe you coyotes wouldn't have been able to beat that bloodsucking bastard Darian, the mutt Alexander and that bitch Elise…but we tigers would have been able to do so."

A rich, deep smooth voice penetrated the room. "So why didn't you?" asked Richard, the coyote Pack's Alpha, as he stepped into the room.

His dark chocolate complexion glowed beautifully in the twinkling lights of the overhead chandelier. Beads of water cascaded down his strong muscular pecs and abs as he toweled off his arms and legs.

"Enjoy your swim, Richard?" Scott asked as he looked adoringly at his Pack Alpha.

"It was very relaxing," Richard responded. He returned his attention to Elizabeth, whom he did not favor. He felt that she didn't know her place as an underling and spoke entirely too much without the knowledge to back up her statements. To sum it up, she annoyed him greatly. "Elizabeth, please 'enlighten me' on just how much more your Pride is equipped to deal with our adversaries?"

Elizabeth groaned. "I don't need to prove anything to you!" she rose from the sofa, heading toward the door.

Richard grabbed her by the arm, preventing her from leaving. "Don't have an answer?" he challenged.

Elizabeth snatched her arm away, glaring at him. "Fine, I'll give you an answer! Our queen is generous!" She tossed Scott a scornful glare, then returned her attention to Richard, who only chuckled. Annoyed, Elizabeth stormed out of the room, leaving the three men alone.

"What a bitch!" Scott said in a hushed voice.

"Why are you whispering?" Richard asked through chuckles.

"Well, I didn't want her to hear me really." Scott smiled.

"Who gives a fuck if she does." Julian made an offhand gesture. "Just ignore her, she's pissy that way."

"I really could care less." Richard said as he tossed the towel over his shoulder, letting the rest of his naked body air dry.

Scott's blue eyes roamed over Richard's powerful physique, drinking in his beauty.

Richard smiled menacingly. "Don't look at me in that way."

Embarrassed, Scott looked away. "In what way?" he asked softly, shyly.

"Fine, play innocent." Richard smirked as he relaxed more comfortably on the soft suede cushions of the recliner. Scott remained silent for a few more minutes, then very boldly, he rose from the sofa and walked over to Richard, who opened his eyes. He kneeled beside Richard's chair, resting his folded arms on the armrest of the recliner.

"You know why I look at you that way?" Scott asked Richard who remained silent, waiting for the younger man to continue. "Why won't you give us a try?"

"Because, I'm not-"

Scott interjected. "You'll never know if you don't like it unless you give it a try. Are you trying to tell me in all of your years, you never thought about it, just once?"

"And if I did? Doesn't mean I have to do anything with you. You're overstepping your boundaries, Scott. We've discussed this before. I don't share those kinds of relationships with my Pack members."

"That's a weak excuse and you know it!"

"Not an excuse, my reasoning. Don't ask me again."

"If you'd give us a chance, I could make you happy," Scott whispered imploringly as he slid his hand over Richard's thigh, his fingers slowly caressing his groin. Richard reached down taking hold of Scott's chin, lifting his face to his own. He leaned over until their lips were almost touching. Scott tried to inch forward, but Richard held him at bay.

"My final answer is no," Richard stated, shoving Scott away from him, hard enough to put a distance between them, but not enough to cause pain.

Scott regained his balanced. "I just wanted to prove to you how much I care!"

"You're disrespecting me and my wishes. I don't like it. Don't ever do it again."

"For crying out loud, Scott, give it a rest already!" Cory said as he entered the living room with two mortals in his possession. One mortal was an eight year old boy with sandy brown hair and light brown eyes. The second was his older brother, an eighteen year old with matching hair and eyes. His older brother, his hero, had been treating him to a night on the town by taking him to the theater to see his favorite cartoon on the big screen. After that, they were planning on eating ice cream together. But then, before they could get to his brother's Viper Solstice four-door economy sedan from the theater, they were kidnapped and brought here, for reasons neither he or his brother were aware of.

"I've got the perfect fresh meat for Jaric!" Cory said with a wide grin.

"I'm sure Jaric will be pleased." Richard rolled his eyes. "This entire plan reeks of weakness, cowardice and it isn't in the least bit honorable."

"If you're so against it, why are you helping?" Cory asked, still holding both struggling humans in his grip.

"I'm simply doing my part because you need me. I'll be more than happy when all of this unsavory business is over and done with." Richard pointed to the two humans. "Why does Jaric want these two?"

Christopher struggled in Cory's grip, but Cory tightened his fingers around his arm, causing pain and bruising, so much so, that he cried out.

"Didn't like that? Stop struggling then, it'll do you no good anyway," Cory warned, then he looked at Richard. "All I know is, this was a part of the big plan. I want this territory, so like you, I'm just doing my part."

"I told you all in good time," Jaric said upon entering the room, glancing at the two humans Cory had brought with him. "You did well, exactly what I wanted."

"Good. Whatever you have planned better work. We don't need another half-ass job done like before. Every delay means more hours I have to spend with you!" Cory said, sneering at Jaric while shoving Christopher, the eighteen year-old, onto the blue sofa. "This is his little brother, Brandon." He held onto Brandon, as the eight year old continued to struggle wildly in his grip.

"Don't worry. The amount of time we have to spend together will be shortened very soon, trust me. Until then, I forbear," Jaric stated. He approached Christopher. "They're perfect."

Christopher glared up at him. He was terrified, but refused to show fear. He didn't know what they wanted with him or what they were going to do to his little brother, but he would be brave. He promised himself that he would be brave.

"What do you want with us?!" Christopher demanded an answer.

Jaric laughed softly. "Spirit, I like that. I suppose it's only fair to tell you why you're here."

Christopher remained silent, waiting.

"You will be our 'front man', so to speak. You will go on a mission to inform our 'friends' of their current predicament."

"Are you some cowards, you can't do that yourself? Why involve us?" Christopher was enraged, on top of being frightened. *They kidnapped him to do some of their dirty work? What the hell was going on?!*

"Cowards? No, of course not. Is it cowardice to outsmart your opponent, leave them completely baffled? I don't think so. We're strategists." Jaric moved around until he was standing directly in front of Christopher. "You must understand, our enemy is crafty, so therefore, we must be crafty. You however, are expendable, so if they chose to kill you, it won't cost us much, but the job will at least be done." He smiled wickedly.

"Fuck you, I'm not doing shit for you!" Christopher yelled defiantly.

Jaric pursed his lips, brows furrowed. "Oh, I think you'll change your mind. See, your little brother here, he's so young, so innocent…" he walked over to Brandon, his eyes locked onto the child's as a mental connection penetrated his tender mind, making him pliant, calm. He rubbed the boy's soft, tender cheek with the back of his fingers.

"Don't you touch him, you son-of-a-bitch!" Christopher yelled. "What did you do to him?!"

Jaric's gloating smile grew wider. He looked down at Brandon. "Tell your brother to play nice."

Brandon smiled at his brother, Christopher. "Play nice, Chris," he said in a soft, angelic voice that made Christopher fear the worst for his brother's life.

"Don't you hurt him!" Christopher demanded.

"Oh, it won't be us who will hurt him, but you," Jaric replied in a calm tone.

"What are you talking about?!"

"See, it's very simple, Christopher. You are going to tell our 'friends' what we tell you to tell them. You do that, we'll let you go."

"That's if they don't kill you first," Cory stated with a chuckle. Christopher tossed Cory a ferocious glower before returning his attention to Jaric.

Jaric kneeled beside Brandon, his right hand brushing a lock of the boy's hair from his eyes. "If you don't, your refusal will be what kills your brother. But that's not all, I'll make sure to have a little fun with him first."

Richard watched the interaction, disgusted by everything that had happened up to that moment. He rose, wrapping his towel around his waist. "Enough, Jaric. This is unnecessary! It's time for us to issue an *Official Challenge for Territory*."

"Are you challenging my authority in this situation?" Jaric rose, facing Richard. "You know you can't take me, so unless you want me to rip your heart out of your chest-"

"Don't you fucking threaten me!" Richard stormed over to him, stopping only a matter of inches apart. "I don't fear you, Jaric. I don't fear death. Don't ever make the mistake of thinking I'm an easy target."

"You'll be easy for me. You're no match, you know it. This is a part of the plan, you don't like it...leave, abandon your Pack."

Richard stared at Jaric. He thought about his promise to help them, they were depending on him.

"Good. I'll take your silence as a sign that you're on board." Jaric turned toward Christopher. "Back to you."

"Do I have your word that you'll let us go, all of you?" Christopher asked.

Jaric's eyebrows raised. "Why did you phrase it that way?" he asked, intrigued.

"I just want to make sure that my brother and I will be let go and left alone when all of this is done. And I don't want you touching him at all anymore! Do I have your word?" Christopher asked in a controlled manner.

Jaric nodded. "You have my word."

Christopher rose from the chair. "Fine. Where do I have to go, what do I have to say?"

Jaric's wicked grin returned. "You have to go to Chicago. I want you to contact Alexander Peterson, inform him that we have three of their friends. We want you to schedule a meeting with one of his Pack members, the youngest. Once you meet, you will tell them of our demands."

"Which I think are very reasonable," Elizabeth declared as she walked back into the living room.

"Nobody cares what you think," Richard commented. Elizabeth glowered at him, but said nothing.

Jaric watched the two as they exchanged looks. "Are you two finished?" he asked.

Richard sat back down, observing the situation. Elizabeth walked to a chair, sitting down as well, settling her attention on Jaric and what he was "arranging".

Jaric looked at Christopher. "After you've given them our demands, you'll be free to go. Come back here and you can take your little brother home to mom and dad. Sound fair?"

Christopher huffed. "This wasn't fair from the beginning, but I'll do this. Remember, your word, you aren't going to harm him or touch him, right?"

"We promise, he will be unharmed, untouched," Jaric reiterated.

"Okay, I want to get this over with. What are your demands?"

"Wonderful! Here." Jaric handed Christopher a folded white piece of paper along with two hundred dollars.

"You will contact them via a pay phone and set up a formal meeting, this is their contact information. Once you're face to face with them, simply tell our 'friends' that either they hand over their territory or their loved ones will be tortured. Body parts will be sent to them on a daily basis until there is nothing more to send. Once we're done with the three, we'll pluck them off one by one, taking their territory by stealth and force. Tell them that we are the threat they can not see coming, nor can they stop. They have until sunrise to leave."

"You're awfully sure of yourself, aren't you?" Christopher asked. Not quite sure what to think of this situation.

"I'm simply confident. Oh, and please inform them that following you will be detrimental to the health and safety of their friends. Now go. There's enough money there for you to take a cab."

Christopher rose from the sofa and walked toward the door. Jaric called out to him, which made him turn around.

"If you even think about betraying us, we will kill your brother, then your entire family," Jaric warned as he sat down on the sofa. He gestured for Brandon to sit next to him, which the boy did, still showing no emotion. The vampire looked at Christopher. "Do we have an understanding?"

"Please, I'll do this, just don't hurt them…Please," Christopher pleaded.

"You keep your end of the bargain, we'll keep ours. Now off you go."

Christopher looked at his little brother, so trusting in the vampire's presence. He watched his brother for a long moment before turning to leave.

"You could have done this little mission yourself. You could have called them and given the message," Richard pointed out, disgusted.

"I'm sure I could have. But even you have to admit…this is way more fun." Jaric smiled.

"Can you really trust him? What he if tries to tell them about us, where we are?' Elizabeth asked once the teenager had left.

"He won't remember where we are. All he knows now is his mission," Jaric replied.

"You put the whammy on him, didn't you?" Julian asked, smiling.

"Of course. Couldn't risk the chance that he might want to be a superhero." Jaric began to stroke Brandon's cheek.

"Remember your promise, don't touch the boy," Richard reminded.

Jaric looked at him, a sneer on his lips. "Rather I touch you?"

"I'd rather you didn't. When the boy returns, send them home. The honorable thing to do would be to erase his memory, although, I don't see you doing the honorable thing."

"You'd be surprised. I always pay people back for doing me favors." Jaric smiled.

Richard turned away, walking into the bedroom. As Elizabeth watched him walk away, she chuckled. They waited in the hotel for Christopher to return.

CHAPTER ELEVEN

Christopher followed their instructions and took a cab to Chicago. For some reason he couldn't put his finger on, he was unable to remember the names of the people he was doing this errand for or the address of the hotel where they held his brother captive. All he could remember was what he had to do to save his brother's life. Once he reached the city limits an hour later, he searched for a pay phone. He found one, located in front of a little restaurant that served all sorts of fast foods. He reached into his side jeans pocket, removing the piece of paper given to him by the man holding his brother hostage. He looked at the number on the paper, then dialed. He waited for a few seconds, hoping that someone would pick up the telephone quickly.

After three rings, Warren answered his cell phone. "Hello, who's calling?" he asked, He knew by looking at the caller ID display on his cell phone, that this particular call came from a pay phone. He hoped that it was Matthew, but didn't expect that it would be.

"Hello?" Christopher's voice was caught in his throat. Here he was, talking with a complete stranger. He was to tell this stranger, a person who had never done a mean thing to him, this horrible information, this threat. Never in all of his life did he ever imagine himself in such a horrible predicament. He took a deep breath, releasing it slowly.

"Who is this?" Warren asked once more.

"Hello, I have something to tell you, but I want to do it in a very, very public place," Christopher said. He knew that for sure, he would not want to meet these strangers in anywhere but a public place. If he was going to be killed for being the bearer of such bad news, then by God, he wanted witnesses!

"Who the fuck is this?" Warren asked, thoroughly agitated now.

Christopher took another deep breath before answering. "My name is Chr-Christen," he lied. He thought about it and came to the realization that he did not want them to know his real name. Just in case they wanted to hunt him down at a later time where spying eyes wouldn't be able to see and testify in court.

"Okay, Christen," Warren repeated his name as if he knew that it was fake. "Why are you calling?"

"I have some information about your, ummmm, friends," Christopher said, not quite sure as to who these people were or who their enemies had as hostages, and who they were to these strangers.

"Tell me more," Warren said.

"In a public place." Christopher wanted to be able to tell him over the phone, but for some reason, something urged him to request a public meeting.

"Very well, where?"

Christopher thought long and hard about the perfect place. Populated enough to ease his anxiety, yet quiet enough for them to talk. Chicago wasn't a city he knew well, having only visited the city on three occasions while preparing for college. He remembered a restaurant he and his family had eaten at while visiting the college of his choice that had accepted him on a full academic scholarship.

"Why don't we meet at *Sandy's?*" Christopher suggested. He remembered that he loved the steak dishes served at that restaurant. His father had eaten two, which was a first for him.

"*Sandy's?* Very well. I'll meet you there in about twenty minutes. Who do I look for?" Warren asked as he surveyed the others around the hotel room. Darian was watching with a slight smile on his face.

"Hmmm, umm, I'll be wearing a black leather jacket, a green "Vampire's Suck" t-shirt and blue jeans." Christopher gave as his description. He looked down at his t-shirt and only now, did he think it appropriate but unfortunate to have been caught wearing it on this day.

"Good, see you there." Warren ended the call. He looked at the others.

"Well, he sounded as if he didn't know what the fuck he was getting himself into," Adrian commented on the tone of Christopher's voice.

"Why the hell are you smiling?" Sergio asked as he looked at Darian.

"Because they're not sure what to think of us. It was quite evident that this person is afraid to meet with you. These tactics are those of beings who fear us."

"Correct. In fact, I believe that he had no idea who he was speaking with," Xander said.

"I wonder how he got my cell phone number?" Warren pondered.

"Probably from Matthew if your number is in his cell's phonebook," Daniel said.

"Yeah, that would be a way." Warren nodded.

"Go Warren, meet with him," Elise said, then she looked at Darian. "Perhaps you should go with him or send someone."

Darian nodded. "If he is a powerful shifter, there won't be anything I can do as far as reading his mind. But if he is human...well, you know." He rose from the sofa, looking at Warren. "Shall we?"

"We shall," Warren said as he pulled on his brown leather bomber jacket. He and Darian left. Outside of the hotel, Warren motioned for the valet attendant to bring one of the SUVs around. The man nodded, sprinted around the corner into the garage to retrieve their vehicle. He pulled the towering SUV in front of the hotel hopped out and gave Warren the keys. Darian tipped the him handsomely, then climbed into the passenger's side. Warren drove toward the popular but expensive restaurant. His thoughts began to run rampant regarding his lover, Matthew. He was worried beyond all rationale, yet he'd been forcing himself to stay focused. It was what Xander expected and what they all needed. But inside the SUV, heading to a meeting with one of "them", he could no longer contain his emotions.

"I'm going to try my best not to kill this son-of-a-bitch on sight!" Warren growled through gritted teeth.

"Well, hopefully, at least not before we can get information out of him," Darian said.

Warren looked at him inquisitively. "How can you, a Master Vampire, be so calm considering all of the shit that has happened in the past twenty-four hours?" He knew that Darian was as much in love with Natasha as Xavier, yet as he'd watched the two men throughout the night, he noticed that they possessed two completely different frames of mind. Xavier seemed to be near the brink of hysteria at the very mention of Natasha's name or predicament. An emotion that Warren was all too familiar with himself at this moment. Yet, the Master Vampire seemed calm, composed as if he had not one worry. Warren thought back to the only time he had witnessed him completely lose his cool, so to speak, and that was when he thought Xavier was going to die.

He was curious about Darian even more now.

Darian looked at Warren, studying him for a few moments. "You have answered your own question, Warren. I am a Master Vampire. Think you that I should break down at the very sight of opposition...hardship?"

Warren shook his head. "No, of course not, but...I don't know. Last year, when Xavier was almost killed, I don't know, I mean, I saw you there...you panicked."

Darian smiled. "I don't have to be able to read your mind to know your thoughts. I am calm because I know that Natasha is alive and that no harm has come to her that would cause her great pain. I love Natasha very much and I am angry regarding our situation. Fear not, Warren, these imbeciles will have hell to pay for what they've done. Now is not the time, but they will. Keep yourself calm when speaking with this person tonight, do you understand?"

"Yeah, I understand." Warren smiled, now satisfied with Darian's answer. He continued to drive until he reached the restaurant. Both men climbed out of the truck. The valet immediately approached them.

"Hello gentleman, may I park your vehicle?" the young man asked.

"No," Warren flashed his S.U.I.T. badge.

"Oh, officer...mmm, we'll leave it right there. Will you be long?"

"No." Warren slipped his wallet back into his pocket. "Thank you." He walked into the restaurant. Darian followed behind him, but he had allowed enough distance between them so that no one would think of him as Warren's companion.

Warren approached the hostess. "I'm looking for someone. No need to seat me," he said as he scanned the restaurant looking for his contact.

Once he saw him, he walked over to the young man who looked like a teenager wearing the described outfit. Darian was seated by the hostess near the window, across the room from Warren and Christopher. He thanked the hostess with a tip as he settled comfortably into his seat. He spied on the two men inconspicuously from his position. He now knew who and what Christopher was and that his younger brother was being held prisoner by their attackers. However, he didn't know where their attackers were, how many or anything else that would be useful past what they already knew. That information was missing from Christopher's memory, erased. It bothered him that he couldn't retrieve this information. This was indeed unexpected.

Warren stood next to the table as Christopher looked up at the six-foot-two inch shape-shifter. His eyes bulged from his sockets as he scanned over Warren's physique. Terrified, he gestured for him to sit down. Warren sat in the booth opposite Christopher, never taking his eyes off of him. He knew that he was human, he could smell his fear, and knew that it ran deep.

"Well, I'm here. What do you have to tell me?" Warren asked in a stern, steady voice.

"First off, I'm not your enemy. I was...," Christopher trailed off. He wanted to tell Warren about his brother and that he was given this mission, but something deep inside his conscious told him that would not be a good idea. He feared a threat, a warning, but couldn't remember who gave it. But he somehow knew that his betrayal would be detrimental to him and his family. Attempting to seek help was not an option. He decided not to tell Warren anything about that night. "I was sent here to give you a message."

"Stop beating around the fucking bush, what's the message?" Warren said in a no-nonsense tone.

Christopher was taken aback, becoming more frightened. The message that he had to deliver was sure to enrage this stranger in front of him. He was even more grateful that he had decided to meet the stranger in a public place.

"The people who sent me wanted me to tell you that they had your loved ones and as long as you do what they say, they won't kill them."

"Go on."

"They want you to leave the city to them and to never return. If you don't agree to their demands, they promised they will send you..." Christopher paused. The stranger's penetrating stare unnerved him, but he continued. "They will send you your friends' body parts every day until you agree to leave. If you don't, they will kill you all, one by one until they've taken this city by force. You have until tonight to leave." He hated what he was doing and wished he could tell this person the truth, possibly ask for his help. Problem was, he didn't know the whole truth, not anymore. He thought about telling this stranger what he did know, even a little might help. But would this stranger trust him enough to help him?

"Who sent you?" Warren asked.

"His name is...is..." Confusion swept over Christopher. He struggled to remember something, anything about the person who sent him, but couldn't. "I...I don't know his name," he stated. "I'm sorry." It was true, he was sorry.

Warren nodded. "Is that all that you have to tell me?"

"Yes."

"Is that all that you want to tell me?" Warren asked imploringly, hoping to persuade the young man to divulge more information he might be holding back. He could tell that the young man didn't want to be there, he knew he was afraid, and his fear was palpable. Being surrounded by people didn't seem to ease the young man's tension.

"That's all that I can tell you, that's all I know. Listen, I want to leave before you do."

"I'm not going to hurt you," Warren said.

"I still would feel better if you would let me leave first. Besides, I was told to tell you, if you try to follow me, they'll kill your friends."

"Very well. Go." Warren watched as the young man who called himself Christen walked away, leaving the restaurant quickly. Darian exited the restaurant in time to see Christopher climb into a waiting cab and drive off. Darian kept tabs on Christopher. He was glad that he had come instead of one of his younger coven members. They would not have been able to create a mental lock with him and hold it over great distances. Warren exited the restaurant, walking over to Darian.

"So, what did you gather?" he asked him.

"What he told you is true, it was really all that he knew. The memory of those who sent him has been erased, as well as their location. This is a very powerful vampire we're dealing with. One who is able to perform a selective memory block."

"You guys can do that?"

Darian chuckled. "So much more you need to learn, young wolf." He walked to Warren's truck and climbed inside.

Warren climbed in behind the wheel. "I know that I need to learn more, so tell me. You guys can do that?"

"Yes. Only those who are powerful. John would not be able to pick and choose the memories he would want another vampire or human to possess. Xavier however, can but he can not control his connection over great distances, which is why he is not able to channel in on Natasha. However, I'm glad that this little trick was used on the boy. It lets me know that we are dealing with vampires as well as shape-shifters and these vampires are powerful."

"Damn, it's like every time we pull back a layer, there's another layer! So what do we do next?" Warren asked while he navigated the truck through the light traffic as he raced back to the hotel.

"I have a connection with him. Once his memory is restored, I can gather his location and we can attack."

"Why would he be going back to them?"

"Because they have his younger brother. Both he and his brother were abducted by them earlier tonight. It was programmed inside his brain that he shouldn't tell us anything, or even to ask for help. Betrayal would have meant the death of his family."

"Shit! Poor kid."

"He's eighteen, his brother is eight."

"So once we get the information we need, we can save them and our own asses, right?"

"That's the ideal thought, Warren."

"You think something's up? Like there's more?"

"I just don't think it will be that easy. These supernaturals took a lot of strong measures while implementing their plan to attack us. I don't think following the boy is going to lead us to the source, thus allowing us to destroy our enemies. Does that make sense to you?" Darian looked over at Warren.

Warren thought about what Darian had said. Although, he wanted it all to end, he had to agree. It would be too easy if that were the case. And nothing was easy about their situation. "I see your point. But what if they still think you're all dead?" Warren pulled the truck in front of the hotel. The two men climbed out, tossing the valet the keys.

Inside the elevator, Darian answered his question. "Natasha's not in this city and that boy lives in Naperville. These supernaturals are keeping to two locations."

"I see, I get it now. All bases covered."

Darian nodded.

"With what I've learned tonight, may I ask a favor?" Warren asked in a soft voice.

Darian smiled. "You want to know if Matthew is alive, if he's unharmed?"

Warren nodded. "Thought you couldn't read our minds."

Darian chuckled. "It's written all over your face." He watched the numbers light up on the elevator with each passing floor. "Matthew is alright and so is Sebastian. However, I'm not able to penetrate their minds. I can just sense that they are alive. I believe they are as heavily sedated as Natasha."

"Have you told Sergio and the others this information?" Warren asked.

"No."

"Why not? This is important information, Darian."

Darian smiled wryly at Warren. "You asked me earlier, why my manner has not quite mirrored that of Xavier's. Just now, you have discovered my flaw. I have been concentrating solely on Natasha, so much so, that I neglected to connect with the others."

Warren nodded. "I honestly have to tell you that I am in awe of your power, Darian. I see why they really wanted to take you out."

Darian studied Warren, but said nothing.

Warren smiled at him. "But it's nice to see that you're not so perfect after all." His smile widened as the elevator doors opened.

Both men walked off of the elevator. Warren felt a lot more relieved than he had been only moments ago when Matthew's condition was still unknown to him. He respected Darian even more than he had before. He'd always had respect for the Master Vampire, but on this night, he saw a different side of him and he liked it. They entered the penthouse hotel suite.

"What happened?" Justin asked anxiously.

"Well, he's being used by both vampires and shape-shifters. They have his little brother and threatened to kill him if he betrayed them," Warren said as he sat down on one of the cushioned chairs. He continued to bring everyone up to speed on what the situation was.

"I'm going to rip their fucking balls out through their fucking throats!" Sergio flared in anger after hearing the fate of his son if they didn't give the city over to them by dawn. He stormed out onto the balcony. Madeleine followed him. She too was worried about their son, her first born, but she knew that they would have to stay calm until it was time to make a move. She walked out onto the balcony. Sergio's hands gripped the railing so tightly, the steel gave away under his fingers.

"Sergio, you need to calm down. When you're like this, you don't think straight and you owe it to your son to be in the best frame of mind you can possibly be in. Anger will only cloud that."

"I can't deal with this, Madeleine!" Sergio turned around to face her. "I'm sick and fucking tired of everybody telling me to calm the fuck down! I don't want to calm down! I want to rip these sons-of-bitches to pieces, literally. I want to throw something, I want to punch something, I want to hurt somebody, Madeleine!"

"I know, Sergio. Do you think this isn't driving me crazy?! Sebastian is my son, too! But I know that going off in rages isn't going to save him. Staying calm and focused on forming a rescue plan will."

"What plan, Madeleine?" Sergio made a wide gesture with both hands as if to say they have nothing. "We're sitting ducks here, we don't have a fucking plan!"

"Come back inside, we have new information that might help us form one. Come on." She grabbed Sergio's hand and led him back into the hotel room. He plopped down on the sofa, an angry frown on his face.

Darian looked at him, then his gaze scanned over to the others. "I have something to say." When he thought that he had everyone's attention, he continued. "Sebastian, Matthew and Natasha are alive and unharmed. They're not in Chicago or even in Illinois any longer."

"What a bunch of cowards!" Devin exclaimed. "These assholes are using the dirtiest, most cowardly and underhanded tactics I've ever seen!"

"Keep living, you'll meet other individuals who are far more devious," Xander stated. He returned his attention to Darian. "This is good news, thank you."

Darian continued with what he was saying. "I've also made a connection with Christopher." He began to tell them what he saw mentally in Christopher's mind. "Right now, he's being controlled, much like a marionette."

"What do you mean?" Xander asked curiously.

"I mean, that his mind is being blocked and controlled, he is not aware of his travels. He is still riding in the cab now, and does not know where he's going. The cab driver is being controlled as well. It's a strong connection and I dare not interfere."

After a few seconds, the mental bond he had made began to fade.

"My connection is fading," Darian announced.

"Why, how?" Carmen asked disappointedly.

"Because, if I were to make a stronger connection, I would be discovered. What I've done is make a surface connection, creating a fragile link between us. This other vampire has him under his complete control, he would feel my invasion if I were to linger on or pry deeper...do you understand?" Darian asked.

"I do now," Carmen replied, even more disappointed. "The closer he gets to this vampire controlling him, the stronger their mental bond is, right?"

Darian nodded. "I'm going to withdraw for the time being," he said, ending his connection.

"When are you going to reconnect?" Xavier asked, softly.

"In about an hour, I'll check back with our young friend."

Darian settled comfortably into the cushions of the sofa. He looked at the others in the room. His human servants had fallen asleep on the floor, one leaning on the other. He smiled warmly at them. He was proud of them for risking their lives to save his coven. He rose from the sofa and walked over to them. He looked at John, Tony and Gary.

"Let's put them to bed," he said as he reached down and lifted

Billy in his arms. The other three vampires lifted the others and followed Darian as he led the way to one of the numerous bedrooms in his penthouse. The vampires laid the humans very gently on the bed and sofa inside the room, making sure not to awaken them.

Darian knew that the humans felt safe in their presence and would sleep throughout the night. The vampires walked out of the room and rejoined the other supernaturals. Many lounged on the thick carpeted floor, while others relaxed in the many chairs in the penthouse. Darian sat on the sofa next to Xavier, who remained composed.

He took Xavier's hand into his own, squeezing it reassuringly.

Xavier looked at him. "Our time is limited. If we aren't able to make the next step, then we're going to have to leave the city, if even for pretense, and who's to say they will release them?" he said in a strained voice.

It was a thought that had crossed Darian's mind and the others several times, but no one wanted to speak of it. It was an outcome that not one of them wanted to accept or even entertain.

"That's not something that's going to happen, no one is going to take our land from us, not without a fight," Elise stated with the utmost confidence.

"Exactly. We can not run. If we do, we will have to continue to run. This night will be long and arduous, but it is nowhere near over." Xander's voice was filled with passion, conviction. He honestly believed that they would be able to make the next move, all they had to do was wait until the time was right. Patience was ever a virtue.

"Xavier's right, there's no telling if they will give us back our family. It's not like they've shown themselves to be upstanding individuals," Carmen said, somewhat dejected.

"What's your point?" Adrian asked curiously.

"My point is-" Carmen began.

"Whatever happens, we make them pay for it!" Sergio

interjected, staring blankly forward, obviously consumed by his own thoughts.

"We'll make them sorry!" Justin said, making a fist and punching the palm of his other hand for visuals. He pouted. "That was kind of clichéd, wasn't it?"

"Yeah, it was, but I wasn't going to say anything." Daniel commented. "I say we stick with this kid, he's going to lead us to something, and when he does-"

"My point is…!" Carmen looked around the room making sure she had everyone's undivided attention. "How can we insure we'll get them back?"

"We can't, Carmen. We honestly have to accept that they may still kill them." Devin's statement sent the room into an uproar.

"Calm down, everyone!" Xander said, ordering the others to silence.

"Look, I know no one wants to even think about it, but we need to. Sitting here pretending like it couldn't happen is just dumb. I want them back as much as the rest of you. They're my family and friends, but I don't want to base our whole strategy on something that might be fruitless. All I'm saying is; let's have alternate plans, just in case." Devin looked at the others who seemed to be contemplating what he said.

"Devin is right," Darian said, "but regardless, we'll make them pay. One thing everyone is forgetting. They think my entire coven is dead, this gives us an advantage. Right now they don't know that I'm spying on this human. We need to stay focused and not to despair in any case."

"All I know is I'm fucking somebody up," Sergio said, pulling his thoughts together.

"You had me at 'we'll make them pay'," Warren added.

Darian smiled slightly as he watched the others psyche themselves up for battle. He could feel their energy flowing through the room. It filled the area up with a delicious heat that seemed to wrap itself around them. All of them decided to discuss other matters.

"When this all over, that damn son of mine will be in a heap of shit so high, he'll need scuba gear!" Sergio declared.

A few of the others chuckled.

Justin was confused. "I don't get it." he stated innocently.

"It means he'll be punished until he's eighty, and we're not talking cat years," Sergio said, clearing up any confusion. They started to talk about other issues, various scenarios and strategies while Darian let the hour pass before he reconnected with Christopher.

CHAPTER TWELVE

Christopher didn't know how he had arrived back at the hotel room, but he was there nonetheless. He looked at Jaric, who was still sitting next to his brother. He began to remember why he was there, he wanted his little brother! He did what they'd wanted him to do, now it was time for them to keep their word.

He approached Jaric boldly. "I did what you wanted me to do, can we go now?" he asked, looking directly into the other man's eyes.

Jaric admired the boy's bravery. Young, strong, courageous humans were Jaric's favorite kind of prey. They would fight until the very end, just before their lungs drew in and then released their last breaths. They would pull Jaric's hair, claw at his flesh, and still... their bodies would give into the inevitable pleasure of his bite. He loved to watch the uncontrollable surrender in their eyes. He would pause in his feeding to gaze into their dying faces, reveling in his own power as the light faded from their eyes. What he loved best though, was not that they were surrendering, but that they were capitulating completely against their will. It was always evident in the eyes; their indomitable will to live slowly replaced by terror and despair as they realized that very moment was going to be their last. It was delicious to him, simply because, no matter how great that desire to live was, in the end, he had always conquered their spirits and left them defeated on the cold, wet streets to rot until their decaying corpses were discovered.

Jaric smiled wolfishly at Christopher, who grew more nervous.

"Can we go now?" Christopher asked once again, his voice becoming shaky.

Jaric tossed a glance to Scott, who lowered his head, chuckling. Elizabeth smiled as she speculated on what the next move of Jaric's was going to be. Christopher became more frightened. He reached for his brother, but the vampire grabbed his hand in such a powerful grip, it was painful to him.

"Ow! Lemme go!" Christopher demanded.

"I think that I'll be the only one making the demands around here, not you," Jaric said. Rising from the sofa, he spun the boy around, pinning Christopher's arm behind his back.

The young boy shook his head. "No, no! You said that you would let us go, you swore that you would let us live!" Christopher desperately reminded the vampire of his promise.

Jaric nodded. "Yes, I remember my words to you and I will keep them. I'm going to let both you and your little brother go, but not without a parting gift!"

Without any warning, his other hand gripped a handful of Christopher's sandy brown silky hair, jerking his head backward, baring his neck. Jaric's long, dagger-like fangs extended from his eyeteeth. He drove them deeply into Christopher's vein making the eighteen year old scream in agony. Christopher's knees buckled from the initial pain of the bite and he fell onto the cushions of the cream colored suede loveseat opposite the sofa. His little brother looked on, still unable to move. Jaric fell on top of him, still attached to his throat and feeding greedily.

"No...no...," Christopher mumbled weakly as he felt his life being drained away. He lowered his gaze from the ceiling to his little brother. He watched as tears ran in streams down his brother's soft, plump cheeks. With the last bit of strength in his body, he smiled at his brother, not wanting him to worry. A tremendous wave of pleasure rippled through his body causing his limbs to jerk and twitch weakly as his body released an orgasm. Soft whimpers emanated from his throat as Jaric drained him to the point of death. His body fell limp in the vampire's arms, his eyes rolled up into his head so that only the whites were visible underneath his half closed lids.

"Oh cool!" exclaimed Crystal as she entered the room, shoving her hotel key card into the back pocket of her super tight blue jeans. "Are you making a vampire?! If so, I came just in time!" she sprinted across the room, jumping onto a large ottoman, landing on her knees, smiling.

"Yes, you are just in time." Jaric smiled as he lifted his wrist to his mouth, piercing his flesh with his razor-sharp fangs, making a wide gash. Blood gushed from the open wound, dripping onto Christopher's green, "Vampire's Suck" t-shirt. Jaric's grin widened as he watched his blood stain the black words red. He grabbed a handful of Christopher's silky locks, lifting his head to his wrist, pressing the bleeding wound forcibly against the younger man's open mouth, smearing blood over his lips.

"Is he drinking yet?" Crystal asked with excitement. She had never seen a vampire being made and this was, in fact, the moment of a lifetime for her.

"Not yet, but he will." Jaric continued to hold his wrist against Christopher's mouth until he began to feel the gentle pull of his new fledgling's feeding. "Ahh, that's it...drink. Be one of us."

"Wow! This is so fucking cool!" Crystal was in awe as she watched Christopher's rebirth, knowing that her own would be on this night.

"Argh!" Jaric grimaced in pain as Christopher's pull became more fierce, animalistic. The young man's hands wrapped around Jaric's wrist, gripping all the harder as if he were afraid that the vampire would snatch away at any moment. Short, harsh grunts were coming from Christopher as he began to sit up. Jaric's breathing had become ragged, he began to tremble as if in sickness. He gripped Christopher's hair, yanking his head backward, as he freed his wrist from his mighty grip.

"That's enough of that!" Jaric ordered feebly through pants as he moved away from Christopher.

He stood over him, watching the shock and confusion spread over the young man's face.

Jaric laughed outright, pleased with himself. "My gift to you for a job well done."

Christopher was speechless, but that was not his only problem. He began to feel an intense pain burning and coiling within him. He yelled, doubling over on the cushions. He felt as if molten lava was traveling through his intestines. He cried and screamed as he rolled into a fetal position on the sofa, hands gripping his stomach tightly.

"It's only your weak, pathetic human body transforming into something extraordinary. So stop carrying on as if you're dying. It'll all be over in a few more minutes," Jaric scoffed as he watched Christopher's suffering.

"Does that always happen?" Crystal asked curiously.

Jaric nodded. "It does, and once it's over, it will be over for all eternity." He looked at Crystal mischievously, "but there are many ways to cause a vampire pain and misery." He smiled.

"Is that what you plan on doing?" Scott asked as he finished off his seafood platter.

"No, but he belongs to me now and there's nothing he can do about it." Jaric laughed again.

"He has my sympathies," Richard said, coming out of the bedroom, pulling his coat on over his muscular shoulders.

"Give me a break, don't give this poor dope your sympathies now. Don't you think it's kind of late for that shit, Mr. High-and-mighty?" Elizabeth commented.

Richard didn't respond verbally, he sprinted across the room faster than Elizabeth could see. He struck her hard across her left cheek, knocking her from the chair, sending her crashing into the end table beside the sofa.

She glared up at him, her eyes teary – a mixture pain from the blow as well as the anger she felt from her embarrassment.

"How dare you!" she growled.

"Don't ever speak to me as if we are on the same level!" Richard snarled, baring his teeth in a dominant manner.

Elizabeth remained silent, glaring at him from the floor with a less intense stare than before when he had first slapped her.

Richard turned his attention back to Jaric. "Just don't fucking jeopardize what we're doing here. I don't want all of this time and effort we've put into this to be wasted because you want to be petty."

"I have only one master. I don't take my order's from you. Don't worry about what I do, worry only about your Pack, make sure that they don't jeopardize our goals," Jaric responded cockily.

Richard stared at him a moment longer, then turned to face Scott and Crystal.

"Man, is it getting tense in here or what. Take it easy guys... and girl," Crystal said, trying to decrease the amount of negative energy that was flowing throughout the room due to the rise in tempers.

Jaric smiled at her. "Tell me, Crystal, did you have fun seducing the young Sebastian Giovanni?"

Crystal thought about her answer for a moment, then chuckled. "Hell yeah! He was so cute, and it was his first time. He was so nervous, terrified!" She giggled even more as she thought back to the moment they were in her bedroom. She had lied to Sebastian, telling him that her parents were out of town on a family emergency. She had told him that he was the hottest boy in school and that she wanted this to be 'the night'. Infatuated with Crystal, Sebastian believed this beautiful girl. The very girl that no other boy in school had been able to touch. Here she was, wanting him, they were going to 'do it'. The last thought that had run through his mind as he'd collapsed afterward, exhausted and sated in a way that he'd never known was possible, was how lucky he was.

"Well, you did an excellent job," Jaric stated.

Crystal's grin widened. "So, are you going to do it?" she asked. For her, the possibility of become supernatural was a dream come true. She found amazing attributes in both species, and didn't really see any downsides. Quite frankly, she didn't care what she turned into, as long as she would be one of them afterwards.

"No, not me, Scott will," Jaric answered. He looked at Scott, who had been staring lustfully at Richard the entire time. He desperately desired his Pack Alpha, he wanted him so badly. The vampire had made him a promise for his part in the plan. If he'd turned Crystal, he'd get the chance to bed his Pack Alpha, even if it was by force.

"I don't think so, my Pack won't be a part of this scheme. We came to fight, not-" Richard was cut off by Jaric.

"Does your complaining have no end!"

"I don't want any part of my Pack involved in this situation."

"Too late, Scott made his decision, didn't you?" Jaric looked at Scott.

"Yeah, it's okay, Richard. I volunteered."

Richard gaped at him, aghast. "Why?"

"Because, I want this territory," Scott answered, not being completely honest.

"At any cost?" Richard asked.

Scott remained silent.

Richard turned to leave, shaking his head in disgust.

"Where are you going?" Scott asked.

"Going to the others." Richard left the hotel room, silently shutting the door behind him.

"Fucking prick!" Elizabeth belted out after a few moments had passed, when she thought that Richard would no longer be able to hear her.

"Oh, don't get courage now!" Scott teased.

"You shut the fuck up! At least I'm not all hard up for his ass, like you, you punk bitch!" Elizabeth cursed.

"With a mouth like that, I'm surprised you still have teeth left!" Scott retorted.

"Enough!" Jaric interrupted. "You two end this annoying bickering this minute, or I'll kill you both and swear it was an accident!"

Both Scott and Elizabeth remained silent, each one believing that Jaric was a man of his word, considering the threat.

"Good." Jaric looked back at his newborn fledgling and smiled. "There, you should feel all better now."

"You asshole!" Christopher screamed, knowing full well what was done to him was done out of spite.

Jaric grimaced. "Such ugly language in front of your new Master. I'll not tolerate it." He took hold of Christopher's chin, squeezing it slightly. "Allow me to show you the first lesson's consequence." His fangs extended and he lunged for his fledgling's throat once again. This time, there was no ecstasy, no pleasurable surrender. Christopher's fierce blows were in vain, nothing seem to stop Jaric. The draining was painful, torturous as the vampire feasted harshly, taking back what he'd given him, leaving him panting and weak on the cushions. Jaric licked his lips as he gazed down at his weakened fledgling.

"Now, you may go." He walked away, releasing his mental hold on his brother. Brandon ran to his elder brother's side, tears flowing down his face as he witnessed his brother's pain. Christopher lay on the sofa, weak and starved. A great deal of the blood in his body brutally taken away, leaving him suffering in a way he had never felt before. He looked at his brother, he could smell the tantalizing child's blood flowing through his small veins. It sickened and enticed him that he wanted this blood more than anything. He wanted so desperately to push his brother to the floor, and in one vile maneuver, rip his throat out and gulp down the precious blood that would no doubt come gushing from the open gash. He turned away, pushing his brother away from him.

Jaric laughed once more, throwing his head back in vicious delight. He walked toward Christopher again. Once his laughter settled down, he gazed down triumphantly at him. "I guess you're going to have to feed soon enough." He leaned forward, looking closely into his pain-filled expression. "You don't want to make a mistake and kill innocent people, do you?"

Rage boiled inside of Christopher. He wanted nothing more than to rip Jaric's head from his body, but he knew that he didn't have the strength. Not wanting to stay in Jaric's presence any more than he wanted to be in the others', he rose weakly from the floor, steadying himself on the armrest of the sofa. He didn't turn to look at his brother, he only beckoned to him. "Come on, Brandon, let's get the hell out of here." He held his hand out to his brother, who slipped his smaller hand into his cold palm. Without looking back, Christopher left the hotel suite. In the elevator, he told his brother to stay on one side as he moved to the opposite side and, leaned against the mirrored wall. He opened his eyes. From his reflection he could see the changes that were taking place because of his transformation. His eyes seemed to collect the light from the elevator lamps. His skin, though pale, appeared to be much smoother, clearer, to the point where his pimples were no longer apparent. He could feel his hunger pangs raging inside of him and he fought against them with all his strength. He knew that he would have to get his little brother to safety, for he didn't know how long he would last before he had to feed his hunger. Exiting the hotel, he took his brother's hand, hailing a cab to the nearest police station.

***

Back at the hotel, Jaric smiled as he recalled his actions of the evening. His lover and Master, Cassandra, contacted him mentally. She wanted to know if everything was going as planned. In the same manner, he responded, informing her that all was going as they had expected. The remaining members of the opposing Pride and pack had received their demands. The ball was now in their court. If they left by sunrise, there would be no blood shed. If they didn't…well, the consequences had been well presented.

Excellent, my love, Cassandra whispered seductively into his mind, making his smile widen.

I'll be there beside you tomorrow night, we can make love until the sun rises. We will celebrate our victory, Jaric stated with assurance.

We shouldn't celebrate too soon, my precious. Our victory is not yet sealed," Cassandra reminded.

Jaric chuckled. *Either way, if they surrender, it will be our victory, if they don't, then the deaths of their members, one by one, will be our sweetest victory.*

Ah, my love...I do relish the way that your wicked brain rationalizes. Your lust for violence is as strong as your lust for blood.

But neither are as strong as my lust for you, he replied.

Of course. Nonetheless, you are correct, it will indeed be our victory either way. I await your return. Cassandra ended her connection.

Jaric looked at Scott. "Why don't you get on with what you need to do."

"Don't forget our deal," Scott replied.

"What? You mean allowing you to have your wicked way with Richard? Don't you worry, he's put quite a damper on my fun for the evening. Setting him up for you is good enough payback." Jaric smiled, thinking of how devastated the coyote Pack Alpha would be the moment he realized the betrayal.

"Fine." Scott said, satisfied with Jaric's answer.

"Well, I'm off. Think I'll join the others, I don't need to stick around to see this," Julian said, rising to his feet and stretching. "See you, soon." He waved nonchalantly as he made his way to the door.

"I think I'll follow you," Cory said and he made his exit.

Scott turned, facing Crystal, who was growing impatient. "Your night's just beginning," he said.

Crystal Malloy was what the "normal" people called a groupie or pet, depending on what kind of supernatural fits your fancy. If you liked hanging out in vampire bars, you were referred to as "groupie". If shape-shifters were more your choice, then you were known as a "pet". She enjoyed hanging out with both. She would let the vampires feed from her, and even went so far as to taste of their blood, simply for the delicious delirium that soon followed. She gave her body to both. She would thrash in rapture as the powerful pounding of a shape-shifter sent waves of pleasure throughout her limbs. She had long since fantasized about such beings even before she knew they were real. When only the movies and entertaining vampire and werewolf novels written by authors with vivid imaginations were the only source of knowledge she could attain. The bookshelf in her bedroom was lined with these types of sci-fi, fantasy/fiction novels. Her movie cabinet was full of such "horror" DVDs. Still, it wasn't enough, she needed the real thing.

Her time came one night nine months earlier while she was partying way into the early hours, right before dawn. Mark-Anthony had come to her. He seduced her, they had had sex in the last stall in the men's bathroom. Afterward, he asked her if she wanted to be one of them, a shape-shifter. It was the words that she had always wanted to hear. She told him that it was "her greatest desire, her only desire, to become something superhuman." This pleased him. He took her number, said he'd get in contact with her when the time was right.

That time came three months later, when they had set up an identity for her and a school transfer. Crystal was twenty years old, but could easily pass for a high school student, which was what they needed her to be.

She was to seduce and trap the son of a very powerful shape-shifter from a very powerful and well connected Pride. In addition to that, she was to help lure a shifter to the location where he would be kidnapped. This request, she thought, was an easy one and one she was more than happy to fulfill. It didn't take long for her looks to attract the young and impressionable Sebastian. Now, she had done what they wanted of her. She had been patiently awaiting her reward; patience that was coming to an end.

"I'm ready," Crystal said with anticipation.

"I just bet you are," Scott muttered. Jaric chuckled, watching as Scott began to remove his clothes. He eyed the shifter's strong physique with lust. He did enjoy men, but was only allowed to be with them with Cassandra's blessing. If she did not approve, he was not to touch them. She had not approved of any of the males in their camp. This he found disappointing. There were at least six males within the Pack and Pride that he felt desires for. Dejected, he only watched Scott as he began to change into his half-man, half-beast form.

Scott stood before Crystal with the face of a coyote. His body, completely covered in tan fur, towered over her smaller frame by more than three feet. Crystal's eyes widened as she tried to brace herself for what was to come.

Scott reached for her. Lifting her off of the ottoman, he breathed in her scent, allowing the smell of her fear and anticipation to whet his appetite. He opened his mouth, revealing a frightening sight. His mouth, or rather partial snout was filled with razor-sharp teeth with serrated edges.

"My! What big teeth you have!" Jaric joked from the sofa, chuckling even as he said it.

Scott ignored Jaric as he held the woman tightly by her arms, but not enough to cause her pain. He leaned toward the bared flesh she had exposed for him. Opening his mouth wider, he plunged his canines deeply into her right shoulder, causing her to scream. He immediately pulled away, letting her fall back onto the ottoman. He began to change back into human form. The silky tan fur that covered his body began to recede as his body grew smaller, less muscular. Once in human form, he looked her over. She had begun to tremble and sweat profusely, definite signs that the gene was working inside of her, changing her.

"Hand me a bucket and towel!" Scott demanded.

"Argh! I say let's leave her by the trash. If she survives, then her dream is fulfilled, if she dies, then at least she won't be our headache any longer!" Elizabeth stated with a cold demeanor.

"Unless you want her puking all over the furniture, get me a fucking bucket or something!" Scott reiterated.

"Oh fine!" Elizabeth rose from the chair, grabbing the nearest wastepaper basket. "Here!" She thrust the basket into Scott's hands and not a moment too soon. Scott heard Crystal gagging. He rolled her over onto her side, placing the basket under her mouth in time to catch the stream of multicolored vomit that spewed from her stomach in a continuous flow.

"Shit, I told her not to eat! That makes it worse!" Scott fussed under his breath.

"Perhaps she was hoping I'd turn her and wanted one last good meal," Jaric stated unconcernedly.

"Yeah, maybe that was it. Whatever the case, she's a mess now," Scott said, holding her head over the wastepaper basket.

"Here," Elizabeth brought a cold, wet towel for Scott to place over Crystal's forehead.

His main objective was to fight the ferocious fever that was now boiling within her. Elizabeth returned to her seat, watching as Scott attended to Crystal.

"This is disgusting," Jaric commented, then he rose from the sofa. "I'm going to my room." With that, he disappeared into the master bedroom, leaving the shape-shifters to their new convert.

CHAPTER THIRTEEN

I only have five dollars, can you-" Christopher was cut off by the cab driver slamming on the brakes.

The cab driver looked at him through the rearview mirror. "I'm sorry, but I can't take you-"

Christopher interrupted. "Please, we need help! Here, take my watch!" He began to remove his watch from his wrist, only worth twenty bucks, but it was all he had.

The cab driver shook his head. "No, please get out of my cab or I'll call the cops!"

"Yes! Yes! Call the cops! Please!" Christopher exclaimed. "Because I'm not going anywhere!"

"Fine!" The cab driver radioed for the police to assist him.

Brandon, still terribly frightened and confused looked at his brother with wide, innocent eyes. "Chris, what's going on now?" he asked softly.

Christopher forced himself to look down at his brother. He had been avoiding eye contact for fear that he would lose control of his will power. He knew that he was hanging on by a thread. Even the cab driver was smelling appetizing to him. It was both seductive and disturbing to him because it seemed so natural. "Help is on the way, stay calm," he advised.

A black Anaconda Pavilion pulled up beside the cab. John opened the passenger side and climbed out. Frightened, Christopher looked at the cab driver, who now seemed to be in a trance. He sat behind the wheel, motionless, receiver still in his hand.

"Shit!" Christopher cursed under his breath. "Let's get the hell out of here!" He opened the car door closest to his brother, and pushed the boy toward the curb while he climbed out after him. When he stood up, John was standing right in front of them. Christopher stepped in front of his brother. Facing John, he looked him in the eye in spite of the indescribable gnawing pain that swirled around his stomach.

"What do you want?" Christopher asked defensively.

John held his arms up in a non-aggressive manner. "Hey, take it easy." He turned, leaning into the window of the cab. "Cancel that distress call and leave."

The cab driver did as he was told, pulling off instantly.

"You didn't answer my question," Christopher said as he watched John closely. Every few seconds he darted glances toward the luxury automobile, wondering who was still inside.

"We're not here to harm you. We want to help you, but we need your help in return," John responded.

"What do you need from me?" Christopher asked, agitated. He was getting sick and tired of people "needing" him for one night.

"Your master has your mind blocked. We need to know where they are." John gestured toward the Anaconda Pavilion. "Please, come with us."

"Do I have a choice?" Christopher asked.

"No, not really."

Christopher didn't argue, he could tell that the man in front of him was the same as he was…a vampire and stronger. It amazed him that he could sense this vampire's power. It unnerved him also. It seemed like everyone was stronger than him at this point. He took his brother by the hand and opened the back passenger door of the luxury car, climbing inside. John climbed back into the front passenger seat.

"Who are you? And what do you want with me?" Christopher asked the man sitting in the driver's seat, watching him in the rearview mirror. He thought the driver was a good-looking man, one of the best looking men he'd ever seen. It's not that he was attracted to men, but this particular man's beauty was noteworthy to say the very least.

Darian turned around, facing him. "My name is Darian, I want to know what you know about the ones who did this to you tonight. Tell me what you remember."

Christopher studied Darian a little longer. He hoped that he'd turn around and drive them to safety. Since it didn't seem like he was going to, Christopher decided to answer his question. Before he could speak, a violent spasm ripped through his body, causing him to cry out in pain as he doubled over in the leather back seat. His little brother reached for him, but John held him back.

"Now is not the time to get close to him." John reached under the boy's arms, lifting him out of the backseat, seating him in the armrest space between himself and Darian.

"Don't...hurt...him!" Christopher managed to say between pain-filled pants.

"What do you remember?" Darian asked once more, attempting to get the information he needed.

After a few moments, Christopher was able to speak. "God...," he panted as the painful spasms subsided a little.

"That will end once you've fed. Tell me what I need to know." Darian's voice had grown stern. He turned back in his seat as he resumed driving.

"They're staying at a hotel," he said, giving them the description and the general directions he could remember since Jaric had erased the name of the hotel from his memory.

"I know that hotel," John said the name.

"What are you going to do to them?" Christopher asked, wincing slightly as another stab of pain struck his stomach.

"What we've been wanting to do for the past twenty-four hours," John said, smiling, finally thrilled that they had made a breakthrough.

"Are you going to kill them?" Christopher asked, his voice hopeful.

"Yes," Darian answered as he mentally contacted the others who were in the vicinity, through Xavier. He told them which hotel to go to.

"How did you find us?" Christopher asked curiously.

"Through your thoughts, though some have been sealed off completely, so tightly, that I dared not dig too deep. I didn't want to be discovered. That's why I needed you to tell them to me."

"You can read my mind, too?" the newborn vampire asked.

"Yes, but now that you are a vampire, your maker has more control over your thoughts and willpower than you know," Darian informed him. Then he looked at John. "I want you to take care of Christopher, he's your responsibility."

"Whoa, I don't want him 'taking care' of me, whatever the hell you mean by that!" Christopher said defensively.

Darian chuckled, though John seemed slightly disappointed. The thought of having to be responsible for training Christopher annoyed him, but it was his Master's orders and he would follow them without question.

Darian knew this and did not comment on it.

John turned around, looking at Christopher. "What he means is that I'm going to teach you what you need to know in order to survive. Like tonight for instance...you need to feed or you're going to be in a worse situation."

"I just need to get to a grocery store so that I can pick up a couple bottles of Synblood," Christopher said, believing that he had the answer to his hunger problems.

Darian snorted, but remained silent. His thoughts on synthetic blood and its drinkers were not favorable.

"There's more to it than that, much more. Look, to make it easy for you to understand, Darian is the Master of this entire state, though he's a generous man and doesn't mind sharing this territory with smaller covens. Chicago is ultimately his, and he governs all. There are rules you are going to have to learn for the sake of your own survival. Don't fight me on this, I don't have the patience for it," John stated matter-of-factly.

Christopher remained silent as he reflected on what John was saying to him. He decided not to be stubborn, taking into consideration that he was alive, his brother unharmed, and that they were willing to help, but above all, they wanted to kill the ones who had condemned him to an eternity of nights and an unbearable thirst for blood. He nodded, signifying that he understood. John smiled his approval.

Darian listened to the two vampires talking. When he thought enough time had passed by for the others to make it to the hotel, he decided to join them. "John, take him hunting." With that, he pulled the car over, climbed out and vanished before their very eyes.

"Holy shit!" Christopher gasped in shock.

"Yeah, Darian can fly faster than you can blink. Listen, we don't have much time, you need to feed before the sun rises."

"Look, tonight, just let me drink the Synblood. I don't have time to...," his voice trailed off. The thought of hunting humans was unnerving him.

John watched him for a few moments then he nodded. "Very well, only tonight." He climbed into the driver's seat, then drove Darian's car back to their hotel.

"Can I ask you a question?" Christopher's voice was strained as he fought his urges.

"Sure."

"If this asshole who turned me tonight can control my thoughts...do you think he knows about what you're going to do? What about us having this conversation?"

"If he listening in to your every thought, and I think he might be, then yes."

"What's going to happen?"

"I don't know," John responded, not really knowing what else to say. He only hoped that they had a big enough of a window of opportunity for Darian and the others to get to their enemy's hotel in time.

CHAPTER FOURTEEN

Sergio, Adrian, Nagesa and Xavier bypassed the elevators, going straight to the staircase following the scent of a coyote. Twenty-five seconds later, they were on the thirty-fourth floor, their keen sense of smell leading them right to the room they knew to contain more than one shifter and at least, one vampire. They could hear the other supernaturals inside scrambling as if they knew who was there and they were preparing for their attack. Sergio kicked the door open, the others following him into the room.

Jaric had not spied on his new fledgling after he allowed him to leave. It was only his curiosity that egged him on to peek into his mind before the sun rose, just to see how he was dealing with his newborn hungers. It was then that he spied Darian and the other vampire, John and knew that more were coming having been tracked down through his fledgling. He was furious and in shock to discover that they were alive still. He informed Cassandra of their predicament. Her response was as he expected, she was incensed! He only had a few minutes to tell the others of what he'd learned. It was at that time they became aware their hotel room was surrounded, they could smell the shape-shifters. Jaric could sense Xavier's aura coming closer. He was ready for battle. He allowed his nails to grow into claws so that he could rip these beings into shreds. Scott and Elizabeth had changed into their most powerful half-beast forms, standing by the door, waiting. When their enemy entered the room, they launched a full-on attack.

Jaric was too fast for them to see and far too powerful for them to counter. Immediately, he struck Nagesa, tossing him against the wall, destroying the wallpaper and plaster. Picture frames crashed to the floor, the glass breaking into thousands of pieces. Sergio had changed forms, rushing his change, which weakened him a bit. He took hold of Elizabeth as she clawed at his chest, nails slicing through a layer of his skin. He jumped back, out of her reach before she could follow up with another assault. Unfortunately, he was caught from behind by Jaric, who dislocated his arm in a moment too fast for him to react, causing him to gasp. The vampire laughed as he witnessed Sergio's pain. A second later, he tossed the leopard into the wood and lacquer bar, destroying dozens of expensive liquor bottles and glasses.

Xavier held Scott against his chest as the coyote struggled against his powerful grip. Xavier's eyes grew red with anger as his clawed hand ripped Scott's vocal cords from his throat, cutting through the shifter's windpipe.

Adrian leaped over a sofa and chair, landing softly in front of Scott. He plunged a finger from each hand into the other shifter's eye sockets, deep into his brain. Scott tried to force a scream from his mangled windpipe as the agonizing pain throbbed inside his head, but only a gargled growl came through. A second later, his body grew limp in Xavier's arms. Adrian pulled his now bloodied fingers away. Xavier let go of Scott, letting his warm corpse fall to the ground. Nagesa had regrouped and was now charging toward Elizabeth. She had tried to attack Sergio while she thought he was defenseless. Sergio now had her neck between his thighs, squeezing with all his might as she struggled. She was able to free one of her hands from his grip and she grabbed hold his groin, digging her nails in deeply. Sergio cried out as blood gushed from his groin, but he held tightly to his attacker, refusing to release her from his grip. When Nagesa reached Elizabeth, he broke her arm, releasing Sergio from her clutch. She let out a dry scream as she struggled to breathe. Sergio was then able to twist her head, baring her neck as Nagesa sliced her throat open with his clawed hands. Blood gushed from the wound in a torrent, splattering Nagesa as it flowed over Sergio's legs. He then finished her off, ripping her head completely from her neck in a violent spray of blood.

In a matter of seconds, Jaric had watched the three shifters and vampire kill his companions with a keen fascination. He thought about intervening again, then decided against it. He didn't like either one of them anyway.

"Well, four-to-one...now it's fair." Jaric smiled wickedly.

Without waiting for one of the others to make a move, Jaric charged Adrian, picking him up with amazing speed and strength. With one great thrust, he tossed him through the large glass sliding doors, shattering the glass. His body continued sailing over the balcony. Adrian screamed as he free fell down several stories until he was able to grab hold onto a railing on an eighteenth floor balcony. Jaric and Xavier charged each other. Jaric immediately overpowered him, digging his claws under his chin, causing blood to gush from the wounds. Both Nagesa and Sergio knew what Jaric was trying to do and they rushed over to Xavier's side before Jaric could decapitate him.

Jaric saw them approaching and he released Xavier, tossing him against the two running toward him. The weight and velocity of Xavier's body knocked the two men to the ground. With more amazing speed, Jaric advanced on the three men, snatching Nagesa up from the pile. He punched the wolf several times, striking his face, abdomen and chest, before dumping his bruised and beaten body onto the floor, leaving him gasping in pain. Sergio was able to push Xavier off of him, just in time for Jaric to slice his inch long razor-sharp claws across his throat, barely missing his jugular. This time, Xavier managed to push Sergio out of harm's way in time, sparing him serious injury.

Jaric's viselike grip wrapped around Xavier's neck, tightening as he lifted the vampire to his feet. Jaric opened his mouth, baring his fangs. Xavier clawed at the hand locked around his throat, but to no avail. The other vampire leaned forward, toward his neck, then he froze. He looked toward the balcony, seeing Darian standing amongst the broken glass.

"So we meet face to face, finally," Jaric smiled wickedly, tossing Xavier into the dining room. His body crashed on top of the heavy redwood table, sliding across the surface and landing on the other side with a resounding thud.

Nagesa manage to pull Sergio away, into the safety of a corner farthest away from Jaric. "I'm going to pop your arm back into joint," he whispered into his ear.

Sergio nodded, gripping onto Nagesa's thigh with his uninjured hand, bracing himself for the pain. Nagesa snapped Sergio's arm back into its joint as the leopard growled in pain, but stayed still. Hotel security and the manager barged into the room, demanding to know what was going on. Jaric laughed as he advanced on the three men, taking the manager into his arms.

"What do you say, Darian Alexander. You seem to have a soft spot for these humans. One can only assume, with your pretty Natasha, and all. I'll let these humans go if you leave." Jaric held the security personnel under his spell as he bargained with Darian.

Darian chuckled softly. He looked at Xavier as he rose from behind the table, recovering from Jaric's attack.

His eyes scanned over the others, seeing that they were injured, but healing. He did notice that Adrian was nowhere to be seen and that was cause for concern.

Darian shook his head and he took several steps closer to Jaric. "Your time of hiding behind humans has long since passed with the last breath of your human rebel shield." He tilted his head sideways slightly, smiling wickedly. "His blood was sweet on my tongue."

Jaric laughed deeply. "I don't give a shit about him or his useless band of rebels!" He broke the Manager's neck, dropping his body, then immediately grabbed the nearest security guard. "Although, I did half expect them to be able to kill a coven of sleeping, oblivious vampires with some measure of success. I guess you can say that I expect too much from people." He laughed.

The man in his hold cried and pleaded for his life. He had a wife and four children, the youngest was three years old. The other security officer was a single father and a good one at that. He was unable to aid his partner due to Jaric's mind spell, but he was fully aware of what was going on before him. He knew that he might be next to die.

"They're family men, Darian. Are you going to make his wife a widow?" Jaric said, jerking the man in his arms. He looked at the other human. "You want to make both of their children orphans?" He poised his fanged grin over the pulsating artery in the security guard's throat.

"Of course not," Darian said and before Jaric had time to kill the second man, Darian appeared behind him, slipping his arm between Jaric and the guard, pinning the vampire to his chest. Jaric's arms were pressed to his sides, unable to move. Darian's other hand gripped Jaric's chin, tilting his head upward so that the vampire had to look into his eyes. Darian didn't say another word before plunging his fangs painfully into the vampire's vein. Jaric struggled as hard as he could in Darian's unyielding hold, but he couldn't loosen his grip. Darian feasted quickly as he pried freely through Jaric's most heavily guarded thoughts. Once he had drained him completely, he wasted no time in killing him. Doing exactly to Jaric what he had attempted to do to Xavier. He slid his claws under the vampire's throat, digging his nails in deeply. In one quick upward jerk, he ripped the wounded flesh, tearing the head off completely, releasing several spurts of blood from the torn arteries. He tossed both the body and head onto the floor. The head rolled to a stop, eyes staring forward, empty. Darian didn't turn to face the security staff as he erased the incident from their minds and told them to leave. The two security staff walked away as if there was nothing wrong.

Adrian walked past the two men. As he reentered the hotel room, he looked around at the carnage. "Shit! That motherfucker was strong as hell!" he exclaimed.

"Tell me about it! I didn't even know he was behind me, the next thing I knew, that son-of-a-bitch damn near rips my fucking arms from my damn body!" Sergio commented, surveying the damage.

Darian looked at Xavier. "Are you alright?" he asked softly, full of concern.

Xavier nodded. "I am. Were you able to gather more information?"

Darian nodded, smiling. "The others are located in Florida. It's dawn there already and Cassandra does not know that her lover's dead. We have to get there before nightfall if we are going to save the others and end this war."

"Have Sebastian and the others woken up yet?" Sergio asked, hoping to find out more about his son.

"Not yet, they are keeping them heavily sedated. I am unable to contact them at this point. Not only that, but Natasha's thoughts are still unclear, confusing. I can not read them effectively," Darian stated.

Sergio turned, looking at Crystal who lay on the ottoman, her body trembling as she was racked through and through with a fever that held a 105 degree temperature. He walked over to the ottoman, staring down at her.

Nagesa decided to inform Sergio of who Crystal was. "She was the one with your son."

"I know, I can still smell his scent all over her." Sergio leaned down, so that he could look into her face more closely. He could see why his son had been so swept away. What angered him more than anything was that she had never cared for his son, only used him and endangered him in order to become a shape-shifter.

"Are you going to kill her?" Adrian asked. The others watched Sergio in silence.

"Hell yeah, I'm gonna kill this bitch! It's because of her ass that my son is in danger." Sergio looked up at the others. "The funny thing is, if this was all she'd wanted, had she been true and they fell in love, Sebastian could have given it to her in a few years without her having to sell her soul." In a lightening-quick movement, his clawed hand slashed her throat open, spilling blood onto the ottoman and carpeted floor. "That, of course...was strictly personal." He flicked her blood from his fingertips with a quick jerking motion. Her body twitched several times as blood poured from her wounds before falling still. Sergio watched her die, then he joined the others.

Xavier was watching Darian, he knew that something troubled him by the way he studied the damaged room.

"Darian, is there something else that you want to tell us?" Xavier asked as he stepped closer to his lover, placing his hand gently on the other man's arm questioningly.

Darian turned toward him, smiling warmly. His other hand coming up to caress the side of Xavier's face lovingly. "You know me all too well, my love."

"It's because I love you, that's the reason why I know you all too well. There's something wrong, this I can tell."

Darian studied Xavier for a few seconds more before he reluctantly pulled his hand away. "We need to return to the hotel before sunrise, we don't have time to waste."

"Darian, what's-" Xavier began, but Darian cut him off with the wave of his hand.

"I'll explain further once we get back to the hotel," he stated then he looked at the shape-shifters. "We will meet you there." With that, Darian flew out of the window so fast it seemed that he disappeared into thin air.

Xavier followed him back to the hotel, flying behind him.

"Damn, I wish I could fly," Adrian commented. "We've got to weave through traffic and shit."

"You forgot already? Ten minutes ago, you did fly," Sergio stated as he walked toward the door.

"That was low as hell, and you know it," Adrian said, shoving Sergio lightly.

"At least we're one step closer to ending this. Come on, we only have about an hour, less than an hour until sunrise. Whatever Darian has to say, we need to be there to hear it," Nagesa said.

They took the staircase back down to the lobby. Once they were back inside their car, they drove as fast as they could back to their hotel. When they reached the hotel, Adrian tossed the valet the keys as the others entered the hotel, heading straight for the elevators.

"What do you think Darian has to tell us?" Adrian asked as they rode the elevator up to the penthouse suite.

"I don't know. But I didn't like the expression on his face, did you guys notice it?" Sergio asked as he glanced from Nagesa to Adrian.

Nagesa nodded.

"Yeah, I did catch his expression, that's why I know whatever it is that he has to tell us, can't be good news," Adrian said as he waited for the elevator doors to open. When they did, all three men stepped out. They walked toward the double doors. Just as they reached the doors, Devin opened them up wide to allow them entrance. Nagesa closed the doors behind them then walked over to update Xander on all that had taken place. Sergio told Elise and Madeleine that he had killed the female responsible for Sebastian's kidnapping.

Adrian was watching Darian from across the room. He noted that Darian was quiet and appeared to be in deep thought. He thought at that moment, it would be the perfect time to ask the right question. "Darian, what was it that you were going to tell us?" he asked.

Darian looked at him, then nodded. "I had tried to read Jaric's mind before I killed him, but couldn't. His deepest thoughts were heavily protected and not by him, another force, more powerful than him. I suspect it was his Master. It wasn't until I fed from him, was I able to penetrate those thoughts. The members of his coven... Cassandra's coven are very powerful."

John's expression grew fearful even as he fought to contain his emotions. "What does this mean for us?" he asked in a soft but apprehensive tone.

"It means that you don't stand a fucking chance toe-to-toe against these guys," Sergio answered.

"How much stronger?" Xavier asked as he studied Darian's expression.

"Let me put it this way, the youngest member of her coven has been a vampire for fifty-two years, whereas the youngest member of my coven has only been one for two years."

Gary pouted. "I'm twenty-three."

Tony chuckled softly as he shook his head. "He's not talking the human years it took you to reach the age legal enough to enter bars, baby."

Gary turned to Tony but said nothing. He was beginning to understand how high the odds were stacked against them.

"Their oldest?" Xavier asked.

Darian turned to face him, taking a deep breath and exhaling it slowly through his nostrils. "Three thousand."

Xavier's mouth dropped open, shocked. He sunk further into the cushions of the sofa. The situation had just escalated into a worst case scenario.

"What's wrong, what's going on?" Devin and Justin asked at the same time.

"This coven master will either match my strength, or top it," Darian said, then he fell silent as he allowed that information to sink into their minds.

Xander leaned forward, elbows resting on his knees. "What do you think your chances are against her and her coven?" he asked, his stunning silver eyes locked on the forest green of Darian's gaze.

"I honestly do not know," Darian answered. It was true. He had never faced a vampire of his own strength, let alone one stronger than himself. The reason, he told himself, why this situation had never occurred in the past was because of his reputation, one he had fought hard to maintain. Being the Master vampire of a large city was not an easy feat. There had been plenty of challengers who had come to oppose him, but none had been so devious as the enemy he was facing at the moment. He knew what he was going to have to do if he was going to give his coven a fighting chance.

"Master?" John asked, growing more afraid as he observed Darian's uncertainty.

Darian looked up at him, but said nothing.

John's blue eyes gazed at him. "I will fight, live or die with you, you have my allegiance."

April tied a rubber-band at the end of her thick braid, tossing it behind her back. She looked at Darian. "I think I speak for us all when I say that we share John's sentiments. We await your decision, although, I don't think we have much of a choice."

"You can always leave the city, they said they'll let the others go," Christopher said. Everyone turned toward him. Now that he'd sated his hunger with a few bottles of Synblood, he was able to be near his brother Brandon, who was curled up in his arms safe and fast asleep.

"You're young, so we'll let that comment slide," Annabelle stated.

"But if you guys try to fight them and die, what good will that shit do?!" Christopher responded as he looked around the room at the others.

"Young one, tell me, from your own experience with this enemy, are they honorable...trustworthy?" Xander asked.

Christopher thought about Xander's question, then he responded. "Honorable, no. However, they did let me and my brother go."

"Yeah, after he killed you," Sergio said, sardonically.

Madeleine struck him hard on the arm. He looked at her, instantly realizing his blunder and regretting it. He returned his gaze to Christopher.

"I'm sorry, that was heartless of me. I shouldn't have said that. It's just I've been under so much stress in the past twenty-four hours, I sometimes say things without thinking. I'm sure the last thing you wanted to hear was that shit," Sergio apologized, hoping Christopher understood his sentiments.

"Yeah, not that it wasn't true. When you put it that way, I can see why you guys don't trust their ultimatum. He did kill me, turned me into something that's not human. Needless to say, I'm glad that son-of-a-bitch is dead," Christopher looked at the others.

"I honestly don't think we have that ultimatum anymore. Now that Jaric's dead, all bets may be off," Nicole stated.

"I don't see why you just can't call the S.U.I.T. and tell them what's going on. Seems like this is something they would handle," Christopher said.

Adrian scoffed. "The S.U.I.T. doesn't work *for* supernaturals, Chris, it works against them."

Warren turned toward him. "Hello, standing right here, S.U.I.T. officer right fucking here! Don't talk about shit you don't know, Adrian. You have no idea how hard the S.U.I.T. tries to protect both humans and supernaturals."

Nicole interrupted. "Wait a minute, before you two get all deep into the whole 'are they assholes' debate, let's stick with the problem at hand," Her statement stopped both men from arguing. The two men nodded.

"Well, can the S.U.I.T. deal with this or not?" Christopher asked, wanting an answer.

Elise shook her head as she approached Christopher, slipping her hand underneath his chin, lifting his face to her own. "When another supernatural issues you a challenge, your only option is to fight. If you run, you'll be running forever. And every supernatural will challenge you, simply because they'll think you're weak."

"Besides, running away never solved anything for those that have done so," Devin stated, then he looked at Darian. "What about the shape-shifters, do you know how strong they are?"

Darian nodded. "Ranging from over three-hundred years old, to newly bitten."

Xander sat back in his chair, fingers coming together to form a triangle as he pondered the situation. Elise turned sharply, facing Darian, her mouth slightly agape as she thought about the strength of their adversaries.

"Shit!" Sergio cursed under his breath. "If these guys are stronger than us, why don't they just face us?"

"Because up until they kidnapped our members, they had no idea how old we were and still they are not aware of our full resources," Darian stated.

"Tell me, Darian, who is the mastermind of their plan?" Xander asked.

"Cassandra, but Jaric suspected that she knew she could not take over the city with just her coven alone, and that's why she sought others that wanted Chicago for their own. They made an agreement to share the city once they took it over. What they don't know is that Cassandra was planning on killing them off once she had established herself here. Well, let me clarify that. She was planning on keeping the Matrons of the tiger Pride, Milan and the coyote Pack, Katrina," Darian said.

"Do you think these women know that Cassandra was planning on killing off their Pack and Pride?" Elise asked.

"Yes, they are aware of it. Also, Cassandra read the minds of our members, but like me, because they were drugged, she's getting only bits and piece, incoherent thoughts and she can not be sure what is true and what is not. Which is why they are sticking to their original plan and have not attacked us full on."

"But why would she even try? I mean, Darian, your reputation as a kick ass vampire Master is well known. Why would she even bother?" Justin asked.

"Shit, why not, Chicago is a kick ass city!" Devin declared.

"A fledgling of mine, Eliana...," Darian looked at Warren whose expression let him know that he thought he remembered who she was.

"You mean that female vampire that went on a killing spree with the werewolf almost two years ago?" Warren asked, surprised.

Darian nodded. "I don't make a habit of telling every vampire I sire my age." He looked at Xavier and smiled. "With one exception."

"That's true, I never knew how old you were until Natasha threw you the birthday party," John added.

"Exactly. I do this to protect what is mine. There are many vampires who would seek me out for my blood, along with the power and strength that I could give them."

"But I thought only a vampire from your line could gain power by feeding from you?" Carmen asked.

"That is true, but my line doesn't end nor did it ever begin with me. Vampires from the main line would seek me out and others like me for extra strength. It is what Eliana had done. When I didn't give in to her, she left me and searched out one who would."

"But didn't you read her mind before you killed her, did you see this plan?" Warren asked.

"I did read her, but this plan had never been revealed to Eliana, she wasn't a part of it. She was being used even as she thought she was using them. Jaric was the one who had given her his blood. I only knew of him what Eliana did and she knew very little."

"Jaric must have read her mind when he shared his blood with her. That's how he got the information," Xavier said as he pieced together the carefully laid plan.

"Exactly. Cassandra shares the same line as I do, but I don't know her," Darian stated.

"So when do we attack?" Gary asked, attempting to rouse himself for battle. He had never seen battle, he only heard the tales and it was not something he was at all eager to engage in. But he would defend what was theirs to defend. He would fight alongside his lover, Tony, his Master, Darian and the rest of his coven.

Darian chuckled. "My dear Gary, you must stay here. I want you to look after Christopher and his brother until this is over and we return," he said, the last part of his statement filled with confidence.

"But I want to fight," Gary protested.

"My order has been given." Darian looked at Gary, who lowered his head, nodding. "Good." He rose from the sofa.

Xavier grabbed his hand. "Is there anything else?" he asked as he gazed up at him.

Darian took a deep breath then released it. It was a sign that Xavier knew all too well. It meant that he was going to have to do something he would not have done otherwise.

"Darian?" Xavier asked, gently urging him to continue.

"I am going to do what must be done." Darian turned, looking at his coven. "We must make haste before the sun puts us all to rest. I will give those of you from my lineage my blood to strengthen you."

"Really?!" John asked excitedly, unable to contain his delight. He knew that the situation was gloomy, however, the opportunity to drink from Darian was a rare one. To John, seeing a lunar eclipse would be more probable.

Darian chuckled. "Yes, John." He turned to the others. "I will need help."

"Why?" Devin asked.

"In order to sustain them throughout the feeding, I'm going to need to feed to replenish what I lose. The sun is rising now, and I don't have time to waste. Being shape-shifters, you will heal fast as I feed from you. Who will assist me?" he asked.

"Oh, I'm all for that," Devin said as he rose from the foot stool, but Sergio reached out, stopping him.

Devin turned to face Sergio. "What's wrong?"

Sergio looked at Darian, then back at Devin. "You're too young for this job, you wouldn't be able to heal as fast as I would. I'll do it." He rose from the chair.

A few of the others were in shock, everyone knew how Sergio felt about being fed from by a vampire and a male one at that. Sergio's "touch" of homophobia was a secret to no one. For him to volunteer for such an act left many of them surprised.

"You?!" Devin exclaimed

"Yes, me!" Sergio answered, mocking Devin as he approached Darian.

"But you hate the thought of being 'food'!" Daniel added as he was equally stunned. Madeleine and Elise remained silent, both knowing why Sergio was doing it.

Sergio looked back at Daniel. "My son is out there. He's scared, unaware of his surroundings or he could be hurt and wondering why he's not here with us. If this is what Darian is going to need to get the motherfucking job done, then that's all I need to know." He turned back toward Darian. "Okay, let's do this."

Darian glanced around the room. No one else said a word, only watched. His gaze settled on Sergio. "Let us go into the bedroom." He led the way as Sergio, John, Xavier, Miko, April and Annabelle followed closely behind him. Annabelle closed the door after they were all inside.

"Damn, I would have never thought I'd see the day Sergio opted to feed a vampire!" Devin said.

"Enough Devin, now is not the time to make light of this situation," Elise chastised.

Devin nodded, acknowledging that his behavior was inappropriate. He sat down on the sofa.

Elise turned to Xander. "We should arrange for our jets to fly us to Florida so that we will be in their territory in time for nightfall. When Cassandra and her coven awaken, they will not have enough time to plan a counterattack. I'm sure they wouldn't be expecting us to meet them at their front door."

"Indeed. We just have to be cautious about one thing. We have to make sure that we are not in an area that they or other shifters would frequent. We definitely don't want them knowing that we are there," Xander added.

"Excellent." Elise nodded, as she pulled out her cell phone. Tatiana did the same. Both of them called the companies that maintained their private jets. They requested that their jets be ready for take off within the hour. Then Elise looked at Christopher. "Why don't you call your parents. I'm sure they are completely worried about you. Tell them to come and get your younger brother."

"Why can't I go with them?" Christopher asked.

"Because, you're new and not properly trained. The scent of their blood would drive you insane the moment you wake up tomorrow night. You'll be starved and you'll want to feed immediately. And unless you want your entire family to be your first meal for the evening, it'll be best if you stay here," Tony said, his eyes on Christopher, making sure what he said really registered.

Christopher was thinking about what Tony told him, and he knew it to be true. He remembered how he'd felt around his little brother, the lust and thirst he'd felt for the blood flowing through his brother's veins. He hated feeling that way. He wanted control.

"I see your point," he said as he looked at his brother sleeping soundly. He slid from underneath his brother, placing him gently on the seat cushions and walked over to Elise, who held out her cell phone for him to use. "Thank you," he said, taking the cell phone from her, clicking it on. When he called home, someone picked up the phone on the first ring.

"Hello, who is this?" his mother asked anxiously.

"Mom, it's-" Christopher was cut off my his mother's screaming.

"Christopher! Oh my god! "Thank the lord! Is your brother alright? Where are you?"

"Yeah, Mom, Brandon's alright."

"Your father and I have been worried sick about you and Brandon, we've been going out of our minds! We've called the police, hospitals, homeless shelters, everywhere we could think of! Do you know how much we've been worried?!" his mother asked breathlessly.

"Mom, I-"

"No you don't, you have no idea! Your father has been patrolling the streets looking for you for hours. He's still out there!" his mom paused for just a second as she struggled to contain her emotions. She was thrilled and relieved to hear from her son, and wanted him home. "Where the hell are you? We're coming to get you right this minute!"

"Mom, I need you to listen to me very carefully, please don't interrupt. Do-"

"What's the matter? Are you and your brother okay?"

"He's fine, he's here with me. Mom, please let me talk."

"Alright, Christopher, go ahead."

"Something happened to me tonight. On the way home from

the movie theater, a guy grabbed me and Brandon and threw us in the trunk of his car."

"Oh my god!" his mother gasped as her hand covered her mouth.

"I'm alive, Brandon is unharmed. He took us to this hotel, and when we got to the room, a guy told me that he wanted to use me as part of their plan to flush out the local supernaturals in the city and state."

"What?! What happened?"

"They were supernaturals too, the guy who wanted me to do this. His name was Jaric, he was a vampire. He threatened to kill me and Brandon if I didn't, so I did. When I went back to the hotel to get Brandon, he bit me and turned me. I'm one of them now, Mom. I'm a vampire." Christopher paused, giving his mother a chance to let all of the information sink in.

"My baby, my poor baby!" his mother's voice was shaky, Christopher could tell that she was crying. "We're coming to get you, sweetheart."

"That's just it, Mom. You can only come and get Brandon. I'm not safe around you yet, I have to get control of what I am now. I'm staying here."

"No, absolutely not. You're coming home where you belong. We're not going to leave you in some strange place, sweetheart."

"Mom, I can't. Please understand that it's for the best that I stay here-"

His mother interrupted, "Where are you, and why do you need to stay there? Can't you learn control in your own home, where you'll be safe?"

"I'm with some people that will help me, Mom. They're vampires too and they're going to help me so that I can come back home and not do you any harm. This is important to me, Mom. Please understand. Look, the sun's rising, and I'm starting to feel weak. I might not be awake when you get here, but please come and get Brandon. Let him know that everything will be alright, I promise." Christopher did not wait for his mother to respond before he gave her the address to Darian's hotel and the room number. "Mom, I have to go, I...,"

Before Christopher could say another word he had fallen asleep, dropping the cell phone at the same time.

Carmen caught both the cell phone and Christopher before they hit the floor. She laid him on the sofa, and checked the cell phone seeing that the call had ended. She handed the phone back to Elise.

"So, we should be expecting his father at least, very soon," Elise stated.

"He's a brave kid...well, young man. I hope that he can embrace what he has become," Tony said as he laid Gary's resting form next to Christopher's on the couch. "I'm next, I can feel it."

"Well, you better lay down on something, cause if you fall out, we might not catch ya," Adrian joked, making a few of the others chuckle.

"Can you explain to me how vampires sleep at different times?" Justin asked.

Tony plopped down heavily into the chair beside the sofa. It was becoming harder for him to concentrate on what was going on, but he was able to answer Justin's question. "The youngest or weakest sleep first. The sun doesn't even have to be up for them to rest. The older or stronger a vampire is, the later he can stay awake. For instance, Darian has only about ten minutes to feed John before he falls asleep. Xavier, about thirty, whereas Darian can actually watch the sky lighten...or so I've been told. I am resting during the times he's awake."

"That explains it. Thanks." Justin smiled. Tony nodded, then lay his head back against the cushions, his eyes closed and he stopped breathing. Everyone knew that he was resting, and would be doing so until the next nightfall. The others continued to converse as they waited for Christopher's parents to arrive.

CHAPTER FIFTEEN

Inside the bedroom, Darian had removed his clothes. He stood before the others, naked. "We must hurry, so please do not try to savor the moment," he told them, then he lay back on the bed, his eyes staring up at the ceiling. The other vampires climbed onto the bed, taking positions around his body. Xavier leaned forward, kissing Darian lovingly on his full-shaped lips.

"I love you," Xavier whispered.

"I know." Darian smiled.

John looked at Darian's body lustfully, secretly missing the times they used to share, although he kept his thoughts to himself. "I can't wait for us to get the others back."

Darian nodded, then looked toward Sergio who appeared to be having second thoughts. "Sergio?"

"Yeah?"

"Have you lost your nerve?" Darian asked.

"No, I'm just mentally preparing myself for this shit. This is the gayest thing I have ever done. It's not easy for me to let another man give me an org-" Sergio paused, then shook his head. "Come on, let's get this over with while we still have time." He climbed on the bed, gazing out of the window at the light purple sky. Time was running out.

"If it's any consolation, I've never done this before, either," Darian admitted.

Sergio looked down at him. "No consolation whatsoever."

Darian smiled, then looked down at the vampires surrounding him. "Do it," he instructed his fledglings and they followed his orders. Each drove their sharp fangs deeply into his flesh. He arched on the bed, his body feeling the pain of each piercing fang. Then he began to relax as the pain of their bites transformed into pleasure.

John, the youngest of his fledglings, had bitten deeply into his nipple and was now feasting greedily. Xavier's fangs were buried in his carotid artery. Xavier's eyes were closed as he drank from his lover. Annabelle had chosen his wrist. She locked her mouth around the fount that spurted up through the puncture wounds her fangs had created. Both Miko and April had taken places between his legs, feeding from the main vein near his groin.

Sergio watched the vampires feed, feeling slightly uncomfortable as he listened to the sounds of their sucking and their moans of ecstasy as they fed. "This is truly the freakiest shit that I've ever done," he mumbled as he waited for Darian to motion for him.

Darian arched on the bed one more time, bellowing in pleasure as his vampires continued to feed. His skin had become pale, his fangs extended and Sergio took that as a sign. He held his wrist over Darian's mouth. Instantly, Darian bit into Sergio's flesh, sinking his fangs deeply and sealing his lips around the bite.

Sergio gasped as he lay next to Darian's head. He began to pant as indescribable pleasure rippled through his body, causing his penis to harden. He thought back to when he had given his blood to Xavier, which had been amazing, but Darian's bite was far more potent! He was beginning to wonder if Darian had ever bitten Elise, a tinge of jealousy flashed through his mind as he wondered about the pleasure they had shared. He banished the thought. Elise was with him now, and Darian was happy with Natasha and Xavier and that was what all of this was about. Getting everyone and everything back to the way it was supposed to be.

Sergio felt an orgasm building within him. He fought against it, but to no avail. His entire body tingled with the oncoming power of his climax. The fingers of his left hand gripped the sheets on the bed as Darian continued to drink from him. When he could no longer hold back, his body quaked as the pleasure Darian's bite had created exploded throughout his being. He cried out over and over again as his bodily fluids drained while his orgasm intensified.

He collapsed onto the bed, panting breathlessly and still feeling his orgasm cascading inside. Darian continued to feed, creating another powerful wave of pleasure inside them all. John forced himself away from Darian, declaring that he could take no more. April was next, pushing herself away. One by one, they began to release Darian, Xavier being the last as he shared one more climax with both Darian and Sergio, then he pulled away, resting his head on Darian's chest.

Darian continued to feed from Sergio until he had replenished the blood he had lost. Sergio's penis had grown hard once more as a third orgasm began building inside both of their bodies. A few seconds later, their bodies lit up with inexpressible pleasure. Both moaned as their bodies rocked with their orgasms. Once Darian was full, he retracted his fangs, releasing Sergio, who lay motionless. The vampires had sprawled on the bed, each one falling under the spell of the rising sun. Sergio had fallen asleep as well, and only Darian was left awake. He looked at the others, smiling as he noted Sergio snoring and the look of serenity in his expression. He looked at Xavier, pulling the younger vampire into his arms, feeling the heat in his body cool. He decided to concentrate on his connection with Natasha. She was awake, but still groggy.

This pleased Darian.

Natasha, we are alive and well.

Darian? Where am I? What's going on? Natasha was frightened. She didn't remember how she'd gotten there or even where she was. All she knew was that she was alone.

Calm down. I can not tell you much, but you are being held hostage by our enemies. We will save you, trust in me. I will explain more later, right now, I must rest. Be brave, my darling.

"I trust you," Natasha said aloud. She knew Darian heard her, simply because she had to think the thought in order to say it. She felt the connection with Darian fade, then disappear. The room in which she was being held was dark,. The windows were boarded and the door felt like metal as she ran her fingers over its surface. She listened carefully, and could hear footsteps approaching. The sound of voices grew louder. She backed away from the door as she heard a key open the lock and the knob turn. A bright light filled the room, blinding her as she struggled to see her captors. Before she could react, they had grabbed her, holding her down as she screamed and struggled. One of them pricked her skin with a needle, injecting into her veins the very same drug that had rendered her unconscious. A few seconds later, Natasha ceased to struggle. Her eyelids grew heavy, so heavy that she could no longer keep them open. Her fearful thoughts faded away to mental rambling as darkness surrounded her.

CHAPTER SIXTEEN

Adrian looked at Tony. "Shit, I feel like crashing like that right now. I'm exhausted," he stated, yawning loudly. "I know what you mean, we've actually been up for damn near forty-eight hours!" Warren added.

"I can't believe that all of this shit started last night during the *Lunar*. So much has happened," Devin stated.

"It's not over yet," Xander spoke in a low voice. "We'll wait for Christopher's parents to pick up their son, then we'll place Darian and the others in coffins. We've already made preparations for our flight."

"What about guns?" Adrian asked. Being one of the Pack's enforcers, he had used guns on rare occasions when battling certain enemies, but never on this level, never over territory. He was wondering if his father would allow it.

"Adrian, how can you even ask that question? This is about integrity. Your father would never allow such a thing, not in this situation," Tatiana protested.

"But Mom, these sons-of-bitches have been using humans and every dirty trick in the book to try to defeat us. Let's give them a taste of their own medicine!" Adrian argued.

"Enough!" Xander looked at his son. "Let us not insult ourselves by stooping to their level. Territorial battles are to be fought with integrity, as your Mother stated. Integrity, wisdom and strength, it is tradition. It is how we survive, how we won our territory in the first place."

"But Dad, who's to say they don't already have that figured into their plans? We go in there, unarmed...we could get slaughtered," Adrian said as he knelt down in front of his father's chair.

"Are you so terrified of them, Adrian…that you would disgrace yourself and Pack?"

"Fuck, Dad! It's not about that!" Adrian rose from the floor. "I don't want anyone else to die!"

"Think you that I do?" Xander asked, his eyes locked on Adrian's.

Adrian shook his head. "No."

Xander continued. "Adrian, if we fight with weapons…don't you see, we weaken our defenses. It opens the door for all shifters to attack us with weapons. If they hear about how we defended our territory with firearms, that's what the next challengers will use against us! Our strength doesn't come from a manmade object, but from what we are…who we are. Do you understand? We must keep with tradition, it's the only thing that will give us leverage. It will also prove to other challengers the measure of our power. It will prompt them to think twice before approaching us."

Adrian gazed at his dad, he now understood what his dad was saying. He hadn't thought it was possible for him to feel any more admiration for his father, but he was wrong.

"I understand, Dad." He smiled warmly.

"Good." Xander was proud of his son…he knew that his son would have what it took to run the Pack when the time came.

"Well, I must say that I agree with Xander," Elise said with a charming smile.

Justin and Devin looked toward the bedroom door. "Think they're done?" they asked at the same time.

"I don't hear them moaning anymore," Warren said, shrugging.

"All I know is; it sounded really hot," Carmen added.

"Please." Xander shook his head, holding his hand up to silence the curious shifters.

Devin, Carmen, Warren and Justin nodded, they would spare Xander.

Warren looked at his watch, then walked to the window, parting the curtains ever so slightly. The sky had turned a shade of blue, he could see the sunny horizon approaching. He closed the curtain, looking back at the others.

"Oh yeah, they're done alright. The only ones that might be awake are Darian and Sergio," Warren said.

Elise rose from her chair and walked toward the bedroom. She opened the door slightly, peeking inside. She saw all of the vampires lying on the bed. Darian and Xavier were spooning each other as Darian held him close. Sergio was also asleep, lying on his stomach at the head of the bed. Elise chuckled at the thought of Sergio being put to sleep, sated after a "vampire's kiss." She closed the door, walking back to her chair.

"They were all asleep, including Darian and Sergio." Elise chuckled once more.

"We should pack Sergio an extra pair of pants and underwear," Devin said, genuinely trying to be helpful. Then the deeper meaning of his comment struck him as funny, and he began to laugh out loud, falling over on his side.

The others watched him, some chuckled.

"I'm telling Sergio you said that," Daniel threatened.

"Tell him, I don't care. As I see it, I'm the only one caring about his ego." Devin smiled wickedly.

"Or you could just be making fun of him," Madeleine pointed out as she held her daughter, Mia.

"Nonsense!" Devin threw his hands up into the air, exasperated. "I was honestly trying to be considerate, but when I thought about it...well...I thought it was funny."

"Not that it wasn't true," Miranda stated. "Why don't you go and pack him that change of clothes, Mr. Considerate."

"I'm sure Darian won't mind you borrowing a change of clothes from his wardrobe," Elise suggested.

"Okay." Devin rose from the dining chair and walked into the bedroom where Darian and the others were resting. He approached the bed, looking down at Darian's nakedness. His curiosity was piqued and a wicked thought entered his mind. He ran his fingers along Darian's chest, down to his stomach, stopping himself just before his fingers brushed the master vampire's crotch, thinking it was in poor taste.

"Having fun?" Darian asked softly, startling Devin. He jumped back as if he had been burned, hand over his chest, as if he were having a heart-attack.

"Oh shit!" Devin panted, his heart still racing, pounding fiercely. "You scared the shit out of me!"

"I wasn't expecting to be molested in my sleep." Darian chuckled seductively. "Shouldn't you be fondling John?"

"Well, yeah. Don't tell him, please. I was just curious. I wanted to know what your skin felt like." Devin was embarrassed at having been caught. He had seen Darian in the hangar, and just wanted to touch him while he was naked. As the realization of his act settled on him, he became ashamed.

"Just my skin?"

"Yeah, I wouldn't have dared to go any further! I swear! I respect you, Xavier and Tasha too much to have gone any further!" Devin said in his defense.

Darian watched him for a few seconds. "Don't worry. It's not a big deal. I'm actually flattered and it doesn't change what you feel for John. I won't tell him, although, I don't think he would care if I did."

"I'm sorry," Devin apologized.

"Don't be." Darian smiled as he closed his eyes, returning to his rest.

"Good job, Devin...you and your damned curiosity!" He chastised himself as he returned his attention to the clothes in the closet, grabbing a pair of pants for Sergio to change into. He turned back around, looking at John. He approached him, leaning over, kissed his lover gently on his lips. They were cool, but soft, yielding.

"See you later, baby," Devin whispered, then he left the bedroom.

"In there doing some shit you weren't supposed to be doing, weren't you?" Daniel teased him.

"Yeah, you got busted!" Justin added with a mischievous chuckle.

"Oh, shut up!" Devin spat back as he returned to his seat.

Elise smiled, but said nothing, figuring that Devin had learned his lesson. They waited for Christopher's parents to arrive. Fifteen minutes later, their hotel telephone rang, waking a few of the shifters who had drifted off to sleep. Elise walked over to the telephone, picking it up on the third ring.

"Hello?" she said in greeting.

"Hello. This is the front desk, you have two guests. They said they were here to pick up their son. Shall I send them up?" the female clerk asked. Normally, a hotel guest would have to greet their visitors in the lobby. Since these particular guests were staying with Mr. Alexander, the owner, she allowed for a little extra convenience, and hoped she'd made the right decision.

"Yes, please," Elise instructed, then she hung up the telephone. "Finally, they are here." She walked over to the front door and waited for them to arrive. When she caught the scents of two humans approaching, she opened the door. A man and a woman stood before her. The man's hand was raised as if he was going to knock.

"Please come in," Elise invited, opening the door wider, stepping aside. Both parents entered, they looked around at all of the strange, but lovely faces, not fully understanding what was going on.

The mother decided to ask. She turned to Elise and demanded, "What's going on? Where are my sons?"

"Please stay calm, we're here to help your sons. Here they are." Elise gestured to the chair where Brandon slept and the sofa where Christopher rested. The parents ran toward their children. The father ran over to Brandon, scooping him up into his arms, while the mother rushed to Christopher, kneeling beside him. She touched him gently, but pulled her hand away as she felt the coldness of his flesh. Shocked. She looked at her son closely. Tenderly, she ran her fingertips over the smooth lines of his jaw.

She looked at Elise. "What's wrong with him?"

Elise stepped closer to the mother, who cringed away slightly. "There is nothing wrong with him. Right now, his body is in its resting phase. He'll awaken when the sun has set completely. He is a vampire and during the day, he must rest where the sun can not touch him. Sunlight would kill him."

"Oh! This is ridiculous! I'm taking him home right now!" The mother gestured for her husband to help her lift Christopher's body from the sofa.

Elise placed her hand gently on the woman's shoulder. The woman jerked as if the touch of Elise's hand was scorching hot. "Please listen to me. If you take him home, you'll endanger your entire family. Is that what you want? Right now, he has no idea how to control his urges. He can't be trusted around humans at this point. Please, let us take care of him. We know how to help him."

The mother focused on Elise, believing that she was sincere in her words. She looked sadly at her son. "When can he come home?"

"That, I can not answer. It is all up to your son and how well he can control his hunger. He's a very brave young man and I think he will be alright," Elise said as she glanced between the mother and father.

The mother ran her fingertips along her son's cheek, gently brushing some of his brown curls from his eyes.

"Who would do this to him? He's a wonderful person, smart, friendly...what kind of monster would do this?" The mother fought to control her anger. At this point, she hated all supernaturals for what happened to her son.

"A monster," Elise stated. "I assure you, we had nothing to do with what happened to your son, but we can and will help him."

The mother looked up at Elise, tears in her eyes, sliding down her cheeks. "Can you give me back my beautiful son? The one who had a future?! Who wanted children and a wife?!" There was rage in her voice.

Elise understood her feelings. She tried her best to console his parents. "I can not take away what has happened, no one can. But his life is not over, not by any means. Please, take your youngest home and let us help Christopher," she pleaded softly, her French accent lacing every word, adding a gentleness to her tone.

The mother lowered her head as she cried. The father looked around the room, noticing all of the other shifters, not knowing what they were, or who.

He looked back down at his wife. "Come on, darling. We should go...let these people help Christopher. We don't have a choice. We need to take Brandon home now." Her husband reached out, placing his hand on his wife's shoulder gently. "Come on, darling. Let's go."

His wife kissed her son tenderly on the forehead before reluctantly rising from the floor. She wiped her tears with the back of her hand as she looked at Elise, but said nothing, only turned and left. Her husband turned to Elise before he left.

"Thank you for helping him. We'll be keeping in contact with him and all of you. We love our children and he will always be our son. Please send him home soon." The father did not wait for a response as he closed the door behind himself.

"You handled that very well," Tatiana praised Elise.

"It was still hard to see their faces and tell them that their son was going to have to drink blood for all eternity," Elise said, feeling sorry for his parents and Christopher.

"Well, at least they know that they still have both of their sons," Warren stated. "Some parents aren't so lucky. I see it everyday."

Adrian looked at Warren but said nothing. He only thought about Warren's words.

"Do you think Darian still hunts humans?" Devin asked.

"Yeah, he's pretty old, he might want to cling to the old times a little longer," Justin commented.

"I don't know," Warren said.

"Would you ever arrest him?" Nicole asked. She had fallen asleep and had been awakened by the telephone ringing, along with several other shape-shifters. Now she was intrigued by the question.

"I don't think the S.U.I.T. could, even if they wanted to. But something tells me, if Darian still hunts, we won't have to worry about him or his coven killing innocent people like Christopher," Warren replied.

"I have to agree with you on that," Madeleine stated.

"We need to discuss more important matters," Nagesa interrupted.

"Exactly, the boys' parents have come and gone. Now, we must get going. We have the coffins. Place Darian and his coven in them. Tatiana, darling, have a valet bring our vehicles to the front, we don't want to have to wait otherwise. Elise, we need a rendezvous point for when we arrive in Florida," Xander said. The others began to load the vampires into the coffins.

Elise nodded. "I agree. I know of a place twenty miles from their location and it's outside of their city." She named the location. "I don't think they would be expecting us to be there."

"Excellent," Xander said, nodding.

Adrian looked at his father. "Dad, before you call for the trucks, do you think we should order something before we leave?"

"Are you hungry?" Xander chuckled.

Adrian shrugged one shoulder. "Well, yeah, I'd be lying through my teeth if I said I wasn't. But that's not the only reason I think we should eat. We need to regain our strength. We're going to be meeting them head on. The stronger we are, the better chance we'll have."

Xander nodded. "Indeed. Very well, order something, but let's not waste too much time. We should be leaving within the next two hours. That should give us enough time to order and eat."

Adrian dialed room service and ordered their deluxe breakfast meal for everyone present. It was an expensive dish specially created to satisfy any shifter's immense hunger. "They said it should be here within the hour."

"Good," Xander said.

Everyone had finished loading Darian and his coven into the coffins and were now waiting for room service.

"I'll be happy when all of this is over," Tatiana said. She had settled beside her husband. Her mind was preoccupied with the previous night's events and their upcoming battle. She was nervous, even though she was by Xander's side. She had been witness to and survived only two territorial battles. Those had been easy victories for Xander, on both occasions. Only the Alphas of each Pack had challenged him. Her husband had always arranged his battles so that only he would be challenged, leaving his Pack unharmed. But now, they were all going to be fighting and she feared that many were unprepared for such a confrontation, even herself. She didn't want to let her Pack down and she prayed that she wouldn't.

Xander was silently watching his wife. He knew what she was thinking about. He knew her well enough to recognize the signs that she was in distress. He took her hand into his, squeezing it gently. "Don't worry, darling." It was all that he could say. He couldn't promise them a victory. He couldn't promise that no one else would be harmed or perish in their battle. All he could do was comfort her as best he could.

Tatiana nodded, but remained silent. The entire room was silent as they all reflected on what was going to happen. Before long, their meal arrived via room service. Devin opened the door, allowing the four men to push the food carts inside. Several shifters crowded around the four men and the carts.

Annoyed, Xander spoke up. "For crying out loud! Must you all crowd around the food like a pack of wild animals?" His voice was moderate, but a hint of anger laced his words.

Elise chuckled, he had beat her to it. She was on the verge of reprimanding the younger shifters before he spoke up. She admired him for his take-charge personality. Xander was one of the few Alphas that she could respect for how he protected and cared for his Pack. He was dignified, a true traditionalist, much like herself.

She also respected his wife and Matron, Tatiana. The woman reminded her a lot of herself. Both women carried themselves with such poise and each put their families before all else.

"I'm sorry. I guess, we're just really hungry, Xander," Justin said in their defense.

"I'm not denying that you're hungry, but this is simply ridiculous. At least allow them to place the platters on the table." Xander was calm when he spoke, forcing the others to calm down themselves. The shifters backed away from the carts, allowing the servers to set the plates on the table. Finally, when they were done, they left.

Xander, Tatiana and Elise were the first to prepare their plates then the others followed. They ate quickly, finishing their meals in a matter of minutes. They began to leave, loading the coffins inside the trucks. Elise took the liberty of ordering food for Darian's human servants. Next, she entered Darian's bedroom gathering an outfit for him. Then she entered the bedroom where the humans were sleeping, waking Billy up with a soft nudge on his shoulder. He opened his eyes, immediately sitting up, alert.

"What's wrong?" he asked.

Elise smiled softly. "There isn't anything wrong. I woke you up because we're getting ready to leave. While you were asleep, we found out where our enemy is hiding. We're going there and I need you to watch over our children, along with Gary and Christopher."

Billy's eyebrows creased in confusion before asking, "Who's Christopher?"

"Oh! That's right. A lot has happened while you were sleeping. Christopher was turned earlier tonight by one of our enemies. Darian took him in, so now he's a part of his coven. At least for the time being."

"Oh, I see. Shit, a lot did happen. I wish someone would have woken me up before now."

Elise gently touched his shoulder. "There was nothing you could have done. Besides, we needed you to get enough rest, because we need you alert. I'm leaving my babies here with you. Madeleine's Mia and Tatiana's Mariah are also going to need your care and protection."

Billy nodded then placed his hand over Elise's. "Don't worry. We'll protect them with our lives."

Elise smiled. "I know. That's why I'm trusting you four with this responsibility. Everything you need is here for them."

"When will you all be back?"

"Hopefully, we'll be returning tomorrow night." Elise started heading toward the door.

"And if you don't?" Billy asked, stopping her in her tracks. He was worried.

Elise didn't turn around when she spoke. "Take care of them." With that, she left the hotel room, rejoining the others. She climbed into the truck beside Daniel. Looking in the back seat, she saw Sergio sleeping, head resting in Madeleine's lap.

"Everything okay?" Daniel asked.

Elise nodded. "Let's go."

The huge SUVs sped to their separate private airstrips. When everyone had climbed on board, Elise had Darian and three members of his coven. Xander had the other three, Miko, Annabelle and April. Once they had settled comfortably on the jet, they took off, heading toward Florida.

Daniel looked at Sergio sleeping on the sofa and chuckled. "I've never heard him snore before."

"That's because he's never snored before, not that I can remember," Elise said with a soft chuckle.

"They really did a job on him, knocked him the hell out." Devin laughed as he made himself more comfortable by curling into a ball on the sofa beside Madeleine.

"We have a few hours before we get to Florida, now would be the perfect time for all of us to get some rest," Elise said as she pulled her legs into her chair, tucking her feet between the cushion and armrest. She assumed Xander would be suggesting the same for his own Pack. She was correct. All of the shifters decided sleep was a good idea and did just that as they flew to their destination.

CHAPTER SEVENTEEN

Richard pulled his car into the driveway of Cassandra's huge, luxurious mansion. He climbed out, making his way toward the front door. When he knocked, one of Milan's Pride members answered. Without saying a word to each other, Richard entered the mansion when the other man stepped to the side.

Richard turned toward him. "Reno, where's Katrina?"

"Asleep," Reno answered with a condescending tone. He closed the front door, walking away.

Richard released a long sigh. He wasn't enjoying his current company and was regretting ever agreeing to this invasion. "I didn't ask you what she was doing, I asked you where she was."

Reno turned. "If I'm not mistaken, coyotes have a great sense of smell. Why don't you put it to good use? I'm not a part of your Pack, I don't keep tabs for you." He continued to walk away, leaving the Alpha even more incensed.

Richard used his sense of smell, following Katrina's scent to an upstairs bedroom. On the way there, he ran into Ryan, a bitten member of his Pack, turned only six months ago. She approached him, smiling widely.

"Hey Richard. Glad you're finally back." She wrapped her arms around his strong, muscular shoulders.

He returned her embrace, hugging her tenderly. "How have you been?"

Ryan stepped back, looking up into his brown eyes. "Okay, I guess. I get the feeling that I'm not wanted here by the vamps and the tigers are really getting on my damn nerves. One of them keeps hitting on me and Katrina."

Richard rolled his eyes, annoyed. "I've been wondering if I made a mistake by teaming up with these...," His voice trailed off. He began to walk past Ryan, but she reached out, taking hold of his arm. He looked at her. "Yes, Ryan?"

"It wasn't just your decision. Katrina was pushing for this more than anyone. Besides, Chicago is prime territory, you said it yourself. Definitely worth fighting for."

"We haven't actually begun fighting for it yet. All of these unscrupulous tactics are leaving a foul taste in my mouth."

"Oh, I know. If you had it your way, we would have rung their doorbells and told them to come out for that ass whoopin." She giggled.

Richard smiled, caressing her face lightly. "I don't think I would have put it so bluntly. But yes, a more direct, honorable approach would have been much more to my liking."

"Hey, don't fret. If what I hear about them is true, then maybe it's best that we did approach this challenge like this," Ryan said, hoping to comfort him.

"If we didn't think we could beat them, Ryan, we should not have bothered." Richard pulled his hand away. "Listen, I need to speak with Katrina."

"Okay, she's in there." Ryan pointed to a door down the hallway. "I'm going to get a few hours sleep as well. If you want, you can join me," she offered imploringly.

"No, Ryan, I don't think that I will be joining you. But I do want you to get some sleep. Rest easy." He walked away without waiting for a response from her. He was one Pack Alpha who avoided sexual relations with his members as much as possible. He believed that sexual interaction with his Pack would only complicate their lives. In the past, when he had engaged in sex with his members, jealousies had arisen and fights had broken out. He would not abide that amount of jealousy and dissension within his Pack, not ever again.

Disappointed, Ryan nodded, then turned, heading toward her bedroom without saying another word. She had hoped that since Richard had not taken Katrina as his mate, but only his Matron, that she would have a chance at becoming his lover. She wanted to tell him that she loved him, that she would be his perfect mate. At first, she thought because she was bitten and not a natural born, that she would never have a chance to be by his side, never be a Matron. However, Richard had deviated from that tradition. She knew it was because he and Katrina didn't really make good lovers, and lately, it seemed they were barely getting along. Shot down this time, she wouldn't give up on him.

Richard turned back and watched her walk away, then he went to Katrina, entering her bedroom, switching on the lights. "I need to discuss something with you."

"What do you want, Richard? You interrupted a very good dream," Katrina complained as she turned toward him, shielding her eyes from the bright light.

He sat on the edge of the bed. "I think we should pull out of this arrangement. I sense something isn't right."

Ignoring him, she attempted to change the subject. "It's eight o'clock in the morning! I just went to bed about thirty minutes ago."

"Katrina," Richard paused, hoping to get her undivided attention. She looked at him. "I don't think we can trust Cassandra, not that I really did in the first place."

"What are you saying? Why do you feel as though we can't?" she asked, trying to ascertain whether he had discovered anything detrimental to her and Cassandra's plans.

"I don't know." He turned, sitting on the edge of her bed, elbows resting on his knees, hands clasped together. "There's too much animosity between us. It doesn't feel like a unit, or even that we're working together. We've been at odds from the beginning. I'm just wondering what our standing will be once this is over."

"Is that the only thing that's bothering you?" Katrina asked, with a chuckle.

He turned toward her. "Don't make light of this. My gut is telling me we can't trust them."

"Richard, I think you're seeing problems where there aren't any. So we don't get along. That's nothing noteworthy. We're just a group of people that gathered together for one purpose only. Once we get what we want, we can all go our separate ways. I've told you this. It's what we've agreed upon, remember?" Katrina sat up, looking directly at him.

He nodded. "I know our arrangement, but-"

"Listen, don't flake on us now. We need you. You help us get this territory, and you can go on your way. That was the deal."

"I just want to make certain that I'm not leading my Pack into danger."

"Nonsense. I can take care of the Pack and I'll find another Alpha who will help me control it. You can be free."

She leaned forward, placing her hand on the side of his face. "Isn't that what you wanted?"

"I don't want to leave you in a worse predicament. I tell you, Katrina. I don't trust Cassandra, or the others for that matter. Everything that's happened has been orchestrated by her. The humans, us being a part of turning that young girl, all of it is what she wants! We were not asked our input, or opinions. We were only told that everything was in order. Why did she not incorporate us?" Richard rose from the bed, arms folded across his chest. The more he thought about everything that had happened, the more he wanted to leave.

"She needed help taking over Chicago. For that reason alone, she sought us out. We made a deal and things are going as originally planned. Why are you bringing all of this up now? We have them right where we want them!"

"Do you honestly believe that she will share the territory with you? Who'd really want to share a territory with two bickering supernatural groups?" he asked, hoping to make Katrina really think of the possibility of a betrayal.

"I trust her, Richard. She's a master strategist, but I believe she will keep to her word. I'll say it again, you're thinking too much about what's not there. You're making me nervous. Listen to me, we've made an investment in this plan. It's already underway and moving along smoothly, let's see it through. Stop being so paranoid." She lay back down on the bed.

"I'm not being paranoid, Katrina. Something just does not feel right to me." Richard studied her, not understanding why she was so trusting of their companions. He didn't know quite what to make of it.

"Well, it's too late to turn back now with a clear conscience. We've laid the tracks along with everyone else and I'm not going back to Kansas, ever!" She turned over on her side, her bare back facing him. "Now could you please turn off the lights and let me sleep."

Richard watched her for a few more seconds, then he left, turning off the lights before closing the door. He walked around the mansion, which was for the most part, quiet. Only a few shifters and human servants were awake and walking around doing various activities. His stomach began to growl and he made his way to the kitchen to make himself something to eat.

He decided upon three cheese steak sandwiches loaded with all of his favorite toppings. As he sat and ate, he just couldn't shake his growing suspicions. He wanted the Chicago territory for his Pack. He also wanted to live there in peace. In the very beginning, he had urged them to issue a *Challenge of Authority*, facing their enemy in a designated location where they could do battle without prying eyes. Katrina had convinced him that Darian would kill their Pack if they attempted the "Traditional" approach. Unknown to him, Katrina, Cassandra and Milan had made arrangements for one of the Pride to be the liaison between them and the human rebel group for their primary attack. Upon finding out, Richard was vehemently against it, but the others insisted that it was the "only way to go". They used convincing words such as; "necessary and essential" even going as far to say, "vital". Richard had given in, but he insisted on monitoring the proceedings, making sure no harm ever came to the three humans they had in their possession.

He had chastised Ignacio for injuring Matthew. Ignacio had insisted that his actions were just. He claimed that Matthew had attacked him, firing his automatic at him loaded with the specially manufactured silver-nitrate bullets. He assured Richard that he only "punched him, no bones were broken, no stitches needed."

Still, Richard didn't think it was necessary for a shape-shifter to strike a human when they could be so easily overpowered. The more he learned of his new companions, the less he wanted to share territory with them. He thought his feelings were most likely mutual across the board. Would Chicago become a battlefield of a warring Pack, Pride and coven? He didn't know and the possibility haunted him. He finished his sandwich, looking up in time to see Ignacio walking past the doorway. He called to him. The coyote entered the kitchen, eyes peering into Richard's now empty plate.

"Steak, cheese, peppers, that's what I call good eating," Ignacio said as he walked toward the refrigerator.

Richard chuckled. "Hungry?"

"Always."

"Help yourself, there's plenty."

"Oh, I will." Ignacio pulled several items from the refrigerator and began making himself something to eat. He sat down at the counter opposite Richard.

"Listen, about yesterday...I'm sorry. You were right, I shouldn't have hit him. He just, well, he kind of pissed me off when he shot at me like that," Ignacio confessed as he took another bite of his sandwich.

Richard chuckled once more. "You were kidnapping him, what did you expect? For him to go with you quietly and peacefully? He's S.U.I.T. for crying out loud!" He began to laugh softly at the absurdity of it all.

"I see your point, Rich, you don't need to rub it in. I feel kind of childish about it already. My manhood...is a little bruised."

"I'm sure your shape-shifter pride has something to do with it as well."

"Okay, you've got me there, too." Ignacio finished off his meal, licking and sucking his fingers clean of all the mixed juices. "Hey, by the way, what did you want to talk to me about? Why did you call me in here?"

Richard studied him for a few seconds, making the other man nervous.

"What? Come on, Rich, what?"

"Nothing...nothing, don't worry." Richard decided not to bring up his concerns to him. He was going to ask him if he was getting the same uneasy feeling he had, but thought it would reflect negatively on him. He was their Alpha, their leader, they would follow him. He thought it best to withhold judgment until the smoke had cleared.

"Are you sure?" Ignacio asked, concerned.

"Yes. Go ahead, relax." Richard rose from the stool, turned and walked toward the doorway. He paused. "I'm going to take a nap. I want you to call the hotel. Check on Scott, see how Crystal is doing and let me know when I wake up. Also, see if you can contact Eric, I've been trying to get in contact with him all day."

"I thought he was with Scott?"

"Scott said he'd left, I think his exact words were 'to get laid'. I'm just concerned, so let me know if he made it back to the hotel."

"Sure thing." As Ignacio watched Richard walk away, he felt his hunger still and decided to make something else to eat.

***

Richard entered the bedroom he shared with Katrina. She woke up when she felt the bed give under his weight. "What now?" she asked in a slightly irritated tone.

"Nothing, go back to sleep." He was becoming increasingly annoyed with her as of late. He didn't appreciate the manner in which she spoke to him or how she'd been treating him. However, it wasn't just Katrina whose behavior had changed. He was noticing several of his members growing ever more belligerent. He didn't like it, but he suspected it might have been brought on by the stress of their current situation. He decided to ignore her attitude as he climbed under the soft covers. He allowed his body to relax, his eyes closed and he felt a deep sleep come over him.

Richard had no idea how long he had been asleep when he felt someone shaking him awake. He knew it was Ignacio even before he opened his eyes and saw him. "What is it, Ignacio?" he asked in a groggy voice.

"Rich, I've been calling the hotel phone, cell phones and I'm still not getting any answer," Ignacio said, there was a definite nervous tone in his voice.

"What time is it?" Richard asked.

"Nine-thirty."

"They're probably asleep. Jaric is resting for sure," Katrina said, then she closed her eyes.

Ignacio looked at her. "They should have woken up instantly when the damn phones rang. I don't care how sleepy they are!" He looked back at Richard, who was now sitting up in the bed, thinking.

Richard picked up the telephone that was sitting on the nightstand. He called the hotel's front desk and waited for an answer.

"Good morning, *West Montecore Hotel*, how can I help you?" The male clerk made the greeting in a pleasant sounding voice.

"Good morning. I'm trying to reach the party that is staying in room thirty-two fifty-eight," Richard said, using his smoothest, friendliest voice.

"One moment, sir. May I put you on hold?"

"Yes." Richard was very concerned. He expected the clerk to simply transfer his call to their room.

Because he was put on hold instead, it left him with a sense that something had happened to them. A few minutes later, the hotel manager picked up the telephone. He asked him if he was still there and Richard replied.

"I'm sorry, and I regret that I have to inform you that the guests who were staying in that room had an unfortunate incident earlier this morning. I think it's best that you contact the Illinois S.U.I.T. division."

"What happened?" Richard asked.

"I'm sorry, Sir, but I'm not at liberty to divulge any more information. Please contact the S.U.I.T."

Richard was silent for a few seconds as he contemplated the situation. "Thank you." He ended his phone call.

Katrina had risen while he was speaking with the hotel manager. She was now more alert than ever before. "I suppose they were discovered."

"It would seem as though they have been," Richard said, running his finger along the width of his bottom lip.

"But isn't Jaric with them? He should have been able to protect them," Ignacio said.

"He has no allegiance to my people or Milan's. If something happened, who's to say he didn't think only of himself?" Richard stated.

"I see your point. Besides, we still don't know the measure of their combined strength," Ignacio said.

"But with the vampires dead, would the other shifters be able to defeat him otherwise?" Katrina asked. "He's a very powerful vampire."

"I can't answer that. I don't know. All I do know is that no one can be reached at this time. If it happened before dawn, you'd think Jaric would call here simply to report the incident," Richard said, slightly irritated.

"Can't we just call the S.U.I.T.?" Ignacio asked.

"I don't think that's a wise idea. If we inquire about the occupants of that particular hotel room, we'd automatically be placed on their radar. They have systems that could track us down, and we'd immediately be brought in for questioning at the very least via the S.U.I.T. division here in Florida," Richard replied.

Katrina snorted. "I doubt they are that advanced."

"They are. The S.U.I.T. is not to be underestimated. Do you honestly believe that their officers consist solely of humans? I hope you are not that naïve," Richard retorted. Katrina rolled her eyes, but remained silent. When he had first chosen her as his Matron, he had hoped that one day, they'd fall in love. But something always held him back. Now he was beginning to see what that "something" was. He was relieved that he hadn't committed himself to her in that fashion because of it. One of the reasons why he was leaving this Pack was because the two of them didn't get along, and his Pack had taken quite a liking to her, more so in the past months. The other reason was, he was just tired of it all and wanted peace.

"What do you want me to do?" Ignacio asked, getting back on track.

Richard looked at him. "Wait a few hours, then try to contact them again. If you still can't reach them, we are going to have to wait to see if Cassandra can connect with Jaric."

"Okay." Ignacio left the room, leaving the two of them alone.

"They're probably dead," Katrina said softly, feigning concern.

"We will know for sure soon enough," Richard said as he lay back on the bed. He closed his eyes, forcing his worry for his Pack from his mind so that he could rest. If something did happened, he wanted to be in his best mental and physical state so that he could deal with it accordingly.

CHAPTER EIGHTEEN

Justin rolled over on top of Warren, his foot hitting him in the stomach, waking him up. He grunted and pushed Justin off of him, agitated. Xander chuckled as he watched them. Justin woke up when Warren shoved him.

"Dang, Warren! You could have woke me up and told me to get off of you," Justin said as he readjusted himself on the sofa.

"You kicked me in the stomach! Sorry if I was too busy gasping for air to take your feelings into consideration," Warren retorted, rolling his eyes.

"I kicked you in the stomach?"

"Yeah!"

"Oh," Justin lay back down on the sofa.

"Is that all you're going to say to me?" Warren asked, lifting one of Justin's eyelids up, opening one eye.

"Yep, " Justin replied with a chuckle. "Now let go of my eyelid."

"You're hopeless." Warren left him alone.

"The two of you might as well be siblings," Xander said, smiling in his own charming way. His smile was one of his best physical features.

"I think he has more in common with Devin than me," Warren said.

Justin opened his eyes at the mention of Devin's name. "Yeah, I can see why you said that. Sergio is always saying how we're like twins or something."

"Yes, I'd have to agree with him, it's almost uncanny," Tatiana chuckled.

"I love Devin like a brother. I'm sure he feels the same way about me," Justin said, smiling.

"Well, you've spent so much time together, your feelings for him aren't unusual," Xander commented on the two men's relationship.

Justin nodded, then he looked at his watch. "Either the plane is flying very smoothly, or we're in Florida already."

"We landed about forty minutes ago. I woke up earlier, but decided to let the rest of you sleep," Nagesa said. "We have about four hours until nightfall, you should get some more rest."

"Why don't we attack when their vampires are still resting?" Justin asked.

Xander smiled at him. One thing he recognized in both Devin and Justin was their almost childlike innocence. He found it rather refreshing. It proved that they still had so much more to learn about the world and that they harbored a thirst for knowledge.

"I don't think that would be wise. We need Darian and his coven more than ever. Not only are we outnumbered, but several members of their parties are stronger than both of ours," Xander said. "You should really get some more rest, there is nothing that we can do until nightfall."

Justin nodded, reflecting on what his Alpha said. It frightened him that he might be facing his own death in a few short hours. Being a Natural Born, he knew that his life would include territory battles and everything else he'd experienced up until that point. Belonging to an honorable and powerful Pack, he felt honor-bound to fight, but that didn't stop him from being scared out of his mind. He decided to take Xander's advice and get some more rest. He lay back down, using Warren's back as a pillow. The older shifter looked at his younger Pack brother, but said nothing, only smiled. Warren could smell Justin's fear, almost all of them had that same scent with the exception of Nagesa. He looked at him sitting in a chair by the window, composed, his expression serene as he watched the clouds float by. Warren wondered what he was thinking. He didn't bother to ask him. Instead, he decided to go back to sleep, regain his strength.

Tatiana woke up again an hour later, she raised her head from her husband's lap. She looked at him. "Hello sweetheart."

Xander smiled. "Hello darling, sleep well?"

She nodded as sat up, kissing him tenderly on the lips. "My, I had no idea how tired I was until now." She stretched her muscles.

Xander watched his wife, never taking his eyes away from her. He loved her with all that he was and then some. She was his soulmate in every sense of the word. They shared everything and were extremely happy together. Now, looking at her, he knew she was scared, but he also knew she'd never show it. She'd stand by his side until the very end.

Tatiana's eyes were locked to her husband's, she smiled. "Xander?"

"Yes, darling?"

"What are your ideas for our attack?"

"I believe our best approach would be to flank them, to surround them. But not at the same time. We should present the first offensive. Once we've engaged them in a battle, the rest of our team should converge on them from behind."

"I think that is a wonderful plan, but I expected no less."

Tatiana slid off the sofa, looking around the plane. Only Nagesa was still awake, but he paid them no mind.

She looked at the others, sleeping so peacefully and wondered if they truly understood what awaited them.

Xander rose from the sofa, stepping behind her, slipping his arms around her waist.

"What's the matter, Tat?" He kissed her temple softly, then her cheek.

"Whatever happens, I want you to know that I love you," she said.

"I know, I love you, too." He turned her around in his arms, then leaning forward, kissed her passionately.

Afterward, Tatiana pulled back, smiling mischievously at him. "Follow me," she said as she led the way toward the jet's bathroom.

"What is it?" Xander asked. After the words left his mouth, he knew his answer. He could smell the sexual scent rising from her body in waves. It washed over him, her arousal, immediately driving him crazy with lust. She was irresistible!

Tatiana led him into the bathroom, locking the door behind them. She turned around, wrapping her arms around his neck, kissing him passionately. "We have to be quiet," she whispered after she broke the kiss.

Xander chuckled seductively. "I can not make any promises." He smiled wolfishly as he began to unbutton her blouse, revealing her purple lace and satin bra. He pressed his lips against hers once again as he continued to undress her. He removed both her shirt and bra, letting the clothing fall to the floor. Tatiana ripped open his shirt pulling it off his shoulders hastily. Xander didn't care, he crushed her to him, his mouth exploring her flesh, tongue seeking her nipples. Her hands caressed his muscular back, fingers running over the smoothness of his skin. She traveled further, coming around, fingers undoing his belt buckle, button and zipper of his pants. Xander removed her jeans while she helped him by stepping out of them. His hands slid behind her, caressing her buttocks, lifting her with ease, pressing her back against the wall. She wrapped her legs tightly around his waist as he freed himself.

"I love you!" Tatiana panted breathlessly. Xander kissed her as he slid inside of her. She shook with passion as he began thrusting in and out in one smooth rhythm. His skillful mouth suckled her neck, moving lower to her breasts, he teased her nipple with gentle flicks of his tongue causing her to gasp. He continued teasing her until she begged him to go further. He smiled, then covered her nipple. The wetness and heat of his mouth, sucking and stroking the sensitive flesh, sent tingles throughout her limbs. He pushed deeply into her, matching his thrust with hers until she cried out. Her body jerked uncontrollably as a powerful orgasm rushed through her body like a tidal wave.

Xander rode her faster, harder as she clung to him. It pleased him that he could make her feel that way, him and only him. They belonged to each other, this was their moment. As he continued, he began to feel his own orgasm building deep within his groin. He felt it growing more powerful with every thrust, causing his knees nearly buckling. He placed a hand against the wall for balance. Soft, husky moans began to seep from his throat as he quickened his pace. Tatiana smiled as she sensed his climax approaching. She constricted her muscles, caressing him all the more. He threw his head back, moaning loudly, unable to contain his pleasure any longer. Tatiana chuckled lustfully as she took hold of his head, burying his face into her neck, muffling him. A low guttural moan emanated from him as the last waves of pleasure flowed through him causing his body to jerk uncontrollably. She ran her hands through his long silky hair, fingers entangling in his locks.

He collapsed against her, falling to his knees, sated, but unwilling to pull himself away from her. They stayed there for several minutes in each other's arms. After a while, Xander lifted his head, he kissed her passionately. Once they broke the kiss, the two simply stared into each other's eyes, never saying a word. Their love was unconditional.

He would gladly die to protect her, his wife, mother of his children, Matron of his Pack. He prayed that he would be able to hold her in his arms again.

"I love you," Xander whispered once again.

She giggled delightedly, so happy to be there with him. There was a sudden knock on the door. They looked at it, each chuckling.

"One minute," Tatiana called out. They quickly washed up, then dressed. Xander tried his best to look presentable in spite of his torn shirt. They stepped out of the bathroom, looking around at the others. All of the shifters were awake, many looked away, some smiling knowingly.

"There's nothing to see here," Xander stated with a smirk.

"Seeing is the last thing I'd want to do. Hearing it was bad enough. I think my young impressionable mind is just scarred for life," Adrian said, teasing his parents.

"Oh, you should be one to talk," Warren ribbed Adrian, who turned to face him. "Only reason why you and Nicole aren't trying to sneak in a quickie is because they beat you to it." He pointed at Xander and Tatiana.

Adrian rolled his eyes playfully. "Yeah, now the bathroom is contaminated."

"Oh hush, boy!" Tatiana said as she walked past him, smacking him playfully on his muscular biceps on her way to the galley.

Nicole watched Tatiana walk toward the galley. She rose from her chair to follow. "Yep, that's a good idea, cause I'm so hungry right now." She followed her Matron to help prepare what might turn out to be their last meal.

Xander settled comfortably on the sofa once again. He looked over at Justin who was smiling at him mischievously.

"Whatever is it that you want to say – don't."

"What? I wasn't going to say anything, honestly," Justin said, still smiling.

"Good, keep it that way," Xander said, then he leaned his head back against the pillows. His eyes panned over to Nagesa who was in the same position he was before. He didn't say anything to him, letting him deal with their situation in his own way. He closed his eyes, feeling more relaxed.

Adrian sat beside his father, causing the other man to open his eyes. "Dad, all jokes aside, I want to ask you a question."

"Ask," Xander said, turning toward his son.

"Do you think our chances are good?" Adrian asked, gaining the attention of the other shifters in the room.

They looked at the two men, many were surprised that he asked the question, but it was one that they were all thinking. Even Nagesa turned toward Xander, awaiting his answer.

Xander didn't answer his son right away. He thought about what he knew of their opposition's strengths and weaknesses, then he answered. "Yes, I do."

Warren sat up straight in the chair he was lounging in. "Well, I know it's not because good must triumph over evil."

Xander chuckled, shaking his head. "No. History has proven that ideology to be less than true. Although it is most unfortunate, but bad things do happen to good people, while good things happen to bad people. We must make our own fate in this world. It's because we work as a team, we care about each other, we have integrity and loyalty that we have a chance to survive this battle. I sense fear in all of you. This is perfectly normal. But understand and believe in this: We face our enemies with something they do not have...and that is courage."

Xander's speech had done what he hoped it would do. It was rousing pride and hope. He could plainly see their worried expressions transform into that of determination. He was willing to bet that Elise was most likely making a similar speech to her Pride as well. Fifteen minutes passed before they could all smell the delicious aromas of their meal cooking. They all loved Tatiana's cooking and they were most certainly anticipating it.

After an hour and a half, Tatiana announced that their food was ready. She, along with two other shifters, covered the table with numerous platters loaded with everyone's favorite dishes. In an orderly fashion, they made their plates and ate greedily.

"That was sooo good! Who made the mac and cheese?" Justin asked, scraping the last of the cheese from his plate.

Nicole giggled. "I did."

Justin smiled, pointing at her. "You've got a gift, lady."

"Wait till you taste her ribs!" Adrian boasted, thinking about this girlfriend's signature dishes.

"I'm there!" Justin exclaimed, giving Nicole a "thumbs up".

Xander chuckled as he listened to the numerous conversations that the others shared. The topics were ranging from their favorite current movies, actors, and games to music. He thought it was a good idea to have lighthearted conversations. It was taking away some of the anxiety they were all feeling. After a while, they all heard a knocking on the airplane door. Xander rose, heading toward the door. When he opened it, Elise stood there.

"It's almost time," she said, motioning to the setting sun.

Xander nodded. "Why don't you bring your people here so that we can go over our final preparations."

Elise nodded and left, returning minutes later with her entire Pride and the three coffins with Darian, Xavier, Tony and John inside. They set the coffins down next to the other three and settled wherever they could find comfort.

"What did you do over there?" Justin asked Devin.

"Of course, we slept and ate all day, as we cats like to do," Devin replied, jokingly. He walked over to the dining table and saw all of the empty platters. He could still smell the mouthwatering aromas in the air. "Damn, what did ya'll eat over here?"

Justin bragged about their meal.

Sergio snorted. "Is it that serious?"

Justin looked at him. "Yeah, to me it is. So what did you eat?"

"Food," Sergio replied dryly. A few of the shifters chuckled.

Devin decided to brag for his Pride. "We had a smorgasbord of food, from Carmen's exquisite Spanish dishes to Miranda's Mac n' Cheese."

"I wish you two would shut the hell up talking about food and shit!" Sergio said, lounging even deeper into the chair.

"I wasn't talking about shit," Devin joked.

"Disgusting," Justin commented, chuckling.

"But you were going on and on about food," Carmen said.

Devin shrugged.

"Discussions about food making you hungry again, Sergio?" Elise asked.

"Yeah, you could say that." He gave her a soft smile. His mind wandered to the upcoming battle. He was relieved that they had been able to get the information they had needed to get to the point where they were. Like everyone else on the plane, he was hoping he survived, at least long enough to save his son. The other shifters continued to converse amongst themselves as they waited for the sun to set. Once the sun began to sink beyond the horizon, they knew the moment had come. A few minutes later, Darian's coffin opened and he climbed out of it. As he looked around at the others, it didn't take long for him to realize that he was naked...again.

Elise approached him. "Hello, Darian."

"Hello Elise. Is everyone alright?" he asked, looking at the others. Everyone answered him in their own way. Some only nodded while others were more vocal.

"I took the liberty of bringing you something to wear. Do you need to feed?" Elise asked.

"We know that we don't have much time to spare, but we're prepared to feed you and your coven," Xander offered.

Before Darian could respond, Justin jumped up from his seated position, beating Devin who was still trying to untangle his legs. He sprinted up to Darian, smiling.

"You can bite me," he said, baring his neck.

"Thank you." Darian gave him his most charming smile, then he leaned forward, toward the bared flesh. His razor-sharps fangs extended and he drove them swiftly into Justin's artery, causing the shifter to gasp, back arching from the momentary pain. Once he began to feed, the pain Justin was feeling melted into the most exquisite pleasure he'd ever felt. He gripped Darian, pulling him closer, his fingers gripping handfuls of Darian's hair, pressing his face hard to the wound as if he could increase the pleasure by such a simple act. Darian wrapped his arms around Justin, adjusting the angle of his head so that he could bring more blood into his mouth. Soon, their pleasure grew more intense, they felt it, a mingling of preternatural auras coiling within them. Both men began to moan in ecstasy, Justin louder than Darian. A second later, the pleasure erupted, filling them completely as it washed over them. Spasms ran through their bodies as they rode the final waves until Darian withdrew. Justin's grip tightened as he struggled to keep Darian close to him, his hand pressed on Darian's head, trying to force it back toward his throat.

Darian chuckled lightly, vibrations flowing off of the surface of Justin's skin, tickling him, arousing him. "Get a hold of yourself,

Justin. It's done." He released the young wolf, pulling away even as Justin struggled to keep them together.

Finally, Justin relented, stepping back. "That was unbelievable," he panted. "Can we do it again some other time?"

"Perhaps," Darian flashed him a dimpled smile.

"I feel like I can take another nap," Justin admitted softly as he sat down, regaining his strength.

"Weakling, amateur," Devin taunted. "I did both him and his master before I passed out."

"Back to more important matters," Elise said, giving both men scolding looks. They understood, lowering their heads. She returned her attention to Darian. "We should be leaving now. As your other members awaken, we'll feed them along the way."

"My, my, you've all thought of everything," Darian complimented.

"Ah, let me fill you in on what we think is a feasible attack plan." Xander began to tell Darian about their strategy to approach their enemy from two positions.

"Good idea, come...let's go," Darian said.

"Umm, Darian...don't you think you should get dressed?" Sergio said, pointing at his body.

Darian looked down. "I almost don't care, but I suppose you're right."

"Here." Elise handed him the fresh change of clothes and he dressed quickly. They removed the resting vampires from their coffins, wrapping them in blankets to protect them from the soft rays of the setting sun and carried them to the SUVs they had arranged for, storing them in the cargo area with the tinted windows. As they drove toward Cassandra's mansion, the other vampires began to rise. The shifters greeted them with bared throats and wrists. They knew that time was of the essence and they were only a short distance away from their destination. Darian watched intently as Xavier fed from Devin. He drank deeply as the young leopard moaned. Both shared a powerful orgasm as did the others who were donating and feeding. When the feeding had ended, Xavier had climbed from the cargo area into a space beside Darian in the back seat.

Xavier leaned over toward Darian's ear. "You're worried that she and the others will flee before we get there, aren't you?" he asked, wondering why they didn't want to wait until they had all risen to feed while still on the airplane.

"It took us a long time to get this far. I don't want to take any chances that would allow them to slip past us," Darian replied.

Xander tossed them both a glance. "Not only that. We wanted to get there before she and her coven had a chance to feed. Chances are they might not be at their full strength."

"Yeah, I doubt if these other shifters are as generous as we are," Devin stated.

"They might be weaker having not fed. Unfortunately, some are strong enough to not feel their hunger as intensely as say... John, Tony, and Annabelle do at first rise. That means the stronger vampires don't need to feed immediately," Darian said, darting glances between John, Xavier and Tony.

John looked at his hands, astounded. "Wow, I feel so much more stronger than before!"

"That's good, we're going to need every ounce of that power," Xavier said as he flexed his own muscles.

John looked at Darian. "Thank you, Master."

"You're welcome. I just wanted to give you all a fighting chance," Darian said, then he looked out of the window, watching the city pass by in a blur.

CHAPTER NINETEEN

Richard stood in the doorway, leaning against the frame with both arms folded across his chest. He watched Cassandra and Milan argue. Milan wanted to flee to another safe house, Cassandra wanted revenge. It began the moment she woke up. She was enraged by the loss of her lover and Second-in-Command, Jaric. She knew that Darian and his coven were still alive and that her initial plan had failed. Richard himself was sickened to discover that Scott had died and he was still unable to reach Eric. Julian and Cory had returned once they realized what had taken place at the hotel. Neither knew how it had happened, although they were relieved that they'd left before the hotel was attacked. Scott's death had been the Pack's first casualty and Richard was beginning to wonder if such a loss was worth it for all that he was experiencing. The other thing that bothered him was how Elizabeth, Jaric, and Scott had been killed. He knew how powerful the three were and apparently, they hadn't had a chance. He was growing more intrigued by each passing minute as he watch the two women argue.

"We don't know where they are or what they're doing right now! You said that Darian is still alive, your plan failed!" Milan yelled, enraged.

"Don't you mean our plan, Milan?" Cassandra looked at the other woman accusingly.

"Leaving the vampires to the humans was your idea, darling. I told you to let my Pride handle the heavy lifting!" Milan's tone was bitter and sarcastic. "But noooo, you wanted to use those pathetic humans which is most likely the reason they know about us now!" She brushed a lock of her black, bone-straight hair from her almond-shaped light brown eyes. A mixture of Asian and Egyptian blood gifted her with beautifully delicate, petite and exotic features.

Cassandra smiled wickedly. "We stay!" she declared, not caring that her female cohort was frightened.

"Didn't you say that Darian is our biggest threat?! That means he and only he alone could have killed Jaric!" Milan tried to reason with her.

"And that's why I will make him pay for every drop of blood he spilt last night that belonged to me." Cassandra's blue eyes bored into the light brown of Milan's. The women gave each other venomous glares, each wanting their own way.

"Cassandra, listen to me. Darian must have read Jaric's mind. He knows our plans! We should take some time to regroup," Milan suggested, hoping she was getting through to the other woman.

Richard laughed. "Don't you mean run?"

Milan whipped around to face him. "Prepare!" she said the word as if it were poison she spat out to harm him.

"This entire predicament is preposterous. We should have issued a *Challenge of Authority* from the very beginning. All of this sneaking around and deceit is demeaning." Richard approached the two women. "In fact, the only logical reason I can ascertain for it is fear. You fear Darian for some reason."

Before Richard could move to defend himself, Cassandra had him by the throat, slamming him hard against the wall, pinning him there. "Don't presume to understand me, dog!"

Richard grimaced as he struggled for air. "Take your hands off me, corpse!" he spat back with as much malice as he could muster under the circumstances.

"I should kill you where you stand!"

"But you won't. Now let me go!"

Cassandra looked at him, her luscious full lips turned up in a sneer. She released him a second later. "I do not 'fear' this vampire." She turned toward Milan. "You may leave whenever you want. That territory will be mine before it's over!"

Richard watched Cassandra, not trusting her one bit. He turned toward Katrina when she entered the room.

"I take it there's been a change in plans?" she asked, looking at the others.

Before anyone could answer her, Cassandra held up her hand, silencing the room. "I do believe they are here," she announced.

"Great! Just great! This was supposed to be an easy takeover!" Milan complained through gritted teeth.

"Nothing worth obtaining is ever easy," Richard remarked, leaving the room heading toward the front door.

Milan and Katrina followed him.

"Where are you going?" Katrina asked.

"I'm going to introduce myself to our company." Richard unlocked the front door, opening it wide. He saw two Sidewinder SUVs pulling up onto the manicured lawn, crushing a beautiful bed of multicolored, exotic flowers.

He chuckled as he thought about how upset Cassandra would be when she saw her lovely flowers flattened under the rubber wheels of the behemoth vehicles. Richard walked down the steps followed by Ryan and Ignacio. The others stood in the doorway, waiting for the perfect moment to attack. Cassandra stepped out onto the third-story balcony of her master bedroom, giving herself a birds-eye view of the impending battle.

Cassandra stared intently as she watched Darian and several others emerge from the trucks. They were correct about one thing, her vampires hadn't had a chance to feed. Darian studied the other supernaturals, especially the three who confronted them first. Then his gaze traveled upward, to Cassandra, whose own gaze was locked on him.

"Welcome to my home. Have you come to pay me *Homage?* Or perhaps to give up your territory before we kill you?" Cassandra smiled evilly.

Darian chuckled. "Nothing of the sort. You've caused us a great deal of inconvenience…" He shook his head, "…and that just doesn't sit well with us." He made certain to match his own arrogance with hers. Elise stood beside him, silently observing their enemy.

Cassandra mentally calculated the total amount of supernaturals she saw before her. With the information she'd had from the beginning, she knew that some were not accounted for. This was good news. She didn't see Xander and only five members of his Pack were present. She also noted six members of Elise's Pride and four members of Darian's coven. Smiling inwardly, she thought the others had been slain in their numerous attacks. It pleased her to know that her camp greatly outnumbered her adversary's.

"So, I can assume that you've come here to challenge me?" Cassandra asked.

"Not to challenge, but to defend what is rightfully ours," Darian stated with conviction.

"Ah, and destroying my lovely flowers...what purpose did that serve?" she asked, leaning over the railing to gain a better view.

"Oh this?," Darian pointed to her crushed flowers. "That was just for fun." He smiled devilishly.

Cassandra's smile faded, her boasting ceased. This vampire enraged her. She couldn't feel his aura and that bothered her. She did not know how old he was and his aura would have been able to give her an idea. Looking at him, she did have to admit to herself, the rumors of his beauty did not do him justice. Nevertheless, he was still her enemy, and she would rip those stunning forest-green eyes from their very sockets when the moment presented itself. Darian and his comrades possessed something she wanted...their land.

Richard watched Darian and Elise, the two leaders of their groups. He was impressed with their straightforward approach. They had integrity and courage. It was more than he could say for his companions. "I see no need for this conversation. You came to defend, we are all here to challenge, let us begin our battle," he said, officially issuing a *Challenge of Authority.*

"We accept," Elise agreed, intrigued that one of their members opted for a traditional challenge.

"Excellent." Richard didn't wait for a response before attacking. He charged Elise, but ended up striking Sergio who had stepped in front, protecting her. The other shifters followed Richard's lead, attacking their enemy with brute strength and speed. Cassandra watched from above, biding her time. She'd mentally contacted her coven, ordering them to wait until she gave permission to attack. Ryan snuck up behind John while he was engaged in a power struggle with Ignacio. She was unable to change forms, but she still had supernatural abilities; speed, strength and agility. She kicked him, her foot making contact with his left temple, startling him.

Ignacio used that split second to push John to his knees, but April came up behind him, kicking Ignacio hard in the groin, bringing him down to his knees. Ryan attempted to kick John again, but he was ready for her this time and able to retain his balance. Using his speed, he avoided her attack. Appearing behind her with a speed that surpassed her own, he slashed his razor-sharp nails down the length of her back, slicing her open. She shrieked, turned and fumbled to the ground, shrinking away from him. John approached quickly, hissing, fangs bared as he went in for the killing blow. He lunged forward. She was unable to escape. Just when his nails were inches away from her throat, he was wrenched back, snatched by his lovely blonde hair, causing his head to jerk backward painfully. Stunned, John looked up to see who had thwarted his attack. Before him stood Richard, well over six feet tall.

Richard reached down, wrapping his hand around John's neck before he could scoot away. John hissed, snapping his fangs at the Alpha coyote as his nails clawed at Richard's flesh, struggling to free himself from the other man's grip. Richard punched John four times in different areas with a speed and force that broke several of his ribs and left him dizzy. Richard lifted the vampire off the ground, well over his head, then tossed him into a huge thick redwood. John struck the tree, his back breaking from the power of the impact, leaving him paralyzed until his bones could mend. Richard started toward John, to finish him off, when he was tackled from behind by Sergio, causing his knees to buckle. Both men tumbled to the grass.

Sergio crawled up his frame, his claws ripping at Richard's flesh, shredding his shirt in the process. Richard took hold of Sergio's wrists, keeping him from further attacking him. With a powerful buck, he propelled Sergio away, sending the younger shifter skidding across the lawn.

In the heat of the battle, Katrina had changed into her strongest form, her half-human, half-beast figure. Charging in to the battle, she grabbed Elise from behind, pulling her away from Carrie, a coyote from her Pack. Katrina dug her nails deeply into Elise's arms, trying to pin her against her chest so that she could crush her.

Elise, being nimble, managed to twist inside her embrace, so that the two were facing. Using more of her catlike agility, she was able to free one arm. Slashing downward across Katrina's face, she sliced the woman's jaw open. Katrina released Elise, staggering backward while pressing a clawed hand to her bleeding wound. Elise used the time she had to morph into her own half form. Her own Pride followed her initiative and began to change as well. Every member of each group assaulted their enemy with vicious attacks, trying to kill their opponent. Richard was getting double-teamed by Sergio and Adrian. The men lunged for him, but he sidestepped their attack. Turning around, he grabbed Sergio, spun him around and tossed him into Adrian, sending both men crashing to the ground. Before he could capitalize on the damage done to the two men, Xavier plunged his clawed hand into his back. Richard howled in pain, twisting around, freeing himself from Xavier's claws. Without missing a second, Xavier grabbed him by the throat, giving Adrian and Sergio a chance to grab each of Richard's arms, holding him for an attack. Richard, as he struggled against his two captors, found it impossible to break free. Xavier plunged his razor-sharp nails into Richard's chest, attempting to push his hand further in an effort to rip the shifter's heart out. Before he could inflict this life ending injury, Ignacio and Ryan came to Richard's aid, knocking Xavier to the ground. Ignacio bit Xavier, burying his two inch teeth deeply and ripping away a chunk of his shoulder. Xavier screamed, but managed to punch Ignacio, knocking the shifter away from him.

Richard used that time to toss Adrian with one arm, sending him flying into a large fountain on the front lawn. The impact of his body crashing into the concrete statue destroyed the structure. Adrian lay in the ruins, unable to move, his body racked with intense pain as his broken ribs and shattered collarbone began to heal.

Xander and the other members of their party snuck up behind the battle and watched Richard and Adrian as they fought. When they were near, they charged into the battle, taking many of the others by surprise. Cassandra's eyes bulged as she witnessed their strategic assault, she was impressed. Richard had Sergio in the air, the leopard was unable to maneuver out of his grip. He slammed Sergio's body sideways over his knee, re-injuring his ribs. Sergio cried out in pain as he was tossed to the ground. Richard then kicked Sergio hard, breaking two more of his ribs.

Xander came up behind Allison, a member of Richard's Pack. Before she could protect herself, he had her, his teeth already embedded in her throat. He jerked his head back, snapping her spinal cord and ripping away her jugular, severing the connection to her aorta. His clawed hand finished her off, tearing her head from her body. Tony and Nagesa worked back to back, fending off shifters from Milan's Pride. Each man was able to injure the less powerful beings with each attack.

Milan had Devin underneath her, pinning him to the ground with her knees. She held his head in an iron grip as she slid her claws into his torso like daggers sliding through a roast. Devin cried out, tears of pain welling in his eyes as he struggled in vain. Smiling, she ripped away flesh and muscle, exposing the white of his bones. Miranda saw this and instantly enraged, she rushed toward them. Thrusting her nails into the back of Milan's neck, severing her spinal cord, immediately paralyzed her. Blood gushed from Milan's wound as Miranda tried to pull her head from her neck. A member of Milan's Pride came to help her, punching Miranda hard across the cheek, knocking her to the ground, dizzy. Milan was helped from the ground and pulled away from danger. Richard noticed Miko getting ready to kill Katrina. Instantly, he ran over to them, leaving Sergio wallowing in pain. He took hold of the vampire in his powerful grip. He reared his head back then bit Miko, locking his jaws around her vital arteries.

Darian turned in time to see this. "Stop! Don't!" he called out to Richard, who looked up. His reddish brown-golden eyes focused on the vampire, his teeth still embedded in Miko's throat, poised to take her head within an instant. Darian was gratified to see that he had the Alpha's attention. He looked around, taking note that the vampires of Cassandra's coven hadn't entered the battle. Those of his own party were badly injured and not healing as fast as they could due to fatigue. He had to do something to turn the tide. "Look!" he pointed toward Cassandra who was watching the battle with a self-satisfied smile plastered across her face.

Richard looked up at Cassandra, but he hadn't released Miko, he only pulled his teeth free from her throat, which gave her some relief. He took the time to look around and see who was engaged in the battle and who was not. He saw members of his own Pack struggling against their enemy. At that point, they were outnumbered. Their enemy worked well together, as a team. That teamwork gave them the advantage, the same advantage he had hoped his own group would have, but they could not get along. He looked back at the vampire...giving him his attention.

Darian continued. "When I took the blood from her lover, I discovered all of her secrets. Richard, she will kill you and all those loyal to you." He approached Richard, so that they were eye to eye. "Once she's taken over our territory, she will not only destroy you and your entire Pack, but her Pride as well." He pointed to Milan who was cowering behind the vampires to give herself time to heal. Around them, the others continued to fight, not pausing to pay any attention to the two men talking.

Richard's eyes narrowed as he listened. He was in his strongest form and was unable to talk, so instead, he growled low as if to say "Go on."

Darian continued. "She will not share that territory. But you knew this, didn't you? You suspected as much. You must have."

Richard was silent, neither confirming nor denying Darian's assumption.

"Well here's something you didn't know. Both Katrina and Milan were in on it, leaving you and all of the others in the dark."

Katrina turned in time to see Darian revealing their secret. In a rage, she ran toward him. Darian sensed her coming and moved out of the way so fast, she wasn't able to stop herself from crashing into the tree he had been standing in front of. Richard watched her shake her head free of the cobwebs. Darian reached for Katrina, determined to end her life, when Cassandra finally made her move. Flying toward him, she punched him in the stomach, knocking him to the ground. He regrouped fast, climbing to his feet instantly, facing her.

Richard thought over what Darian had told him. It was as he feared. He would have denied such an allegation had certain circumstances not been present. His Pack's growing resentment toward him, Cassandra withholding herself from battle until both of their forces were weakened and just his overall feeling. He released Miko, pushing her away from him as he reverted back into his human form.

He turned toward Katrina. "We leave now!" he declared. Ignacio stood beside Ryan, protecting her, both looked at him, confused. "This is not our battle!"

Richard's Pack ceased fighting their opponents and approached him, surrounding him. All but Ryan and Ignacio, who simply looked on. Katrina stood before Richard. "This isn't your Pack anymore, Richard. It's mine! And they'll follow me, not you."

Richard grimaced. "This is mutiny!" he growled through gritted teeth.

"We like to think of it as a new day, independence. We're tired of living under your rule, we all want things you're not willing to give us. If it were up to you, we'd still be in Kansas! Besides, Cassandra is the only mate that I need...that I want."

Richard's face contorted in rage. "I will not abide this betrayal!"

"You don't have a choice! You can't fight us all!" Katrina smiled, triumphantly.

Richard stood still, anger boiling within him like lava inside a volcano. Katrina rushed toward him with intent to kill. The others followed her lead. Sergio, having witnessed their exchange, raced to Richard's rescue, tackling one of the Pack members, knocking him to the ground. He buried his face in the other shifter's throat, biting down hard and yanking back, pulling away the shifters windpipe, instantly ending his life. Ignacio and Ryan ran to Richard's side, facing off with their ex-Pack members. Richard was now battling two of his former Pack members, injuring them badly.

All of the supernaturals had heard when his Pack turned on him, they heard the words spoken. For some of them, it was good news. It meant that they had more allies, to others, it meant that they now had a new and dangerously formidable enemy. Richard, Sergio, Ryan and Ignacio fought the shifters of the Pack. Katrina herself, had scurried away when Richard punched her, knocking out one of her teeth. He had tossed her against a tree, injuring her. There were many dead and wounded shifters strewn across the lawn. Milan had rejoined the battle. She had double-teamed Madeleine, shredding her flesh as one of her Pride held the woman down.

Elise's eyes narrowed as she stealthily advanced on the duo, pouncing on Milan, bringing her down. While on top of her, Elise straddled the tiger, without letting another second pass by, she began to shred Milan with criss-cross patterns. Her curved nails hooked into the other woman's flesh with ease. She ripped chunks away slowly killing the tiger who wasn't able to get Elise off of her. Her own nails were not doing enough damage to save herself. Once Milan was dead, shredded to pieces, a bloody mess, Elise rose to help heal Madeleine who had been able to kill her opponent once the match had been leveled.

Tatiana was giving her healing blood to Nagesa who drank deeply, healing his life-threatening wounds rapidly. While her back was turned, Vincent, a cunning and powerful vampire from Cassandra's coven converged on her. He bit her from behind, running his embedded fangs along her throat, attempting to sever her jugular. She screamed as she tried to push his face away. Xander tried to rescue her, but he was held down by another powerful member of Cassandra's coven. Before Vincent could make a killing blow, Richard came up behind him, grabbing the vampire's head. Unfortunately, Vincent took hold of Richard's hand, preventing him from decapitating him. Realizing that his initial plan wasn't possible, he did the next best thing. Breaking the vampire's neck which didn't kill him, but it gave Richard time to save Tatiana. As Richard picked her up, their eyes locked and she silently thanked him for saving her life. He nodded and released her. She ran over to her husband, both double teaming the vampire that had him pinned.

Vincent healed quickly and was back on the offensive. Springing up before Richard, he slashed his claws across Richard's throat. Blood splattered their faces as the Alpha fell backward, hands gripping his wound. With no Matron's blood to drink, he would heal slowly. Vincent's bloodlust intensified and he lunged for the coyote, fangs bared.

Ryan screamed, and threw herself on top of Richard, taking the full force of the attack, leaving her spine broken in two places. She cried in pain as she lay crumpled on top of Richard. Incensed, Vincent went in for another attack only to be yanked back by Xavier. Before he could counterattack, Xavier buried his fangs into his vein, sucking greedily and quickly, rendering the other vampire weak. It was a trick Darian had taught him only a few months before, a nifty attack to use in confrontation with another vampire. Vincent fell to his knees, his limbs growing heavy. Xavier pulled away, but he continued to hold the other vampire. Without having to worry about the other man fighting back, he was able to slice his nails across Vincent's throat, then he ripped his head from his neck.

Decapitation was the quickest and most reliable way to kill a vampire. In a bold move, he tossed Vincent's head at Cassandra, who had been knocked down by Darian. She looked at the rolling head, then at Xavier who winked. She growled low, enraged that she was not able to capitalize on this battle as she had hoped. She looked at Darian, he was stronger than she had anticipated. She had gathered very little from Natasha. She thought she knew of his age, flickers of a birthday party and memorabilia was all she had seen when she had looked into the other woman's memories. But there had been nothing to prepare her for a vampire half her age with all of her strength!

In the meantime, Tatiana had knelt beside Richard. Since he was without his Matron, he would have trouble healing. Her own blood would help his healing process. Not as much as one from his own Pack, but enough.

Ryan lay still beside Richard, unable to move. She looked helplessly up at Tatiana with pleading eyes. "Please help him... please! He's a good man, please!" Tears ran freely from her eyes down her cheeks. Tatiana looked at her, then nodded. She cut her own wrist, pressing it against his open mouth. Ignacio came to his aid, licking Richard's wound as he drank the healing blood that flowed into his mouth.

Across the lawn, Xander had just killed the vampire who had injured his son. Adrian grimaced in pain as he lay in a fetal position, holding the insides of his stomach in by sheer will. Xander rushed to his son, prying away his hands so that he could get a better look at the wound.

"Oh God! How bad is it?" Adrian asked his father as he examined the wound.

Xander pressed his hands against the opening, attempting to push his son's intestines back inside. Warren ran over to them. He was also still in half beast form, so he immediately began licking at the wound.

Realizing that his injury was fatal, Adrian did the only thing he had enough strength to do. "Mom!!!" he called out to Tatiana.

She turned away from Richard, looking in the direction of her son's voice and saw that he was in danger.

"Go to him," Richard whispered weakly, letting go of her wrist.

With no prompting needed, she was at her son's side in an instant, giving him her blood to drink.

In the chaos of the battle, Benito, a shifter from Richard's Pack and Alec, a vampire from Cassandra's coven ran back inside the mansion, both rushing through the halls toward the holding cells where they kept their captives. The two men witnessed the betrayal, the turn in the battle and they wanted insurance. Benito felt the betrayal more. Richard was as deep in the plot as any of them, how dare he fight alongside their enemy! It angered him more, because he had been leery of the Alpha's participation from the beginning. Richard had protested every move they'd made. He would belittle them, basically calling them cowards without ever actually saying the word. But then again, Richard always had a way with words. Benito didn't like him and was looking forward to killing him once they got their land. He tolerated him being on their team because Richard was a strong warrior, well over three-hundred years old. That was impressive for a shape-shifter. He was the strongest among all of the shifters in their party, not to mention, he was stronger than half of the vampires. The moment the tide had turned, Benito witnessed Richard single-handedly kill three shifters in a matter of seconds. It was at that moment, when he knew how badly he wanted to live, he thought to use their human captives as a shield or possible bargaining chip. Whatever would help him get away. Alec had seen him flee and decided to follow his lead.

It was the only wise choice the two could think of. Cassandra wasn't able to defeat Darian as easily as she had hoped or even bragged about. They had all assumed she could kill him. She was three-thousand years old, an amazing age for vampires, many of whom were either killed or committed suicide long before that age. How could a vampire half her age be her equal?! Milan was right, they should have left to regroup and prepare for another attack. Too much was falling apart too soon; they had underestimated their foes. Both men ran to their prospective target's rooms. Each opened the doors they were standing in front of. Benito looked in on Matthew, who was awake but still a bit groggy from the drugs he'd been given. Matthew scooted across the floor to the furthest corner of the room. He knew that he would not be able to outrun or out muscle his captor, but if he had anything to do about it, he wasn't going to make it easy for him.

Benito stepped closer to Matthew, who was now rising to his feet with his back pressed against the wall.

Matthew's eyes were slightly blinded by the light that poured into the room from the open doorway. He had sat in the darkness for so long, he'd become accustomed to it and was having a difficult time focusing on Benito's movements. When the shifter drew close enough, he tried to make a break for it, running in a zig-zag pattern toward the doorway. Benito caught him from behind, grabbing him around the waist, and tossing him over his shoulder. As he made his way toward the exit, he saw Alec a few steps ahead of him with Natasha thrown over his shoulder. She struggled wildly, arms and legs flailing as she pounded Alec's back with her petite closed fists. Matthew's own movements mimicked those of Natasha's, although both struggled in vain.

Outside, the battle raged on. Richard was now fully healed and fighting a vicious interlock with one of Cassandra's stronger vampires. Elise and Tatiana had taken on the role of healers more so than soldiers. They ran to the aid of their members who were fatally injured, giving them blood as they licked their wounds.

In the one-on-one between Cassandra and Darian, the fight was fierce. Darian had punched her, his fist connecting with her face, but he was unable to knock her off balance. Her eyes locked onto him, a low, menacing growl oozed from her throat. It disturbed him, but he held his ground, recognizing a scare tactic for what it was. Although he was surprised by her strength, he couldn't get a killing blow on her and it infuriated him. Each time he would go for a fatal attack, she would counter as if she were able to predict his every move.

The same could be said for him. Cassandra had grown increasingly agitated by the younger vampire. He was smart, cunning and powerful. She stared hard at him, making certain to keep eye contact. Then in a last ditch effort to frighten him, she released the full force of her aura which she had been holding back, hoping to knock Darian down with her preternatural power. After the wind settled and the petals fell back to the ground, she saw that Darian was unmoved. This enraged her even more! Her lips parted, revealing her pearly white fangs. Her stare grew more intense as her jaw muscles tightened. Darian, although unnerved, stood his ground, matching her intense stare with his own.

"Darian!!!" screamed Natasha as she was carried out of the mansion. She didn't have much time to take in her surroundings before Alec decided to use her body as a shield protecting him from Nagesa's attack. The wolf was able to pull back his assault, preventing serious injury to her. Alec smiled, pleased that his plan had worked.

He hoped that he could hold them at bay until he could get away. Darian wanted to run to Natasha, but he refused to let his guard down, knowing all Cassandra would need was a split second to kill him.

Impatient with the turn of circumstances, Cassandra decided to attack Darian, appearing behind him. He managed to block her slash at his throat, but was caught on the chin by her left hook, sending him crashing into a nearby tree. She advanced on him. He was able to climb to his feet, dodging her follow-up attack, but just barely. Her claws swiped across the tree, ripping away a four inch thick chunk of the bark instead of Darian's head, which was her actual target. With a snarl she began to stalk him, keeping him on the defense.

As she chased him around the lawn, she began to do something vampires rarely do; she changed into her demonic form. Letting the demon blood that flowed through their veins take control of her appearance as the power was unleashed. Darian dodged another of her attacks, stumbled, but managed to catch his footing, pressing his back against a tree.

He watched her complete her change, shocked. He'd never been in a battle with another vampire that dared to take such a form.

Unlike shape-shifters, when a vampire changes form, they don't have to worry about being incapacitated until the change is complete. This was something Darian hadn't anticipated. She approached him, her body two feet taller and broader, more muscular. Her ears had become long and pointed, much like those of bats. Her mouth was filled with razor-sharp fangs with her incisors growing even longer. Her fingers elongated, nails turning into talons, curling over with sharp points. Her red glowing eyes bored into Darian, attempting to hypnotize him into surrendering.

Everyone paused at the sight of Cassandra in full demon form. The other vampires in her coven followed her example and began to change as well. Leaving little time to marvel at such a noteworthy spectacle, Miko and Xander combined forces, killing one before his change was complete. The two took him out with speed, strength and agility, Miko attacking high, Xander attacking low, snapping the vampire's spine as they ripped his head from his body. Xavier and Sergio had ganged up on the last member of Richard's Pack, killing her after a long struggle, leaving both men exhausted and well battered.

Xavier was worried now more than ever as he saw that Cassandra had taken their strongest form, giving her the upper hand. The only thought that comforted him was this: she feared Darian.

Looking around the lawn, Xavier saw that Benito had Matthew by the neck, threatening to kill him if Nicole and Carmen didn't back away. Carmen put her hands up in mock surrender. She and Nicole stepped back, pretending to let him pass. He began to sidestep, dragging Matthew with him toward the forest. Xavier used all of the speed and strength he had left and advanced on him. Grabbing the shifter by his neck and arm, he pried him away from Matthew, who ran toward the trucks once he was free. Xavier held onto Benito, who was struggling, while Carmen, in her half-beast form lunged forward, claws out before her. She slashed across Benito's stomach, spilling his intestines onto the blood-soaked grass. Nicole jumped in as well, biting deeply into his throat, ripping away a large chunk, spraying blood in all directions. Without his Matron to save him, he was as good as dead. Within seconds, he passed away. The two women gave into their bloodlust and began devouring his body to regain their strength. When Xavier scanned the area, he saw that Alec held Natasha. He was swinging her violently from side to side as he fended off the others who had crowded around him.

Natasha screamed as she was jerked savagely by her captor. She was terrified by the carnage she was able to catch glimpses of, dozens of bloody body parts strewn over the lawn, supernaturals lay dead everywhere! She was terrified.

Adrian, Miranda and John had ganged up on Alec, attacking all at once, not allowing him any time to harm Natasha. She screamed as they converged on him, claws slashing, fangs and teeth biting and ripping. Blood splattered on her flesh, even though they were very careful not to touch her as they dismembered Alec. Once she was free, she ran toward Xavier who was calling her name as he ran toward her.

Unsuccessful against her assault on Darian, Cassandra quickly decided on another tactic. She saw Natasha running toward her lover from the corner of her eye. With lightening-quick speed, she intercepted Natasha, scooping her up in her arms and holding her tightly. Xavier didn't hesitate as he jumped on Cassandra's back, digging his claws deeply into her forearms, attempting to force a release. Before Darian could run over to help them, Cassandra lashed out one arm. Xavier was thrown with such force, he was propelled into the air, landing on a splintered tree trunk that had been split in half during the battle. He bellowed a gurgled scream as he lay impaled on the jagged wood that jutted out through his chest, covering him with blood. Pain was all Xavier was now aware of, and a possible death. John, Xander and Sergio ran to his aid, gently lifting him off of the jagged tree trunk. They laid him on the ground. John immediately opened a vein, shoving his bleeding wrist against Xavier's mouth, forcing him to drink. He yelled at Xavier, urging him to drink, hoping that he was strong enough to save him. Miko had seen what happened and she ran over. Pulling John's wrist away, she replaced it with her own.

"John, pour your blood over his wound!" she ordered. John obeyed, cutting himself deeply, letting the blood flow into the grotesque hole in Xavier's chest. Sergio grabbed John's wrist and began milking the blood from his veins, speeding the flow. They watched as his wound began to heal, giving them a sense of relief. They were still concerned as he hadn't begun drinking the blood that had filled his mouth.

"Let's work his throat, he needs to swallow. I don't think he can do it on his own yet," Sergio suggested, letting go of John's wrist. He tilted Xavier's head backwards and began to stroke his throat. The motion was inducing him to swallow, working the blood down his esophagus. Seconds passed, seeming like hours before Xavier began to suck gently at Miko's wrist. They sat back, relieved as he began to feed. Darian wanted to go to his lover. He tossed glances in their direction as he monitored their actions. He wanted to take Xavier in his arms and save him, to feel his blood flow into his lover's mouth, but he was caught in a stand-off. If he made the slightest ill-fated decision, they could all die. He kept his attention on Cassandra. She still had Natasha and was threatening to fly away with her if he made a move.

"You love her. I can see it in your eyes!" Cassandra taunted. Her voice didn't sound like her normal voice, it was deep, like a growl, an effect of the transformation.

Darian knew that in his current form, he was no match for Cassandra. She would be able to see his movements before he could make them. "I see using humans as shields is very popular within your camp. Let her go, it's me you want."

Natasha screamed and struggled vainly in the woman's arms. She looked to Darian, seeing that he was caught at an impasse. She feared that he wouldn't be able to save her. Choosing to have a hand in her own fate, Natasha worked up the nerve to attack Cassandra. With both hands clenched tightly, she mustered all of her strength and thrust her fists upward, slamming them against the vampire's jaw, catching her by surprise. Justin, Elise, Madeleine, Devin and Rachel seized the opportunity, and pounced on Cassandra, preventing her from getting away. It was becoming increasingly difficult to contain Cassandra and protect Natasha at the same time. When Darian had jumped into the cluster, he was able to free Natasha from the vampire's grip. Outraged, Cassandra bucked and swung her arms, sending everyone backward in all directions. Darian collided against Xander, both men falling to the ground. Elise and Tatiana ran toward Cassandra, trying their best to bring her down.

Darian watched the struggle, and without wasting another second, he forced his change. His body began taking on his strongest form, one that was very similar to Cassandra's. He ripped out of his clothes in the process, as Cassandra had done and he stood before her, naked in full demon form. Xander looked up at Darian, the vampire was suddenly unrecognizable. His skin was no longer smooth or baby-soft, it now looked to be as hard as tanned leather. His claws were now more like talons, his mouth had grown wider, filling with long, dagger-like fangs. His fire-red, glowing eyes stared forward at his target.

Cassandra grinned, baring her own fangs. With a sharp spin, she managed to toss both Elise and Tatiana, propelling one into the other and sending both crashing against a truck. Natasha had run over to Xavier, burying her face in his chest as he comforted her. He was now completely healed and watching the final battle as they all were. Everyone was exhausted. Many didn't have the strength to even rise from their prone or sitting positions.

The two master vampires charged each other at speeds the others couldn't see. She dug her nails deeply into Darian's chest, attempting to reach his heart and rip it out. He grabbed her wrist with one hand while his free hand slashed her across her face, ripping her left eyeball from its socket. Blood splattered over his chest as it gushed down her face. Cassandra screamed, pulling her hand free of Darian's grip and pressing it to her now empty eye socket.

"I'll kill you!" she roared.

"Do your worst!" Darian shot back, the sound of his voice much like hers, unrecognizable.

She lunged for him again, talons hooking into the flesh of his chest, shredding his skin and muscle as she dragged them downward. Darian grimaced, crying out in excruciating pain, but he refused to lose his focus. He wrapped his hand around her throat, stabbing her flesh with his own talons, causing her to grab his arm. He used her own momentum to sling her body to the side so that he was on top. He punched her several times as her claws raked down his face. Darian grabbed one of her hands and bit down hard, yanking his head backward, pulling three of her fingers away. Cassandra screamed and looked down at her injured hand as blood spurted from the jagged joints where her fingers used to be. Darian spit the digits out as he punched her again. Cassandra lunged forward, head-butting him, catching him by surprise enough to grab hold of his groin, digging her talons into his crotch.

Blinded by pain, he screamed as she laughed. Instinctively, he caught hold of her hand, preventing her from injuring him further. At that point, when he saw his chance, without hesitation he buried his face in the crook of her neck, and bit. Feasting faster than he ever had, he weakened her enough to bite harder. A second later, he pulled his head back, ripping out her throat, leaving her incapacitated. The moment had come! He sliced his talons across the remains of her throat, severing her head, finally killing her.

Sitting back on his heels, he caught his breath as he waited for his body to heal from its numerous wounds. He looked down at Cassandra's corpse, smiling. The others remained silent. Not only had Darian's appearance unnerved them, the fight itself had them scared as well. It could have gone either way. If Cassandra had won, they could only imagine what that would have meant for them. Darian rose to his feet, standing eight feet high. He turned, looking at Natasha who was crying hysterically. Xavier was unable to calm her down. She watched as Darian approached them. She screamed in terror before losing consciousness, falling limp in Xavier's arms.

Darian quickly changed forms. Kneeling beside his lovers, he kissed Xavier deeply, overjoyed that he had survived the battle. He then checked on Natasha, brushing her long, dark brown hair from her face.

"She'll be alright. I think this was a little too much for her. We just have to get her to a scene she recognizes," Darian said, smiling sadly.

"Before we leave, let's do a final sweep," Adrian suggested.

"I need to get my son," Sergio said, as he made his way toward the mansion with Madeleine by his side. Once inside, they followed the scent of their son, leading them toward one of the locked rooms in the basement. Sergio knocked down the door, freeing Sebastian, who ran to his parents, falling into their welcoming arms. Madeleine held onto her son tightly, kissing his hair, forehead and cheeks. Sergio took his turn hugging his son as tightly as he could without harming him. He ran his hands lovingly over Sebastian's shoulders, checking him for injuries.

Sergio brushed the red bangs from Sebastian's eyes. "Are you okay?" he asked.

Sebastian nodded. "Yeah, I'm okay." Tears ran down his cheeks as he continued to embrace his parents.

"Oh my God! I'm so happy that we've found you! I've been worried sick to my stomach! Let's get you out of here," Madeleine said. She hooked her arm around Sebastian's waist, pulling him toward her, afraid to let him go. The three exited the mansion, shoulder to shoulder and joined the others in making sure their enemy was destroyed.

No one had any idea that Katrina was still alive. She had pretended to be dead in the confusion of the battle. No one had paid attention when she lay down face first on the bloody grass. She had witnessed the death of Cassandra. And now her enemies were checking the dead bodies, leaving no one alive. She knew, now that the heat of the battle had died down, they would hear her heartbeat, smell her blood flowing. They were focused and now hunting for survivors…hunting for her! She would not be able to sneak away. She had to make a move and soon! She looked around, checking for something, anything, to help her get away. Seeing Matthew sitting in the back seat of one of the SUVs gave her a desperate idea. Quickly, she rose and running over to the SUV, ripped the door off the truck. She snatched Matthew out of the back seat before he could scoot away. She sprinted off into the swamp, hoping the murky, alligator filled water would help cover their scents. She knew that the others had seen what she'd done and were right on her tail. With all of the noise Matthew was making, their trail might as well have been lit up in neon lights. She cursed under her breath over her current situation. She heard several voices, as well as their footsteps splashing in the water behind her. They were closing in! She started to panic. Matthew's screaming and struggling made it very hard for her to flee easily. She also had no idea that right above her, Darian hovered. He landed softly behind her. When she turned at the slight sound, he punched her, sending both her and Matthew crashing into the swampy water. The others caught up, surrounding her.

Katrina rose, jerking Matthew to his feet. She pressed her back against a large tree. Still in half-beast form, she used it to her advantage. She pressed her nails against Matthew's jugular, puncturing his flesh, but not deeply, just enough to open negotiations.

Richard stepped forward; he had changed back into his human form. "Let him go, Katrina. There's nowhere else for you to run. Let's end this."

Katrina shook her head, unable to use words, she had to rely on short growls and grunts to communicate. Only Richard and his members could understand her. Each breed had their own way to communicate in that particular form, leaving the others in the dark.

"What did she say?" Nicole asked.

"She's not willing to let him go. As far as she's concerned, Matthew is her one-way ticket out of here," Ignacio translated.

"She also insulted the entire lot of us," Ryan added.

"You're out of options, Katrina. Turn him over and we may spare you. If you keep fighting us, you'll leave us no other choice," Elise pleaded.

Katrina communicated again, directing her comments to Richard.

"You're afraid, Kat. The scent of fear oozes from your pores like sweat. End this, it doesn't have to go any further. You know that harming him will mean your death," Richard replied, taking one step closer. Another growl from Katrina, and he paused.

"Can someone please translate?!" Warren demanded. He wanted to know what was being said concerning Matthew's welfare. Because he was a wolf, he couldn't understand the coyote form of communication.

"She said she could smell our lies, then she told Richard not to move," Ignacio continued translating.

Katrina eyed her enemies. She could smell their hate, their distrust. She knew they wanted her dead and any promise they gave her would be a lie. She feared Richard the most. She had betrayed him and she knew he would want his revenge sooner or later. Everything that she had fought so hard for was gone and it was far too late to think about what could have been done to prevent it. Her gaze zeroed in on Warren who had stepped forward, hands out before him in a submissive position.

"Please let him go," he beseeched.

Katrina growled several times. This time, Richard translated. "She wants a confirmation that he's your lover. She said she can smell your scent all over him. She wants to know if you love him."

Warren nodded. "Yes, he's my lover and I love him very much. Please, just let him go, this really doesn't have to end badly for anyone else," he said. He began to move closer, but Nagesa grabbed his arm, holding him back.

"Please Katrina, let him go and you can go," Xander pleaded with her. No one wanted to make a move that would end Matthew's life, the situation was just that tense.

Katrina growled and grunted again. Richard's eyes bulged, he lunged for her, but it was too late. She bit Matthew on the shoulder, ripping away a large piece of his flesh, and swallowing it.

"Noooo!!!" Warren yelled as he rushed forward.

Before she could go for a killing blow, Richard came up behind her, forcing her hands away from Matthew. Warren caught the falling mortal in his arms.

Richard didn't give her a chance to counterattack. He broke her neck. Then, growing his claws long, he slashed them across her throat, severing her head. Blood splattered his face. He wiped it off with the back of his hand, smearing it slightly. The vampires fought their urges to feed, now was not the time.

Tatiana ran to Matthew. A violent fever had taken hold with amazing speed within him. His body shook uncontrollably in Warren's arms.

"Warren, let me see him!" Tatiana urged, prying Warren's hands from Matthew. She leaned over him, seeing that his eyes were rolling inside their sockets and his lips were turning white. "We have to get him someplace cool. We need to leave, now!"

The others agreed. Knowing she was right, that Matthew's condition was quickly becoming serious, they began to make their way back to the SUVs. Warren carried his lover, he was extremely worried, not sure if Matthew would survive the course of the change or not. When he heard the telltale gagging, he immediately stopped running. Placing Matthew on his feet, supporting him, leaning him over just in time.

Matthew vomited the contents of his stomach into the murky water, causing a splash. It seemed to go on forever until he started to give dry heaves. Warren picked him up again and ran toward the trucks. He placed him inside, cradling his head as one would do a baby. Together, they all made their way back to their airplanes. Many were naked and all were covered in blood and bits of flesh. Darian had hypnotized the pilots so that the aircraft would be ready for take-off upon their arrival. When they got to the planes, they all boarded immediately. Everyone split up, climbing on either plane regardless of who owned it. All three leaders allowed Richard and his remaining members to join them. Once they were on board, Tatiana immediately began attending to Matthew, placing cold compresses on his forehead and the back of his neck. Warren knelt beside Matthew, dabbing his face with the cold compress.

Adrian approached him, laying a hand on his shoulder, trying to reassure him that everything would be alright. At least, that is what he hoped, but nothing was written in stone. He knew well enough that most people bitten by shape-shifters rarely survived the turn. Most shifters victim's bodies went into shock as the shifter gene traveled throughout their system. The gene induced the fever, which often brought on seizures. Many fell into comas before they died. Matthew had a great deal of their gene in his system. Adrian prayed that he would be able to live through his transformation.

Darian walked over to the sofa, where Matthew had been settled. He looked down at the shivering form lying there and frowned. He understood perfectly well why Warren was so distraught. It didn't look good. He suspected Matthew had only a few more hours to live, if that long, based on his current condition. "Is there anything that I can do?" he asked.

Tatiana looked up at him. "Thanks Darian, but there really isn't much you can do. Besides, I think Natasha needs you now." She gave him a sweet, sad smile.

Darian nodded. "Alright, but if you need anything..." he let his voice trail off, letting her know that he was available if they needed him.

"Thank you, Darian." Tatiana turned her attention back to Matthew. "We need to lower his body temperature right now! Adrian, Devin, get some ice cold wet towels!" she ordered. The two men ran off to the bathroom, snatching the towels and wash cloths from the racks. Running into the galley, they soaked them with the cold water from the refrigerator. They poured ice cubes into one of the wet towels, making sure it was cold. While they were doing that task, Warren undressed Matthew, tossing his clothes on the floor beside them. The other two men came out of the galley, arms full of cold, wet towels. Tatiana layered the towels over Matthew's body.

Nicole lowered the thermostat on the airplane, hoping the

cooler temperature would help. They made certain to monitor Matthew as they continued to keep cold compresses on him.

"Think he's going to barf again?" Devin asked.

Warren shook his head. "Not likely. He pretty much emptied his stomach earlier." He couldn't take his eyes off of Matthew. He was so upset, he felt nauseous himself.

"We're going to do everything we can, Warren...try to relax, alright," Tatiana patted him on his hand. He looked at her, nodding slowly.

Darian sat by Xavier as he cradled Natasha's head in his lap. She was still unconscious. After checking her vitals, he knew that she would be alright, at least physically. He hoped he could say the same about her mental state.

"Should she still be unconscious after this long?" Xavier asked, concerned.

"It's only been about thirty minutes. She's been through an ordeal and needs rest to recover from it. Let's worry if she doesn't wake up in six hours or later." Darian gave him a slight smile. Xavier nodded.

A few minutes passed by before Adrian received a phone call on his cell. He looked at the caller ID then answered. "Hey, Nagesa, why are you calling me from Rachel's phone?"

"Because my cell phone was ruined in the battle." I called for a more important reason. Elise needs to speak with Darian, can you give him your cell?" Nagesa asked. Adrian agreed, handing Darian his cell.

"Yes?" Darian asked.

"I have some terrible news, and I need to ask a favor of you," Elise began.

"But of course. What's wrong?"

"I had hoped that no more of our friends and families' blood would be shed on this night, but that was not the case. I lost a member of my Pride, Marianne."

"I'm sorry to hear that, Elise," Darian said, giving her more comforting words.

"Thank you, Darian. I expected casualties in this battle, but I also hoped my expectations were wrong. I suppose one could be grateful that more of us didn't perished this night. By the way, how is Matthew doing?" she asked.

"Not well, but it's not over yet."

Elise exhaled with a sigh. "Let's hope for the best. I wanted to know if we may borrow one of your coffins to transport Marianne's body in?"

"Yes, of course. Consider it yours."

Elise thanked him before ending their conversation. Darian informed the others of the Pride's loss, which upset them all. Marianne had been a sweet, good-natured woman. Devin had witnessed her death. Her throat ripped out by Katrina and he had been unable to help her. Even the memory was too much to bear. He sat on the edge of the sofa, tears flowing down his cheeks, his heart heavy with their loss. They all mourned her in their own way.

An hour passed before Adrian walked over to Warren. "Come on, man, let's give him some room. Crowding around him will only add more body heat and that's something Matthew doesn't need right now."

Warren nodded, but was unable to move from his lover's side. Adrian watched for a few seconds, then he walked away, sitting down on one of the chairs. He understood how his Pack brother felt, and he wished he could do something about it other than just watch.

While on the flight home, they all took turns in the bathroom, washing as much of the congealed blood from their bodies as they could, some with little success.

"I never thought I'd say this, but...I look gross as hell," John said as he emerged from the bathroom with bits of bloody flesh still entangled in his hair and several dried splotches of blood caked on his chest and arms. "We're clean out of soap and the water pressure is way down, this is the best I could do with what we've got in there."

Devin walked over to him, wrapping his arms around his waist. He'd been attached to John the moment they boarded the plane. He had witnessed his lover being thrown into a tree, his back being broken in the process. Because of that fact, he still harbored a grudge against Richard, and he was grateful that the Alpha coyote was on the other plane.

"I love you so much, I was so terrified when I thought you were going to die. That drove me insane!" Devin said.

John chuckled. "It hurt like a son-of-a-bitch, too. Don't worry, baby, it's going to take more than a broken back to kill me." He kissed Devin passionately. After their kiss, the two sat side by side in a window seat, with Devin snuggled closely to him, content.

"What are we going to do about Richard and his people?" April asked.

"That bastard better be glad he jumped to our side! If he hadn't saved Tatiana...," Devin grimaced.

"Shit, I saw him in action in a first hand account! You better be glad he jumped on our side. That motherfucker is strong! I had no idea a shape-shifter could be that strong!" John said.

"Oh, you think because you guys have endless years to build up your strength, that we can't compete?" Devin rolled his eyes, exasperated. "I swear, you arrogant vampires!"

"Now, hold on, that's not what I mean, smart-ass. What I meant was; his strength was greater than Xavier's! And Xavier is pretty damn strong. How old do you think he is?"

"Darian, didn't you say one of them was like three-hundred or something?" Nicole asked.

Darian nodded.

"It must be him, which means he has the strength of a vampire who may possibly be seven-hundred years old, I think. Regardless, he was a big help. It's because of him that we were able to walk away with only one fatality. Although, I would have much rather preferred no deaths from our side," Miranda said.

"I get the feeling that he wasn't really a part of what happened, ere by circumstance," Xavier said.

"eah, I get you. Like when his Matron betrayed him, you tally see the pain in his face," Carmen said.

"I don't know about you, but I was grateful for that betrayal. He killed four of his own Pack members, three of those tigers and two vamps. It's a good thing he stopped to listen to Darian at that moment. His killing them made it easy for Elise and my mom to heal us whenever we were injured and man!, that was often! That puts him in good standing in my book," Adrian said, lounging more comfortably in the chair.

Daniel finished the last of his bottled water before screwing the top and tossing it into the garbage. He looked at the others. "Whatever the case, that son-of-a-bitch played his part!"

"Thank you! That's what I'm talking about. He was a part of all that deceit. Besides, why are we even talking about his ass anyway?" Devin said, scowling.

"Because he's in the other plane coming with us to Chicago. Our leaders..." Xavier made a gesture toward Darian, and Tatiana. "...might say that he and his can stay."

"He's earned it," Tatiana whispered.

"He's earned nothing! Have we forgotten about how much trouble he caused us?! He almost killed some of us!" Devin protested, outraged by the possibility that Richard might be allowed *Sanctuary*.

"Hey baby, calm down," John said, getting Devin's attention. "Yeah, I know that you're still fired up and this is pissing you off, but the guy was also the reason why some of us didn't die, like Tatiana. And according to my calculations, he didn't actually kill any of us."

"Yeah, but not for a lack of trying, though!" Devin argued.

"Devin...Darian, Xander and Elise are wise enough to know if letting Richard live is a mistake or not. If they grant him *Immunity*, then it was for a good reason, one we need to trust," Tatiana said.

"Besides," Darian added. "He fought for his Pack, and we fought for what was ours. What is done is done."

Devin studied the others, but said nothing. He laid his head back on his lover's chest, silently rejoicing in the fact that he was alive and they were together. Another half an hour passed before

Natasha opened her eyes, blinking repeatedly, trying to focus her vision. Once her vision cleared, the first person she saw was her very handsome lover, Xavier, smiling back at her. She was still slightly disoriented as she struggled to rise.

"Shhh, lie still. Don't worry, Tasha, you're safe, everything is alright," Xavier reassured her as he pressed down gently on her shoulders, forcing her to lie still in his arms.

"I feel dizzy..." She made a sickened expression. "...and a little nauseous." She swallowed hard, her throat felt scratchy from all of the screaming she'd done earlier.

"You just need to relax, darling...you'll be alright," Xavier said, comforting her.

"Where am I?" Natasha asked, looking around, confused.

"You're on an airplane, we're going back to Chicago."

Darian walked into the galley to fetch a bottled water for her. He returned, handing the bottle to Xavier, who assisted Natasha in sitting up so that she could drink the water. Gingerly, he tipped the bottle to her mouth, she took two swallows then stopped, coughing slightly.

"Oh God! My throat hurts so badly!" she said, rubbing her throat softly.

"That's from all of that screaming you were doing. I was on my cell talking with a Hollywood agent...I think you have just enough talent to be the next Scream Queen," Devin joked, trying to make her smile. It worked.

She chuckled softly, wincing a little.

"Is everyone okay?" she asked, looking at the others, knowing that all of her friends weren't on the plane with her. "Where are the others?"

"The rest of us are on Xander's plane, this is Elise's," Xavier said.

"Where's Xander?"

"On his plane, we just kind of boarded which ever one, didn't really matter at the time," Nicole said. "And everyone is pretty much okay. We only lost one person, Marianne, which is very unfortunate, I'm really pissed about that, she was cool as hell."

"We lost Alex from our Pack," Adrian said, he lowered his head, saddened.

Natasha was shocked, she mouthed both shifters' name. She'd liked both. She'd gone on a lot of "Girl's Night" outings and bonded wonderfully with Marianne. Alex had been fun to be around as well, he'd had a great sense of humor. She began to cry. The others gave her time to grieve, not wanting to rush her. She had a lot to take in. In addition to learning of the two deaths, she was told of Matthew's condition. She was extremely worried about him. She cared a great deal for him and wanted him to pull through. Tatiana had told her there was nothing she could do to help when she offered and for her to remain calm. After a while, when she was able to regain her composure, she looked at her two lovers. Her eyes scanned over Darian, who was still naked but completely recognizable. She remembered what he'd looked like in his other form, the form Xavier had once warned her about. He'd said she wouldn't ever want to see that form. He was right.

Darian knelt beside her, brushing a few strands of hair from her eyes. "How are you feeling?" he asked. His Greek-accented voice was smooth, sensual and calming.

"I guess I'll be alright. I still feel a little shaky from all the drugs and everything else." She leaned closer toward him, whispering, "Was that really what you look like? I know what I think I saw what I saw when I saw it, but...I don't know." With eyebrows furrowed, she settled back into Xavier's comforting embrace, looking at Darian. "I think I'm still a little loopy."

Xavier smiled. "You think?"

Darian smiled sadly. "It's not a side of myself that I like to present, but it was necessary. It was me. It's what's really inside of me. Inside every vampire, there is the demon that gives us our power, our eternal life...our thirst. It's important to me that you understand that. I hope you can accept this truth."

Both men looked at her. She looked at them, seeing their warm, loving expressions, their concern. She knew her answer.

"Why wouldn't I be able to accept it?" she asked, perplexed that Darian would question her love for them.

"Because, it's something you've never seen before. A side of us we never wanted you to see. It's one thing to know that we have demon blood flowing through our veins, it's another to see it for what it is," Darian said.

Natasha smiled sweetly. "I'm not stupid, Darian." she looked off to the side. "Okay, granted, you scared the shit out of me-"

"Not literally, I hope," Adrian said, teasing her.

Natasha looked at him. "That's disgusting! I'm sure if he did, you'd be the first to know," she quipped playfully.

Adrian laughed for the first time since the sun had set.

She returned her attention to her men. "Now, as I was saying, I'm not stupid. I know that sometimes I may seem like I don't fully understand certain things about your lives, and maybe I don't, but I'm still learning. I do, however, know that the special element inside of you isn't anything human, or natural, and I don't care. I love you, both of you. And it's going to take a whole lot more than seeing your full beastie form to change my mind or heart." She smiled warmly, hoping she'd put them at ease. She now understood why the question was asked. They thought she'd want to leave them. *Never*, she thought to herself.

Her two lovers kissed her, each taking their turn. She was relieved to be in their presence, in Xavier's arms. She wanted to sleep more than anything. Ever since the day she had been kidnapped, she hadn't really enjoyed a good night's rest. She'd suffered an onslaught of nightmares from visions that ran rampant and became something unusual, tangled with that which wasn't reality. She knew it was because of the drugs they'd injected into her system that she was in such an uncontrollable state. She was happy to finally be going home.

Tatiana kept monitoring Matthew, she and Warren were still struggling to lower his body temperature. The others kept watchful eyes as they discussed a number of things as to pass the time away on their flight.

***

On Xander's plane, which had taken off a few minutes before Elise's, they were mourning the loss of their Pride member. Sergio had placed Marianne's corpse inside one of Darian's coffins. It made traveling a little better, by not having to see her body laying in plain view. Sebastian was reminiscing about their life with Marianne, all of the fun and loving things she had done with them and for them.

"Remember what she went as for our Halloween party?" Sebastian asked his dad.

Heartbroken, Sergio couldn't give him an answer. "I don't want to talk about it."

"We can't hide her death, or shove it under some rug and hope the pain goes away! She died for us, her life wasn't in vain. Battles always have casualties, any one of us could be dead right now. Marianne was my best friend and it really hurts that she's not here to celebrate our victory with us-" Rachel was interrupted by Sergio.

"When I said that I didn't want to talk about it, that also meant that I didn't want to hear about it. Don't tell me how to grieve, Rachel." Sergio looked at her, his expression was full of pain, and exhaustion.

Rachel looked at him. "Fine. I know that you don't take death well when it's someone you know. We'll have more time to honor her when things settle down." She sat down by the window, looking out at the passing clouds. Tears flowed freely down her cheeks as she remembered her best friend.

The airplane was silent for a while as they thought about the battle and what they'd gained and lost. Xander was thinking about Alex, how he'd sent for him. How he'd protected him and taught him their ways. Alex had been so grateful to have been rescued and so eager to learn everything he'd had to teach him. He was family and now he was dead, murdered by hate filled humans who had no idea what their purpose was in this scheme. The mood on the plane was somber.

Tony felt he needed to lighten it just a bit. He pointed to Sebastian. "You are in so much trouble. Enjoy your freedom while you can, because the way your dad was talking, you'll be grounded until you're eighty!"

Sebastian chuckled nervously. "Yeah, I know," he replied. He was just happy to be alive and back with his family. He knew one thing, he would never lie to his parents ever again. Of that, he was certain. He suspected that his father, once calmed down, would lay down a punishment fit for the very worst of offenses. He decided he'd worry about that when it happened.

Ryan, Ignacio and Richard were sitting together on the plane, silent, not really certain how to deal with their current situation. Richard was looking out of the window and when he felt the extra attention, he turned to see several pairs of eyes staring back at him. He decided to make himself open for questions.

"I realize that many of you have questions," he said, pausing to allow them to begin the barrage of questions he knew were coming.

"Why did you fight along with us? You could have just run off?" Rachel asked.

"Because it was clear to me that you were going to need my help and I owed it to you," he answered.

"Why did you attack us in the first place?" Justin asked.

"It was what my Pack wanted. Kansas was our state, but they grew bored of it. Then Katrina met Cassandra and the two decided that Illinois would be the best territory. I wanted to make my Pack happy, I wanted them to be stable and comfortable, so I agreed. It was going to be my last duty-"

"Last?!" Ryan asked, interrupting Richard.

He looked at her. "Yes, Ryan. It would have been my last duty before I left."

Ryan's face slackened, sadness creeping in. "You were going to leave us?" she asked softly, as if she didn't want to believe it.

Richard nodded.

"Why?" Ignacio asked, equally surprised by the sudden news.

Xander and the others looked on, awaiting his answer as well.

"I was tired. Tired of being challenged at every turn. I've been a Pack leader for over two-hundred years, it is time for me to step down. And I didn't want to spend the remaining years of my life battling the very people I'm supposed to protect and care for. Katrina assured me she would find a worthy replacement, but she insisted she needed my help to take over the territory," Richard said.

"So you were going to fight and then disappear in the middle of the night or something?" Ryan asked, a tear rolling down her face.

Richard reached over, wiping the tear away. "Yes, once I knew you all were safe. Although, I hadn't planned on simply vanishing into the night. I was going to announce my departure."

"So what now?" Ignacio asked. "Are you still going to leave us?"

Richard looked at him. "No. I'm all that you have. Another Pack may not want to take you in. They might even assume you're rogues or orphans and kill you. I can't allow that to happen." He looked back at Ryan who seemed to be recovering from the shock that the love of her life had almost abandoned her.

"What was your part in their plan?" Elise asked.

Richard looked at her thoughtfully. He had been impressed with her from the very beginning. He thought she was strong, intelligent and beautiful. He had been awed with her fighting skills on the battlefield. He'd seen very few feline Matrons take such a strong stance in battle. From his experience, most left it up to their kings to defend their Prides.

He answered her. "It was brought to my attention, after the fact, that we had contacted the female who was to seduce the boy, Sebastian." He pointed to him. "In return for her participation, she was to be made one of us. I was against her being turned by us, but one of my Pack members decided to do the honors. That was the extent of my knowledge as far as their overall plan."

"That can't be entirely true," Nagesa said. "At Warren's home, we caught his scent." He pointed to Ignacio.

"Hey, it wasn't anything I wanted to do, but per Katrina's agreement, we were to collect the 'human bargaining chips' as she called them. I just did what I was told," Ignacio said in his defense.

"I urged Katrina, Cassandra and Milan to issue a *Challenge of Authority*, but they refused. I did not approve of the cloak and dagger tactics. They were cheap and demeaning, but I was outvoted," Richard said.

"You could have walked away, why didn't you?" Annabelle asked.

"Because the plan was already in motion. And as I said before, I didn't want to abandon my Pack when they needed me. The others were most adamant about going through with it. Besides, I had already made a commitment. I'm a man of my word and I was going to keep my promise to them."

"Too bad none of your loyalty rubbed off on them," Rachel said.

"Did you know that one of your Pack members was the one who contacted the human rebels?" Xander asked.

Richard's expression proved that he hadn't been aware of it. He shook his head slowly.

"What are you talking about?!" Ignacio asked incredulously.

"Boy, did they pull the wool over your eyes!" Justin said, shaking his head in disbelief. He'd never even heard of such betrayal. He was even more grateful that he belonged to a Pack that cared for and loved each other. He now understood why Xander was the kind of Alpha he was, he appreciated that even more.

"This may have been Katrina's doing. It was gathered through our own means that the leader of the human rebel group had a connection with one of your Pack members. We later discovered that the human leader was afflicted with a fatal disease and he was promised to be turned if he cooperated. The other members in his group hadn't known about the trade," Xander said.

Richard sat back further into his chair, thinking over the new information.

"It had to be Katrina and Eric! They were always going off somewhere and many times, Eric wasn't around when you were looking for him. I never made the connection until now!" Ryan exclaimed. She hated Katrina and the others in her Pack for betraying Richard. She believed was the greatest and most honorable man she'd ever met.

"It's not your fault...it's mine." Richard looked at the others. "I should never have played a part in it from the beginning. I did something I didn't want to for the sake of others and almost paid a very heavy price. I know that now..." His voice trailed off as he reflected on the past. "...I think I knew it from the beginning. I just kept telling myself, 'it'll all be over soon'." He shook his head, disgusted with himself.

Xander gazed at Richard thoughtfully. He understood why Richard had done what he did. He had thought he was doing right by his Pack, as any Alpha would try to do. "You saved many of our members tonight. You could have left and never looked back. But you didn't and I thank you for that. You saved my wife and I do owe you a debt of gratitude."

Richard held up a hand in protest. "It was the very least I could do for all that you've been put through."

"Speaking of Eric, where the hell is he?" Ignacio asked.

"Dead," Elise said. "When Darian read Jaric's mind, he was able to obtain every little detail of their plan. Eric was used as a message to us. His body was found in a suburb in Illinois the day before yesterday. He'd been shot by silver bullets."

"He was going to warn you, and that was the price he paid," Xander added.

"My God!" Richard whispered, horrified.

"Not only that, but that other guy, Scott, he was helping them because he wanted to have sex with you. Jaric made him a deal if he held up his end of the bargain by changing Crystal, he'd get to have his way with you," Justin said.

"Scott was planning on raping you?!" Ignacio was disgusted. He looked at Richard, who seemed to still be reflecting on everything.

"I want you to know, and I believe that I speak for all of us with this offer; if you would like to stay in our territory, you may," Elise said.

"That means a lot to me to have your trust, considering the terms in which we met," Richard said, smiling with relief. "I'd like to stay, start over. Thank you."

Ryan and Ignacio were thrilled, both delighted and relieved that he wasn't going to leave them. They continued to find out more about each other for the remainder of the flight, in hopes of easing the last of the remaining resentment and mistrust.

CHAPTER TWENTY

Gary had refused to take Christopher out hunting. Number one reason, Darian didn't instruct him to do so. His own personal reason was that he knew he wasn't strong enough to restrain Christopher if he had lost control during feeding. He was more than happy that the human servants had taken David and the little infants to another hotel room. He wanted to make sure they were safe from the fledgling's new hunger. Unfortunately, both he and Christopher had to settle for Synblood, which he only liked when drinking one of Tony's three specialty beverages.

Christopher was developing a strong distaste for the bitter flavored food substitute. He grimaced as he swallowed the last of the bottle's content. "I swear, I'd rather starve than drink that shit one more night. Isn't there another drink that we can have? Something that tastes a whole lot better?" he asked, in hopes that he could have a variety of blood substitutes.

"I'm afraid not. If you're looking for a selection in the synthetic blood category, you're fresh out of luck. The former, and now deceased, owner somehow managed to lock in the copyrights or whatever they call it, on all edible synthetic blood for global marketing. Pretty smart if you think about it. I don't know how all that stuff works, so please don't ask me about it. So until someone finds a legal way around the copyright, it's Synblood or nothing. That is, of course, if you want to deny your nature," Gary said, lounging lazily on the sofa.

"What do you mean by that? 'Deny my nature'? I thought it was illegal to kill humans?" Christopher asked.

"Well, yeah, if they find out about it. But really, forget what you've heard or read. Vampires don't ever really have to kill their victims if they don't want to. All it takes is a little self-restraint on your part. You have to be able to drink slow at first, savor their essence and have the control to pull back before it's too late."

"But how will I know if it's too late?" Christopher asked, leaning forward, intrigued.

Gary sat up, facing him. "See, that's one of the things that you have to learn. Darian is the master of this city...well, actually this entire state. But he allows smaller covens to gather here, especially if Illinois was their home state. Darian is going to assign someone to teach you everything you need to know."

"But you're here now. Why can't you do it?"

"Well, because he didn't tell me that I could," Gary answered, almost innocently.

"Do you have to obey everything that he says? Can't you make up your own mind, make your own decisions?"

Gary laughed. "Whoa! Slow down there! What are you, union? This isn't a democracy, we didn't vote Darian in. You bet your ass I obey his every word, and you'd better, too, if you want to survive."

"So is it like it is in the movies and books? The master vampire controls all of the lesser vampires?" Christopher sat back, awaiting an answer.

Gary shrugged one shoulder. "More or less, but Darian is so cool! You'll like him. He's one of the most laidback vampire masters you're ever going to find, I promise you." He nodded, smiling. "Oh, and another thing, I don't consider myself a 'lesser' vampire. I'm just not as strong."

"Oh, pardon me." Christopher smirked. "I can tell by looking at how you guys respond to him that you admire him." He was remembering the conversations they'd had that he'd witnessed before he fell asleep. All seemed to respect Darian and vice versa from his observations. Knowing what he knew, he was going to give Darian a chance...not that he had a choice otherwise.

Gary nodded. "I have nothing but the utmost respect for Darian. You will, too, once you get to know him."

Christopher thought about his new master. He didn't know if he would like Darian the way Gary and the others did, but he knew he liked him a damn sight better than the vampire who'd made him. He looked at Gary, he could tell by the aura the other vampire was giving off that he was weaker than himself. He wanted to know a lot more about vampires, especially about the ones within his "new" coven.

"Gary, tell me about a few of the vampires here?"

Gary smiled. "I thought you'd never ask. Xavier was once a wannabe gangster. Now he's Darian's lover and Second in Command. He's also Natasha's lover, but she's not a vampire-"

Christopher interjected. "Whoa, rewind that. Are you saying what I think you're saying?"

Gary nodded. "Yeah, I think I am. Natasha, Xavier and Darian are in a relationship together. It just kind of worked out that way. I ain't mad at them, though, just more to love."

"Tell me about it," Christopher said, shaking his head in disbelief.

"Oh, well, that's a long story, about two years ago-"

"I didn't mean that literally, just a saying."

"Oh." Gary chuckled bashfully. "Good, 'cause I didn't want to have explain that old tale anyway. Miko is older than Xavier by about forty years, but she's not stronger. In her time, she was an assassin for the Meji government in Japan during the late 1880s, when Darian turned her. April came into the coven around 1938. Darian came upon her right before some men got a chance to do some very unsavory things to her, if you catch my drift. He saved her. Annabelle was an abused housewife and now she's Miko's lover. John was saved by Darian one night from some gay bashers, then he just got lucky. Tony came to Darian a few years back for protection, so he took him in. Me, I'm Tony's lover. If you want to know anymore about them, you're going to have to ask them personally."

"Wow, based on that alone, it seems as though Darian is some kind of vampire hero."

"I know he is to a lot of the people he's saved," Gary said, smiling.

"Now, you said you and Tony were lovers?" Christopher asked, one eyebrow raised.

"Yeah?"

"And Darian and Xavier are lovers along with Natasha. And Miko and Annabelle are lovers..."

Gary laughed out loud. When he settled down he answered him. "Okay, I think I know where you're going with this. All of the vampires in this coven are bisexual...all of them, regardless if they were gay or straight before they were turned."

"Why? Does becoming a vampire make you bisexual? If that's the case, I don't feel any different."

"You're straight, right?"

Christopher nodded. "I wasn't really going to say anything, I didn't want to insult anyone. I have nothing against it, I was just curious."

"It's okay. Well, to answer your question, no, becoming a vampire doesn't change your sexuality. You may still prefer to be with the opposite sex. But it's Darian's own philosophy that vampires shouldn't limit their own existence. He says there are 'endless pleasures to indulge in and to deny oneself even one is an abomination'. Basically, we're going to live forever and ever and ever, unless someone or something kills us. We're free to enjoy life without the fear of viruses or diseases. We can't impregnate anyone either, so might as well take pleasure in both sides. Sexual orientation means nothing to us because of that fact. We're free in that sense. Right now, you're still holding onto your human morality, your *mortal coil*. You'll come to understand that much more as you get used to what you are."

"Don't worry, I get what you're saying. I have another question. You said that Xavier was Darian's Second in Command, is that because he's his lover?" Christopher asked.

Gary shook his head. "Oh no. Xavier earned his position. He has what it takes to fill Darian's shoes in his absence. It has nothing to do with favoritism. He's the second strongest within the coven, Miko's the third."

"I see. How did he become stronger than Miko if she's older than him?" Christopher asked perplexed.

"That's because Darian shares his blood more with Xavier than Miko."

"So, it is favoritism."

"How do you figure?"

"If Miko was getting more blood, she'd be strong enough to be Second in Command."

"You could look at it that way. Fact of the matter is, Miko doesn't want that responsibility. She feels she's more dangerous lurking in the shadows than she is standing in the spotlight. Besides, Xavier is Darian's lover, has been for almost a century, it goes without saying he gets to share blood with the master more than the rest of us."

"I get it. Okay, tell me something, how did you become a vampire?"

"Ah, you finally got around to asking the obvious." Gary chuckled. "Now that is a most wondrous and splendid tale. One for the ages to be passed down from generation to generation."

"Un-hun, Was a magic ring involved?"

"Depends on the kind of ring we're talking about." Gary smiled lecherously.

"Damn, I'm sorry I asked that question."

Gary laughed. "Okay, okay, I was just having some fun. I've only been a vampire for a little over two years, almost three. I chose to become a vampire."

"What?! You're kidding me right?"

Gary shook his head. "No, I'm not kidding you. Let me tell you why. The supernaturals had just been exposed and it was still pretty new and scary, but mainly exciting…it still is. *Desires Unleashed* was one of the well known and most popular hot spots to hang out if you wanted to meet one. A few of my friends and I were drunk as hell and naturally we decided to go to a supernatural smorgasbord for shits and giggles. The line was excessively long so that was a good sign in our book. When we finally got in, the place was amazing! Music was blaring, bodies thumping, it was hot! Unfortunately, drunk or sober, we didn't know what a supernatural looked like. So the thrill of going to the club to find werewolves or vampires was fading quickly."

"What did you expect them to look like?" Christopher asked, intrigued by the story.

"Hell, I didn't know! Not like us! It was stupid. I mean, when I think about it, they looked like us all of this time, that's how we didn't know they existed in the first place." He chuckled. "At that time, that reasoning never dawned on me."

"Yeah. I bet you expected them to be all fangy or hairy," Christopher said, laughing.

"Maybe I did. Dumb ass notion, though. Anyway, I had decided to keep the buzz going, so I danced my way to the bar and that's where I saw him…Tony. He was mixing drinks, using all kinds of jazzy tricks, tossing bottles and spinning around, just some really cool shit. I still didn't know that I was looking at a vampire, I just thought he was hot as hell! Then he turned and saw me, he started walking toward me. He asked me what I wanted to drink, at the same time, he flashed me that smile."

Christopher laughed. "This is so gay…but please go on."

Gary rolled his eyes dramatically. "If I may…without any further interruptions."

Christopher made a sweeping gesture indicating that he wanted him to continue. "Go on, I won't interrupt."

"Okay. Well, I told him that I wanted him and he laughed. That night I continued to dance in front of the bar, making sure he was watching me. He was. We hooked up later when he got off work and one thing led to another. We just fell head over heels for each other. I told Tony that I wanted to be with him forever. By this time, I knew what he was and it didn't matter. No, that's not true. As a matter of fact, it did matter because he had the power to make my wish come true. He didn't want to at first. Told me, 'I didn't know what I was asking for'. He said that it 'wasn't like it is in the movies'.

I was finally able to convince him that I knew perfectly well what I was asking. He finally turned me with Darian's permission and we've been together ever since."

"Do you miss being human?" Christopher asked softly. He was already missing his humanity. He no longer felt human and that saddened him greatly. He wanted to know how Gary handled it.

"Well, sometimes, but it's a fleeting thought. Being with Tony is much more important to me. There is so much we as supernaturals are able to see and do, it's actually a gift. I know you probably don't feel that way now, knowing that it was forced onto you, but there really is a bright side to immortality."

"Like what?" Christopher asked, not believing Gary entirely. "I'll never have a family complete with a wife and children, or see the sun again or even taste food again, or-"

Gary interrupted. "Stop right there. That's all trivial bullshit and incorrect. Let me explain something to you. You can have a mate at any time. Also, once you've reached a certain age, all of that other shit comes around again. You'll be able to taste food and go out into the sun. Although, from what I've heard, a lot of ancient vampires no longer prefer human food, but that's not to say you'll feel that way. I'm also aware that you may feel that your nights are endless, but if you open yourself up to your nature, you'll discover that there's beauty in the night. For one thing, it's when the city comes alive. There's passion and lust in the air and now that you're a vampire, those two emotions make an enticing aroma. The night throbs with an energy that only a vampire can appreciate."

"That's all fine and dandy, but I wanted to accomplish things in my lifetime! I'm in school now on a full academic scholarship in a place that doesn't cater to vampires. The classes I'm in don't take place at night. I'm going to have to drop out of school and lose everything I worked so hard for!"

"You can still get a degree. There are other schools that do offer night classes," Gary said, trying to offer him other options.

"Non-Ivy league schools! That's not good enough. I didn't score fourteen-hundred on my SAT to go to a school one step up from a community college!"

"Now, wait, hold on now, don't knock community colleges!"

"Those schools don't have the reputation of the school I'm going to now."

Gary was silent for a few seconds then he spoke. "You don't have much of a choice. Tell me, what did you want to be? What are you going to school for, what's your major?"

"Long story short, I wanted to be a doctor, a neurosurgeon, to be exact."

"Wow, well all I can say is don't let being a vampire stop you. That's taking the punk way out."

"Please tell me what hospital will hire a vampire doctor? Furthermore, what patient would want a vampire operating on them? They'd probably be terrified that I'd find them appetizing and eat them while they're under anesthesia!"

Gary chuckled without really meaning to. The mental image of Christopher donning green scrubs and a white lab coat leaning over a patient on an operating table, feeding, tickled him.

Christopher smirked, head cocked slightly sideways. "That's so not funny."

Gary laughed harder, unable to contain himself. He held up his hand as if to excuse himself. "I'm sorry, I'm sorry...I didn't mean to laugh, honestly," he said through chuckles. "It's just the mental image that I got was hilarious. Listen, if you look for walls to come up, then they're going to come up, blocking you from living your life, however long it is."

Christopher started to protest but he paused, thinking about what Gary had just said. The reasoning was so simple, it held significance for him.

"Chris, er...may I call you Chris? Christopher seems so formal and-"

"Don't worry about it. Yeah, you can call me Chris."

"Great. Listen Chris, you have eternity to be whatever the hell you want to be. See, back in the old days when supernaturals were just monsters in movies and books, it was much harder for us to find things that we could do. You have the luxury of freedom, choice and most importantly the law. You can go to any hospital and get hired. If they don't hire you because of your being a vampire, it's discrimination."

"What you're saying makes sense, but let's be real. Even if I suspected they wouldn't hire me because I'm a vampire, they'd just claim that they passed me up for other reasons. I never thought about it before...mostly because it didn't affect me, but the laws are pretty shitty toward supernaturals."

Gary nodded. "That's true, there's no way I can deny that. However, the laws, as biased and shabby as they are, still opens doors for negotiations, especially if you have a good lawyer. And for the record, there are plenty of supernatural lawyers. Some are out in the open, some still covering it up, but best believe they're great at what they do. Many have had centuries to perfect their craft and the same can be said about supernatural doctors. But you can help people in a number of ways. Hell, you can even open up your own hospital or clinic. The point of the matter is, you have time on your side, not like the rest of the human world, that is your gift...," Gary lay back down on the sofa, relaxing his muscles. "...Or curse. However you choose to look at it. You can see hope or despair. But if you're going to pout and mope about, I don't think you'll survive very long. Most vampires who despair choose to die early."

Christopher studied Gary in silence, amazed by how insightful he was. Everything he said made sense to him. One thing he wanted was to live. He enjoyed life, enjoyed being around his family. He decided right then and there that he would learn from the other vampires if they were willing to teach him to survive his immortality.

"Gary, thanks for taking the time out to talk to me. When I was turned, I thought my life was over. I know that there's still a lot I need to learn, and I'm willing to learn it." Christopher smiled.

"Anytime. You're one of us, now, and the really cool thing is, you're a part of Darian's coven. Now that's prestige!"

"Is that because he's the master vampire of the city?"

Gary nodded his head vigorously. "The vampires in his coven are pretty privileged, more so than those who aren't. We get into *Desires Unleashed* free...," his voice trailed off as he thought about what he was saying. "Now that I think about it, we do get in free because we all work there, which kind of takes the shine off." He laughed.

Christopher laughed as well. "Well, I guess you could say it's the thought that counts. What else puts you on pedestals?"

"Well, none of the other vampires can touch you. Some vampires try to pick on the younger ones for whatever reasons. Not to mention we do get in free to other supernatural owned establishments, complete with the VIP treatment. We're kind of like celebrities."

"Ah, now I understand. I guess that's cool," Christopher said, smiling slightly. He thought about the future of his new life, one thing was clear. If he was going to survive, the first thing he needed to do was embrace his nature, accept what he was. He and Gary continued to converse about many topics as they waited for the others to return.

CHAPTER TWENTY-ONE

The two airplanes landed at their designated airstrips located in different suburbs a few hours later. The nighttime sky was still dark and countless stars twinkled above. They loaded their trucks with their belongings, coffins included. Darian was wearing one of Daniel's favorite jogging suits. He didn't like wearing the outfit. Not only did he look unusual in the clothing, but he felt uncomfortable.

Natasha looked Darian over as he held the truck's door open for her, she had to smile to herself. He looked almost *Hip-Hop*, in her opinion. The vampires were dropped off at their hotel first. Taking the private elevator from the garage to their suite, Darian and his coven carried their remaining coffins back to their room. When they entered, Gary flew into Tony's arms, kissing his lover several times over his face. Tony chuckled softly as he embraced the love of his life, returning his affection. Gary told Elise and Xander which room their children were in and the Pack and Pride gathered their young ones before going to their own mansions.

"Did you miss me?" Tony asked, joking.

"A nervous wreck, is what I've been! I'm so glad that you all made it back in one piece. What happened?"

Gary glanced at all of the vampires, then back to Tony.

"Gary, listen, we're all pretty worn down, achy, weak...shit, you name it, we feel it. Can I give you an update tomorrow?" Tony asked.

"Now that you mention it, I can see just how tired you all are. Okay, I can wait until tomorrow...Natasha!" Gary walked over to her, taking her into his embrace, hugging her tightly. The two had become very close and he was ecstatic to see her alive and well. They released each other, smiling warmly.

"I'm so glad that you're okay," Gary said. He was so happy that his coven was intact.

"You have no idea how happy I am to be here. It was horrible! Marianne's dead and Matthew's been bitten! They don't even know if he's going to survive, but I'm praying that he will," Natasha said as she sat on the sofa next to John. He had collapsed onto the cushions. When she moved his legs out of the way, he looked at her, then let his head fall back down, too tired to jest or even complain.

"That's so fucked up! Marianne was cool as hell! I can't believe this!" Gary sat down on the end table. He looked up at Darian who was walking by. "Master, is it all over?"

Darian nodded. "It's over. We're safe from any further attack from that particular party."

"Good." Gary let loose a sigh of relief.

Tony sprawled out on a chair, draping one leg over the armrest. "God, I don't think I've ever been this tired!"

Gary chuckled. He suddenly remembered something important. "Master, Billy and the others are still in room 1427. They thought it was best to keep the young ones away from Christopher," he said.

Darian nodded. He was pleased by their initiative. "I know. I heard when you told Elise and Xander where to gather their children."

Right after he said that, his human servants entered the suite. Each greeting Darian in their own respectful way.

Billy stood in front of him. "Master."

Darian smiled. "I'm very proud of all of you. The initiative you took during this crisis has impressed me and you will be rewarded accordingly."

His servants smiled, pleased with themselves. Billy bowed slightly before taking a seat along with the others.

Darian looked at his newest member. "Christopher?"

"Yes, um, Master?" Christopher responded, saying the word "Master" as if he wasn't sure if that's what he should call him.

Darian looked at him for a few seconds, making him nervous. "Were the rules explained to you?"

"Hmmm, I guess. You're the master vampire of the city and well, that means...well, members in your coven get perks...um, no... not really." Christopher looked down, embarrassed after struggling to remember if Gary had told him the rules and he just hadn't paid attention.

Darian turned his gaze toward Gary, irritated. Gary cringed and scurried over to Tony, sitting down on his lap.

Tony chuckled, finding the situation slightly funny that he would run to him for safety from their Master, as if he could protect him.

"Why haven't you explained to him my rules?" Darian asked.

"Master, I started to tell him, but the conversation kind of veered off into other topics that seemed to trouble him. I was sidetracked, I'm sorry," Gary apologized.

Darian sighed. "Doesn't matter anymore, and I'm far too exhausted to stay angry." He turned toward Christopher. "Tomorrow night, as discussed, John will be your guide. He will teach you how to feed and everything else you'll need to know. You'd be wise to listen to him. You will stay here until I feel that you are ready to roam freely in my city." Without waiting for his response, he walked into his master bedroom.

Christopher looked at the closing bedroom door, then at the others.

John chuckled. "Don't worry, we're all just really drained. I'll look out for you tomorrow, everything will be fine."

"Thanks," Christopher said softly.

"Right now, though, I'm going to bed, I don't care if the sun hasn't risen or not." John rose from the sofa and walked into one of the empty bedrooms. Stepping back out, he said, "Christopher, if you want, you can sleep in the bed with me."

Christopher tossed him a suspicious look. "Thanks, but I think I'll be okay."

John laughed. "Hey, take it easy. I'm not trying to make a move on you, loosen up. I just wanted to offer you a more comfortable place to sleep, but suit yourself." He went back into the bedroom, closing the door. A few of the other vampires chuckled before going into the bedrooms themselves.

Xavier and Natasha were still awake for the time being. She looked at Christopher, not knowing who he was.

She leaned over, whispering to Xavier. "Who's he?"

Xavier glanced at the young vampire then back at Natasha. "Ah, that's right, forgive me. I completely forgot to introduce you two."

"Don't worry, I understand. I figured I'd get to know everyone sooner or later and under less stressful conditions," Christopher said.

Xavier studied him for a moment. He had been so preoccupied with the situation that he hadn't given the young vampire much thought at all. Now that he was speaking with him on a personal level, he found him to be very mature for his age. He respected that about him.

Xavier made the formal introductions. "He was turned last night because of a series of unfortunate events and now he's with us."

"Did one of you turn him?" Natasha asked, curious.

"No, of course not. Our enemy did as a punishment, or some sick satisfaction," Xavier said.

"Oh." Natasha looked at the teenager. "I'm sorry to hear about what happened to you."

"It's okay...it's done. Now, I just have to figure out what it's all about," Christopher said. He felt a bit awkward with the others in the room. He didn't know any of them well, but he knew all that would change soon enough.

"I hate to cut our conversation short, but we're going to call it a night. There will be plenty of time for us to get acquainted tomorrow," Xavier said, rising to his feet. Natasha took his lead and rose as well. They said their "good nights" to Christopher before joining Darian in the bedroom. Darian was already resting, lying on his back, hands on his stomach.

Natasha chuckled. "I bet he doesn't even know that he looks like a dead man when he lays like that."

Xavier laughed. "I'm going to tell him you said that when he wakes up."

"Good, maybe he'll find another position." She grinned.

Both of them showered before climbing into the bed beside Darian. They closed their eyes, letting their bodies relax into a blissful sleep.

Christopher decided to watch television now that he was the only vampire still awake. Billy was the only human servant still awake, but he seemed to be in his own world, reading a magazine. Christopher flipped through the channels until he found something he wanted to watch. He looked toward the bedrooms. He'd had no idea that vampires grew tired, not to mention, exhausted! He found that detail interesting. He was also taking note of his own being. He felt powerful, strong, his senses heightened to a level that confused, disturbed and excited him. Another thing he felt was Darian's power. He suspected the vampire master wanted him to feel it. He was beginning to understand why Darian was the master. He didn't know how he was going to get along with the rest of the coven, but he was willing to find out.

***

Elise practically fell to the floor as she opened the front door to her mansion. Everyone was past the mere feeling of exhaustion and were basically dead on their feet. The others barely made it to their bedrooms before collapsing. Daniel stored Marianne's body in their walk-in freezer to preserve it until they could have her funeral. Elise and Sergio walked to the nursery to put their infants to bed. Leaning over the cribs, they placed the twins inside gently.

"They did a great job. I was kind of hesitant with leaving the kiddies with them, but I knew we didn't have a choice," Sergio said as he gazed lovingly at his children.

Elise chuckled softly, she looked over her shoulder at him. "Darian trusts them with his life and the lives of his coven. That fact alone gave me some sense of comfort in leaving our children in their care." She turned back toward her sleeping infants. "I'm so happy to be here, back in our home with them."

"I know, baby. I know." Sergio lowered his head, kissing her softly on her shoulder. His son slid a thumb into his mouth, sucking gently. Sergio chuckled as he reached into the crib, plucking the thumb out.

"Don't want him to get used to that, bad habit, causes bucked teeth," he said, chuckling still.

"What's so funny?" Elise asked, looking at him suspiciously.

Sergio looked at her, innocently. "What? Nothing."

"Oh no, you're not getting off that easily, what's so funny?" she asked once again.

"It's nothing really."

"Tell me, I want to know."

"Nosey woman! Very well, I just had a funny thought pop into my head. Made me think about Devin, that's all. Like I said, it's nothing."

Elise thought about Devin's features. "He doesn't have bucked teeth."

Sergio laughed. "That wasn't what I was thinking about when I pulled his thumb out of his mouth." He turned to leave before he could be subjected to the chastising glare that he knew would be on Elise's face.

Elise shook her head, chuckling softly at Sergio's own unique humor. She turned back around, looking lovingly at her babies. After a few minutes, she leaned over the crib, kissing each one on their tiny foreheads. She left the nursery, heading toward her bedroom. When she opened the door, Sergio was already lying down, the satin covers pulled over his shoulders. His hair was still wet from the shower he'd just taken. She undressed and showered quickly before climbing in beside him.

"I never thought a bed would feel so good to me," Sergio said, snuggling closer to Elise, inhaling her scent.

"Aren't you glad I spent three-thousand on this mattress?" Elise mumbled.

"I am now, feels like a cloud. I don't think I've ever been this tired, do you?"

"Not that I can remember," her voice was soft, fading as she drifted off to sleep.

***

Xander looked down at Matthew's shivering form, monitoring his condition. Warren sat in a chair next to the bed, his eyes never leaving his lover. Tatiana sat on the edge of the bed dabbing a cold compress over Matthew's face and chest. Adrian entered the room, carrying an electric fan. He set the fan down beside the bed. Turning it on to high, he positioned the cool air toward Matthew.

"There really isn't much more that we can do but try to keep him cool. The air conditioning is on high, he's got this fan…he's going to have to pull through this on his own," Tatiana said, looking up at Warren.

"He's strong, he'll pull through, I know he will," Warren said. He hoped he was right and not trying to convince himself of something that wasn't possible. He wasn't willing to give up on his lover. He could see that his Pack didn't think Matthew would pull through. He saw it in their eyes whenever he looked at them, which is why he was now avoiding eye contact.

"Warren?" Xander called, just to get the younger man's attention. Warren looked up at him slowly. "What are you going to do about your job? Shouldn't you call in for both yourself and him…that is, if you're planning on staying here?"

"Shit! You're right." Disappointed that he had to leave his lover's side, he had to agree with Xander, he had to tell his Captain something. He rose from the bed, and left the room, entering one that was more quiet. He called his boss and waited for her to answer.

"This is Captain Lawrence," she answered.

"Hey, Capt, Warren, I'm calling-"

"Where the hell are you?! And where is Matthew? You two were supposed to check in earlier! I've been paging you for hours! " Captain Michelle Lawrence was furious, but also relieved to discover that at least one of her best was alright. Now, she was ready to "tear them new assholes."

"That's what I'm calling to tell you. I'm going to need about three days' sick time. I can bring you a doctor's note when I get back." Warren made certain to pretend he was sick, allowing his voice to sound hoarse, even faking a gagging noise when he coughed.

"You sound horrible and very gross. It's convincing, but not convincing enough. I need your asses in here right now. The chief has been calling, wanting an update on the case. Early this morning, there was an attack at the West Montecore Hotel, three shifters, a vamp and a human were killed. Not to mention the slaughter we found yesterday. The killers tried to cover it up by setting fire to the building," the Captain said.

"We can't make it right now-"

"What do you mean? I assigned you two to this case for a reason. You're two of my best, I don't want to hear about how you can't make it, Davis!"

"I'm sorry to disappoint, but we can't. If you want to know the truth, we were injured. While we were investigating a lead, both Matt and I had an unfortunate tumble down a flight of concrete stairs. I didn't want to say anything because it's embarrassing, but right now, neither one of us can walk. Listen, just give us a day, just one day. Put Johnson and Weinstein on the case if you have to, just to cover us. Please, just this once," Warren hoped she would buy his story.

"If I do this for you, you're going to owe me big. I want this case closed within seventy-two hours. I'm only giving you one day. You're on a high-profile case, so even if you have to crawl out of bed and get around on crutches, I want you out there. And don't think I won't be expecting a doctor's note excusing this, the moment you step foot into this precinct."

"Well, I hope you'll allow me to take several more steps with my feet to your office so that I can give you the note," Warren said, sarcastically.

"I see you're not in too much pain to make smart-ass comments. I want you both here tomorrow. Oh, and Warren...?"

"Yeah?" Warren waited for her to continue, silently chastising himself for being a smart aleck.

"Don't wait till the last minute to call in next time. You know better than this," she advised.

"Sure, don't worry, I won't."

"Is Matthew there with you now?" she asked.

Warren was caught off guard. "Hum?"

"I'm quite sure he's there with you. Is he as badly injured as you were?" she asked, sarcastically.

Busted! Warren thought. Not only did she not believe his story, but she knew about him and Matthew. "Yeah, he's pretty fucked up, too. He won't be coming in tomorrow, either." This time it was the truth.

"Alright, just this once."

"I'll let him know that. Can I ask you a question?" Warren asked.

"What is it?"

"Why did you assume Matt was with me?"

"I didn't get my position being oblivious to details. If I didn't think the two of you were best together, I would have split you up by now. I'd rather be concerned with the state of my job than my officer's private relationships. As far as I'm concerned, as long as it doesn't interfere with our mission, I'll look the other way."

She had figured out the two men had become lovers a while back, although, it had been her suspicion for some time. Her first inclination was to find them different partners, knowing the S.U.I.T. organization frowned upon interoffice relationships. But she felt it'd be hypocritical to intervene, when she had her own secret relationship with the S.U.I.T. pathologist, Marshall Galen.

"Thanks for everything, Captain. I won't forget this." Warren said, knowing full well why she hadn't bothered them about their relationship. He remembered the first time he had smelled her scent all over Marshall and vice versa.

"You better not forget it! As soon as possible, get in contact with Johnson and Weinstein to get caught up. Remember, you have seventy-two hours from this moment to get me results, or I'll have your balls as paperweights!"

Warren laughed, it felt good to finally have something to laugh about. "Your desk wouldn't be able to stand under the weight!"

This time, it was Michelle's turn to laugh. "I'm hanging up now," she said before hanging up.

Warren felt a sense of relief that he didn't have to worry about their jobs, they were secure. He knew that he would have to come up with something for the dead shifter they'd found three days ago. Getting down to the bottom of that crime had nothing to do with the law. The massacre the S.U.I.T. found in the hotel room and the SOH hideout were just adding to the case. And once the Florida branch got wind of the bloody battlefield they'd left behind, there was no telling how fast or hard the shit was going to hit the fan. He hoped that he could make it a cold case or find a way to tie the messy ends together. He walked back into the bedroom where Matthew was struggling to live. Tatiana was still applying cold towels to his overheated body. Warren could tell that she was exhausted, they all were. He walked over to her, gently touching her shoulder.

"Tatiana, please get some sleep. I can keep an eye on Matt," Warren said.

She was looking up at him. "Are you sure? This is a constant thing, making sure he stays cool."

Warren nodded. "Yeah, there isn't much more we can do for him anyway, right? You said it yourself, the real fight is up to him."

"For the most part. I've given him a thousand milligrams of acetaminophen, that should take effect soon. I'm hoping it will help bring down the fever at least." She rose from the bed, aided by her husband and Warren.

"Thanks, Tatiana." Warren leaned forward, kissing her softly on the cheek. He loved her as he had loved his own mother. She'd taken him in, loved and nurtured him as she had done her own son. He was grateful for what she'd done for Matthew. They left, leaving Warren alone with his lover. He sat down in a chair beside the bed, continuously refreshing the cold bath towels. He took Matthew's temperature, his heart sinking when he saw that it hadn't gone down. He wasn't ready to say goodbye to him. Warren struggled to stay awake, keeping himself busy by wiping the sweat from Matthew's body. He also paced the room, did push-ups, anything that could keep him alert. Five hours passed before his legs finally grew tired. He sat down in the chair, his bloodshot eyes lazily blinking tiredly at Adrian when he entered the bedroom.

Adrian stopped short, staring at him. "You look like shit, why don't you get some rest? I'll keep watch." Warren began to protest, but he stopped him. "Hell naw, don't even try to fight me on this one. Now, I can drag you out of this room, kicking and screaming, but I hope it doesn't have to get to that point. You need rest. You may be supernatural, but that doesn't mean you're invincible."

Adrian stepped to the side, then pointed toward the door. "Get out, go to sleep and when you wake up, take a fucking shower. Seriously."

Warren rose, he walked toward Adrian. "Will you-"

"Don't worry, I'll wake you up personally if his condition changes. I promise."

Warren nodded. He was tired, and secretly relieved that Adrian had come to help him. "Thanks." He left the bedroom to get some sleep.

Adrian tended to Matthew, doing what was necessary to get his body temperature down. He was relieved by Nagesa three hours later. He was grateful, for he'd only been able to get five hours of sleep before he'd relieved Warren. Nagesa administered more medication, hoping it would break Matthew's fever. He also applied more cold towels. They made sure that Matthew was under constant surveillance. Each shifter knew how crucial the first twenty-four hours were. If the fever didn't break within that time, chances are it never would and the person affected would go into a coma and then die within forty-eight to seventy-two hours. Tatiana entered the room carrying a cup of ginseng tea for Nagesa who took the cup gratefully.

"How's he doing?" she asked.

"Not good. We should probably start preparing Warren for the worst," Nagesa said, then he took a sip of his tea.

Tatiana looked at her watch. "Well, he's not out of the danger zone yet. I spoke with both Natasha and Elise earlier. Everyone is very concerned. I figure in a hour or so, I'll check his temperature again. For the time being, I can watch over him."

Nagesa nodded, rose and left. Tatiana took his seat. An hour later, she checked Matthew's temperature. She looked at the thermometer and she smiled in some relief. His temperature had begun dropping. It didn't mean that he would live, but it was a damned good sign!

CHAPTER TWENTY-TWO

Sergio walked into the bedroom he shared with Elise, carrying a platter loaded with four huge multilayered sandwiches. Plopping down next to Elise, he watched her feeding their twins. The toddlers sat between her legs as she spooned puréed bananas and apples into their tiny mouths. Elise looked at him, smiling.

"It's about time I got those back," Sergio joked, pointing to her breasts.

Elise rolled her eyes, chuckling softly. "You're almost too ridiculous for words."

Sergio laughed, then finished off one sandwich. Elise looked at his plate, then back at him.

"Why are you looking at me like that?" he asked.

"You know full well why."

"Hey, this isn't being greedy right here, I'm hungrier than a hostage! But see, I thought about my baby, too. One of these bad boys is yours." He smiled wolfishly.

"Just one?" Elise asked, both eyebrows raised.

Sergio swallowed the first bite of his second sandwich. "Oh, alright then. If you're going to make a big fuss about it, you can have two."

"You're such a humanitarian." Elise smiled, then leaning over, kissed him. "I love you."

"Baby, I don't think there are words to describe how much you mean to me. To say I'm happy we survived is an understatement. I don't know what I would have done if you...," his voice trailed off, not wanting to even contemplate Elise's demise.

"I know, sweetheart, I know." She kissed him once again.

Sergio continued to watch her feed their babies. He leaned over, kissing both toddlers on their tiny foreheads and noses. When his son, Cicero, had taken all that he wanted from his sip-cup, he dropped it on Elise. Releasing several burps causing his parents to laugh lightly. Sergio scooped his son into his arms, turning him over and tickling his belly. Cicero laughed and cackled as he wiggled playfully in his father's arms. He let his son crawl and climb over him, laughing happily as he did this. He looked over at his daughter, Annette-Naté, who was now eating the remainder of her brothers meal.

"She's got an appetite!" Sergio declared with glee as he watched his daughter lean forward, mouth open to take in the spoon full of apples.

"I know! She's like Mia!" Elise agreed as she balanced her daughter on her lap. With her free hand, she reached over, taking up one of the sandwiches and began eating.

"Did you call Natasha and Xander?" Sergio asked.

Elise nodded. "I did. Natasha's doing fine and so is their newest member. Matthew, however, isn't looking so good. But we're going to keep our hopes up. He's in good hands over there."

Sergio nodded in agreement. "Warren must be at the end of his rope."

"I'm sure that he is. But he's keeping in good spirits about it."

"I'm sure Tatiana and Xander are helping him stay grounded." Sergio sat back against the pillows. "You know, it's funny."

Elise was curious. "What?"

"Xander...Tatiana, both are pretty regal if you think about it. Obviously, they're aristocrats. Adrian's dad is this stiff upper lip British nobleman and his mom is a dainty French dame, like yourself."

"Yes..." She waited for him to continue.

"How the hell did they end up with a son like Adrian?"

"What do you mean?"

"Now, don't get me wrong. We get along great. Adrian is a hell of a guy. But he's nothing like his parents."

Elise giggled. "There is more than meets the eye to Adrian."

"I don't know, I guess I half expected him to be a little like them." Sergio shrugged one shoulder.

"Ah, like you? You inherited a great deal of your parents personality traits," Elise teased, knowing that Sergio's family was a well known and feared Pride in Sicily, that also happened to be Mafioso. He had no doubt inherited his parents no-nonsense attitude. Not to mention his strong sense of honor and loyalty to family.

"What's that supposed to mean?" Sergio asked, one eyebrow raised.

"Oh, nothing really, only that I love you just the way you are." She leaned forward, kissing him softly on the lips.

Pulling back, she picked up the other sandwich and began eating. A few seconds later, there was a knock on their bedroom door.

"Come in," both said in unison.

Sebastian entered the room, head bowed low in shame. Sergio looked at his son, but remained silent.

"What's the matter, Sebastian?" Elise asked.

Sebastian looked up, his gaze darted toward his father. "Mmm, about what happened...I'm sorry."

Elise looked at Sergio, waiting to see what he would say or do. She knew he was still very disappointed in his son for his dishonesty. "I think I'll take the little ones to their playroom," she said. Climbing out of the bed, she helped the twins to their feet so they toddled with her. The three left the room, leaving the two males to speak in private, father to son.

Sergio sat up straight on the bed, keeping his stern glare on his son. He was ready to deal out punishment now that his son was free and clear of danger. "What you did was not only dangerous and foolish, it was insulting."

"Dad-" Sebastian started to grovel, but his father stopped him.

"No. No excuses. You don't have one good enough to suffice." Sergio swung his legs off the bed, so that he could better face his son. "Sebastian, this isn't about you getting kidnapped. I have no doubt that they would have caught you one way or another, it was a part of their plan. I'm upset with you because you lied to me about where you were going. Do you have any idea what your mother and I have been through?"

Sebastian shook his head, his hands in his blue jean pockets.

"Not knowing where your kid is, if they're safe, or hurt or dead is a sickening feeling. I'm teaching you everything I can about being a man and a great deal of that is being honest with your family and to yourself, being accountable for the choices you make and being responsible enough to make the right decisions. I would be lying if I said that I wasn't disappointed in you."

"I'm sorry, Dad." Sebastian lowered his head again, too ashamed to look his father in the eye.

"Sebastian, look at me."

He raised his head, eyes on his father. "Are you mad at me about Crystal?"

Sergio chuckled softly. "That you lied to me because you wanted to have sex, yes. That you did, no. I was prepared for you to explore your sexuality. Why do you think I gave you all of those father-son pep talks along with a few boxes of condoms? To tell you the truth, I'm kind of surprised, but pleased that you hadn't been sexually active until this moment. I know how hard it was for you, I was once your age."

Sebastian nodded with a slight smile. "I thought you'd be mad that I didn't wait for marriage or something like that."

Sergio made an off handed gesture. "No, of course not. You're a shifter, it may take you years and years to find the perfect mate. When I left my Pride at eighteen, I was on my own and searching for another Pride to join. I've been in about four different Prides, and after a hundred and twenty-six years, I finally found the woman of my dreams. But in that time, I'd been with many females, mainly to perform my duties as a stud within those Prides, but other times, just for pleasure."

"Oh, I feel better knowing that," Sebastian said, relieved that he hadn't disappointed his father by having sex on top of lying about it.

"But what I can't figure out for the life of me, is why you felt that you had to lie to me? I've always been honest with you about everything and I expected the same in return. It's a sign of total disrespect when a child lies to a parent, and it's even worse when a man lies, period. A real man should be able to tell the truth and stick by his actions, no matter what the consequences. Now, what do you think I should do regarding this situation?" Sergio asked, putting the responsibility in his son's hands.

Sebastian looked at his dad, he knew it wasn't a trick question. "Everything you said was right."

"I know. I'm your father, I'm always right."

Sebastian chuckled. "I was wrong to lie to you. I was scared that you'd get mad at me for having sex with a girl."

Sergio looked confused. "Why would I be mad at you for having sex with a *girl?*"

"Oh, wait, I didn't mean it like that. What I meant to say was; I thought you'd be mad at me for having sex with a human."

"Oh...that. Well, you're young, and you haven't gone through your change yet. Once you do, you'll discover the differences between a shifter female and a human one. You can make your own decision on the kind of person you want to be with, be them female or male, human or supernatural."

"Wow, you're being pretty understanding about all of this," Sebastian said, surprised by his father's outlook.

"Well, I've had time to change my mind about humans, having met some decent ones, ya know? Besides, I can't project my choices onto you. Now back to your punishment." Sergio rose from the bed, walking toward his son.

"Oh...that. I guess I deserve to be punished." Sebastian's shoulders slumped despondently, lips pouted slightly.

"You're damn right you do! Lucky for you, I'm not going to. I already know that you're sorry for what you've done and berating you was satisfaction enough for me. With the kidnapping and everything else, I'm sure you've learned a valuable lessen. To be honest, I'm too happy to have you back with us to punish you further." Sergio wrapped an arm around his son's shoulder, pulling him closer, hugging him tightly.

Sebastian smiled as he held onto his father.

"Okay," Sergio said, breaking their embrace, holding him at arm's length. "As long as we understand each other?" He looked at his son directly, making eye contact.

Sebastian nodded. "No more lying, no matter what."

"Good." Sergio ruffled his son's hair before he let him go. As both men left the bedroom, Sergio went to find Elise and their twins. They were in the den with a few of the others. The twins were laughing and playing with a few toys along with Mia. Elise was sitting on the sofa, the others were crowding around her as they discussed arrangements for Marianne's funeral. They had their own private graveyard on their property, so looking for a funeral home was the least of their troubles. The real worry was what they were going to say to her family and friends, those who knew about her being a shifter. These few were the only ones who had really stayed in contact with Marianne.

Elise knew she would have to give them the terrible news, and she was dreading having to do so. Sergio sat down beside Elise, rubbing her leg reassuringly.

"Well, baby, how are we going to break the news to her family?" Sergio asked. "They're human and aren't going to fully understand what it means to have a territory war."

"They'll probably wonder why we didn't just go to the S.U.I.T. when Sebastian and the others were kidnapped," Madeleine added.

"That's true. We're just going to have to figure out a decent enough lie. I think telling them the truth would be too traumatizing and most likely, unacceptable," Daniel said.

"Whatever we come up with probably won't be good enough. If we tell them she was murdered or whatever, they're going to want an investigation. And if we tell them it was natural causes, they're going to want to know what kind of natural cause can kill a shifter?" Devin said.

"Our best bet is to tell a shadow of the truth. Just enough to quench their curiosity, but not enough to cause a greater amount of concern...well no more than necessary. We don't want them going to the S.U.I.T. on Marianne's behalf. That's trouble we don't need or want," Elise said. She sat back in her seat, contemplating their situation. She was fortunate to have never come across this situation in the past. She had to admit to herself, her former king and husband had honored his Pride by fighting for them in territory battles, but she also had to thank those who challenged them, for accepting such arrangements. This was the first time her entire Pride had to fight. She was very proud of how well they had handled themselves.

"We don't have a choice, Elise. We're going to have to tell the whole truth. Telling a lie or even half the truth will just make matters worse. Besides, it isn't respectful to Marianne. Let's just hope they'll understand," Sergio said.

Elise nodded in agreement. "You're right. I'd better make the telephone call."

Sergio touched her lightly on the shoulder, gaining her attention. "I could call her family, you've done enough."

Everyone froze, looking at Sergio. They all knew that he was a man of very, very few words and all were extremely straightforward.

Elise placed her hand over his, smiling sweetly. "Awe, that is so sweet of you, darling, but I can make the call."

She rose, heading out of the room.

"What? You don't think I can deliver the news in a gentle way?" Sergio asked, suspicious of her reluctance and everyone's stares.

Elise turned toward him. "It's not that...well, yes, it is that. Darling, you're the most loving man I know, but it's no secret that you lack tact."

"Yeah, Sergio, let's just say your choice of phrases can be brutally honest," Carmen said, teasingly.

"Yeah, I mean, I love that about you, Sergio, but sometimes you're so cut and dried, you come off as…well, a little heartless," Madeleine said.

"What's wrong with being honest? I just got through telling my son that's the only way to go. Lies hurt and they don't fix anything," Sergio said in his defense.

"Tell me something? When Sebastian used to draw pictures when he was a little kid, did you tell him his crazy looking pictures were just that, or that they were masterpieces?" Devin asked, laughing as he spoke.

"Fuck you," Sergio retorted, rolling his eyes. He looked back at Devin. "I told him they were masterpieces, alright. He needed encouragement. And, by the way, I'm a doctor, I have experience with delivering bad news. But hey…," He held his hands up, surrendering, "if you want to do it, fine. No skin off my Johnson."

"Case. In. Point.," Devin said with a boyish grin. Sergio smirked.

"I still love you, Darling," said Elise, smiling as she left the room. She went into her bedroom, sitting down comfortably on the satin sheets. She picked up the handset and dialed Marianne's mother's number. On the fifth ring, her mother answered. Elise greeted her, and explained who she was just in case the woman had forgotten, which she doubted. It's not an everyday occurrence when your only child has to join a Pride of supernatural shape-shifters in order to survive.

"I know who and what you are. You didn't have to remind me. How is my daughter?" the mother asked.

Elise could tell that Marianne's mother didn't like her any more now than she had when they'd first met. She braced herself for the anger, pain, sorrow and no doubt, recriminations that she assumed would be directed at her after the revelation of her daughter's death.

"There is a reason why I've called you today, Mrs. Calloway. I wish that I didn't have to make this phone call, but I have terrible news. Marianne is no longer with us...she was killed." Elise paused, letting what she said sink in.

There was silence over the line for a few seconds, then the mother spoke. "What are you telling me? I don't...I don't understand?" The woman's voice was shaky, soft.

"I am so sorry, we both lost someone we loved very much. There was no easy, less painful way to tell you. I too, loathe that a dear friend and fellow Pride member is dead, she was family to us. Please, I beg you to understand that the circumstances surrounding her death could not have been avoided," Elise said, hoping to relay how much her daughter was loved and appreciated within her Pride.

"Circumstances?! Circumstances?! I'm sorry, Ms DuPre, but there isn't a 'circumstance' good enough to explain or excuse my daughter's death!" The mother paused as she struggle to contain her emotions. Tears ran down her cheeks, her hand quivered as she held it to her mouth as if trying to keep her screams locked within.

Elise could imagine how distraught Marianne's mother was. As a mother herself, she couldn't fathom the loss of one of her precious children. She wished she didn't have to make such a call even more now, than before she'd made it.

"You have the audacity to call me...you tell me my only child is dead and you beg me to understand the 'circumstances'!?!" The mother was incredulous.

Elise understood the woman's anger, she was willing to overlook the rudeness...to a point. "Her death was not in vain, Mrs. Calloway-"

"Oh yes it was! I begged Marianne to come home, to live with us. I wish she had listened to me instead of trusting you people...she would be alive now if she had!"

"Maybe, maybe not," Elise said, taking off her kid gloves, figuratively speaking. "Your daughter, as much as you would like to believe, contrary to all evidence, was no longer a human being. She was bitten by a leopard through no fault of our own. Had she remained alone, others of our kind would not have recognized her as someone with a human family, only that she didn't belong to a Pride. They would have tried to kill her. I took her in, taught her how to survive, made certain that she understood what she had become. I loved her and cared for her...protected her-"

"Not enough!" The mother interjected, her tone heavy with sorrow. "Not enough to keep her alive. I want to know, what kind of 'circumstances' are responsible for my daughter's death, I want to know that much." Mrs. Calloway was furious, her heart ached in ways she hadn't known was possible. She was shattered. Her daughter was dead. She had hated it when she had found out that Marianne had become one of them. For years, her family had had to live with that fact. They had grown to accept it. She hadn't agreed with her daughter when she'd come to them, declaring that she had to move in with the local Pride, a group of supernaturals like herself. She didn't understand then, and she didn't understand now. She listened to Elise tell her about a territory battle, only halfway understanding its true devastation. It was as she suspected; not a good enough reason. Unable to continue the conversation, her voice caught in her throat, she simply placed the handset back on its base, disconnecting the call.

Elise suspected that the mother blamed her personally for Marianne's death. She knew that the woman would not be able to comprehend what a territory battle meant to any supernaturals involved. She was happy that she was able to tell the mother how brave and strong her daughter had been. She hoped that it would mean something.

She sat there in silence, staring at the telephone. Sergio came into the room, sitting beside her on the bed. She looked at him, her king, her mate. She was so proud of him and wanted to tell him. "Sergio, last night, I was so proud of you." She placed her hand over his chest. "Your heart is what makes you such a wonderful man. I couldn't be happier than to be your Queen, I love you."

Speechless, Sergio crushed Elise to his chest, kissing her passionately. As he caressed her tongue with his own, feeling her against him, his heart swelled. He reveled in her heat, her presence. They cuddled together for a long time before leaving the comfort of their bedroom. They still had to tend to Marianne's funeral arrangements, in the event that the parents didn't want to hold the funeral. Elise would extend an invitation to her parents and family members. She was certain, despite their differences, they'd want to come to their daughter's funeral. If the parents were going to hold the funeral, Elise wanted to attend, along with her Pride. She'd have to contact the mother once again to see if they were going to handle the arrangements or not. A few hours later, after everything on her end was set, she decided to take a nap, her body was calling for it. She climbed back into her bed, pulled the sheets over her head and went to sleep.

CHAPTER TWENTY-THREE

When John opened his eyes, the first thing he noticed was that he wasn't in his own bedroom. Beside him sat April, reading a magazine. She turned, looking down at him.

"Finally decided to open your eyes," she teased.

"I still feel like I just got my ass handed to me on a wooden chopping block," John said, climbing out of the bed slowly, feeling his new strength inside him. "I thought my body would be stiff or something, but at least it doesn't ache like it did yesterday."

"Tell me about it," April said, turning the page of her fashion magazine.

"And just my luck, I have the dubious distinction of training our newest member," John complained.

April chuckled. "You should be happy that Darian has that much confidence in you."

"I am. Don't get me wrong. It's just that, well…I don't want to." John chuckled. "I just want to be lazy. I want to spend my nights with Devin. But I should get dressed, he'll be up soon and ready to feed." He walked into the bathroom, showering quickly. As he dressed in a pair of black jeans, white v-neck pullover shirt and black boots, he began to feel a gnawing inside his stomach indicating that he, too, needed to feed soon.

"I can hear your stomach all the way over here!" April teased.

"And…?" John retorted, smirking cockily.

April looked up at him, winking coyly. He shook his head as he tied his boots. He grabbed his black leather bomber jacket and left the bedroom, heading toward the living room where their newest fledgling was still resting. Tony and Miko were discussing the battle they had survived and everyone's amazing fighting skills.

John tossed a glance at them, then at Christopher. "I guess I'm not too late."

"He's young, first to rest, last to rise, you know how it is. Gary's still out, too," Tony said.

"Yeah, I know. I'm just ready to go hunting," John said as he approached the sofa. Leaning over the younger vampire, he peered into his face. "He's cute."

"Don't get any ideas," Miko said.

John tossed her a look. "Don't worry, I won't. I was simply making an observation." He looked back down at Christopher, waiting for him to rise. He thought about what April had said, about Darian trusting him. The longer he looked at the resting vampire, the more he began to feel a sense of pride that he had been picked to educate their newest member. He finally understood.

John sat down on the sofa beside Christopher's head, waiting for the younger vampire to rise. Fifteen minutes more passed before Christopher opened his blue eyes, immediately startled to see John looking down at him.

"Jesus!" he exclaimed as he scrambled to sit up, arms and legs flailing. Once sitting upright, he looked back at John. "You scared the shit out of me!"

John's eyebrows arched. "What are you trying to say?"

"He's trying to say that ugly-ass monster mask you call a face scared the shit out of him, so don't do it again," Tony jested. He turned, facing them. "I tried to tell him myself, but he didn't believe me. Maybe now, he'll stop leaning over people, looking at them while they rest." He smiled wickedly, exposing his pearly whites. He burst into a fit of laughter as John stuck up his middle finger.

Christopher caught on to the joke, relaxing, he began to laugh as well.

John smiled. "Screw the both of you." He looked at Christopher. "Come on, you. We've got to cover a lot of ground tonight."

"What do we need to do?" Christopher asked innocently.

"Well for starters, we need to eat. You need to learn how to hunt, among other things. Come on." John gestured for him to get off of the sofa. "You should shower first."

"Wait, I don't want to kill anybody!" Christopher protested.

John smiled. "Don't worry, you won't. Now come on, get ready before I decide to leave your ass."

"I don't have anything clean to change into."

"I can help in that department. You can borrow an outfit of Gary's. Let me get that for you," Tony offered, rising from his chair. He went into the bedroom and emerged a minute later with a pair of blue jeans and a plain t-shirt. He handed the items to Christopher. "Here you go. You can keep these."

"He won't be mad, will he?" Christopher asked, taking the clothes.

"Trust me, Gary is so not going to want these clothes back after you're done with them." Tony smiled wolfishly.

Clueless as to the meaning behind Tony's statement, he nodded and went into the bathroom to shower and get dressed. John waited for him to finish. Once he was dressed, he stepped out of the bedroom. His hair was still wet from his shower.

"Well, it's good to see that the clothes fit. Okay, let's go, the night won't wait for us." John rose from the sofa, heading toward the door.

Christopher looked around. A few of the other vampires were watching him, which made him slightly nervous. He still didn't know them and everything seemed to be moving very fast. He turned and followed John out of the hotel room. They stepped onto the elevator and John pressed the Ground Level button.

"It's not as bad as it sounds…hunting. It doesn't mean that you have to kill," John said as he watched the numbers light up on the indicator for each floor they passed.

"So what does it mean?" Christopher asked.

John looked at him. "Well, you have to find your…hmmm, there's no nice way to put this and if there is, I don't know it. So I'm going to cut to the chase, no sugarcoating. You're going to have to find your own victims to feed from. You're young and since you don't want to kill, you're going to have to feed from three or four people a night so that you can leave them alive, unaware of what happened to them. Hell, you might have to feed from two people even if you did kill your victims because you're a fledgling. The good news is, the older you get, the less you'll need to feed, but you'll still need to feed."

"Well, can't I just drink the Synblood?" Christopher asked, then he thought about the taste of the alternative drink. He shook her head. "Never mind."

John laughed, knowing what made him change his mind. "I thought you'd change your mind. I think the only reason why they don't try to improve on the taste is because there aren't enough vampires requesting 'better taste, more filling'. The only vampires that are content with that shit are the ones who hate what they have become anyway, so the taste is probably a welcome form of torture for them. Self-flagellation, this is just my opinion."

"It does taste really bad."

John nodded. "You can always tell the difference between a vampire that feeds on blood and one that drinks Synblood. Vampires who drink fake blood are always pale, gaunt. They actually do look like the walking dead, so not attractive and they're weaker." He was glad to know that Christopher wouldn't be settling for the synthetic beverage. *There's hope for the young man, yet,* he thought to himself.

"Look, don't worry. Tonight is going to be a very fun learning experience. Just listen to me and follow my lead and everything will go smoothly." The elevator stopped, the two men stepping off when the doors opened.

"Where are we going?" Christopher asked once they were outside of the hotel.

"Since we're already downtown, which is a good location spot for hunting. We're also close to some of the seedier parts of the city, which is also good hunting grounds. For now, we can just walk around," John said, heading north.

"Why walk? I mean, where's the car you had yesterday?"

"In the hotel garage. We have a lot more cars back at our partially destroyed mansion. I'm really pissed off about that shit, too! That mansion was beautiful! We had everything we could ever want. There's no telling how long it's going to take us to get things back to the way they were. Hopefully, not long." John looked at Christopher. "Why'd you ask? What? You don't want to walk?" He chuckled.

"No, not really. My stomach is really starting to hurt, so walking wasn't high on my list." Christopher caressed his abdomen, rubbing it softly. "Not to mention, you're walking pretty fast, it's hard for me to keep up."

"Don't worry," John said, slowing his pace. "We'll find someone soon, you need this experience." They turned left on State street toward the Humans-Only district.

"So back to what you were saying, since the mansion is destroyed, we'll be living at the hotel? Man, I don't even want to imagine the hotel bills!" Christopher shook his head.

John laughed. "Darian owns that hotel. We're staying there for free."

Christopher looked at John in complete awe.

"Darian is dirty, grimy, filthy, stinking, wretchedly rich. If Entrepreneur Elite would get that stick out of their ass and start listing supernaturals in their magazine, Darian would be one of the top richest business men in the world."

"Not the richest man?"

"Oh, hell naw, " John said, chuckling. "Darian's Uber-rich but there are some who are far older and richer than he is."

"Oh, I see. So Darian takes care of all of you?" Christopher asked, trying to get a better understanding of how the master controlled his coven.

"In the most simplest of explanations, yes. But we all work it off somehow."

Christopher nodded. "I think Gary mentioned that you guys work for Darian at his club. Is that how you work it off?"

John nodded. "Yeah, the club is the business of choice. It's the perfect hotspot for everyone, regardless of species. That's why we choose to work there. But Darian has other businesses, not including the hotel. I also know that he, along with several other supernaturals are forming a board of directors to create a university that will cater to both supernaturals and humans."

Excited, Christopher reached out, grabbing hold of John's forearm, stopping him in mid-step.

"What?! Please tell me I heard what I think you said."

"I take it a university for supernaturals excites you," John said, jokingly. "Yeah, it's something that's been in the works for a while. A few shifters and vamps who were students and professors came to Darian with their proposition. Seemed like a good business venture, so he agreed."

"When will it be…I mean, how long, er, when…" Christopher stammered for the right words through his excitement.

John flashed the young man his megawatt smile. "Not too much longer. Possibly in the next year or so. And you can bet your ass it's going to be Ivy League. Don't worry, you're not alone in your anticipation. Gary had to drop out of college because the curriculum wasn't designed to suit vampires. Same with Tony, although, his situation's a bit different. Anyway, eventually there will be a higher level of education for everyone."

"I'm so happy that it's going to be Ivy league." Christopher smiled, seeing his future looking up.

"Yeah, the teachers are going to be both human and supernatural. Besides, who can better educate you than someone who was around during the first open-heart surgery or who fought in the Civil War?" John began walking again, with Christopher following behind him.

"Will I be expected to work at the club or one of his other businesses?" Christopher asked.

John nodded. "Probably. That decision is up to Darian. But if he does put you to work, you better hope it's the club. Xavier runs the entire club, Gary strips, Annabelle manages the strip club,

Tony tends bar, April is Darian's personal secretary, I manage the dance section, Miko manages the bord-" he stopped, wondering if he should reveal the secret sections of *Desires Unleashed.*

"What? Why'd you stop?"

"Promise you can keep a secret?"

"Sure, I know how to keep a secret. Besides, I'm part of the coven, right?"

John nodded. "True. Okay, Miko runs the bordello and I also oversee the back room. There's also a coliseum which is Darian's haven, but I'm not going to get into too much detail over the last one."

"The back room? Do people get high there, or have sex or something?" Christopher asked, becoming increasingly curious.

"Well, in a manner of speaking, yeah. It's basically a safe spot for vamps and everyone else to go. There are a lot of people who love to get bitten by us. So, they get their desires met, we get our needs met, everyone gets their rocks off, and all can go home safe and satisfied."

"Oh, I get it."

"Yeah, it's a pretty cool setup. Darian expects us to work five days out of the week, but we're doing what we love to do, so it's cool, no real pressure."

"Do you get paid?"

"Yeah, playtime money really. Like, if we wanted to go on vacation or buy tons of clothes, that's what our money is good for. Darian provides us with all of our wants, needs and desires. For instance, if we want a large screen plasma projection TV, then he'd buy it, no questions asked. He feels responsible for us and our comfort. He controls the environment in which he presides and he wants everything to be luxurious. I think you'll really like him a lot once you get to know him."

"Everyone keeps saying that. Okay, you've praised him a great deal, you all have. Please tell me something that you don't like about him?" Christopher was trying to get a better understanding of his new master, pros and cons. He knew no one was perfect.

John chuckled, tickled by Christopher's curiosity. "Maybe you're asking the wrong person, because there's nothing about Darian I don't like. He's brilliant, calm, cool and collected. He's sexy, gorgeous, powerful and he doesn't take shit from anyone."

"I can see why you find him admirable. I guess I'm going to have to determine for myself my own feelings about him. I want to see for myself if he's as wonderful as you all say he is," Christopher said, keeping his pace with John.

"That's a wise idea." John smiled warmly.

Christopher looked around. "Where are we?"

"Gold Coast area."

"What's over here besides a bunch of yuppies?"

"Have you heard about the Gold Coast Rapist?" John asked, tossing a glance his way.

Christopher nodded. "Yeah, he's been in the news every day for a week. They said he raped and killed four women. At least, those they could tie to him that they've found."

"Well, tonight, his playtime will be over."

"Are you going to kill him?!"

"No. Not that I don't want to, I just don't have permission to do so. But we will make him our victim and then turn his punk-ass over to the police." John looked at him. "I've picked him for your first time, because I think it'll be easier for you to feed on someone who really deserves it. The scum of society is always the best choice for a meal. As a matter of fact, it's your only choice. In Darian's territory, feeding on innocent blood is a punishable offense, punishable by death. Only those who are willing or criminals, no one else."

Christopher thought about John's words. He shrugged one shoulder. "I suppose that makes sense. How are you going to find him?"

"I'm a vampire. I can zone in on a human in the area I'm in at any time. I'm not strong enough to do it from a greater distance. I have to be closer to my target in order to connect, which is why we're just walking around this area. This is where he stalks his victims, so this is where we'll stalk him," John enlightened him.

"How do you connect?"

"I can search the minds of people in this area, read their thoughts. It's kind of bothersome because you get a rush of mental voices and you have to filter through them for the one you want. I don't do it often because I, personally, find it annoying."

"I can see how that would be a lot to deal with, even over the span of a short distance, all of that deciphering, trying to determine who's who."

John nodded. "Exactly, but this is a special case." He stopped walking. Standing still, he closed his eyes, concentrating. He paid very close attention to the mental images and voices that flashed into his brain, fragments that told stories of the people he was scanning. Five minutes passed before he found the one they had come for. Their intended target was only three blocks away at a bar. He had found his own victim for the evening, a five-foot-two blonde college student. Her big, round brown eyes scanned the bar, looking at all of the patrons that occupied the bar. She had no idea she was being stalked. She hadn't even noticed when he switched from the bar to a table to gain a better view of her. She was waiting for someone and by the way she checked her watch every few minutes, it was evident that this person was either late or not going to show up. The stalker was thrilled, he didn't want any interruptions. Little did he know, he would soon be interrupted anyway.

The murdering rapist's blue eyes peered at the girl as she slid her slender arms into her blue leather jacket, freeing her long blonde hair from beneath the collar. She grabbed her purse and left the bar, walking south toward her apartment. He left the bar as well, following her. He wanted her so badly...so badly that he could taste her sweat on the tip of his tongue. He grew hard as he fantasized about her helplessness as he visualized himself pressing the sharp, jagged blade of his six-inch long dagger against the tender skin of her throat. He flexed his fingers, keeping pace with her. She had no idea of what he had in store for her. He would first come up from behind, covering her mouth with a chloroformed-soaked cloth, rendering her unconscious. Next, he would drag her off, pretending that she was his intoxicated friend. No one would question it. They would actually praise him for being such a trustworthy and loyal friend, as had happened in the past. Once she was in his car, he would drive her to the place he had taken the others. There, he was going to have his way with her.

She would be blindfolded until he was ready for her to see the face of her fate...her death. Her wrists and ankles would be bound, tied to the bedposts. She would struggle wildly to break free, but the barbed wire constraints would only bite into her skin, shredding her flesh until the excruciating pain would force her lie still. At that point, he would climb on top of her, as he had done with the others, running his dagger along her body, meticulously slicing into fair skin, drawing thin lines of blood. He didn't want to bleed them, just make them feel enough pain to keep them terrified. Their fear excited him so, making his lust for them nearly unbearable. Their screams and pleas only heightened his ecstasy. When their bodies were covered with blood and sweat, he would shove himself deeply into them, over and over again, ramming as hard as he could until he was spent, sated. After that, he had no more use for them. It was at that point, he would remove the blindfold so that when he wrapped his hands around a soft, narrow throat, the last thing she would see would be only him as he would squeeze the life out of his victim. This one was so pretty to him. The way her hips swayed when she walked, the way she brushed her hair from her shoulders, she was seducing him! Of that, he was certain. She wanted him to take her, she would be happy that he chose her, she just didn't know it yet.

John opened his eyes. "Let's go." He now knew how and when the rapist would attack the girl and they didn't have a second to spare. He ran slowly enough to allow Christopher to keep up. Within a few seconds, he turned the corner, purposely bumping into the young lady. "Oh!" he exclaimed, hands out, grasping the young woman, helping her regain her balance. "I'm sorry, are you okay?" he flashed her a charming smile.

The young woman blushed, John was just her type of man. "Yeah, I'm fine."

"Great. Let's keep you that way." John sent a mental message to her, commanding her to take the cab he had mentally hailed for her, and to go straight home. He ushered her toward the waiting cab. She climbed in and the cab drove away. Christopher was amazed by the show of John's ability. He wondered if he would be able to do the same things. John turned toward his victim. The killer who enjoyed raping, had been stalking the girl who was just rescued, and was now ducking into a doorway, watching her climb into a cab. He saw the cab drive away, greatly disappointed that he had been interrupted, robbed of his chosen victim, robbed of satisfaction. Angered and frustrated, he turned, heading back down the street. He was beyond enraged, his plan had been thwarted! The two vampires followed him. He began to notice he was being followed when he tossed a glance over his shoulder and saw the two men watching him. One looked confused, while the other had the eyes of a predator. It was a look he knew all too well, it was one he saw when looking at his own reflection. The things he was beginning to sense from the predator-like male made him extremely nervous.

"George," John called softly, startling the man, who stopped walking. The man turned, facing him.

"I don't know you," George said. He spoke softly, unable to conceal his mounting fear. How did this man, whom he'd never met, know his name and speak it so boldly?!

John stepped closer to him, smiling viciously. Christopher stayed behind, watching in silence, unsure of what would happen next.

"Ahh, but I'm a lot like you. You see, I like to gaze into the faces of my victims, too. It's music to my ears when I hear their screams of fear as I sink my fangs into their veins slowly before I drain their lives away." John's smile widened, revealing his long, pointed fangs.

George stiffened with fear, unable to move because the vampire didn't want him to. John was having a little fun with his prey. He was enjoying the scent of fear that emanated from this man in waves. He led George away from curious eyes into the dank darkness of an alley. Without turning around, he beckoned for Christopher to join them. Christopher did as he requested, approaching slowly as he walked into the alley. He didn't stop walking until he saw the two men standing behind a dumpster. He stopped beside John and both looked at their victim. Christopher was completely unnerved. He didn't know if he wanted to pursue this matter further, or run away. The hunger gnawing away at his insides kept him still.

John turned to him. "It's time now. You need to feed, go ahead." He motioned toward George.

Christopher was horrified. In that brief second, he finally understood what it all meant, being a vampire, having to feed from humans. He didn't know if he could. "Just like that?!"

"Don't fight your nature. Give in to it and you'll see just how easy it is to be what you are. Listen, just take it easy." John stood behind him, leaning closer to his ear. "Get close to him, inhale his scent. I know that you can smell his blood flowing through his veins, you can hear his heart pumping his blood faster and faster. It's intoxicating…delicious, isn't it?"

Christopher was getting seduced by the blood he did hear and smell. He wanted it, every part of him wanted it! His chest began to heave, his thirst raged through him. God, he wanted him so badly! He had to swallow the saliva that had gathered inside his mouth before he'd drool it over his shirt front. He became aroused as the scent grew stronger along with his hunger.

"Take him, he's yours," John whispered. With a gentle nudge, he pushed him forward, closer to George.

Christopher hadn't even realized his fangs extended until the tips poked his bottom lip, drawing a tiny drop of blood. His tongue snaked over his lip, tasting the blood, whetting his appetite. Unable to contain his need any longer, with his thirst demanding to be quenched, he grabbed hold of his victim, pulling him against his chest.

"Take him, " John urged softly.

Christopher closed his eyes. Leaning forward, he allowed his instincts to guide him. A second later, luscious blood flowed into his mouth, so precious...so perfect. He hadn't even realized his fangs had pierced the man's jugular. His lips locked around the wound as he began to suck harder on the blood that pumped into him. He felt himself grow harder with every swallow he took. The blood filled his entire being with ecstasy. He felt pleasure he hadn't known was possible to feel! He wanted it to go on forever. The blood coursed through his limbs, filling him, warming him, sating him in every way. He wanted more, had to have more! Dimly he became aware of someone or something pulling him free from his victim, forcing him to release his bite, ending his pleasure. He cried out as strong hands held him still. John held him against his chest in an unrelenting grip while he waited for the younger vampire to regain his composure. Christopher struggled in vain against the powerful arms that held him captive. When he accepted that he wasn't going to get free, he forced himself to calm down. It was then that he discovered who was holding him.

"Do I have your undivided attention now?" John asked.

Christopher swallowed hard, savoring the taste of the blood that still lingered. "Yeah," he said, still panting.

"Good. Now, I had to stop you before you took too much and killed the asshole." John looked down at George slumbering in a crumpled heap against the dumpster. He scoffed. "Not that I think he'd be missed if you did."

He turned his gaze back to Christopher. "You said you didn't want to kill your victims. That means you're going to have to learn a lot of control when feeding. I knew you were going to go at it just like you did, because we all do our first time. So don't feel bad." He released him and took a step backward.

"I can't believe how good that felt! I mean, good isn't even the right word to describe what that was!" Christopher exclaimed, still exuberant from the blood he had taken in.

John smiled, nodding. "I bet."

"That was amazing!"

"Yeah, I know and it'll be that way for all eternity. Some instances are way better than others. The more control you gain over your feeding, the more you'll be able to enjoy the experience. There's all sorts of tricks of the trade you're going to have to learn. For starters, come here, let me show you one." John knelt beside George.

Christopher squatted beside the two, his eyes on John. "What are you going to do?"

"Hold out a finger, any finger."

Christopher held out his right hand, palm up, extending his index finger. John took hold of his finger and ran one of his long, sharp nails over the flesh, slicing it open.

"Ow!" Christopher yelped.

John chuckled. "Don't worry, it'll heal quickly. Rub your blood over his puncture wounds."

Following John's instructions, he did just that, smearing the blood over the two bruised punctures. He marveled at the magic of it all, watching as the wounds began to heal themselves. Skin cells rebuilt themselves until the wounds disappeared, leaving only a small blood stain. John wiped the blood from George's neck.

"Wow!" Christopher said in a hushed voice.

"Yeah, it's convenient enough. However, if you had actually killed him, you'd need to disguise the wound somehow. Forensics makes getting away with killing people difficult. Let's go, I'm starving and I bet you're still hungry."

"Yeah, I am, but the worst of it has subsided." Christopher rose, looking down at George. "What are you going to do about him?"

"When I get to a pay phone, I'll call 9-1-1. Come on." John started walking out of the alley with his young protégé right behind him. John headed for a pay phone, finding one several blocks away.

"In the age of cell phones, these damn things are becoming harder and harder to find." John looked at the toll. "Damn! Fucking things keep getting more and more expensive, too! Fifty fucking cents! I remember when it used to be twenty-five!"

Christopher laughed. "I see it's been a long time since you had to use one of these." He pointed to the pay phone.

"It's that obvious, hun? It's a good thing this call is free. I don't have fifty cents on me." John smiled as he pressed the three buttons. He told the police where to find the Gold Coast Rapist, that he had tried to attack a young woman that night, but was unsuccessful. He hung up, ignoring the dispatcher's questions, moving on with the night's activities.

He continued hunting, tracking down another victim. This man wasn't a criminal, but he wasn't an innocent either. His personality left much to be desired. John called to him silently as Christopher watched from the shadows. He was in complete awe as he witnessed John "snake charm" his victims. The man came to John easily, willingly. Behind an old, thick tree, John skillfully fed from his victim, inducing the most extraordinary pleasure between them both. His victim shook uncontrollably by the orgasm that rippled through his loins. Once he had taken what he wanted, he pulled away, sealing the wound. He left the man, leaning against the tree, in total bliss but unaware why.

"One more just like that, and I'm good for the night," John said once he was beside Christopher again. "Let's go to *Desires Unleashed*, there's always some willing victims there. We call them 'groupies'."

"Yeah, I've heard about those types of people. I used to make fun of them."

John looked at him, smiling wickedly. "And now?"

Christopher tossed him a knowing glance. "Now, I don't know…if they're as willing as you say they are, then I suppose they're a blessing in disguise, which is good news for me."

John laughed out loud. He was starting to like Christopher a lot and knew the others would also. Once his laughter subsided he said, "You're coping pretty well considering everything that has happened to you in the past forty-eight hours."

Christopher shrugged one shoulder. "As opposed to…?"

"I don't know. I guess I'm surprised. I expected a person in your situation, turned against your will out of maliciousness, would probably brood a lot. You know, a lot of moaning and groaning, whining about 'why me' or crying about being the 'monster' you had become. You know, shit like that."

Christopher smiled regretfully. "I'm not going to lie to you. I think I was very close to being just that at first. My whole life ended when I realized what that son-of-a-bitch did to me. It was actually talking with Gary that put some things into perspective for me. Moping around wouldn't make my situation any better. It would probably make it worse. Besides, how am I going to expect my family to cope with what I am if I can't?" He shook his head. "Naw, whining and crying about it wasn't an option, not for me at least."

John was silent for a few seconds, he was definitely impressed. "You've impressed me, that's not that easy to do. How old are you again?" he asked with a chuckle. Still, he wanted an answer to his question.

"Eighteen."

"Stop lying, really?" John knew that he was telling the truth, but flattery was fun both ways.

"It's true, but I bet you already knew that."

John's eyebrows arched. "Smart as a whip. Yeah, I did," he confessed. "You're mature for a teenager. I don't think I was as mature as you when I was your age."

"Everyone tells me that." Christopher smiled, feeling better and better about his companion and his situation. Things were looking up. They walked on for a few more blocks before he spoke. "So, what's the first thing on the list for me to learn?"

"We've actually started working on the first thing which is… control. You have to learn control before anything else or you'll start making a big mess all over the city. Then, not only will the S.U.I.T. be on you like stink on shit, but you could bet your last dollar that Darian will get to you first. You don't want that."

Christopher flinched. He didn't want to be on Darian's radar any more than he wanted to be on the S.U.I.T.'s. "They're pretty tough, eh?"

John nodded. "Darian being the master of a wonderful, bustling city, like Chicago speaks volumes. As for the S.U.I.T.," he shrugged, "for a group of humans, they are pretty damn tough. They have all sorts of weapons and shit that could kill us in an instant if they're lucky enough to catch one of us slipping. They've managed to arrest or kill a good number of supernaturals since they were established. For the most part, and don't tell anyone I told you this, but I think they do good work. A lot of our kind can be cruel and people need protection. But some of them, I think are power junkies and the power they have with the S.U.I.T. sometimes puts them into overload, to the point it becomes more than a job defending the innocent."

"Why do you say that?" Christopher asked, keeping pace with him.

"A little over a year ago, they arrested Darian on a bogus ass charge of murder. They weren't trying to discover who really committed the murder. They were just in overdrive for having arrested the biggest, bad-ass vampire in the city. Bastards didn't even know how close they came to getting killed by Darian. They were trying to execute him and he wasn't going to have it. We straightened everything out, found the real killers and Darian sued their asses and won!"

"Oh, I see what you're saying. Hey, why wouldn't you want me to tell anyone you said that?"

"A lot of our kind hate the S.U.I.T. and don't see any good coming from them. You'll learn on your own just how biased these so-called *fair* laws really are. For the time being, refrain from praising the government in public. Unless getting into bar fights or long lengthy debates are up your alley." John chuckled.

After five more minutes, they were standing in front of *Desires Unleashed.* Neither man was tired from their long walk, only hungry. John was very much anticipating the time he was going to spend inside. The bouncer stepped to the side when he saw John approaching. John wrapped his arm around Christopher's shoulder, pulling him along.

"Byron, this is Christopher, he's new to the coven. Make sure to take care of him when you see him, cool?" John winked.

The huge, muscular, shape-shifter bouncer nodded his head. "Sure thing, we'll treat him like royalty." Byron grinned.

"Great." John led Christopher into the huge club. Music blared, filling the club with vibrations pounding from the bass of the rap song that was playing. He leaned over toward Christopher. "This place is packed like this every night. That line out there is wrapped around the block, probably twice!"

Christopher smiled as he looked around the hip night club. He was astonished by the grandeur of the décor. Marble floors, slip-resistant dance floor, leather booths, chairs and stools. He looked up at the flashing neon disco lights and strobe ball hanging from the ceiling. The colorful lights reflected off patrons sequined clothing and sparking jewelry, as well as the mirrored walls. The bar was very large, spanning half the width of the club itself. He turned toward John. "Can we drink any of that?" he asked, pointing toward the fully stocked bar.

John shook his head. "Not really. But fear not, my little underage drinker, Tony makes specialty drinks just for us vamps. I don't know what he puts in it, don't really care. All I know is, one shot of his Contender will have me flat on my ass. I normally go for his lighter drink, the TKO. Xavier and Darian like the Contender."

Christopher laughed. "You mean to tell me that you guys, er, I mean we can get drunk, totally blasted?!"

"Yeah, even sick from it, so be careful. You won't have a hangover or anything like that, but you might puke. Your stomach will get all queasy, you'll get a headache. Tony's drinks are the only thing I know that will do that to you...wait, I take that back. Drinking the blood of a lot of high or drunk people will do that, too," John stated.

"Really?"

"Really. Whatever he puts in those drinks has a nice effect on you if you don't abuse it. It lasts for a few hours, depending on how strong of a drink you get."

"You sound like you're talking from experience?"

John nodded. "Yeah, I was still new, but I could hunt on my own by this time. I fed on someone who was sky high off cocaine. I was completely buzzed the rest of the night. Darian just looked at me and shook his head. And another time, I killed and fed on three drunk gangsters, I passed out under a tree in Grant Park. Xavier had to come get me before the sun fried my ass. When I got back home, I was sick and threw up! I didn't even know we could get sick like that! After that night, I never did that again."

"Must have felt shitty, at least you didn't have a hangover."

"No. But Darian scolded me for wasting blood like that by barfing, especially since it was on his expensive 1820 oriental rug. Plus, I was pretty hungry the next night, more so than I would have been had I not lost my dinner. I get drunk off Tony's drinks, too, but I never go overboard."

"I bet he makes a lot of money off those drinks. He's probably really famous because of them, right?"

"Yeah, some consider it his little raison d'être. All I know is, he uses Synblood to mix them, making it the only time I willingly drink that shit. Of course, Darian is the only one who drinks his with real blood, mostly from some kind of animal." John continued to lead Christopher toward the back of the club to the secret room known only to a number of the special patrons who frequented the club.

"Where are we going?" Christopher asked.

"I'm going to show you where you can get an easy meal. I think it's important for you to feed here for your first few months, until you get used to everything." John stopped in front of a black door, two shape-shifters guarding it stepped aside. He turned to Christopher. "Now listen very carefully. This is going to be pretty intense, especially for you since you're new. I'm sure you can already smell and sense what's going on in there." He nodded in the direction of the door.

Christopher nodded as he licked his lips, not really noticing that he was.

"Exactly. I'm going to be watching you in there to make sure you don't fuck up. *Desires Unleashed* is a safe haven for both supernaturals and humans alike. To kill one would mean terrible news for you. I've seen what happens to vampires who think that rule doesn't apply to them. They're no longer existing."

"Darian doesn't like killing?" Christopher asked, confused by the somewhat conflicting information.

"Not necessarily. See, Darian is a hunter, he accepted what he is a long time ago. During his time, hunting and killing was no big deal. Nowadays, we have all these rules to obey if we hope to live openly with the humans and in peace. We had to make some changes in our eating habits, which means no killing. If bodies start popping up all over the place, completely drained of blood, all hell is going to break loose. This isn't 1492, where forensics testing wasn't available and dead bodies were as common as a blade of grass."

Christopher nodded. "I see what you mean now. If I have to kill someone, I run it by Darian first to get permission? If not, a rule has been broken that will cost me my life. Got it." He had a firm understanding of Darian's "No-kill" policy.

"That's right. Besides, he can help you with the necessary steps it's going to take to cover up your kill anyway. I don't think you have much to worry about, and besides, Darian's really laidback. He doesn't want any human drama brought upon his doorstep. The S.U.I.T. suspects he's the master vampire and that all other vampires are under his control in this city. So if they knew for sure, they'd try to hold him responsible for the crimes of those associated with him.

"That's not right at all!" Christopher was surprised. He'd had no idea how hypocritical the government was.

John nodded, then he turned, facing the two guards. "Hey guys."

Both guards greeted them as they walked through the door. The scent of blood and sex was thick in the air. There were seven doors, three on each side of a long hallway and the last straight ahead. Both vampires could hear the sensual sounds of the patrons in the back rooms luxuriating in their pleasures. John kept walking until he reached the last door, the "middle room".

"Now before we go inside, I want you to practice one thing. Try your best to find a technique you can use to stay calm enough to maintain control while you feed. It's going to be very hard, but this is the best place to gain that control." John put his hand on the door knob.

Christopher nodded. He swallowed hard in anticipation of what was to follow. John opened the door. The scent that had called to them both, enticing them to come closer, washed over them like a tidal wave. Christopher's knees grew weak and he leaned against the door frame. Inside were a few dozen people, some in groups of four, others coupled together. There was a mixture of vampires, shape-shifters and humans, all enjoying the vampire's kiss, among other things.

"I can't believe this!" Christopher panted breathlessly.

"Oh yeah! This is one of the highlights of the club. Membership only." John looked at him. "You should remove your clothes. You don't want to mess them up, since those are the only clothes you'll be walking out of here with."

Almost in a trance, Christopher began to remove his clothes. He was unable to take his eyes away from the sights before him. His hunger grew more and more intense as his penis grew harder. John remained fully clothed, but he couldn't help glancing at Christopher's nakedness. He knew that the younger vampire was straight, and he had no intentions of interfering with that, but just had to look...just this once.

"Come this way," John instructed, leading Christopher toward two females. One was a beautiful shape-shifter, a cheetah. The other, a human groupie. Both looked at the two men with glazed vision. The shape-shifter reached out, running her fingers over Christopher's erection eliciting a gasp from him. John chuckled softly. He pushed the younger vampire gently in the direction of the shifter as she guided him down toward the pillow, keeping him beside her.

"I want you to take her, I'll have this one," John said, smiling as he lay on the pillow beside the human woman. She brushed her dyed black hair to the side, revealing her creamy throat, baring an old puncture wound that was still healing. He chuckled to himself, wondering how these people survived in the daylight hours until the club opened. He leaned forward, toward her neck. Looking over his shoulder, he saw that Christopher was on top of the shifter, his fangs buried deeply. He could hear the young vampire drinking her blood strongly.

"I'm so excited! I've been hoping to be chosen tonight!" The human woman squealed in pleasure, anticipating John's kiss.

He tilted his head, so that his lips were close to her ear. "Tonight is your lucky night, baby." He could hear her gasp, smell the wetness that had now gathered between her legs. His fangs extended, and he plunged them deeply into her vein, sealing his lips over the flow of blood. He looked over at Christopher to see that he had mounted the shifter, pumping quickly as he continued to drink from her. John closed his eyes as he fed until he had taken all that he could take from the human woman. He pulled away, holding her as she shook from the pleasure that still tingled inside, her nether region pulsating with intense heat from her climax. John watched her, but felt little arousal. He wanted to be with his lover, only with Devin did he truly enjoy feeding. Only with Devin would he be completely sated and only with Devin did the act of their union mean so much more than just feeding. John laid her down when her body ceased its spasms. He looked over at Christopher, watching as an orgasm rippled through both him and the shifter. Finally, he couldn't take any more blood and he pulled away, fulfilled, satisfied in ways he had never been satisfied before. The female cradled him in her arms until their bodies stopped trembling and the aftermath of their union faded away.

After ten minutes, John rose to his feet. He looked at Christopher. "Come on, let's get you back to the hotel."

He handed him his clothes.

Christopher rose from the cushioned pillow and dressed. Once fully clothed, he turned around to face the shifter. "Thank you, hmmm, it was really great! Umm, When can I see you again?"

The female shifter smiled and winked, but remained silent.

John rolled his eyes, chuckling. "Come on." He grabbed Christopher by the collar of his t-shirt and led him out of the back room.

"I want to see her again!" Christopher stated with great enthusiasm once they were standing outside of *Desires Unleashed*.

"She might be there the next time you go, and she might not. That wasn't a date, you know," John said as he hailed a cab.

"Well, yeah, I know, it's just...," Christopher looked slightly disappointed as he glanced back at the club.

John watched him, a smile creeping across his face. "Was that your first time?"

Christopher turned quickly, looking at John. "What do you mean?"

"Oh, no you don't. Don't play coy now. Was that your first time with a woman?"

Christopher blushed. "Yes."

John threw his head back with laughter. After a few seconds he managed to regain his composure.

"I don't get it, what's so damn funny?" Christopher was slightly embarrassed. It was bad enough his friends made fun of him for being a virgin, now someone he was just really getting to know was laughing at him.

"No wonder you're in love with her!"

"I'm not in love with her, I -I just like her, is all!"

"Now, calm down, don't get so defensive. It's not a big deal. You'll come to realize that. See, our bite is extremely pleasurable. It's better than any drug and that's why we can always find people who are willing to let us feed from them. They can't get any STDs from us or get pregnant, so having sex with a vampire is the safest sex around. So you see, it's a win-win situation for everyone." John managed to get a cab to pull over and the two vampires climbed inside. He gave the cab driver the address to the *Xavier Hotel* and they were off.

"Think she'll let me do it again?" Christopher asked.

John smiled. "Most likely she will. We'll be going there a lot during your training because you need to learn how to control yourself. You need to be able to feed without having sex and leave your victim alive. You should also be able to feed with much more finesse."

"It's really hard to concentrate on those things when I'm in there. So I understand what you mean when you say I need to learn control. I tried so hard not to bite my brother. It was almost impossible because he smelled so good! I had no idea how long I was going to be able to hold out. All I wanted to do was…well, you know."

"Yeah, I do know, that's why I'm making *Desires Unleashed* the training grounds. After mastering your skills there, you'll be a pro!"

"So did I look amateurish in there?" Christopher tossed a glance at the cab driver who seemed to be very interested in their conversation, which made him uneasy.

John chuckled softly. "Very amateurish, but that's to be expected. I remember my first feeding. Right after the pain faded away from my transformation, Darian took me hunting. I remember being totally mesmerized by his sheer skill as we stalked our victim. His eyes never left the man as we followed behind him. The guy had no idea we were even there, watching. Before he could rape another woman, Darian was on him."

Christopher was mesmerized. "So what happened next?"

"Well, the whole time we stalked this guy, my thirst was growing stronger and stronger. The woman ran away as Darian instructed. Once the guy was alone, he beckoned him to follow us into a dark alley…" John paused and looked at Chris. "Dark alleys are our friends. Remember that when you're out hunting."

Christopher nodded slowly, taking in the information. "Considering everything that we've done tonight, I can't help feeling like some kind of wild animal."

"We're vampires, Chris. We hunt, we kill. We're predators. We're not human, and frankly, even they hunt and kill. I'm not saying that you personally have to kill your victim, but you need to know how to take care of yourself out here. Hunting is one of our greatest joys and it is necessary for your survival to hone your skills."

"Is this what Darian taught you?" Christopher asked, genuinely curious.

"Yeah. He taught us what he's learned over the years. You'll be lucky to survive as long as he has. Whatever he wants to teach you, trust me, it's golden knowledge."

Christopher reflected on what John said and nodded.

"Well, Darian let me take the man and I was horrible my first time. I ripped his throat out and he died too quickly. The blood was still good, but nothing like a healthy heart to pump the blood to you. I had to really suck hard to drain the man. Darian teased me about being a messy feeder, said I needed to learn more finesse." John chuckled.

"I wasn't that bad."

John looked at Christopher, smiling mischievously. "No, you weren't, but you weren't perfect either. That's why I paired you with the shifter, I knew she'd survive your feeding. I think I'll continue to do that until you get the hang of it. Better safe than sorry."

Christopher frowned.

"Don't worry. You have an eternity at your side, plenty of time to get wild and have fun!"

"What happened after he teased you?"

John took a deep breath, smiling as he thought back to the moment. "Well, I was so aroused by the kill that I felt as if I was going to explode. Darian knew I would feel that way after feeding, all vampires do, regardless of age. He stepped up closer to me, and it was like I was caught in a trance."

"He hypnotized you?!"

John laughed boisterously. "Darian would never hypnotize anyone into sex. Shit, he doesn't have to! I was just so caught up in the moment, that the very thought of what was in his expression drove me wild."

"I have a question. Are you bisexual, too?"

"Yeah, but I wasn't always bi. If you're going to live forever, might as well enjoy everything you can. For instance, I had never had sex with a woman until I started living with Darian. Annabelle was my first time with a woman and she was amazing! Xavier, Darian's lover was straight at one point in his life. Now, as I'm sure you've deduced, he's bi, too."

Christopher had a mixture of uncertainty and disgust in his expression.

"Why are you looking at me like that?"

"I wasn't aware that I had a specific 'look'. Sorry."

"Well, ya did. It's not what you think. When you're feeding, and you get aroused like you did tonight, it helps to leave your options open. Darian thinks it's ridiculous for vampires, beings that are going to live forever, to hold on to your old way of life. Gay or straight, black or white, he says vampires should just 'be'. That way, you have the best of all worlds. It gives you a freedom unlike anything you've ever known, and I say that from experience."

Christopher shook his head slightly. "Un-hum, Gary said as much last night. I just wanted to hear your take on it. Right now, I'm still getting used to not being a virgin...I'm not ready to start experimenting with anything too radical."

"No rush anyway, but you need to learn how to leave all that petty, trivial bullshit behind you. It'll make your life must easier when you do," John advised, then he continued with his lessons. "Now that you've fed for the evening, we should start on exploring the limits of your powers."

Christopher's face lit up. "What kind of powers, like in the movies?"

"Depends on what kind of movies."

"Well, can I turn into a bat and fly away? Or a wolf even? Can I turn into mist?! Or shape change into other people?!" Christopher's voice grew more excited at the mention of each possibility.

John frowned. "You watch way too much TV. Let's start with the basics shall we?"

Christopher pouted slightly, but nodded.

"Our weaknesses are fire, sunlight, decapitation and of course, getting our hearts ripped out of our bodies. We are not easily destroyed. If you get shot by any kind of bullet besides one of those damn ultraviolet bullets, you won't be harmed. Granted, you'll lose a lot of blood until your skin heals, which happens almost instantly and it hurts like a motherfucker, but you can't die that way. However, one shot from a UVG bullet will kill you. It doesn't even have to hit you in the chest, it could be in the finger. If it explodes under your skin, the gel goes through your bloodstream, and you'll disintegrate instantly. It can't be stopped."

"Holy shit!" Christopher was amazed.

"Exactly. Needless to say that we vampires hate that invention."

"Sounds brutal. Okay, you mentioned something about powers?"

"That's right. I like to talk, and sometimes I go off on a tangent. I'm a little excited because you're the first vampire I've ever had to train. There's so much you need to know, we're not going to get to all of it tonight."

"That's cool. I'm actually enjoying the stories. I don't mind."

John smiled. "One of the things that we can do is hypnotize mortals. You're a pretty strong vampire for your age, and that's because you were made by a powerful vampire. The older you get, the more powers you'll gain. Ancient vampires no longer have to worry about the sunlight. They can stay awake for twenty-four hours if they want to. They can eat human food, but they have to use the bathroom like humans when they do. From what I've heard, most ancient vampires don't eat human food unless they really have to in order to keep up appearances. Fire no longer bothers them either. I've heard that they can walk right through fire and not even get soot on their faces! Man, that'll be the day!"

"So basically, once you reach a certain level of power and strength, you're damn near invincible?" Christopher asked, completely amazed.

"Pretty much. Only a vampire of matching abilities stands a chance. Vampires can fly, but that, too, comes with age and power." John placed his hand on Christopher's shoulder. "You can't fly yet."

Christopher pouted. "What can I do?"

"That's what we're going to find out."

The cab pulled in front of the hotel. John paid him and at the same time, he erased the driver's memory of their conversation. The cab driver thanked him for the generous tip and drove away.

"Tonight was amazing." Christopher said. "I'm starting to see a brighter side of being a vampire. I really want to learn everything that I can, especially control. I want to be able to see my family soon without hurting them."

John smiled and nodded. "Good, cause becoming a vampire isn't the end of the world, it isn't the end of your life. All it means is that you have to have a new outlook on life, it's all good." He looked up at the sky. "The night is so beautiful. Humans can never see its beauty like we can. They can't appreciate it like us. Not their fault really."

Christopher looked up to see what he meant. He saw the stars shining brighter than he ever had in the past. The dark blue of the sky looked so clear, so flawless! When he relaxed, he could feel the electricity in the air, the passion that vibrated with every passing second. It made him feel so alive! "I see what you mean," he agreed.

John smiled, then entered the hotel. A few minutes later, the two men finally reached their suite. He closed the door behind them, gesturing for Christopher to have a seat in one of the plush recliners.

Tony looked at Christopher. "So, did you have fun hunting?"

Christopher turned toward Tony. "Well, it was definitely an enlightening experience. I did have fun, which was surprising to me, didn't think I would. I know there's a lot I have to learn, too."

Tony chuckled. "Yeah, I'm sure. How did you enjoy your first taste of real blood?" He threw one long leg over the arm of his chair, reclining more comfortably against the cushions. His dark blue eyes studied Christopher, the young man intrigued him.

"It was really delicious, I hadn't expected it to taste like...I don't know. I can't describe it, but I guess you know from your own experiences."

Tony nodded. "I do. Well, it's good to see that you're not as depressed as you were when you first got here."

Christopher shook his head. "I'm feeling better about my life now. I was just telling John that before we came inside."

"So where did you go?" Gary asked as he entered the living room, sitting in the chair next to Tony's.

Christopher tossed a glance at John who was lying prone on the sofa, then back to the others. "We went to *Desires Unleashed.* I had always heard about that club, I used to wonder what it looked like inside. It's an awesome nightclub."

Tony leaned forward, one eyebrow raised. "John took you to *Desires Unleashed?*"

Christopher nodded. "Yeah, we went to the back..." he trailed off as he noticed John gesturing for him to be silent.

Tony looked at John, catching the vampire making the 'cut-off' gesture by waving his hand in front of his neck back and forth repeatedly. When John saw that Tony was watching him, he lowered his hand, offering him a boyish grin.

Tony rolled his eyes. "I can't believe you took him to the back room on his first night out."

John scoffed. "Take it easy, he can handle it. I wouldn't have taken him there if I didn't think he would have been able to handle himself. Besides, Darian gave me permission to train him. I thought the club would prove to be a great start. There are shifters there who he can feed on and never have to worry about killing."

Gary smirked. "I see why you would choose the club. I still think it's kind of overwhelming, in spite of it being a controlled environment."

"It is overwhelming, I agree," Tony lightly scolded.

Christopher was silent, watching the three vampires exchange words.

"He'll be better off for it. Tony, back off, I didn't criticize how you trained Gary. At least Chris was able to enjoy himself and see another side of what we are. You two can get off my back now. Everything's just fine. You guys are acting like I took him to an orphanage and told him to go wild!" John retorted.

"No we're not. I just want to make sure things aren't moving too quickly for him. But since everything went smoothly, I'll let it go. I don't feel like arguing tonight anyway." Tony leaned back into his chair. He looked at Christopher. "Did you two do any strength or power tests?"

Christopher looked at John, then back at Tony. "No, not yet. We talked for a long time, I had a lot of questions."

"Yeah, you do." Gary laughed, thinking about all of the questions he'd been asked the night before. "But it's good to be inquisitive." He rose from his chair and walked over to Tony, grabbing onto his hand. "Come on, babe."

Tony looked up at him, smiling as he rose from the chair. The two disappeared into their bedroom, closing the door behind them.

Christopher looked at the now closed door. "Are they going to do what I think they are?" he asked John.

John nodded. "Probably, you know how love is."

"It got kind of heated in here for a minute. I hope that wasn't my fault," Christopher said, thinking about the words shared between John and Tony.

John scoffed. "Naw, that wasn't a big deal. We rarely fight, but we do sometimes get into arguments here and there, but not much. That's just what happens when you live with people. Don't worry."

Christopher nodded, feeling better about what happened. Both vampires looked toward Darian's room when they heard the door open. Darian walked out, making his way across the hotel room. He sat down on the armrest of the sofa closest to where John was resting his head.

He looked down at John. "Well?"

John sat up, turning to face Darian. "Everything went smoothly. We hunted, fed...he has a great amount of control. I don't think it'll be too difficult to teach him."

Darian looked at Christopher. "I'm sure that John explained to you my rules and what a privilege it is for you to be accepted into my coven."

Christopher nodded. "Yeah-yes. He told me everything."

Darian smiled. "Good. Then I don't have to say another word." He rose from the armrest, then looked down at John. "Next time you plan on taking him to the back room of *Desires Unleashed*, let me know first."

John shied away from Darian's stern glare. He nodded his head in acknowledgment. "Yes Master. Okay, since we're on the subject of the back room, can I continue to take him there for his training?"

"He's your responsibility. Train him however you see fit as long as it doesn't violate my rules." Darian walked back into his room, leaving the two alone.

Christopher looked at John. "Wow, that was intense! Is he always like that?"

"Darian always means business, but he's not always like that. It's been a trying seventy-two hours. I think a few of us are still a bit wired. Give him some time to unwind. There's one thing I don't think I've mentioned."

"What?"

"Well, Darian demands loyalty...allegiance, if you will, of his coven members. Which means that basically, we're a family. We stick together and don't betray one another. And if he needs us, we owe it to him to respond. Besides, he's been there for us in a heartbeat. You saw that with your own eyes."

"I did. Well, he's already helped me, the least I could do is follow his rules. Besides, it's not as if I really have a choice anyway."

"Oh, you have a choice. It's just the other option sucks."

Christopher chuckled. "I get your point."

The two vampires talked and trained until the sun forced them to rest for the day. John rose from the couch, stretching. He looked at Christopher and said, "You know, if you want, you could bunk with me?"

"Naw, I'm cool with the sofa, but thanks."

John nodded with a sly smile. "Got a thing about sleeping with other men?" he teased.

"Naw, just you." Christopher joked, his smile broadening as he chuckled.

"I didn't want to share with you anyway." John laughed as he walked into his bedroom to rest for the day.

Christopher lay back on the soft cushions. He closed his eyes and moments later, he was resting.

CHAPTER TWENTY-FOUR

Matthew rolled over onto his back, his eyes opening, his vision began to become clearer than he'd ever seen. He shaded his eyes from the bright sunlight coming in through the exposed window. He looked around the room, seeing a dresser, a closet, a bedpost. When he turned toward the window, he saw Warren sleeping in the chair beside his bed. He knew that he was in Warren's bedroom at the mansion but how he'd gotten there was a mystery to him. The muscles in his body felt extremely relaxed as he shifted positions. The squeaking of the bedsprings under Matthew's weight startled Warren, waking him up instantly.

"Matthew?!" Warren's voice was dry...hoarse. He sprang forward from the chair, reaching for Matthew, wrapping his arms tightly around his lover. "My god, you had me going out of my fucking mind!"

"I'm sorry."

Matthew held Warren a little longer. Moments later, they released each other. Warren sat back down in his chair, never taking his eyes from Matthew.

"Okay Warren, tell me what's happened. Don't sugarcoat it, either, I can handle it." Matthew propped himself up leaning against two pillows. Warren leaned over, adjusting the pillows for him. Matthew playfully smacked Warren's hands away. "I'm not an invalid, Warren...I can sit up on my own, please don't do that, I'm okay."

Warren settled back into the chair, he smiled. "I'm sorry. I know...it's just, seeing you...the way you were, scared the hell out of me. I thought you were going to die and I was terrified...I didn't want to lose you."

"I know that I must have been in a bad situation to have you watching over me." Matthew looked down at his hands resting in his lap. "I don't remember exactly what happened last night. All I know is how I feel right now. This strength...this power flowing through me." He looked at Warren. "My senses are running wild, I can hear all of these voices! All of these different smells! My vision...it's like...I'm seeing things clearer, as if my eyes have been magnified. And I'm so hungry!"

"Matthew...," Warren turned, looking away.

Matthew looked at him. "I'm not so confused that I can't figure out what happened to me, Warren. I was turned, I just don't know what I was turned into."

Warren nodded. "You were turned, but that was two nights ago, not last night. You're a coyote now. Tatiana saved your life, and we've all kept watch over you. During the battle, one of the coyotes, their Matron took you to protect herself from our attack. When she realized her plan wasn't going to work, she bit you."

Matthew winced as if in pain.

"We killed her..." Warren looked down, saddened by Matthew's reaction. "Richard killed her."

Matthew, noting the sudden change in Warren, leaned over, placing his hand over his. "Warren," he began, gaining his attention. "I'm not blaming you or anyone for this happening..." He looked off to the side. "Well, maybe the bitch who bit me. But this was something that none of us could see coming. I'm not mad at you, I'm just glad that I'm still here, alive and with you."

Warren smiled slightly. He leaned over, kissing Matthew full on the mouth then he sat back.

"God! You have no idea how happy I am that you're alright with this." Warren switched from the chair to sitting on the edge of the bed beside him.

Matthew shrugged. "What good would it do me to be sitting here crying about it?"

"Well, it's one thing to be born a shape-shifter and it's another to be turned out of vengeance, or just turned in general. A lot of turned shifters are resentful, some even suicidal. I was worried about you and how you would feel about being turned into a coyote."

Matthew nodded. "I see what you mean." He sighed. "I'm not going to lie to you, Warren. I'm not exactly thrilled by the idea at this point. I'm not sure what this is going to mean for me, or for us. I didn't see becoming a shape-shifter in my future, know what I mean?"

"Yeah, I know."

"But I'm in no way, shape, form or fashion, suicidal, so don't worry about that. I'm far too grateful to be alive. I just have to take some time to get used to everything. Like, right now, I keep hearing all of these voices from everyone else who lives in this house. I can smell food cooking and it's driving me crazy. I don't think that I've ever been this hungry in my entire life!"

Warren chuckled. "I can remedy that right now." He rose from the bed, walking toward the door. He stopped short as Adrian entered the room carrying two plates piled high with bacon, eggs, ham, grits, hash browns and toast.

"Look who's finally awake!" Adrian walked over to the table, setting the plates on the nightstand. "How are you feeling?"

Matthew smiled. "I feel great actually. Strong, energetic, kind of hyper and...just a little hungry," he said modestly as his eyes drifted to the steaming plates of food on the nightstand. He swallowed the saliva that had gathered in his mouth.

Adrian chuckled. "'A *little* hungry,' eh? More like you're ravenous!"

Matthew looked at Adrian. "Well, yeah."

Warren looked at the two plates. "Are those for us?"

Adrian turned toward Warren, smiling. "They are now. I wasn't sure if he was awake, so they were for you and me. I was going to keep you company. By the time I made it upstairs, I could hear you two talking, so they're yours now. I'll tell the others he's alright."

He turned to leave when Matthew called out to him, capturing his attention.

"Thanks for everything, Adrian," Matthew said as Warren handed him a plate.

Adrian smiled. "Don't mention it. Besides, you're one of us. We look out for each other." He left the bedroom, leaving the two lovers alone.

Matthew began eating the food with an almost animalistic ferociousness. Using both fingers and fork to shove heaping piles of food into his mouth.

Warren chuckled. "I've never seen you eat like that. You're normally the one who's a stickler for table manners."

Matthew nodded as he swallowed a mouthful of eggs and bacon. "I know," he managed to say once he'd cleared his mouth. "I've never been this hungry before! I can't help it, I feel like I can't fill up fast enough!" He continued to shovel food into his mouth until the plate was empty.

Warren finished off his plate then sat back, looking at Matthew. "Do you want seconds?"

Matthew looked at Warren, smiling shyly. "Yes."

"I'll get it-"

"Wait, I think I'll get my own food. I'm feeling quite energetic and I really don't want to lie in bed any longer."

"Not even if I lie there with you?" Warren asked seductively.

Matthew tossed Warren a knowing look. "You're not wasting any time, are you?"

A wolfish grin spread across Warren's lips. "I've had to go over forty-eight hours without being close to you the way that I wanted to. Now more than ever, I want to be with you." He began to crawl onto the bed with a predatory gracefulness. He climbed over Matthew's prone form, dipping down to kiss his chest. He paused over Matthew's nipples, licking and teasing them, all the while keeping his eyes on his lover's face.

Matthew moaned softly. "I suppose I can stay in bed a little longer." He wrapped his arms around Warren as they begin to kiss passionately.

***

"I'm glad to know that he's alright," Xander said as he poured himself another cup of English tea.

Adrian chuckled. "He's more than alright." He grabbed a plate out of the cabinet over the counter and began piling on breakfast food.

"Warren didn't waste any time, I see." Justin joked as he finished the last mouthful of cheesy scrambled eggs.

"I'm just so happy that he pulled through. Matthew's very strong. I knew he was going to make it last night. His fever had broken the last I checked on him," Tatiana said with a sweet smile.

Xander looked at his wife, winking. "If anyone could have saved him, it would be you, my love."

"Oh, I helped. Fact of the matter is, Matthew wanted to live," Tatiana stated.

Adrian sat down at the table and began eating. After he swallowed a hearty mouthful of grits, he began to speak. "Personally, I think they are both better off this way. Warren doesn't have to hold back any longer and Matthew is now truly one of us. I mean, don't get me wrong, I accepted him as part of the family before all of this, but not as part of the Pack. I wasn't so sure if Warren would ever turn him on his own or watch him die a mortal's death. Sometimes it's best when the hard decisions are decided by someone else."

"I understand what you are saying, son. It would be a lie if I were to say that I'm not at all happy with this outcome. Yes, this was a catastrophic circumstance, but I do believe that they have been brought closer together because of it," Xander said, his English accent lacing each and every syllable.

"I love the way Xander speaks," Justin said with a chuckle.

"All long-winded, using many big and complicated words to explain the simplest of things?" Adrian retorted, mimicking his father's accent perfectly. "He just couldn't say, 'I agree'."

"I know!"

"Very funny." Xander rolled his eyes as he sipped his tea. Both Justin and Adrian laughed.

Tatiana chuckled softly. "Oh stop you two."

"He's your son," Xander said, nodding at her. She smiled sweetly.

Nicole entered the kitchen, wiping her eyes. "Good morning, everyone," she mumbled. Adrian rose from his seat, taking her into his arms when she walked up to him.

"Hey baby," Adrian whispered into her ear as he nibbled her lobe.

"Hey." Nicole kissed him softly, her lips brushing his lightly. After a moment, the two parted. She began to make her plate, piling on as much food as the others did. "I guess I don't need to ask if Matthew woke up, I could hear them loud and clear. They woke me up. I had no plans whatsoever of waking up this early!"

"Wanna go and make some noises of our own?" Adrian mumbled seductively. The others watched him silently. He looked around, noticing that he was being regarded knowingly by his parents and a few Pack members and decided to change the subject. "So, what are we going to do today?"

Xander smirked as he took another sip of tea.

"Down boy," Nicole teased. "Right now, I just want to eat. After that, I don't know."

Justin chuckled. "Well, I, for one, will be visiting my family. After this whole ordeal, I just want to let them know how much I love them."

"I know what you mean," Nicole agreed. "That gives me an idea! Adrian, I know what I want to do later on today. Something just for the two of us."

Adrian was headed toward the door when he turned, looking at her. "Sure, baby...whatever you want to do is fine with me."

"Where are you going?" Nicole asked.

"Back to bed. I only got up to keep Warren company. But

he's doing just fine now, so I'm going to catch up on the sleep that I missed."

"Good luck," Nicole quipped. He smiled then left the kitchen.

"I know what I have to do," Xander said with grim determination.

"Funeral arrangements?" Tatiana looked at her husband's sad expression. She too, was dreading Alex's funeral. She had adored the young wolf. He had been charming, and extremely naive, but smart and funny. He had been a welcome addition to their Pack and the pain of his death was felt by everyone. Xander felt anger and a sense of responsibility over his death. Tatiana watched him in silence, knowing that he felt guilty for not protecting his entire Pack during their most vulnerable moment. The night they came home, in the privacy of their bedroom, she had tried her best to alleviate his distress. She knew that it wasn't his fault, but he felt that he should have taken some measure to ensure their safety. He had failed his Pack and nothing that his wife had said that night could change his mind.

"I took the liberty of calling Alex's parents last night. I told them of his death. Needless to say that they were extremely upset," Tatiana said as she rose from her chair, walking over to the sink to rinse out her coffee mug.

"What did they say?" Xander asked as he took another sip of his tea.

Tatiana looked at her husband. "They wanted to make sure that we avenged their son."

"Did you tell them?"

"I told them that we did in fact, find the people who had attacked us and took care of them. I did not inform them of the grizzly details. I only told them what I thought they could handle and what they should know."

Xander nodded. "Excellent." He drained his cup, then handed it to his wife, who began washing it out. "You know, darling, that's why we have a dishwasher," he smiled, pointing to the dishwashing machine.

"I know, but I'm standing right here, it's not a bother."

Xander looked at Tatiana lovingly as she rinsed out the ceramic tea cup. He caressed her face lightly. She looked up into his stunning silver eyes. "I love you."

Tatiana smiled. "I know." She raised up onto the tips of her toes as Xander lowered his head to meet her lips with his own.

"Man, I need somebody quick! There's far too many lovebirds in this house!" Justin stated as he rose from the table, slipping his plate into the dishwasher. Xander and Tatiana watched him walk out of the kitchen.

"Too bad Devin has eyes only for John, I think they would have made a good couple," Nicole speculated as she finished her breakfast.

"Why do you say that?" Tatiana asked, genuinely curious.

"I'm going to take my leave now." Xander kissed his wife once more on her left cheek before leaving the two ladies to their female gossip.

"Well, Devin and Justin seem to be the perfect match when they are together, they're like best friends or something," Nicole elaborated.

"It is true that they do have a great deal in common, but that doesn't mean they should be lovers. I think Devin is with whom he should be with and our darling Justin will find someone he is most compatible with," Tatiana said.

"Yeah, I guess." Nicole agreed as she placed her plate into the dishwasher. "Tatiana?" she called out to her as she was heading for the exit.

"Yes?"

"What's going to happen next, you know? With Richard and the others with him? Are we going to let them live here or what?"

"I will talk to Xander about that later on. I wouldn't worry, though. The threat is over and I really do believe that Richard only wants peace between our Packs."

"I suppose so." Nicole appeared to be a bit worried, not really sure of her opinion of Richard and his now downsized Pack.

"Don't worry about it. Xander and I will do what is best for the Pack."

"I know you will." Nicole smiled, finally satisfied with Tatiana's answer. "I think I'll go and take a shower now." She left the kitchen.

Tatiana joined Xander in his study and remained quiet as he made arrangements with a crematorium for proper dispensation of Alex's remains. It had been his wish to be cremated in the event of his death. Xander was going to honor that. He ended the call.

"What's on your mind, darling?" he asked, rubbing her hand gently.

"Nicole asked me a question that I'm sure is on everyone else's mind as well."

Xander inhaled deeply, already knowing what his wife was going to say. He decided to say it first. "Richard and his Pack."

Tatiana nodded. "They are going to live, that was decided, but where?"

"Tat, I'd be lying to you if I said that this situation isn't perplexing. One on hand, he should have died with the others."

"But on the other, he is the reason why many of us are still alive," Tatiana finished his point.

Xander nodded. "Very true. We were overpowered by them. He alone is much stronger than I am, even stronger than most members in Darian's coven. This has opened my eyes...no, I take that back. I was well aware of our strength as a Pack, but this situation has really put our lives into perspective." He settled back comfortably into his leather chair.

Tatiana rose from her chair. Stepping behind him, she began to massage his shoulders, attempting to relieve the tension in his muscles.

"Xander, you are a wonderful Pack Alpha. A position you fought for, because you deserved it more than any other. For a century, you have protected this Pack to the best of your ability...with your life!

We are lucky to have you as a Pack Alpha. This was a hard battle, and it won't be our last. The most important outcome is that we are still here and in our own territory."

Xander caught his wife's hand before it slipped away. He kissed her palm softly. "You are my everything, Tatiana. What would I do without you?" he whispered.

She smiled but remained silent. His feelings were hers, nothing more needed to be said.

After a few moments of silence, he spoke. "Richard can stay here in Chicago. I think it would be good for Matthew to have a Pack of his own to belong to. He's going to need Richard to teach him what he needs to know. If Richard wasn't in the picture, I would be the one to do this, but he is. It's only right for him to take care of his own Pack members. They can share our hunting ground and we can make a peace treaty between our two Packs."

"See, I knew you'd figure out the perfect solution." Tatiana smiled as she leaned forward, kissing Xander on the forehead.

"I just hope Warren will understand."

"He will. He knows it's best."

"I will need to speak with Richard."

"I'll go get him," Tatiana offered. She left the study to search for Richard, whom she found quickly. He was sitting on the back patio, in one of the comfortable tan lawn chairs. He rose when Tatiana approached.

"Morning," Richard greeted her in a strong, masculine voice.

"Good morning," Tatiana replied. "Xander would like to speak with you, please follow me."

Richard nodded and followed her back to Xander's study where she left the two men alone. Xander gestured for him to take the chair in front of his desk, he did.

"I'm sure that you can guess what I would like to discuss with you," Xander said, initiating the conversation.

Richard nodded. "It has been on my mind since we were on the plane. That question is: what's next?"

"Exactly. You've explained your side of the story and I believe you-"

"Xander," Richard held up a hand, gesturing for Xander to pause. "I understand that this situation, my being here, may be growing increasingly uncomfortable with your Pack. I am, however, guilty of trying to take over your territory, there is no denying this fact. I just wanted to make sure that Matthew was going to pull through. We'll leave tonight."

Xander smiled. "You're a very honorable man...I like that."

"So are you." Richard's brown eyes studied Xander closely.

"I'm going to get right to the point. You don't have to leave. Your Pack has been greatly diminished and if you were to return to your old territory, you would easily become a target. Although you yourself are stronger, the other two members of your Pack probably would not fare so well if a battle were to erupt."

Richard gave Xander a rueful smile. "Your points are both valid and discouraging."

Xander chuckled. "I speak only the truth. Fact of the matter is, Matthew is of your Pack, he's a coyote. He is going to need you to train him, teach him the things he must know, he's your responsibility."

Richard stared at Xander, somewhat confused.

Xander continued, "We care a great deal for Matthew, we want him to be strong and well cared for. You are his Pack Alpha. Because you live, it is only right that you take him. You can stay in our territory, feel free to bring your Pack here to hunt in private on the *Lunar* nights."

"How does your Pack feel about this arrangement?" Richard asked, wondering how they would feel about him taking Matthew into his Pack.

"I haven't spoken with them yet. But it is what must be done, it is tradition. The only way I would not give Matthew over to you is if you were my enemy. Are you?" Xander's expression showed that he was serious.

"No, I have no desire to take over your territory, nor do I wish to make more enemies. I will take care of Matthew. Thank you for allowing us *Sanctuary*."

"This does not come without a price."

"And that is?" Richard asked, one eyebrow raised.

"You become our ally. Which means we sign a *Treaty-of-Peace* right here, right now. I don't want there to be a war between our Packs in the future."

"Ah, I see." Richard smiled. "Clever that. You want to eliminate the possibility of a threat."

"It's more civilized than killing you."

"More appealing, too, if I may say so." Richard sighed. "Very well. Knowing a man of your character, I suppose that you already have the papers drawn up and ready to sign?"

"I do." Xander slid a sheet of paper across the desk to Richard. He took it, read over its contents, then signed. Once his signature was on the paper, he slid it back to Xander who signed as well.

"Are we finally in agreement?" Richard asked. He was impressed with Xander. The way that he controlled his Pack and the loyalty that they shared seemed ideal. It was what he wanted for his own. He blamed himself for the dissension previously within his Pack. He felt that he should have known that there was a problem. That perhaps his Matron harbored ill feelings toward him and all those loyal to him, should have been cause for alarm. The signs were there, why had he not paid them attention? Sitting in Xander's office, knowing that most of his Pack members were lying dead in another state left him with a feeling of great sadness. He had failed them as Pack Alpha. He looked up to see Xander watching him from across the dark redwood desk. The younger shifter was giving him a chance to start over and entrusting him with a member they themselves held dear. He was determined that he would do things differently.

Richard rose from the chair preparing to leave Xander's office. He had a request and hoped that the shifter would allow it. "I hate to impose, but would it be possible for the three of us to stay in your home until I can find one of my own?"

Xander chuckled. "I figured as much. You can stay."

"Thank you. We won't stay long, I don't want to wear out our welcome."

"Agreed." Xander rose from his seat and walked Richard to the door. The two alpha males gave each other parting nods, then Richard left. Xander made his way over to the window overlooking the manmade pond in his garden. He smiled when he caught the scent of his wife as she entered his study.

"Did it go well?" Tatiana asked.

Xander turned around. "Better than I expected. The treaty is now in effect. He seems like a very honorable man, I don't see him wanting to betray us in the future."

"Keep your friends close and your enemies closer? Is that your reasoning?" Tatiana stepped closer, her arms encircling his neck as he took her into his embrace.

"Not exactly. I really do believe that he and I may one day become friends. Right now, he seems to be going through a rough patch. He's clever, strong and aggressive. With those personality traits, I don't understand how he lost control of his Pack."

"Perhaps, subconsciously, he wanted to."

Xander frowned, not sure if he agreed. "Do you honestly believe that?"

Tatiana shrugged. "He may not even know why he lost control. He may have sensed that their loyalty wasn't with him. He may have lost interest in his Pack. He's old, sometimes that happens, especially to those that have been Pack masters for many years."

Xander sighed. "I know."

"Do you think he's going to do right by Matthew and his new Pack?"

Xander nodded. "He is, he's too honorable not to. Besides, he owes Matthew."

Tatiana looked up at her husband, smiling. "Did I tell you today how much I admire and love you?"

Xander chuckled. "Well, it has been at least half-an-hour since you last did. I am about due."

Tatiana laughed. "Well, I do."

He leaned down kissing her passionately, squeezing her soft, warm body closer to his.

He released her, slipping his arm around her waist as they exited his study.

"I have to speak with Warren and tell him about the arrangement," he said with a hint of dread.

"Do you want me to-"

"No darling, I can take care of this matter."

Tatiana smiled. "Very well." She walked away, making certain that the sway of her hips kept his attention until she disappeared into the nursery. Xander's seductive grin vanished as he turned to head toward Warren's bedroom. He hoped that the two men were done with their early morning activities. He knocked on the door.

"Come in," Warren called out.

Xander cracked opened the door, just enough to poke his head into the room. "I need to speak with the two of you as soon as possible. Meet me in my study." He closed the door, not waiting for a response. His study was the only room in the house that was soundproofed. He waited for the two men and when they entered, he gestured for them to take the seats in front of his desk as he had with Richard.

Xander made sure that he had their undivided attention. "I'm going to cut right to the chase. Matthew is of Richard's Pack. Therefore, he will be training him."

Outraged, Warren protested. "I don't agree with this, Xander! I mean, did you forget that it was his Pack that did this to Matthew in the first damn place?!"

"I didn't forget."

"Then why the hell would you ever suggest that Matt become a part of his Pack? I thought that we were going to take Matt?" Warren was flustered, angered by his Alpha's decision.

"Because, Richard is Matthew's Pack Alpha. He is a coyote, Warren, not a wolf. Richard has agreed to take him on. They are going to stay in our territory and hunt here on *Lunar* nights. This has been decided, I simply thought you should know. Nothing has to change between the two of you, but Matthew is going to have to learn how to control his instincts and his hunger. You are both S.U.I.T. officers, your monthly day off will coincide now, have you thought about that? You have more pressing matters to deal with than Matthew joining the proper Pack. No matter how much you disagree, this is the right decision."

"He tried to kill us!" Warren argued.

"But he didn't. In fact, the reason why so many of us are still alive is because he fought beside us. His actions have not gone disregarded. He regrets what has happened, he'll do right by Matthew, I know this." Xander's tone was stern as if to say he'd discuss the matter no longer. Warren caught the hint. He slouched in the leather seat, glaring at the papers and books on top of the desk.

Matthew looked at both men. He felt that he should say something about their situation. "Warren, I'm alright with this decision. Xander's right...we are going to have to figure out what we're going to do about our jobs. When you've had to come home on the full moon nights, I've always covered for you or you had sick days. We're just lucky that no one at the S.U.I.T. district office has put two and two together, but with the both of us now calling in on full moon nights..." Matthew trailed off.

Warren looked at him. "I know," he whispered. It was a thought that remained in the back of his mind. He was always worried about being discovered. Matthew had been a great help in assisting him with keeping up appearances, but now with Matthew becoming a shape-shifter, that would leave them both vulnerable.

Xander regarded both men as they thought about their current predicament. Somehow, he'd known that it would one day come down to this. He'd suspected that the love the two men shared would lead Matthew into Warren's world, possibly becoming a wolf to be with him completely. But like the two men, he had not expected it to be so soon.

"Listen, Matt, let us think about that later, right now my mind isn't exactly focused on coming up with a long term plan. Xander's right, your biggest problem right now is controlling your instincts. I don't want the next dead body you see to bring the animal out of you. You don't have time to waste, perhaps you should see Richard today," Warren said solemnly, darting a dejected glance at his Alpha.

Matthew nodded, knowing they were right. If he was going to keep working for the S.U.I.T., he was going to have to control himself. He had always admired Warren for his own ability to maintain control. He hoped that he would be as successful. "You're both right. I'll go talk with Richard right now." He rose from his seat and left Xander's office to seek out his own Alpha.

Warren stayed behind and looked accusingly at Xander. "Why didn't you want to accept Matt?"

Xander sighed. "My wanting or not wanting to accept Matthew had nothing to do with my decision. Richard is strong, he can protect the members of his Pack. And at this point, he is now our ally. I'd spoken with him the night we came back home. He is, in fact, well connected politically, even more so than I am. If, in the event that you or Matthew are discovered, it would be best that we have powerful people who can help you on our side." Xander rose from his seat, stepping around his desk to stand in front of Warren. "We are supernatural beings, but this world is controlled by mere humans. If we are to survive, we're going to have to work within the law. You chose to become a part of this justice system. Now, with the two of you being shifters, there is a very good chance that you will both be exposed. People are not so gullible that they would not notice both of your absences on consecutive *Lunar* nights. You said it yourself, it's what you are trained to do, look for the signs."

"I don't want to lose my job."

"I know. Richard and I will do our best to insure that will never happen. It's going to be tricky, we may even need Darian's help in the case that something goes wrong. It's our jobs as Pack Alphas to keep you safe, and that is what we're going to do. Relax, Warren."

"Xander? Can you trust him?" Warren asked, waiting anxiously for the answer.

"Yes."

Warren nodded. If Xander believed that he'd made the right decision, he was going to stand by him. "Fine, I won't bitch about Richard anymore."

Xander chuckled. "Yes you will, just don't do it while in my presence."

Warren understood what he meant by that. He knew that he could no longer complain about Xander's decision, especially not to him. "Sure." He stood up. "I'm going to call Natasha and Elise, they wanted to know Matt's condition."

"Sounds like a good idea." Xander nodded.

"See ya." Warren walked out of the study, heading to his room to call the two women. He dialed Elise's personal phone number first and waited for her to pick up.

"Hello?" she answered.

"Hey Elise, I just wanted give you the good news. Matthew woke up this morning, he's doing just fine." Warren said, thrilled to be able to say those exact words.

"Oh, thank God!" Elise exhaled as she relaxed her muscles. "I'm so happy to hear that, Warren. I know how worried you were and we were all so very concerned here as well. How is he handling his transformation?"

"Shit, better than even I expected. Funny, I shouldn't be all that surprised. Matthew's pretty level-headed. It's not in his nature to blow stuff out of proportion or whine over what can't be changed."

"That's good to know. The best thing is that you two have been brought closer together." Elise wanted to shine a ray of light on their situation.

"Yeah, that wasn't anticipated, but I'm kind of happy that he's a shifter now. I don't have to worry any more about accidentally infecting him or hurting him. Needless to say, that him being turned took a load off of my subconscious."

"I understand. Warren, I'm overjoyed that Matthew pulled through and thank you so much for calling to let us know of his recovery. I know that the others will be as happy as I am to know this as well."

Catching the hint that Elise was going to end their conversation, Warren decided he would make it easy for her. "Please let them know and thanks for everything, Elise. I'm going to let you go now, take care."

"You too, Warren."

Warren ended the call, then dialed Darian's home. Troy answered the telephone.

"Hello, Mr. Alexander's residence, who's calling?" Troy asked in a pleasant phone voice.

"Hey, Troy, it's Warren, is Natasha around?"

"Yeah, she's in the kitchen. I'll go and get her, one minute." Troy carried the cordless telephone with him as he walked into the kitchen. "Here," he said as he handed Natasha the telephone.

"Thanks," Natasha said then she put the phone to her ear. "Hello?"

"Hey Tasha, it's Warren...Matthew's okay."

"Warren, that's great! Oh my God, I'm so happy that he's going to be fine. I was so worried! I've never seen what someone who's been bitten by a shifter looked like before. It was scary. I thought he was going to die and that just terrified me!"

Warren chuckled softly. "That makes two of us. Of course, I've seen what a person looks like who's been bitten, but not everyone is lucky enough to survive the change."

"How is he doing?" Natasha asked, concerned about Matthew's mental state. "He's not all depressed is he?"

"Matthew? No, not his style. He's taking it in stride."

"Good." Natasha was satisfied knowing that Matthew was going to be alright. "That bitch! I'm glad she's not around anymore after what she did to him and what she tried to do to all of us!"

"Yeah, right now I don't even want to fucking think about her ass. I'm still kind of pissed that Richard is still alive. Not only that, but he's accepted Matthew into his Pack!"

"What? Why?" Natasha was shocked. She'd thought for certain that Xander would have Richard and the other two members of his Pack book out of town.

"Xander decided that it would be wise to keep an alliance with Richard and he also thought it best that Matthew be with his natural Pack." Warren was still sullen about the decision, but he wouldn't challenge it anymore. Xander's decision was final. To challenge that would be to challenge his authority as Pack Alpha, and that he'd already come too close to doing.

Natasha was silent for a few seconds, mulling over what he'd told her. "Well, Warren, if Xander thought that was the best thing to do, I'm sure it is. He doesn't look like a man who makes a lot of mistakes."

Warren chuckled. "He isn't. I don't think I've ever seen him make one."

"Well see, there ya go. No worries." Natasha's tone was chipper, hoping that she could cheer him up.

"I suppose you're right."

"I'm a woman, of course I'm right. Didn't ya know?"

"Ah, of course, how silly of me." Warren chuckled.

"Well, I'll forgive you for your insolence just this once," she teasingly replied. Then she grew serious. "Warren?"

"Yeah?"

"I was terrified the entire time they had me. I actually thought they were going to kill me." Her voice was steady when she spoke. Still, the memories of what she'd gone through still terrified her.

"I know. You should have seen Darian and Xavier when we told them that the three of you were missing. None of us wanted to have to be the one to tell them the bad news. Elise was brave, she delivered it. And even worse, Darian didn't look like he wanted to tell Xavier. Oh, it was ugly as hell, Tasha. I don't think that I've ever been that violent, but I wanted to get you guys back so desperately.

Sergio was like a machine when he wasn't blowing a gasket. He got the job done, though. I can say that with assurance. Elise has a strong king for her Pride, that's for sure."

"Oh, I can imagine how serious he was, they had his son!"

"We did things, Tasha, none of it was legal either." Warren said with a hint of remorse.

"Are you okay, Warren?" Natasha asked, the tone in his voice bothered her. He was one of the best men she'd ever known. She never wanted him to be upset with himself in any way. She knew that when they'd first met it was because he was an officer for the esteemed S.U.I.T. organization. It was a position that he took very seriously. But she also knew that his first priority was to his Pack.

"Yeah, Tasha, I'm fine. We did what we had to do. I'm fully aware that our world is separated from the human world. Couldn't very well call in the S.U.I.T. for this," Warren chuckled.

"I'm glad that you said that, because I don't want you to feel guilty at all about something that you had to do. It was unavoidable." She assured him that he was a good man, a great man and that he was honorable and honest.

"Thanks, Tasha."

"You are all my heroes. I love the lot of ya!"

Warren laughed. "I love you, too. I'm not going to keep you, I want to get back to Matt."

"Oh, say no more. We'll talk later." They said their goodbyes then ended their conversation. Warren went to search for Matthew. He caught up with both him and Richard by the man-made pond Xander had installed a few months ago. Both men turned, watching him approach.

"Hey," Warren greeted them with a smile. He kissed Matthew softly, then turned toward Richard who only regarded the two of them with a slight interest. "Matthew, would you mind giving Richard and me a few minutes?"

Matthew looked at him curiously, but agreed. "Sure." He rose and headed back toward the mansion, leaving the two shifters alone.

Richard straightened his back as he returned his gaze to the pond. He enjoyed watching the beautiful multicolored fish swim in the shallow waters. Without taking his eyes off the pond, he spoke. "Do you have something that you want to get off of your chest?"

"You tell me."

Richard turned to face Warren. "I'm not sure if I understand what you are asking?"

"What's your story? I got gist of the good guy bullshit you told the others on the plane, but I want to know your whole story."

"And why should I tell you any more than what I have already revealed? What do I owe you, young wolf?" Richard studied Warren's expression.

"You tried to kill my entire Pack and all of our friends. Why should I trust you?"

Richard chuckled. "It must really bother you that your Alpha did not banish me."

"Kill you is more like it."

Richard raised both eyebrows. "Think you that he could have?"

Warren remained silent.

"Do you?"

"We'll never know."

Richard smiled as he nodded. "What happened between our Packs, Prides and covens is a part of what we do, it's a part of who we are. Not only as supernatural creatures but as entities in this world in general. Humans themselves have taken land from each other in brutal battles throughout history. Alliances have been formed between numerous formerly warring nations for the sake of peace. It is the same with us. What makes you think that I owe you a reason?" He was curious, thinking Warren was bold to approach him in the manner in which he did, not that he didn't respect it.

"I don't trust you."

"I don't care. I gave my word to your Pack Alpha, we have an understanding. I don't owe you anything personally just because it was your lover who was turned. Be thankful that he was not killed and be grateful that I have accepted him into my Pack. By all rights, his fate is my will. Matthew belongs to me and I take care of what is mine. I do hope that *we* have an understanding."

Warren was silent, slightly taken aback by Richard's candor, but he also knew that he was right.

"Now, only for the sake of argument, what I said on the plane is all that I have to say on the matter. As Alpha, I was trying to look out for the best interests and desires of my Pack. Why I decided to side with the others was purely to have strength in numbers. It was all tactical and nothing more. I didn't agree with their methods, many of which I was unaware of. Now that is all behind us, we all have lost in this war, let it be."

"Will you take care of him, I mean, really care for him?" Warren asked, looking Richard directly in the eye.

"You love him immensely."

"Insanely."

"Then rest assured, I will take care of him and protect him. You have my word."

"Thanks." Without another word, Warren turned, heading back into the mansion. Richard smiled as he turned his gaze back to the pond. He liked Warren, admired his boldness and noble personality. He believed that the two shifters made a wonderful couple. That they were in fact, perfect for each other. He continued to gaze at the fish swimming as he thought about the turn of events. He felt better about their situation. The change of venue and the new treaty offered him a new beginning, one he was all too willing to take.

Warren searched out Matthew, finding him in their bedroom. He climbed on the bed, scooting closer to him, taking him into his arms.

"Did you get that out of your system?" Matthew asked.

"What do you mean?" Warren asked, playing innocent.

"That whole testosterone thing that you do. It's cute, you wanting to take care of me."

"We came to an understanding."

"Oh, did you? What was that?" Matthew looked at him, one eyebrow raised.

Warren shrugged nonchalantly. "Well, I told him if anything ever happened to you, he'd have hell to pay."

Matthew chuckled. "Did you use those exact words?"

"Well, not exactly, but he still got my point."

Matthew laughed. "Ah, well then, no worries, you told him." He leaned forward, kissing Warren softly on the lips, then he laid his head on his chest, close to his warmth and the rhythmic beat of his heart. They lay together in each other's arms, each grateful to have the other.

"Warren?"

"Yeah?"

"I don't know what being a shape-shifter is going to mean to my life now. I know I should probably feel angry about being turned. Most people probably would in this case. But...I think I'm happy about it. I feel closer to you now than I ever did in the past. I think that's because I'm like you now."

"I know. I hated that the decision was made for you. But now that it's done and you're alive, I'm kind of happy about it, too." Warren kissed his lover's temple. The two men lay in bed, happily anticipating the new beginning of their life together.

CHAPTER TWENTY-FIVE
Four Days Later

Oh god, I'm so glad that's over. Two funerals in one week! This is the worst week I've had in a long time." Natasha declared as she kicked off her black high-heeled shoes.

"But they were both beautiful, and gave closure to those who needed it," Xavier added as he picked up Natasha's discarded shoes from the floor. All three walked into their shared bedroom. Xavier placed her shoes on the rack inside her closet, before removing his own.

"I thought the families handled both funerals very well." Darian began to undo his silk black and silver tie.

"Yeah, I know what you mean…I thought for sure Marianne's mom was going to cuss Elise and the whole Pride out. I couldn't believe she and Elise had that whole disagreement about how to handle Marianne's funeral arrangements. Before it got too ugly, Elise said she'd decided the mother should do everything to her liking. I can't imagine what she must be going through, to lose a child…" Natasha's voice trailed off. She shook her head, not wanting to dwell on the matter any longer. "I'm just glad that we don't have to go to any more funerals. I hate funerals." She plopped down on the bed, rotating her neck to relax her muscles.

"Here, let me help you." Darian climbed onto the bed behind Natasha. His strong hands began to gently massage the aching tendons in her neck and shoulders.

"Oooh, yes! Right there," Natasha moaned as he continued to knead the tension from her muscles.

Xavier settled on the bed beside them, watching his two lovers together. "I didn't know what I was going to do if I had lost you," he whispered.

Both Darian and Natasha turned to look at him.

"When they told me that you were kidnapped, I was so enraged, but I was also frightened." Xavier looked at Natasha, his beautiful gray eyes locked on her.

"Xavier," Natasha inched closer to him. Darian moved back, allowing her room to maneuver. She crawled toward Xavier until their faces were only inches apart. "It's over now, I'm safe." She leaned forward, kissing him lightly on the lips. One hand caressed the back of her head, while his other wrapped around her torso, holding her closer.

Darian smiled as he rested his back against the footboard. He watched Xavier and Natasha share their moment in silence. Natasha broke their kiss, then climbed over him to lay in the middle of the bed. She looked at Darian, beckoning him to come closer. He nodded and with the ease and gracefulness that only a vampire could master, he slid up beside her. She felt completely safe and protected between the two men she loved. Their warm bodies surrounded her, wrapping her in their heat. She laid her head back against Xavier's chest as she stroked Darian's wavy jet-black hair.

"Are you alright?" Darian asked. There was an expression on her face that told him that something was on her mind.

Natasha nodded, then exhaled. "Darian, Xavier..." She was asking for their full attention. Both men remained silent as they looked at her, waiting for her to continue. "I've been thinking a lot about our relationship. You know, what it means to me. I love you both so very much. I've never felt so complete before in my life and who could have guessed all I was missing were the two of you. I never want it to end. I'm not sure if I really know what I'm saying, knowing that you are both vampires and I'm only human."

"Natasha-" Xavier began.

"Xavier, let me finish, please."

"I'm sorry, go on." He encouraged her to continue.

She sat up, turning around so that she was facing them both.

"You are going to remain forever young. I'm going to age and eventually die, that's if I'm lucky. I know full well what my mortality means in your world and I'm alright with that."

Darian and Xavier looked at each other. It wasn't too long ago the two had discussed turning Natasha into one of them. Neither vampire wanted to think about her mortal death. Xavier in particular, he loved both her and Darian so much, the very thought of her death was unbearably painful for him.

"This last thing that happened to us really opened my eyes. Life is short and it can be shortened even more, for any of us. I had a lot of dreams, or visions. It was hard to tell which was which, but some were happy. Some were about us, our future together. I've had a lot of time to think since I was rescued from the clutches of death. I know now just how precious life really is. How unpredictable. You know, it's funny, but humans, we really don't think much about life and death until we're close to it." She paused.

"Natasha?" Darian was studying her face.

"I am ready to take that next step...I want to have a baby." She looked at her lovers, trying to read their expressions. Both men seemed a bit shocked by the revelation.

"Natasha, are you sure?" Darian asked. Xavier couldn't take his gaze from her.

Natasha nodded. "I've been thinking about it for a long time. It was the reason why I had asked Matthew to be the donor. I love the both of you with all of my heart. You've given me so much to be thankful for. I want to give you something that only I can give you. A family. I'm ready to share that part of me. I also want a part of me to continue and I know that all of my descendants will be well taken care of when I'm no longer here. I trust you both and I know that you will love and care for our child."

"Oh my God!" Xavier gasped as he sat up in the bed. "Natasha..." His voice was shaky as tears slowly began to stream down his cheeks. Never had he ever imagined that he would be a father to a human child. To be able to nurture that child and watch it grow. He was beyond ecstatic that the possibility he'd long since given up on was now before him.

"I want this." Natasha touched the side of Xavier's cheek with her palm. He nodded.

"I'll always be by your side, until the very end. I love you so much," Xavier managed to say between his laughter and tears. He kissed Natasha again, crushing her to his chest as if in desperation. She giggled then she looked at Darian.

"Darian, how do you feel about all of this?" she asked.

"I honestly don't know. I've been around for a very long time, Natasha. I remember when you first brought the possibility of children to our attention. I didn't know what to think then either. I'm not a man who has confusion about his thoughts. I normally know exactly what I want and how to go about getting it. But you are and have always been an enigma to me. And now you present something that...that...I don't know my own feelings right now." Darian smiled sweetly.

Natasha took his hand into her own. "It's perfectly alright if you're scared or uncertain. Raising a baby, your own child, is going to be a brand new experience for all of us."

Darian leaned toward her. "You have that much faith in us? That we would make good fathers?"

"I wouldn't want anyone else to raise our child. The two of you mean everything to me. You give me tenderness, respect and loyalty, it's all I've ever wanted and I get that from you and then some. I'm so excited about our future! I want to have our child and I want your blessings."

"I love you, Natasha...I want to you be happy, and if this is what you desire, to complete us, then I want it, too. I don't know, right now, what kind of father I would make." He looked at Xavier. "I believe that Xavier would be excellent. It's definitely an opportunity he's been wanting for a very, very long time. I just want you to be sure. Our lives are very dangerous, as you've seen. You'll be bringing an innocent life into our world. One who is going to be completely dependent on us. Are you really ready to make that decision for our child?" Darian asked.

"I don't think there's a mother alive who can promise a safe haven for their child where no harm will ever come to them. All you can do is promise to do your best to protect them. I want to be a mother. I've always seen motherhood in my future. My life is with you, my heart is with you, that's all I know. It's all that matters." Natasha was watching Darian closely.

Darian nodded. "So, our child will have a hyphenated last name, correct?" he smiled, exposing his sparkling white teeth.

"Yes, Richards-Alexander!" she gushed as she snuggled between both of her lovers. They wrapped their arms around her. She glowed with anticipation. The next day, she would keep her appointment at the clinic where Darian had paid to store Matthew's semen for whenever Natasha was ready.

"Natasha?" Xavier asked.

"Yes, Xavier?" She mumbled.

"When are you going to get the procedure done?"

"Tomorrow. Elise and I are going to the clinic. I asked her yesterday if she would go with me. She said she wouldn't miss it for the world. She also said that she couldn't wait for the baby to be born. She really wants to see the two of you as daddies," Natasha giggled.

"Is that so?" Darian asked with a chuckle.

"Yep. She said she really wanted to see you, Darian, change a dirty diaper. Then Sergio said 'the kind of dirty diaper after the baby has eaten a lot of vegetables'. I have to admit, I want to see that myself."

Xavier laughed. "Me too!"

"What do you think I'm going to do? Break down at the sight of a 'dirty diaper'? Flee the room, perhaps?" Darian retorted.

"No, but I do think the snob in you will react in a very funny way," Natasha stated with glee.

"I'm not a-"

"Darian, please don't say what I think you're going to say," Xavier interjected.

Darian sighed. "I'm so misunderstood."

"No, you're not. We understand you just fine," Xavier teased.

"That's right, we do," Natasha mumbled, her eyes closing.

"Are you sleepy already?" Xavier asked playfully. "It's only one o'clock."

Natasha nodded. "In the morning."

"But we're night creatures," Xavier chuckled.

"Which should come in handy during those middle of the night feedings the baby will need," Natasha giggled.

Darian and Xavier looked at each other. They smiled.

"Get some sleep." Darian pulled the satin covers over her shoulders. The two men stayed with her until she drifted off to sleep. Then both climbed out of the bed, leaving her to the silence of the room.

"Can you believe that?" Xavier asked Darian as he closed the door behind them.

"I know, it's truly amazing how she can simply fall asleep so instantaneously!" Darian said.

Xavier shook his head, chuckling. "I meant about her wanting to make us a complete family."

"Ah, yes. She is such a remarkable woman."

"I never thought I would be a father." Xavier's face sparkled with delight.

"Neither did I."

"Darian, are you frightened of becoming one?" Xavier asked with an almost a childlike innocence.

Darian looked at him, smiling. "To say that I'm not nervous would be an out and out lie. It's such a huge responsibility and I'm very honored that Natasha trusts us. Am I frightened?" He chuckled. "Very little actually frightens me, but I'll know exactly how I feel once the baby's born."

"I still think you're going to have a mini panic attack," Xavier joked as he followed Darian to the den. Both men sat down on the comfortable leather sofa next to John and Christopher.

"What are you watching?" Xavier asked John.

"Some vampire movie. It's kind of funny because it's about a vampire hunter that's half human, half vampire. Talk about a turncoat," John said with a shake of his head.

"Well, not really, because he just chose sides," Christopher stated.

"Yeah, but does that mean he should go out and kill his other half just because they're vampires?" John looked at him questioningly.

"He wants to save the helpless humans and keep his humanity."

"You're being awfully defensive. Okay, let me ask you this, if you were half vampire, half human...what would you do?" John asked Christopher.

Darian, Xavier and John looked at Christopher. Darian was amused by their conversation. John had always amused him, even when he was human. He enjoyed John's sense of humor and his bold and lively personality, which is why he had turned him.

Christopher thought about the question then answered. "I'd kill every vampire I saw!" he exclaimed. Then he began to laugh hysterically. "Oh man! You should see the looks on your faces!" He pointed at the three vampires as he doubled over from laughter.

"Chris, jokes like that could get you killed around here," John said with a serious expression.

"Indeed. We don't joke about killing vampires," Xavier added.

"I think I might just kill him. He broke one of my rules," Darian rose from the sofa.

Christopher stopped laughing abruptly. He looked at the three vampires. He focused on Darian and began to panic. "Hey, Master, I was just joking! I...I would never hunt or kill our kind, I swear. I meant nothing by it!"

Darian stared down at him, giving the young vampire his most menacing glare. When it looked like Christopher was going to try and run for his life..., he cracked a smile. Xavier and John burst into a fit of laughter. Once Christopher realized they'd played a joke on him, he began to calm down. Darian returned to the sofa.

"That was so not funny!" Christopher complained.

"Oh yes it was! You should have seen the look on *your* face!" John pointed at him as he continued to laugh.

"That was cruel and unusual punishment, man! I'm still new at this, you can't play jokes like that on me. I take stuff like that literally." Christopher crossed his arms over his chest in a sulking manner.

Darian chuckled softly.

"It was cruel, no denying that. But it was funny as well. So what's your real answer to that question?" Xavier asked, bringing them back to the original question that John had asked him.

"I don't know. I would have all of the strength and power of a vampire, but none of the weaknesses...I would probably just try to live my life as a human, maybe a cop," Christopher said.

"How boring," John teased.

"Well, what would you do?" Christopher asked, putting John on the spot.

"I'd be exactly the way that I am. I enjoy being a vampire, it's been one of my greatest experiences. I wouldn't want to give up on drinking human blood. I also wouldn't turn my back on other vampires. I mean, you haven't had sex until you've screwed an older vampire. They understand exactly what you need, know what I mean?" John looked slyly at Christopher.

"You would say that, but I'm understanding where you're coming from. I just miss being human sometimes, you know, feeling the sun on my skin," Christopher said wistfully.

"You're going to have to get over that, because it's going to be many years before you'll ever see the sun again," John reminded him.

"I know, I know…I'm still getting used to this new life. It's not so bad. Not like I thought it would be when I was turned."

"You can credit that to being in Darian's coven. Vampire life can be pure hell, depending on who's your Master," Tony said as he entered the room. "I ought to know."

"Considering who turned me, I'd have to agree," Christopher said, remembering his maker.

John smiled at Christopher. He really liked him. Then something came to his mind, he turned to Darian.

"Master, you said earlier tonight that you wanted to tell me something."

Darian nodded. "Ahh, yes. I've been thinking. Now that we are exposed to the world, we are being watched more than ever before. Our enemies are many and now is the time when we as supernaturals are going to have to band together, I realize this now. I've already spoken with both Elise and Xander about this and it's decided. On *Lunar* nights, when they are at their most vulnerable, they'll need to be protected. They need someone to look out for them until dawn on those nights. From now on, you will go to Elise's home and Miko will go to Xander's. Is that understood?"

John nodded. "I'm glad that you made that arrangement."

"Worried about your lover?" Tony asked.

John looked at him. "Do I really need to answer that question?"

"Point taken." Tony smiled.

"Good, then it's all settled," Darian said. Rising from the sofa, he exited the room, leaving the others to their vampire movie.

"Look at that, right there. Why is it in vampire movies like this, every vampire knows martial arts?" Christopher asked, pointing to the television, noting the martial arts display in the movie.

"I've noticed that myself," Xavier said with a chuckle.

"Because it's cool! In all martial arts movies, everybody in the movie knows kung fu. Even the drunken wino on the corner knows how to kick your ass," John added.

"Do any of you know martial arts?" Christopher asked.

"Darian does, as well as Miko and April. I know a little, but I'm more of a brawler, so to speak," Xavier said with a sly grin.

"Miko is amazing! She's like Nagesa, you know. I would love to see those two in a sparring match!" John said enthusiastically.

"I don't know...I'd rather like to see Miko and Miranda go at it," Tony stated, nodding his head. "In more ways than one, if you catch my drift." He winked.

Xavier shook his head, chuckling. "I'm going out." He rose from the sofa and left, heading for the balcony to sit with Darian. The other vampires continued to talk about whatever held their interest from horror movies to who was dating whom in Hollywood.

***

Darian sat on a comfortable lounge on his balcony, gazing up at the stars.

"I knew I'd find you out here," Xavier said as he joined him.

"It's peaceful, quiet."

"Quiet being the key word there. I think sending Miko and John to watch over Xander's and Elise's homes is a very noble choice. That's one of the reasons why I admire you so much."

Darian smiled. "It seemed like the best decision."

"When you went to the mansion earlier, did it look salvageable?"

"It is. I've already contacted a contractor to restore our home to its original state."

"Good, I like the mansion better."

Darian turned to him, wrapping his arm around Xavier's shoulders, pulling him closer. He leaned forward, kissing his lover softly, their tongues pressing gently against each other. A low moan emanated from Xavier as he pressed himself closer to Darian. Xavier's hands slid through his lover's long, silky locks as they continued to kiss. When Darian pulled away, Xavier looked at him.

"I admire you as well, my beautiful inamorato. S'apago," Darian said, thickening his Greek accent.

"I love you, too." Xavier smiled as he settled closer to Darian. The two men sat in silence, wrapped in each other's arms as they thought about Natasha and her gift to them.

CHAPTER TWENTY-SIX
The Lunar Night

When John rang the doorbell, Madeleine answered. "Hey, how's everything going?"

She stepped to the side, allowing him entrance. "Pretty good. Things are getting back to normal since we had to deal with all of the chaos from last month. How about you?"

He nodded, understanding what she meant. "Pretty good. My little shadow, Christopher, is doing much better. He actually successfully hypnotized someone last night without letting his thoughts drive them mad. He just focused on one directive and he was able to do it. I was pretty proud of him." He smiled.

"Sheesh, I'm glad that you guys can't do that little mind trick on us. No telling what you'd do," Madeleine teased.

"Yeah, be afraid, be very afraid." John gave her his most menacing look.

"Oh, you're too cute to be scary."

"So you say. Hey, where's my baby?"

"In his room."

"Alright, thought I'd see him before you guys start changing." John rushed up to Devin's room, knocking on the door. When he heard his lover beckon him in, he entered. Right away, he knew that Devin was in the shower.

He walked into the bathroom, smiling as he watched Devin bathing behind the curtain.

"Hey baby!" Devin said, tossing a look over his shoulder.

"Hi there, sexy. Mind if I join you?" John didn't wait for an answer as he began removing his black leather pants, white t-shirt and leather boots.

"I guess you can, since you leave me no choice but to accept." Devin looked at his lover's bobbing erection as he climbed into the shower behind him.

John reached for his soapy washcloth. "You wanna explain to me why you're taking a shower when you're going to change soon?" He began washing Devin's back.

"Well, apart from working in the garden today with Madeleine, planting her batch of strawberries, I always take a shower before my change. It relaxes my muscles so that the change doesn't hurt as much."

"I know a little trick that helps relax your muscles, too," John whispered seductively.

"Really, why don't you show me this trick," Devin said imploringly.

"If you insist." John began to plant soft kisses along Devin's shoulder, trailing down toward his buttocks.

He turned him around, kissing along his abdomen, up toward his nipples. Once he reached the sensitive flesh, he began to suckle them gently, rolling each nipple between his lips, flicking his tongue over their tips teasingly.

Devin's head leaned back as he moaned in ecstasy. He ran his hands through John's silky blonde hair, entangling his fingers in his bangs. Without wasting one more second, John picked him up, hoisting him up to his waist. Devin wrapped his legs around John's hips, securing his position. He gasped in pleasure as John slid inside of him. Their lips met again, kissing fervently as the hot water cascaded down their bodies, slicking their skin. John didn't hold back as he thrust passionately into Devin without reserve.

Devin relished the feeling of being taken by his lover. He grabbed John's cheeks, bringing his face closer to his as they kissed deeply, desperately, neither man wanting it to end. John began to feel his orgasm building faster, growing more and more intense with every stroke. He could feel Devin tense against him, he knew the moment was almost near. They continued their lovemaking until their muscles grew tense, neither man could hold back. At that moment, John's fangs extended and he plunged them deeply into Devin, piercing his flesh, feasting greedily. The intensity of their union rocked their bodies, their combined climaxes rushing through them like twin tidal waves. John's knees grew weak and together, they slid to the floor of the shower, both his fangs and his softening member still buried deep within Devin.

John withdrew his fangs, relaxing against his lover, holding him still. "That...was...intense!" he panted as he struggled to regain his breath.

Devin nodded. "I don't think we've ever made love on a *Lunar* night before. We have to do that more often!"

John chuckled. "Definitely." He kissed Devin several times before he pulled himself free, quaking softly as he slid away.

Devin looked at him. "I wish I could stay with you, just like this."

"I know."

"I have to go, I'm starting to feel the effects. The *Lunar* is very close." Devin rose to his feet, climbing out of the shower. John followed him.

"I'll be here tomorrow night, we can see each other then," John said longingly.

"You bet!" Devin flashed his schoolboy smile, charming him. "Until tomorrow." He turned, leaving the bedroom to join the others in the forest. John dressed quickly before stepping out on the balcony to watch over them.

He smiled to himself as he saw his lover jogging toward the rest of the Pride. Between being a part of Darian's coven and the love of his life, he was content.

***

Richard and Xander led their combined Packs into the forest adjacent to Xander's mansion. Matthew walked side by side with Warren. He was extremely nervous since it was going to be his first change. Many had told him it was going to be the most painful, and the longest he'd ever experience, which left very little to be desired. Warren had told him he'd get used to it and that once it was complete, he'd feel refreshed, free. He was seriously hoping he would. He wanted something good to come out of so much pain. They stood between several trees as Miko looked on from the roof of the mansion. Her eyes scanned their surroundings, she was pleased that all seemed well. She had felt very honored when Darian assigned her to such a task. She knew that he held both the Pride and Pack in high regard, so for her to be trusted with protecting them made her very proud.

Matthew watched Richard approaching. The first month he'd spent with his new Alpha was a very enlightening experience for him. Richard was stern, but fair, very honorable. He didn't mind being in his Pack. He was also grateful that he got along with his other pack mates. He really didn't want to be a part of a group of people who created a lot of drama. It was something he didn't want in his life, so that was a blessing to him.

Richard stood before him. "Matthew, remember what I've told you?"

Matthew nodded. "Just to relax my muscles, don't try to fight it."

"Right. You should be feeling it now. Don't be frightened, you're surrounded by friends and family." Richard smiled warmly.

"Matthew, It's going to be okay." Warren said, when he noticed his lover tensing. "Relax, tensing up the way you are right now is only going to make it worse."

"It's really starting to hurt!" Matthew said, surprised by what he was feeling. There was a subtle pain in his stomach. Suddenly, it began to grow more intense.

"That's all normal." Richard stepped back, giving his young coyote room.

Matthew collapsed to the ground, his body wracked with intense pain. He'd had no idea his body could feel so much pain all over. His muscles twitched underneath his skin as sweat poured from his pores. He gasped as his intestines began to churn and rotate inside his abdomen.

"Oh God!" he began to pant, undergoing his first change. His body began to elongate, growing into a half-beast, half-human form. Silky brown fur sprang out from his pores, covering his body. His head grew bigger, his teeth, longer and sharper. His mouth began to extend outward, forming a muzzle.

The other shifters began their change. They moaned and groaned as their bodies transformed straight into their full animal forms. Matthew remained on all fours, his body still forming. When the other shifters' transformations were complete, they surrounded Matthew who was now experiencing the final stage. His body grew smaller, muscles tearing and bones breaking, shrinking and reforming to those of a full coyote. A long, fluffy tail sprouted from his tailbone, which was extremely painful to him.

A minute later, it was over. Their newest member trembled, his legs were wobbly as he struggled to balance himself. Warren rubbed along the side of him, licking his muzzle. Richard, Ryan and Ignacio walked around Matthew, sniffing his body. They rubbed along the sides of him, marking him as theirs. Ignacio nudged him, urging him on to chase him. The others ran off, prompting Matthew to follow them, so he did. Together, they hunted down a bull Xander had ordered earlier for their *Lunar* hunt. Both Packs combined, ripping chunks off the bull's body, bringing it down. Richard, Xander and Tatiana fed first, taking their fill of the animal. Then they moved away, leaving the rest for their Packs. The others ravaged the animal in a feeding frenzy, ripping bloodied pieces of flesh until nothing was left but bones.

Throughout the night, they hunted smaller game, frolicked with each other, and played with one another, enjoying their freedom. Matthew had never felt such exhilaration, such freedom! He ran faster than he ever could before, keeping up with Warren in his wolf form. Richard watched the two men playing with each other as he walked through the forest. Ryan caught up with him, keeping up with his pace. Once he reached a tree, he sniffed it, then lifting his left leg, marked it. After adding his claim of the territory, he found a nice spot beside a bush, where he could keep his eyes on the others. Ryan settled down next to him, snuggling closer, enjoying their intimacy.

A few more hours passed and they began to grow sleepy. Each Pack joined their mates and together, they snuggled closer to one another to rest. Matthew lay between Richard and Warren. Finally exhausted from his *Lunar* activities, he slept safely in their closeness, enjoying the heat their bodies produced. He was beginning to understand what it meant to be a shifter and to be a part of a Pack.

He understood and...

He was content.

ABOUT THE AUTHOR

D. N. Simmons lives with a rambunctious German Shepard pup and mischievous kitten in Chicago IL.. Her hobbies include rollerblading, shooting pool, bowling, reading, watching television and going out. She has been nominated at Love Romances and More, winning honorable mention for best paranormal book of 2006. She has won "Author of the Month" at Warrior of Words. She was voted "New Voice of Today" at Romance Reviews and "Rising Star" at Love Romance and More. To learn more, and have the opportunity to speak with the author personally, please visit the official website and forum at: www.dnsimmons.com . D.N. is always interesting in meeting new and wonderful people.

975232

Made in the USA